Luke hadn't bargained on the new cook.

Sure, Rosa had asked if her niece could take over while she spent some of her vacation time with her daughter, who was expecting a baby soon. Trusting the older woman completely, he'd said sure.

He hadn't thought about Josie being a *woman*.

It had been so long since he'd looked—really looked—at a woman, that when she'd glared at him from her car, blue eyes narrowed, with the pepper spray can in her hand, he'd been shocked to feel the unwelcome rush of attraction. And she was a self-confessed city girl to boot, which was a huge no-no in his book. He'd married a city girl.

He was no longer married.

So to feel something for someone who wore three-inch spike heels to stomp across a muddy, wet road in the wilds of Montana wasn't a good sign.

But damn, they'd looked good on her, even in the mud and rain.

MONTANA
★ COUNTRY LEGACY ★

HER BIG SKY DREAMS

— ⚒ —

Ami Weaver

Joanna Sims

Previously published as *From City Girl to Rancher's Wife*
and *A Match Made in Montana*

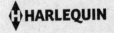

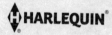

ISBN-13: 978-1-335-46773-7

Recycling programs
for this product may
not exist in your area.

Montana Country Legacy:
Her Big Sky Dreams
Copyright © 2020 by Harlequin Books S.A.

From City Girl to Rancher's Wife
First published in 2015. This edition published in 2020.
Copyright © 2015 by Ami Weaver

A Match Made in Montana
First published in 2015. This edition published in 2020.
Copyright © 2015 by Joanna Sims

This edition published by arrangement with Harlequin Books S.A.

For questions and comments about the quality of this book, please contact us at CustomerService@Harlequin.com.

Harlequin Enterprises ULC
22 Adelaide St. West, 40th Floor
Toronto, Ontario M5H 4E3, Canada
www.Harlequin.com

Printed in U.S.A.

CONTENTS

From City Girl to Rancher's Wife   7
by Ami Weaver

A Match Made in Montana   221
by Joanna Sims

Two-time Golden Heart® Award finalist **Ami Weaver** has been reading romance since she was a teen and writing for even longer, so it was only natural she would put the two together. Now she can be found drinking gallons of iced tea at her local coffee shop while doing one of her very favorite things— convincing two characters they deserve their happy-ever-after. Ami lives in Michigan with her four kids, three cats and her very supportive husband.

Books by Ami Weaver

Harlequin Special Edition

From City Girl to Rancher's Wife
The Nanny's Christmas Wish

Harlequin Romance

In the Line of Duty
An Accidental Family

Visit the Author Profile page at
Harlequin.com for more titles.

FROM CITY GIRL TO RANCHER'S WIFE

Ami Weaver

To my parents, Jan and Nancy. Thank you for all you've done and all your support. It means the world. Love you guys.

Chapter 1

After six hours in a middle-of-nowhere airport, two turbulent flights and a bottom-of-the-barrel rental car, Josie Callahan almost wasn't shocked when she ended up in the ditch on a dark, out-of-the-way Montana road. In what seemed to be a monsoon.

She swallowed what felt dangerously close to hysterical laughter, because at this point, after how awful her day had been, what was the point of getting mad?

Just to check, she dug her phone out of her bag, then almost immediately dropped it back in. No service, of course. It had been hit or miss all day.

Since she had no idea where she was, how far she was from the ranch—this car had no GPS—and her phone wouldn't work, she plopped her head back on the headrest and squeezed her eyes shut. She was hungry, but all she had was a squashed granola bar in her purse and half a bottle of water. No chocolate, unfortunately.

She opened her eyes and gave the rain that was coursing down the windshield a baleful glare.

Where she came from, none of this would be an issue.

Light bounced somewhere down the road. Josie squinted out the rain-streaked window. Lightning? It couldn't possibly be a car out here on this godforsaken road. Could it?

It was getting steadily closer, and she could see the lights were in fact headlights, on what seemed to be a huge truck.

The truck slowed, then stopped on the opposite side of the road, so she wasn't blinded by the lights. Josie scrambled for her pepper spray, her heart pounding. Her hysteria from a few moments ago had turned to a quasi panic. She saw the truck door open, and a tall man stepped out.

She gripped the can tightly. Okay. She was on the road—she hoped—to the Silver River Ranch. Her aunt knew she was on the way. It was possible he was looking for her.

He tapped on her window. She lowered it a few inches and lifted her can of pepper spray so he could see it. The rain splashed in, cold on her skin, but he wore a cowboy hat. The rain ran off the brim. He had sharp blue eyes that caught her attention.

"Are you Josie Callahan?" His voice was deep and a little hoarse, and she blinked.

"I am," she said, holding the can steady. "Who are you?"

"Luke Ryder. Your aunt sent me to check on you."
He stooped a little more and lifted a brow. "You don't
need the pepper spray, ma'am."

Oh, hell. She lowered the can. No, she didn't need it.
Luke Ryder was a well-known retired country star and
her aunt's employer. She dropped it in her lap, thankful
she hadn't accidentally discharged the can. On herself.
The way this day had gone, it wouldn't have surprised
her. "Right. Well. Thanks."

"Why don't you get in the truck and I'll grab your
bags. You're not that far from the ranch, and Rosa is
anxious to see you." There may or may not have been
a note of censure in his voice, and she bristled just a
bit. Rosa had told her to wait, to come in the daylight,
but Josie had had it after everything had gone wrong
and had just wanted to *get there*. Guilt swamped her.
It seemed as if she was always causing people anxiety.
"I couldn't call her. My phone—"

"No service out here for regular cell phones. That's
why she sent me." He opened the door as she hit the
button to roll the window up. She twisted to grab her
coat from the backseat and got her purse and laptop bag.
He extended his free hand and, after a second's hesitation, she took it and he pulled her out of the car. She
was a little surprised at how tall he was—even though
she was in heels he topped her by a head.

Despite the chill in the air, his palm was warm and
rough as it slid over hers. The little shiver that ran down
her spine had to be from the shock of the cold rain in
late August, not his touch.

"Go ahead and get in the truck," he said. "I'll get the
rest of your stuff."

"Thank you," she said, and marched across the sodden, uneven road, her boots with their three-inch heels sinking into the dirt. She was afraid she was going to lose one. They, like her, were made for city sidewalks. In retrospect, probably not the best footwear for Montana.

She climbed into the big red dually pickup and sank into the buttery leather seats. This wasn't what she'd expected. She'd thought it'd be threadbare, dirty, more of a working truck for a cowboy. Which she knew from her aunt was what Luke considered himself now. It smelled like—

Luke.

As he opened the back door of the truck and put her bags in, she got another whiff of the fresh air and rain mixed with the scent of laundry soap and something a little spicy. She stopped herself from taking a deep inhale.

She'd been involved with a celebrity once. It had cost her more than she'd ever expected to pay. She wasn't going to fall into that trap again, not for love or money.

"I took everything out of the trunk," he said, turning slightly toward her so she got the whole effect of those eyes. *Oh, my.* "Is there anything else you need?"

"No, that's everything. Thank you." Her tone was a little prim, even to her own ears.

He arched a brow. "Those are two, full, heavy suitcases. How did you get them on the plane?"

She gave him a tight smile. "Paid extra. Of course." She'd packed a few of her favorite pans and utensils. She wasn't going to explain that to him.

"What about the car?" she asked as he climbed in the truck. "Can we just leave it there?"

"We'll have to for tonight. In the morning I'll come back and pull it out. I'd like to be able to see if there's any damage."

She swallowed a sigh. Damage to the rental car. She'd bought the insurance policy that they offered and she hoped it would cover it in this situation. She'd worry about it in the morning. "All right. Thank you."

"You're welcome." He put the truck in gear and made a series of short turns that eventually had the big truck facing the other way on the road. Josie just sat there, her hands in her lap. It was quiet in the truck, except for the rhythmic thumping of the windshield wipers. If she wasn't careful, it could lull her to sleep. Her day was finally catching up to her. She'd gotten up at four that morning to catch her flight. She glanced at the clock on the dash. It was almost nine now.

Los Angeles seemed like a lifetime away. That was probably for the best. She wondered if Aunt Rosa's no-gossip policy extended to her, too. Had she told Luke about Josie's recent troubles?

She sneaked a little look at his profile, which was il-luminated by the dash lights. His chin was strong and his hair was cut short under that hat. His shirt was soaked, and did a nice job of outlining strong arms. Aunt Rosa didn't say much about her famous employer, but she had said he was a hard worker. Those arms seemed to be proof of that.

Not that she was looking, of course.

She tore her eyes away and fixed them on the bit of road she could see in the swath of light from the truck's headlights. The rain ran in rivulets down the sides of the road, and a washout from that was probably what had pulled her off the road and into the ditch.

"Thank you," she said finally, "for your help. I am sorry for making you come out in this weather."

"You're welcome. Did she tell you to wait until morning?"

Now she heard the note of censure in his tone. But all Josie had wanted was to get away from the airports and into a real bed. "She did, yes."

He glanced at her. "You didn't think that maybe she knew what she was talking about?"

Josie threaded her fingers together so tight it hurt. "Of course I did. I just thought—" She trailed off. She'd thought it couldn't be that bad. That *remote* meant a little ways out from town, that roads were paved, that there'd be people around. Somewhere. That she'd just be *out in the country*, not in the middle of nowhere in a monsoon. She combed her hair back from her face. Her neat knot had given up hours ago. "I was stupid. I'm completely aware of that."

"Stupid can get you killed out here," he said mildly, as if he was pointing out the obvious. "Soon enough this won't be rain. It'll be snow. It could take days to find someone who's wandered off."

A little shiver ran over her skin. She'd be gone before the snow set in, thank God. "Point taken. I'll be careful." Not that she'd be driving anywhere. She'd been driving for almost an hour past the last little town when she'd gone in the ditch. There'd be no quick trips out for anything, clearly.

Not like her neighborhood in LA, where she could

walk everywhere if she wanted. She massaged her temples with her fingertips.

"Rough day?"

She laughed, because otherwise she'd start crying. And maybe never stop. "You could say that." Her past few months had been a series of *rough days*. She was due for something better. Sometime. Any time. It was why she was up here in Montana instead of back at home in California trying to salvage her career.

Which, of course, was beyond fixing, as was her life as she'd known it. Stupid didn't just kill a person. It could cost them everything.

Luke made a turn onto a tiny road that she didn't even see in the rain and the dark, which meant she'd have missed it if she'd been on her own. They bumped along a rutted road for a quarter mile or so before passing through an open gate under an arch. They wound a little farther, and over a rise the house came into view.

Josie couldn't contain her gasp. Even in the dark, she could see the house was a huge log home. Not a cabin—her aunt had referred to it as a cabin! A cabin was smallish. This place was closer to a mansion. Lights were on in many of the windows, and the front porch was illuminated as well, showing a row of Adirondack chairs. Luke pulled the truck off onto a short gravel drive that opened to a parking area. He stopped next to a low stone wall with soft lights set into it.

"We'll have to make a run for it," he said. "I can't get any closer than this." He cast a doubtful eye in the direction of her feet. "Don't break an ankle, please."

She snapped out of her awe and grabbed her laptop bag and purse. "Oh, I won't. I can run in these. I'm a city girl, born and raised." This was not a plus out here in the wilds of Montana, but she'd make it work for the next couple of months.

"That's what I was afraid of," he said, low enough she almost didn't catch it, and got out, opened the back door and grabbed a suitcase. She got the other one, and it bumped along behind her as she half walked, half ran to the porch behind Luke, whose long stride made it impossible for her to keep up without trotting.

The heavy front door swung open. Aunt Rosa was framed in the light from the house, anxiety and relief etched on her face. "Josie! Oh, thank God you're okay."

Josie walked into her aunt's embrace, even though it was awkward with all the bags she was juggling and she was soaking wet. "I'm sorry. I'm so sorry."

Aunt Rosa gave her a fierce hug. "Just like your daddy. Stubborn." Her tone was affectionate, not scolding, but Josie still felt bad. "Let me go grab you a towel. Wait right here." She hurried off, and Josie and Luke came all the way in, the suitcases trundling awkwardly over the threshold. Luke came to a stop right behind her, and she felt the heat of his body. It was an odd sort of awareness, one that made her uncomfortable.

"I'll put this in your room," Luke said quietly, and she turned partway around and nodded, making brief eye contact with him.

"All right. Thank you. For all your help."

He tipped his head at her. "You're welcome." He strode off, and Josie pulled her gaze away when it snagged on his broad shoulders and looked around the room instead.

The place was clearly even bigger than it looked,

with huge vaulted ceilings and a fire crackling in a massive fireplace with floor-to-ceiling stone on the hearth and up the chimney, all the way to the ceiling. There were two full-size leather sofas and a couple deep chairs covered in what looked like chenille. Magazines were stacked on the end tables. A rug in deep colors anchored the space, in an intricate woven pattern. The walls had been left natural, so the logs seemed to fade away, and she guessed the focus was on an incredible view of the ranch and mountains out the floor-to-ceiling windows that covered the back wall. It was a room that could have been intimidating, but somehow felt homey and lived in, and Josie wanted in that moment to curl up on one of the couches in front of the fire and go to sleep.

Aunt Rosa hurried back down the hall with a towel, which Josie took gratefully.

"Thank you," she said, then gestured at the room. "This is—amazing."

"Yes. Actually, this part is the original house his father built. Luke and his brothers added on to it. Tomorrow you'll be able to see the view. I don't know if Luke told you, but this kind of rain isn't typical for this time of year."

She managed a smile. "So I just got lucky?"

Aunt Rosa smiled and patted her arm. "Something like that. Now, let's get these bags to your room so you can get into something dry, then I'll feed you."

Josie pulled the handle on her suitcase and looped the other two bags over her shoulders, waving off Aunt Rosa's extended hand. "I've got them. But thank you."

She followed her aunt's trim figure down the hall past that wonderful fireplace and was surprised to meet an older woman coming out of a room right at the beginning of the hall. She moved slower than her age would indicate, with a walker, and a bag of what appeared to be knitting supplies. Her smile was friendly as she saw them. "Well, hello. You must be Josie. I'm Alice Ryder, Luke's mother."

Josie extended her hand. "I am. Nice to meet you, Alice. Thanks for sharing your home with me."

Alice chuckled. "This is Luke's home. I've got my own a little farther down the lane. I'm a temporary guest."

"Alice had her hips replaced," Aunt Rosa explained.

"The boys insisted I stay here so they can keep an eye on me," Alice said cheerfully, and then her smile faded. "I'm glad you got here safe. This place is hard to find in the daylight, much less the rain and dark."

"Yes. I learned that the hard way," Josie admitted. Luke had been clear on her folly, and he'd been right to call her on it. Sheer stubbornness mixed with exhaustion had colored her judgment, and look where that had gotten her. "It's a mistake I won't make again."

Alice smiled at her. "I'm sure you won't. Now you get settled in and relax."

"This is a gorgeous house," Josie said as they continued on.

Rosa nodded "It is lovely. I love it here. But it's time for me to go spend some time with Kelly."

Rosa's first grandchild was due next week. "I know she'll be thrilled to have you around."

Rosa laughed. "Considering how long she waited to have children, she's not surprised that I want to be there." She paused to open a door a few steps down. "This is your room."

Josie followed her in. The bedside lamps were already on, which gave the room a lovely glow. She set her bags down on the floor, next to the one Luke had already dropped off. She thought she could catch a whiff of his scent lingering in the air. *Crazy.*

"You've got a view of the mountains," Rosa said. "In the morning you'll be able to see it."

"It's a lovely room. So—serene," Josie said. And it was. The walls here weren't log. They were painted a very pale lilac gray, a color that felt a little like twilight. The carpet was cream and very thick underfoot. The queen-size bed had a light blue quilt and a white coverlet folded over the end. There were a few framed photos on the wall, shots of what she assumed was the ranch. A small sitting area rounded out the space, with a television.

And a cattle skull over what turned out to be the bathroom.

"Yes," Rosa said, following her gaze with a good-natured sigh, "the senses of humor around here tend toward warped. I can take it down if you'd rather not look at it every day."

"Ah, no, it's fine," Josie said, eyeing it warily. She was in the West after all. "It lends character."

Rosa gave her another hug. "I'm so glad you're here."

"Me, too." Josie's stomach growled, and they both laughed. "So there's dinner?"

"Oh, yes," Rosa said and smiled. "Change if you'd like, then follow your nose to the kitchen." She left, pulling the door shut behind her.

It took Josie only a few minutes to use the bathroom and put on yoga pants and a long-sleeved T-shirt. She pulled her hair up in a ponytail and stared at her reflection with a wince. Pale, with dark circles under her eyes, she looked as exhausted as she felt. While she'd jumped at the chance to get out of LA, she wasn't sure after her adventures today that she was cut out for this kind of place.

She took a deep breath. She could do it. It was six weeks in the middle of nowhere, cooking for four people. She'd spent the past few years cooking for critics and crowds, her life consumed by her career. How hard could it be?

Chapter 2

Josie slept like a rock, and woke up confused when her smartphone alarm went off. She never slept through the night, in fact had prescription sleep medication that she tried not to take but often had to after several restless nights.

Blinking the sleep from her eyes, it took her a few seconds to remember where she was. The Silver River Ranch. She got up and hurried through her morning routine. Rosa had said she was usually in the kitchen by five, and it was nearly that now.

She hurried through the dark house and nearly screamed when a shadow detached itself from the darkness near the fireplace and hurtled itself at her, panting.

She darted behind a chair and whacked her shin on something hard. She bit back a curse and rubbed her aching leg as the shadow—a dark-colored dog—nosed her, tail going a mile a minute.

"You scared me," she said accusingly, and the dog sat, tail still going, apparently unfazed by her tone.

She sighed and gave the dog's head a quick pat, her heart still racing. She wasn't a fan of dogs. Or animals in general, though she'd taken riding lessons as a teen. She'd never had a pet in any of her thirty-two years. Her parents had been too busy, and she'd followed right in their footsteps in terms of throwing herself whole-heartedly into her work. No time for houseplants, much less a pet.

She moved around the dog, who trotted behind her into the kitchen. It already smelled heavenly, and most important, like coffee. Aunt Rosa looked up with a smile. "Good morning. Did you sleep okay? Ah, I see you met Hank."

"Good morning. I did, thanks." She decided not to mention her little run-in in the living room with the furniture. Getting spooked by an animal seemed like a poor start to her job here. "You let the ranch dogs in the house?" Apparently giving up on Josie, Hank trotted over to Rosa, who rubbed his ears.

"Not the working ones. When they get old or can't work for some reason they'll usually get adopted by a family member. Hank is Luke's dog." To the dog, she said, "Go lie down, Hank." He gave Josie another long look, then meandered out of the kitchen.

Rosa nodded toward the stack of white mugs on the counter next to the huge coffeepot. "Help yourself."

"Thanks." She moved around the island and poured

a cup, adding a little milk and sugar. She closed her eyes as she took a sip. "Wow. This is really excellent coffee, Aunt Rosa."

"Luke wants only the best," Rosa said cheerfully, and Josie's stomach soured just a little. *Only the best* was a familiar refrain. From her parents, from Russ.

She forced her lips into a smile. "Well, he got it here, for sure." She set the mug down with a solid *clink* on the granite counter, eager to get started. "So…where do I start?"

The next hour passed in a comfortable blur of cooking and preparation. Josie enjoyed the chance to cook with her aunt, and the time passed quickly. She eyed the mountain of food on the platters and Rosa, catching her expression, laughed.

"Yep, only three men and then you and I and Alice. But remember, this isn't just a nice meal out. This has to fuel them for hours and they can't just run in and grab a snack. They'll put a hurting on it."

Almost on cue, Josie heard the low rumble of men's voices and they entered the kitchen. Her gaze landed on Luke first. He just had on worn jeans and a flannel shirt over a T-shirt and the same hat as the night before, but her pulse gave a little skip. He gave her a polite nod. Before she could respond, two big guys stepped between them, and she looked up at them, startled. Her first thought was she'd never seen such good-looking siblings. All of them were tall and lean, with similar blue eyes, but their hair color wasn't all the same. Luke's was darker brown and these two were lighter. Still, they shared the same wide smile, similar to the one Alice had given her last night.

"Good morning," the taller of the two said with a charming grin. "I'm Cade, and this is Jake. You must be Josie."

"I am," she said, shaking first Cade's outstretched hand, then Jake's. No little zings or fizzles of awareness. Which was good, of course, but why had it happened with Luke? Maybe she'd just been tired. "Nice to meet you guys."

Behind them, Luke already had a plate, which he was heaping with food. Cade winked at her and said, "Looking forward to getting to know you better. Rosa's said a lot about you."

Ignoring the flirtatious first part of his comment, a little shiver of worry ran down her spine. Rosa didn't gossip, but what had she said? Josie hadn't talked a lot about her relationship with Russ, or the financial woes that had dogged them, but with his outsize personality and popular cooking show, he often made the gossip pages.

Rosa was beside her then, her hand light on Josie's arm. "I talked up your cooking skills," she said cheerfully. "As you've worked hard for them."

Josie relaxed slightly. "Ah. Well, I'm not sure you guys want the kind of food I've been cooking for the past year or so. More for show than sustenance." There may have been the slightest tinge of bitterness in her tone, so she smiled at both men to soften it. "So I'm looking forward to cooking real meals again."

They exchanged a bit more good-natured chatter as

Cade and Jake loaded up their plates and then left for the dining room, where she could hear the clink of silverware and the low rumble of voices.

"I didn't say anything about your personal life," Rosa said quietly as she carried a platter to the sink. "I just said you were between jobs at the moment and could fill in for me temporarily. I don't know all that happened with you, honey, but I know it must have been bad to put those shadows in your eyes and to bring you all the way up here."

The concern in her aunt's voice made Josie want to cry. She blinked away the moisture. "I won't lie. It's been rough. But it'll all work out." She took a deep breath. "What can you tell me about those two?"

There was a slight pause, then apparently her aunt accepted the change in subject. "Cade is a flirt," she said. "Harmless, but a flirt nonetheless. But he won't push you or take it too far. He just loves women of all ages. Luke is the opposite. He won't flirt at all. Jake is in the middle. They're all good boys. Any one of them would be a wonderful catch."

Josie bit back a sigh. While that was good to know, she wasn't looking for any kind of relationship—long-term or temporary. Of all she'd been through personally, the worst had been realizing that *engaged* hadn't meant the same thing to Russ as it did to her. Thank God she'd figured it all out well before the wedding.

She kept her tone noncommittal. "I think it's wonderful that you think so highly of them, but that's not why I'm here." Then she added, "I'm famished. I haven't eaten a breakfast like this in ages." Sad but true. Yogurt and a piece of fruit usually made up her first meal of the day. Eaten in her car on the way to the restaurant. And that was because Russ had made so many comments about her tasting the food. *Be careful. Too many bites will make you fat.* She'd laughed it off at the time, but in retrospect, it made her slightly ill.

Rosa handed her a plate. "Of course, that's not why you're here. But you never know what might develop. If you close yourself off to possibilities, you might miss something special."

Josie didn't fully agree. She wasn't concerned about missing something special. She intended to keep her heart under wraps for the foreseeable future.

Luke hadn't bargained on the new cook.

Sure, Rosa had asked if her niece could take over while she spent some of her vacation time with her daughter, who was expecting a baby soon. Trusting the older woman completely, he'd said sure. He'd listened to Rosa explain with pride that Josie was a trained chef, and had owned her own restaurant in Los Angeles that people flocked to.

He hadn't thought about her being a *woman*.

It had been so long since he'd looked—really looked—at a woman, that when she'd glared at him from her car with her blue eyes narrowed, the pepper spray can in her hand, he'd been shocked to feel the unwelcome rush of attraction. And she was a self-confessed city girl to boot, which was a huge no-no in his book. He'd married a city girl.

He was no longer married.

So to feel something for someone who wore three-inch spike heels to stomp across a muddy, wet road in the wilds of Montana wasn't a good sign.

But damn, they'd looked good on her, even in the mud and rain.

"Don't you think so, Luke?" Cade's question broke into his thoughts.

Luke looked up from the sausage and gravy he'd been demolishing on his plate. "What was that?"

Cade stabbed the egg on his plate. "Josie. She's a looker."

Since she'd just been occupying his thoughts he shook his head, the denial as much for him as his brothers. "I wouldn't know."

Cade looked at Jake incredulously. "He's blind."

"Or stupid," Jake suggested, but there was a glint of humor in his eyes.

"Or both." Cade looked at him hard. "Luke. It's okay to, you know, think a woman is hot."

He shrugged. "She's not my type."

"Maybe she's mine," Cade said thoughtfully, and took a bite of toast.

Luke leveled a glare at him. "Don't even. She's our employee, not a plaything for you."

A slow smile spread across Cade's face and he pointed what was left of the toast in Luke's direction. "You did notice." He turned to Jake, who nodded as he chewed. "He sure as hell did. Well, well. That's a first, isn't it?"

He'd have to be dead not to notice Josie, but he wasn't

going to say that to either of his brothers. Ever. Before he could say anything, Jake held up his coffee.

"Leave him alone, Cade. He wants to ignore her, that's his business and his loss. He's hiding, remember?"

Luke bit back a groan. He'd stepped away from performing, from that life to avoid all sorts of entanglements. His brothers might accuse him of hiding, but he'd wanted to just focus on the ranch, to get it into the black and after years of his father running it on the edge of total ruin. To prove he was more than the kid who couldn't wait to bust out of here with big dreams.

He kept his voice steady. "I'm not hiding. I'm retired. Big difference. We've got a lot to do today. I've got to get that car out of the ditch, so I can't go all the way up to the ridge."

The talk changed direction then, and Luke was more than happy to let it go. His brothers meant well, and they'd tease him, but they didn't know just how destructive his marriage had been—and with the benefit of hindsight, how unprepared he'd been, not only for the spotlight but all it entailed.

He'd learned the hard way he was better off on his own, not caught in the bright lights of Nashville's glare.

Finished with his meal, Luke brought his dishes into the kitchen along with his brothers, who then headed out the door. Josie was on the other side of the kitchen, spooning something into a container. Outside, he could see the peaks of the mountains turning pink with the sunrise.

"Josie," he said, and she turned, spoon in hand, polite expression on her face. "I'm going to get your car. Do you have the keys?"

"I do. In my room. Hang on." She set the spoon down and hurried out of the kitchen. His gaze tracked the sway of her hips as she disappeared from sight.

"Thanks for helping her," Rosa said from her perch at the end of the island, and when he snapped his gaze to her, he realized from the bemused expression on her face that not only had he been staring after Josie's slender figure, her aunt had caught him.

Damn.

He cleared his throat. "You're welcome. Least I can do, after all you've done for us."

Rosa waved his words away. "Nonsense. But, Luke? Be careful. She's fragile. Even if she won't admit it."

Before he could either ask what she meant or deny any interest in her niece, Josie came back and handed him the keys. "Thanks for doing this." Her tone was formal and polite, not the easy one she'd used with Cade and Jake. Just as well.

"You're welcome." A tendril of her short blond hair had escaped from her headband, and he curled his fingers around the keys so he didn't tuck it back in. He added, "That car won't do you much good in a few weeks, though. It can snow here as early as October." It wasn't likely, but she needed to understand where she was. He rubbed Hank's ears when the old dog leaned on his leg.

She frowned, whether at his words or the dog, he wasn't sure. "I know that. It was the only one they had."

He gave Hank a last pat. "We'll take it back. You can

use one of the ranch trucks. It'll save you money and be safer for you on these roads."

Josie's first instinct was to snap at him and say she was completely capable of making that choice on her own, thank you very much, but then she realized he was right. He knew this area and she, of course, didn't, as she'd proved last night. She most definitely didn't want to get herself in a situation where she needed him to fish her out of the ditch again. Or worse. She sighed. "All right. Thank you."

"You sore or anything from yesterday?"

Surprised at his concern, she lifted her brows. Her shoulder was, in fact, a little sore from the seat belt. She touched the sore spot. "A little. It could have been much worse."

His gaze sharpened as it landed on her hand. "Do you need a doctor? There's a clinic in town, or a hospital in Kalispell."

Josie dropped her hand and shook her head. "Oh, no. It's fine. I took a couple ibuprofen." She'd taken a hot shower last night and that had helped, too. It had been such a low-speed accident, it was a wonder anything had hurt at all.

"If that changes, let us know. I'll let you know when I'm back." He left her standing in the kitchen as he went out, and didn't look back.

Well.

She huffed out an annoyed breath and propped her hands on her hips. She could not read him. At all. She'd apologized for last night. She had to work here and live here with him for the next several weeks. It would be uncomfortable if he didn't like her.

Rosa came back in the kitchen with Alice, who dropped a bagel in the toaster, despite Rosa's fussing that she sit and let Rosa do it. Their cheerful interaction told Josie that this was a regular morning occurrence.

"Every day, we go through this," Alice told her with a laugh. "And every day, same result. Don't we, old friend?"

Rose pulled a jar of preserves out of the fridge. "Yes, we do." To Josie she said, "Don't be put off by Luke's grumpiness. He's a good man."

She gave both women a wry smile. "I'm sure he is. He doesn't seem to like me much, though." Not that they'd gotten off to the best start.

Alice sighed. "Give him time. You might remind him of his ex-wife."

Josie gaped at her. "What? How can you say that?" She pictured Mandy Fairchild, the petite platinum-blonde country singer, with her huge brown eyes and bombshell figure. Josie was tall and thin. No curves. They couldn't be more different. "Um. No."

Rosa laughed. "I don't think she meant physically, honey." She looked at Alice for confirmation.

Alice nodded as she spread the rich red preserves on her bagel. "That's right. I meant your background. From a big city, in a new environment. Mandy lasted about a month out here. He doesn't know you and he probably thinks you'll bolt as soon as things get tough."

Josie raised a brow. "I'm not staying for long," she pointed out.

"No," Alice agreed. "Of course not. But you know how things can trigger the memories even when you're not expecting it. It doesn't have to make sense."

"True," Josie said. But she didn't think there was anything up here that would trigger anything for her. It couldn't be more different from home. She looked out the huge window over the sink. There was no glitz and glam, but the pink-kissed mountains scraped the sky and took her breath away. "Wow. Oh, my gosh. Look at that."

Her aunt came and stood beside her and looked out. "Yes. I see that every morning and it never fails to make me catch my breath. I love it up here."

Alice smiled as she came up beside them. "I've lived my whole life in Montana. And I've never failed to be humbled by the natural beauty up here."

Rosa carried Alice's plate and coffee out of the kitchen. A few minutes later, she was back. "She likes the living room, where she can see the views and watch the news, too. That reminds me. It's satellite TV out here and it can be a little hit-or-miss in bad weather. Now, I'm heading out in a couple of hours. Let's get you up to speed. I'll show you what I do and you can take it from there."

They spent a good hour at the little table in the breakfast room off the kitchen, where Josie could see not only the mountains but the barns and people moving around. It was hard to believe just a couple days ago she'd been in one of the biggest cities in the world. "Feel free to put your own spin on anything. This isn't a sacred document," Rosa said with a chuckle. "It's just things that work well for me and hopefully for you, too. Not haute cuisine, I'm afraid."

Josie ran her hand over the torn and faded cover. "I wouldn't expect that out here. There's no reason for it. It's comfort food, and hearty meals." And she could work with all of it, make little changes and tweaks that wouldn't take away at all from her aunt's meals. "It'll be fun."

She'd work around the awkwardness with Luke and remember it was only for six weeks. She was tough. She could do pretty much anything for six weeks. Even learn how to live in the wilderness of Montana.

Chapter 3

Josie called the rental company while her aunt went to finish packing for her trip and made sure she could drop the car off earlier than planned. The problem was, she'd need a ride back from Kalispell. Would a taxi come out this far? It didn't seem likely.

Luke came in the kitchen. He tipped his head in her direction as he headed to the sink to wash his hands and then over to the fridge, where he started pulling out the fixings for a sandwich. "Got the car. It's fine. Some grass and dirt stuck up under the front bumper, and it's muddy, but no actual damage."

Josie expelled a long breath and relief slid through her. She wouldn't have to worry about the money, then. "Oh, good. Thank you."

"Did you talk to the car company?"

Josie turned back to the potato casserole she was preparing for dinner. She'd pop it in the fridge until it was time to put it in the oven. "I did. I can return it anytime."

"Do you want to go tomorrow? May as well get it taken care of." When she hesitated, not wanting to put him out any more than she already had, he added, "I've got to pick up a part for the tractor over there anyway. May as well take care of both things at once."

She nodded. "Okay. As long as you're sure. I can probably make other arrangements."

He chuckled as she covered the pan in tin foil. "No, you couldn't. It'd cost you a fortune."

She sighed. "That's what I was afraid of." And money was at a premium right now. She'd sunk most of it in the restaurant, only to lose it to Russ.

He touched her shoulder as she picked up the heavy casserole pan. She almost fumbled it in surprise. He'd been so cool toward her she'd never expected him to actually touch her. Even if he pulled his hand back awfully fast. "You'll have to get used to it. It's nothing like where you're from."

Before she could say anything, Rosa came in the kitchen, and Luke gave her a hug. They exchanged goodbyes, and before Luke left, he asked Josie, "Is eight okay tomorrow? I'd like to get the part before eleven."

"Eight's fine," she said and tried not to notice Rosa looking between them curiously. Luke left and Josie smiled at her. "Are you ready? You have everything?"

Rosa patted her shoulder bag. "I think so. And the boys gave me a tablet for the trip, so I can watch movies and read. Wasn't that nice of them?"

"It was," she agreed. "I'm sure Kelly can't wait to see you."

Rosa gave her a big hug. "I can't wait to see her and meet my new grandbaby. But I do wish I had more time here with you. Enjoy your time here. Relax."

Josie hugged her back. "I wish we did, too. But Kelly's waiting for you." She didn't touch the "relax" portion of the comment, since it'd been so long since she'd really relaxed that she wasn't sure she knew how to anymore.

"Give Luke time," Rosa said as Josie walked with her through the house. "He'll come around."

Josie laughed. Aunt Rosa was determined to make her point about Luke. "Oh, no. Not going to happen."

Rosa gave her a little smile, then sighed. "I know. I'm sorry, I don't mean to keep bringing it up. I just want to see you happy. Him, too."

Josie stopped in her tracks and looked around for Alice. The last thing she needed was Luke's mother hearing any of this. "Oh, Aunt Rosa. That's nice of you to say, but there's no way I'm staying here. My life is in LA." What was left of it, of course. But she had every intention of salvaging what—if anything—she could and starting over. She didn't need a celebrity chef to give her credibility.

The next morning she had breakfast done and cleaned up in time to leave. She made sure there was sandwich stuff in the fridge from the leftover roast the night before, since she wouldn't be back in time for lunch, but the men had taken box lunches with them when they went out that morning. She heard Luke asking his mother if she'd be okay while they were gone. Patty, the wife of one of the ranch hands, would be in the house, watching TV with her, but Josie understood his hesitation. He didn't want anything else to happen to her.

She waved him off. "Luke. I'll be fine. We are just going to watch *True Blood* and knit. It's not as if you're leaving me for a week to fend for myself. I'm healing well and this place is crawling with people."

Josie shrugged into her sweatshirt with a smile. Luke might be grumpy toward her, but he clearly had a protective streak a mile wide when it came to his mother.

She stepped out on the porch to wait. It was a lovely morning, but not what she was used to. When was the last time she'd stood outside and appreciated the morning? It wasn't really quiet—the birds were chattering up a storm and she could hear some of the hands down by the barns, their laughter carrying on the still morning air. The grass was damp with dew and the air smelled— fresh. No exhaust, food scents, the general smell of a city in a hot climate. Nothing like what she was used to. It wasn't eighty degrees already—in fact, it was cold— and there was no smog or traffic noise.

It was a little unsettling. As was the fact she'd nearly overslept. Again.

The door opened and closed behind her and she turned to see Luke standing there. "Sorry about that. I just had to make sure Mom was okay."

She smiled at him. "No problem. I understand." She wondered what her own mother was doing right now. Of course, her own mother was much younger than Luke's. She must have had the boys at a much older age.

"Let's go, then. You'll need to follow me. It'll be easier for you."

Josie got in the little rental car and followed the big truck down the lane to the road. He was absolutely right that this kind of car wasn't suited to this area. But the SUV she'd reserved at her aunt's suggestion had been given away when she hadn't made it to the rental place before the cutoff time. This was what they'd had left.

The trip in the daylight was eye-opening. The views were killer and she could see, after they'd gone a half hour before seeing another vehicle as they neared the small town of Powder Keg, just how remote the Silver River was. The roads near the ranch were rough, too. She wondered if that was by design, to help discourage people from tracking Luke down. Or if it was simply that the county had other things to do than maintain roads that were hardly driven.

They drove through the little town with its general store that, from the signs on its front, advertised it sold everything, including animal feed, groceries and clothing. There were two bars, a diner, a bakery, a drug store. A couple churches. One stoplight. The streets were wide and the little town seemed to crouch down in the shadow of the mountains. It was a working town, not a tourist town, but Josie thought it had an Old West appeal all its own.

Having left Powder Keg behind, it was another fifteen minutes before they reached the highway that took them to Kalispell. Josie spotted a couple huge elk grazing off the road and figured a collision with one of them would end badly for all involved. Especially in this car, which probably weighed less than one of those elk.

Kalispell was much busier. A tiny fraction of the size of Los Angeles, but traffic was one thing she knew how to navigate without problems, and there was plenty of it here. The town was charming, something she hadn't appreciated when she'd first arrived, thanks to all the drama she'd endured. Luke pulled in the rental car place at the airport and she parked the car beside him. He opened the door to get out but she shook her head at him. "This will just take a minute."

She ran in and went through the process. The guy came out and gave the car no more than a cursory glance over, even though she'd told them on the phone it had slid in a ditch. When she had her paperwork, she hurried back out to the rumbling truck and hauled herself in rather awkwardly.

"Thanks," she said. "Where to now?"

He put the truck in Reverse. "The equipment dealership."

She hesitated a second, then said, "Would it be all right if we stopped at the grocery store, too? I know you're in a hurry, but it won't take me long. There are a few things I'd like to stock up on while we're here."

"Sure. Actually, why don't I drop you off there. There's a grocery store just down the road from the dealer. I'll just come back and wait in the parking lot."

She agreed, and he left her at the store and she went in, pulling her list out. There were a few things she didn't know if she could get that she might have to order. She'd have to ask how that worked—did the delivery couriers come all the way out to the ranch? She wasn't even sure how mail got there. Maybe she could arrange for delivery in town somewhere and then pick it up. She made a mental note to ask Luke when he came back.

She grabbed a cart and wheeled it down the spice

aisle. This store was bright, with wide, well-stocked aisles. They had a surprisingly good collection of spices and fresh items. She loaded up and checked out. When she came out, she spotted the big red truck, Luke at the wheel, his hat tipped back on his head. He pulled forward, stopping in front of her.

"You find what you needed?" he asked as he opened the back door of the truck, and she settled her bags on the floor.

"I did. They've got a lot in there. Just out of curiosity, if I need to order anything, where is it delivered?"

They got in and shut the doors. He put the truck in gear. "Schaffer's—the general store—is where all Silver River deliveries go. Couple times a week someone goes in and gets the mail from the post office and anything that gets delivered. Hungry?"

She hadn't realized it until right that moment, but yes, she was. "Yes."

"There's a good little diner up here. That okay with you or would you rather do a drive-through?"

She laughed. "I can't think of the last time I ate at a drive-through."

He arched a brow in her direction. "Food snob much?"

She shook her head. "Not so much. Just too busy to bother." It was true. It was also true she'd never left the restaurant hungry.

That thought gave her a little twinge.

"Well, this place has great burgers," he said. "And it won't take long. I know you need to get back."

He pulled in the parking lot of a dingy-looking building. The flowers had clearly not been watered in weeks and the blacktop was cracked and weeds grew through them. Luke gave her a full-on grin, and it stole her breath how it transformed his face. Even with the dour expression he usually wore he was handsome. But the smile was something else. "Don't worry. Trust me, okay?"

"Okay," she said, and got out of the truck. The day was starting to heat up. She took her sweatshirt off and tied it around her waist and followed Luke to the door.

Inside it was every bit as small as it looked from the outside. Eight booths and four tables made up the whole place. Three of those were occupied. The floor was cracked vinyl, but clean. The booth the waitress led them to was slightly sticky in the way all diner booths seemed to be, and while it, too, was faded and old, it was clean. The whole place smelled divine. Her mouth watered.

He handed her a small laminated paper. "All you can get here are burgers," he said. "With your choice of fries or onion rings. So there's no real menu, but this is the list of toppings."

Josie took it from him. So this would be an adventure, then. She was game. "All right."

The waitress came back over with tall glasses of water. "What can I get you to drink today?"

Josie chose a diet soda and Luke an iced tea. Then they placed their burger orders. She went with honey mustard, brie and Granny Smith apples on a burger cooked medium. Luke got so many things on his she couldn't keep track.

The waitress left and came back with their drinks.

"So you closed your restaurant?"

His words jarred her. Luke probably thought he was making polite conversation. He had no idea what a minefield that question was. She took a sip of her soda and traced a finger on the laminate tabletop. "It's not quite that easy," she said, settling on a version of the truth. "I had a partner. He has it now."

If he picked up on the bitterness in her tone, he didn't show it. "What made you leave?"

She managed a smile. "It was time to move on. That's why this was perfect timing."

Luke studied her for a second. There was something there she wasn't telling him, but he wasn't going to press. He knew all about keeping things private, and he wasn't going to make her uncomfortable, especially when he didn't know her very well. "Fortunate for us."

Her smile was more real that time and reached her eyes. "I hope so."

She asked some questions about the ranch, and he was more than happy to talk about it, especially since she seemed truly interested in his answers. The waitress delivered two steaming plates of food, and he saw Josie's eyes widen almost comically. "I guess I forgot to mention it's enough to feed a couple people."

She folded her napkin in her lap with a small laugh. "I guess so."

He took a bite of his fully loaded bacon cheeseburger and chewed reverently. There wasn't another place in the world like this. If there was, he hadn't found it. And he'd looked in all the cities he'd played over the years he'd been touring with his band.

"This is amazing," she said, and her tongue slipped

out to catch a dab of ketchup. His gaze snagged on the motion and heat flared inside him, deep and hot. He picked up his tea and took several swallows, hoping the cold liquid would cool him down. He hadn't expected to react to another woman like that—and definitely not another city girl with no plans to stay.

She looked up then, and he was pretty sure she caught him looking at her like something he'd like to eat. She patted her face self-consciously with her napkin. "Did I get ketchup all over?"

"No," he said, and his voice was a little rough in his throat. "No, you're fine."

She gave him a little frown, and he turned his plate and offered her an onion ring to cover the awkward moment. "Want to try one?"

She picked a small one off his plate and took a bite. She closed her eyes as she chewed. "Mmm. Wow. Amazing."

"Not haute cuisine, I guess." It had mattered to Mandy that there was no place, at the time, to get things like sushi in the area. To find a five-star restaurant that wasn't a steak house.

She opened her eyes and frowned at him. "Good food is good food, Luke. It doesn't all have to be fancy and complicated."

He hid a smile. "Sorry. You're right."

She moved her plate out of the way and leaned forward. It was enough to push her breasts up, and he managed to keep his eyes on her face. With great effort. "I'm trained as a chef, but I'm a cook, period. I love to hang out in the kitchen, experiment with recipes and create new ones. Really, the whole idea of haute cuisine doesn't appeal to me. It was part of what led to my split with my partner. Different visions for a lot of things, the very least of which was the menu."

"I understand." He did. She looked at it as an expression of herself, like he had with music. Still did, even if he didn't perform anymore. He wondered if the split had been personal as well as professional, but it wasn't any of his business.

She picked up another fry and nibbled on it. "Do you think I can get a box? I can't take the fries home, but I'd hate to waste the burger."

He'd managed to demolish his. In fact he'd all but licked the plate clean. "I don't know. I'm sure you can. I've never needed one."

She laughed and the sound flowed over him, almost made him smile. "I'm not surprised."

She did get a to-go box and he paid the bill, after she insisted on leaving the tip. They walked through the Montana sunshine to his truck. She made him feel— lighter. She hadn't once referred to his history as a country star. He allowed so few new people into his world it was always a surprise when that happened, because so many over the years had wanted something from him. Or they hadn't wanted him—they'd wanted the country star.

So while it was refreshing to be with someone who didn't have demands or expectations, it was dangerous, too. He didn't want to let down his guard only to learn he'd trusted the wrong person. Again.

Chapter 4

Two days later, Josie couldn't get the trip they'd made to town out of her mind. Or how easy it had been to be with Luke. When he let down the gruff exterior, he was a charming, funny man. Between the laugh lines around those incredible blue eyes and the small dimple in his cheek—

Sexy.

She shook her head to clear the unwelcome thought. She wasn't even going to go there.

"You up for a little walk?"

Josie started and looked up at Alice, who was standing there with a smile. A little thread of embarrassment ran through her. Thank goodness the other woman couldn't read her thoughts.

"Sure. Where to?" She wanted to ask if it was okay

for Alice to do that, but she didn't know the other woman well enough to do so.

As if she'd read Josie's mind, Alice smiled a little wider. "It's okay. We're just going to my house, which is the one down the lane a little way. It's a nice, even path. I need a couple of things. If you don't mind."

"I don't mind at all." She followed Alice out the back door, Hank on her heels. She turned to shoo him back in, but Alice shook her head.

"Let him come. He'll be fine, even if he wanders off."

"Okay." Josie held the door for both Alice and the dog, and watched carefully as the older woman navigated the steps. Hank was very courteous as well, waiting for her to be on the ground before trotting after her and looking back at Josie as if to say, *What are you waiting for?* This late in the afternoon it was comfortably warm out, but not hot. She was still trying to adjust to this weather. Cold enough at night for a fire and a quilt, hot enough during the day for short sleeves. The house didn't even have central air.

"Not long now," Alice said cheerfully. "I go back to the doctor next week. Hoping to get the all clear. Then the boys won't argue when I move back into my own house."

Josie rather thought they'd check on her every hour, but she kept it to herself. Hank stopped to examine a bush, then raised his leg.

"I agreed to stay up here because otherwise they'd be checking in with me every ten minutes. Seemed easier to just be where they are. For all of us," she said on a little laugh.

"That makes sense," Josie said, because even after just a few days she could see how devoted these guys were to their mother. It was a refreshing change. Alice hadn't been kidding—her house wasn't far from the main house at all, but around a curve and behind a copse of trees that made it feel farther away than it was. As a bonus, it added to the privacy for all of them.

"Someday Cade and Jake will build their own houses," Alice said. "For now, they all live in the big house since it's a central location. And—well, and Luke remodeled that house thinking he'd have a big family. That didn't happen. But they each have land on this same property."

"That makes sense," Josie said, caught for a moment on the fact Luke had wanted a big family. She wasn't sure, but she thought his marriage had probably been over before the house had even been finished. But she wasn't going to go there, not with his mother. So she asked the safe question. "How big is the ranch?"

"Almost three thousand acres," Alice said. "Some of that is leased from the rancher to the north. He is dialing back his spread but isn't ready to sell."

Josie's eyes bugged. "Three thousand acres?" She couldn't even wrap her mind around that amount of land. True, she'd seen no other people or signs of people on her drive out here, but given the apparent propensity for half-hidden drives, it was likely she'd missed it. Not many, though. Three thousand acres was an awful lot of land.

Alice laughed. "Yes. It's a big place."

"Wow," Josie said. "I had no idea." She lived in a

condo. With lots of other condos and other buildings. Nothing like this.

The wide front porch was one step up. She followed Alice in and was immediately charmed by the little log house. It had a lovely open floor plan, with the kitchen, dining and living area all open to each other. There was another stone fireplace and the fabrics on the couch and chairs were all soft. There were throws all over and another brightly patterned rug, similar to the one in the main house, was on the floor. The end tables were piled high with books. She could see a bed through one of the open doors at the other side of the room, and the bathroom through the other. The back wall of the main room had sliding glass doors, and Josie could see Alice had an incredible view of the mountains. She wasn't sure there was a bad view anywhere on the Silver River.

If she could build a little house here, this was what it'd look like.

"I love this," she said, and Alice smiled.

"Luke had it built for me. He's very generous. Asked what I wanted. He was willing to go big, bless him, but this is all I need, since it's just me now. It suits me to a T. I do miss the main house," she said with a sigh. "But it was just way more than I needed. I really love my own space, though. So will you help me carry a couple things back?"

"Of course." She helped Alice gather a few items and put them in a bag, which Josie carried. She'd been a little worried that Alice might try to push Luke on her, especially since he'd driven her to Kalispell and they'd been alone for a few hours, but she didn't. Her feelings were decidedly mixed when it came to Luke. He put her off balance, which, for someone who had conceded control unwittingly, could develop into a major issue.

She put him out of her mind as she and Alice walked back to the main house. She'd find a way to deal with this. It wasn't for all that long. It was perfectly okay for her to find him attractive. It meant Russ hadn't damaged her beyond repair.

Alice went back to her room and Josie went back into the kitchen. She had dinner almost done, and the men would be back before too long. She put the finishing touches on the meal and got everything set to be served as they came in through the back door. She was getting pretty good on the timing. She didn't know if it was just luck that had them all coming in around the same time or if this was a common occurrence. Each of the four nights she'd been at the Silver River, the men went back out after each meal until dark. Evening chores, they said. It seemed like a hard life, with long, incredible hours and hard work that never ended and a constant battle with the elements. She'd only been here a week and she had an incredible amount of respect for ranchers and those who chose this life, not to mention a newfound respect for Mother Nature.

She looked again out the long window above the kitchen sink. There were no window treatments and she could see why—the view didn't need anything to enhance it. The sharp peaks, the rolling green pastures, the tiny black dots that she knew were cattle all caught her attention. It was both gorgeous and overwhelming.

* * *

"So," Cade said with a smile as he set his dishes on the counter after dinner, "have you been to the barns yet?"

"No," Josie said. She'd actually been kind of avoiding it. She felt comfortable in the house. Outside—well, that was a whole other story. Even her walk with Alice earlier had been a tad unsettling.

Not seeming to catch her reluctance, Cade said, "Can you come down for a tour tomorrow morning? I've got to meet with a potential buyer for one of my horses at eleven, but if you came down about ten, that would give me time to show you around and you'd still have plenty of time to get your things done."

Josie swabbed the counter with the dishrag. She knew she should go and see for herself how this place was run. Not really seeing any way to decline, she smiled at Cade. "That sounds good. Thanks for the offer."

He told her where to meet him and left the kitchen whistling. She finished her cleanup and the prep for the next morning. Already, she was finding a rhythm here. That was good.

So the next morning after breakfast, Josie dutifully left the house at the appointed time and walked down to the barns, Hank the dog trotting after her. She'd asked Alice if it was okay, and she'd said yes. The yard sloped down to the barn area. It was a good walk. She wore jeans and tennis shoes, not real sure of the proper footwear for a barn tour, but reasonably sure her boots with the three-inch spike heels weren't it.

Hank wandered off as she approached the meeting place. Cade came up while she was looking after the dog, trying to decide if she needed to call him back or not. Alice had told her before to let him go, but she just wasn't sure.

"He'll go back when he's hungry," Cade said, his voice cheerful. "He knows where the food bowl is. Ready?"

She turned her attention to the handsome cowboy in front of her looking at her with a warm smile. She smiled back. "I am."

She followed him into the depths of the huge barn. It was bigger and brighter than she'd thought it would be, and smelled of horses and leather and hay, all things she remembered from her long-ago days of riding. There were a good dozen or so stalls, most with the doors open, unoccupied. It had an indoor arena, with a soaring ceiling and clerestory windows. She stopped.

"Wow. This is amazing." It rivaled the prestigious barn she'd taken lessons at all those years ago, after her mom had gotten a good job and dated the guy who managed the facility. The outside of this barn didn't give a clue to what was inside.

Cade shoved his hat back on his head. "We've put a lot into this. Patty and Jim can train in here all year round. They even hold clinics in here sometimes," he said, nodding toward the small gallery area at one end. "We've all worked hard to build this."

Josie nodded. "I can see that."

Cade was a knowledgeable guide and clearly loved what he did here. They finished in the horse barn and stepped outside, which brought them face-to-face with Luke.

Josie stiffened at his look. His eyes narrowed as he

took in her and Cade. But Cade had a smug look on his face he wasn't bothering to hide as he rocked back on his heels.

Cade gave his brother a nod, but Josie saw Luke's face darken a little. Was he unhappy to see her in his space? That seemed unlikely, but he was hard for her to read. Cade looked from her to Luke, and the smug look turned into a smile.

"You want to finish this, big brother? I thought it'd be a good idea to let Josie get acquainted with the ranch while she's here." He looked at his watch. "I've got to get ready for my client anyway." He touched her arm lightly. "Is that okay, Josie? You'll be in good hands with my brother here."

Luke gave her a nod, but his face remained expressionless. "I've got some time."

"Great. See you later." Cade strode off whistling, and Josie stared after him for a minute, wondering if somehow they'd just been played. Cade hadn't seemed very surprised to see Luke.

Well, of course not. They all worked here after all. And now it was just her and Luke. She looked at him and waited for him to say...anything.

"What did Cade show you?" He was ever so polite. No hint of the fun and humor he'd displayed on their trip to town a few days ago. They were back to the stiffness and formality, clearly. She swallowed a sigh.

Josie turned around and indicated with her hand. "Some of the horses, which he explained was his own business on the ranch. I'm not sure where we were going next, actually."

"Okay." Luke walked toward the back of the barn. "Let me show you something."

Curious, she followed him out of the relatively dim barn into the bright light of outside.

Almost immediately her gaze seemed to hone right in on him, rather than the gorgeous scenery around them. He wore worn jeans that looked as if they'd been made just for him, hugging his rear and legs in a way that made her want to reach out and run her hand over the curve of his butt. Appalled, she jerked her gaze back up to his shoulder blades. His broad back was equally as enticing, with the henley shirt he wore stretched nicely across his back. Goodness. She slid her shades off her head and onto her nose. What was wrong with her? She'd never even looked at Russ that way, as if she just wanted to eat him up, and she'd been planning to marry him.

Maybe that was part of the problem.

Maybe. But there was no way to follow that to its logical conclusion. Frankly, just because she thought Luke was hot didn't mean anything more than that. She stepped up beside Luke rather than walk behind him and get herself in trouble, and headed toward the large, round, fenced-in paddock where a trim woman was working a horse.

"Hey, Nikki," he said as they approached the fence. "How's he going today?"

The big bay horse tossed his head, but didn't break stride as Nikki slowly rotated to keep up with him as he loped in a circle at the end of a long line. She was tall and slim, and in her sleeveless top, her arms were muscular and browned from the sun. Her long blond hair was caught in a loose ponytail under her hat, and Josie thought she bore a striking resemblance to his ex-wife.

But Nikki's smile was wide and open as she glanced at them next to the fence, with no sign of anything flirty. And why that mattered, Josie didn't want to even think about. Maybe after so many years of being on the sidelines and not noticed, being eclipsed by the guy with her, it was just nice to not have another woman look at her as though she was the enemy. "Good. Real good, Luke. I think he'll be ready soon. I already told Cade."

Luke kept his eyes on the horse and Josie sneaked a look up at him. He was clearly assessing the horse's movement, and there was a genuine sparkle in his eye. She nearly peered closer, but that would be rude. So instead she looked back at the horse, who had slowed to a trot. She didn't know much about horses, not really, but she did think this one was beautiful.

"Ready for what?" she asked, leaning on the fence. The smooth wood was cool on her arms. The sun was getting warm on her back, but it felt good. The pound of the horse's hooves on the hard ground was steady background noise.

"Cade trains top-notch cutting horses here," he said. "Nikki's one of the best around."

Nikki made a motion and the horse stopped, but his eye was still on her. She walked over, looping the rope up, and patted his neck as she led him to the fence. "What Luke didn't tell you is he's just as good with the horses as his brother is. Modest to a fault." When Luke shifted beside her she gave him a knowing grin. "You are." To Josie she held out her hand and said, "Nikki Thurman."

Josie took the other woman's hand, felt the roughness and strength of her palm from all the ropes and horses she handled. "Josie Callahan. I'm filling in for my aunt as the cook at the main house."

Nikki nodded. "That's right. So nice to meet you. How do you like Montana? You're from Cali, right?"

Luke ducked under the fence and took the horse from Nikki. She stepped back, but he didn't take him anywhere. Josie watched as he stroked the horse's legs and ran his hands all over the horse's body. The horse didn't flinch.

"I am," she said, shifting her attention to Nikki. "This is—this is different from what I'm used to. Beautiful, though. Overwhelmingly so."

Nikki nodded. "I understand. I came here from a small town in the Midwest—nothing like where you're from—but it wasn't remote like this, nor was it beautiful in this way. Montana, and this more remote area especially, is rugged and wild in a way few places are anymore."

"How long have you been here?" Josie was genuinely curious. Nikki was young and gorgeous. This didn't seem like the optimal place for a woman like her.

Nikki put her hands on her hips and cocked her head. The breeze blew her ponytail back over her shoulder. "Six years? Yeah, six years this winter. Yes, I came out here in the winter," she said on a laugh.

Luke handed the lead back to Nikki. "He's good. Get video of him and get it up on the site in the next week or so."

"Sounds good." To Josie she said, "Nice to meet you.

I'm down here every day if you ever want to keep me company."

"Thanks," Josie said, a feeling of warmth in her chest. Nikki could be a friend. She hadn't expected that out here. "I'll do that."

Nikki flashed her another smile before leading the horse away.

"What kind of site?" She'd known Luke did something with horses, but her aunt hadn't really said a whole lot. And Josie didn't know a lot about this type of business anyway.

"For the horses. When they're ready, they go up on the website. People wait for them to go up."

"So you raise and train them?"

"Some," Luke said. "Some are bought at auction. And sometimes Cade will take on someone's horse and train it for them. But that takes a lot of time. Nikki and Jim, who's not here today, are the trainers, and my brothers and I train, too. Cade really runs this end of the operation. No thanks to our father."

"I see," she said carefully.

Luke didn't look at her. Instead, he watched Nikki lead the horse back to the barn. His tone was almost expressionless, but she saw a muscle tick in his jaw. "When I got back here after—after everything ended in Nashville, the ranch was in bad shape financially. My father had made some risky decisions to try to save this place and then he died before he could really make them pan out—if they would have panned out at all. We almost lost the whole thing because of his carelessness. So when Cade wanted to do this it was a far more calculated risk. He's been known for years for his way with horses. We've all worked together to use our strengths to make this place profitable. My dad never would have understood how something like this works. He wasn't any kind of a team player, even when it came to his kids."

Chapter 5

There was no real way to respond to that, so Josie just said, "How is it doing?"

"Thankfully, really well. It's been going about seven years now. Cade brought Nikki in as soon as he could and Jim right after. The first year was no profit, but we told Cade to stick with it." He turned from the paddock and started back toward the second barn, the one she hadn't seen yet. "I'm glad he did."

"I'm sure," she agreed.

"Do you ride?"

The question shouldn't have caught her off guard, considering what they were discussing, but it did. "I do. Well, I did. It's been many years since I was on a horse." Like nearly half her life ago, actually, now that she thought about it.

"Do you want to ride out with me tomorrow? I'm

going up to the ridge in the northern pasture—" he pointed in the direction "—and it's a pretty easy ride and an amazing view. That way I can show you more of what we do out here."

She snapped her mouth shut before he turned around and saw her standing there with it hanging open in shock. Since he was looking at her expectantly, she said, "Yes. I'd like that."

What did you just do?

Not seeming to notice her flustered state, he smiled at her, the full-on smile that made her forget her own name for a heartbeat. That wasn't good. "All right. We'll ride out after breakfast. Say, eight? That give you enough time?"

"Sure," she said weakly. "Eight's fine." What she should have said was "no, thanks." Josie walked next to him, and in this huge space, their arms still managed to bump into each other. It threw her off a little bit, yet neither of them made any move to walk farther apart.

"You'll need boots," he said, glancing at her sneakers. "If you don't have any that are appropriate, Rosa has a few pairs. They are probably in the mudroom. If not, my mom probably has extras for sure."

"I'll find something," she assured him, trying not to laugh at the idea of her boots, which she'd bought on sale but had still cost her more than six hundred dollars, actually on the back of a horse. They were city-girl boots. Not country-girl boots. She'd nearly destroyed them slogging through the mud when she'd gotten here. The death knell for them might just be an actual horse.

He stopped at the barn entrance. "Thanks for coming out here today."

"Thank you for showing me," she said, and meant it. "Cade thought it'd be a good idea for me to see what goes on here. I'm glad I did."

Hank trotted up then, all wagging tail as he sniffed both Josie and Luke. Luke rubbed his ears. "Hey, boy. You come out with Josie?"

Her heart sank as she eyed his coat, which was wet, dirty and matted in places. "He didn't look like that when he came out. Hank! What the heck did you get into?" The dog wagged harder but didn't answer, of course.

Luke laughed, and Josie was momentarily awe-struck. God, he was gorgeous when he stopped being grumpy. Apparently being around animals made him happy. "There's a pond down the way. Lots of tall grass around it. He went exploring is my guess." He gave the dog another pat. "You'll need to hose him off and brush him down when you get him back to the house."

This time, Josie didn't even try to stop her jaw from falling open. "Hose him off? How am I supposed to do that?"

He gave her that grin. "There's a doggie shower in the mudroom. Use it and stand back when he shakes it off."

Josie thought of the small handheld shower in the mudroom. So that was what it was. She'd thought it was to clean boots. She looked down at the dog doubtfully, who looked right back up at her, tail still wagging. She would have sworn he was laughing at her. She'd never walked a dog, much less washed one. She sighed. "All right. Let's go, Hank."

* * *

She managed to get the dog mostly clean. She also got herself sopping wet—possibly wetter than Hank himself—and dirty in the process. Alice met her in the kitchen and laughed. "Oh, dear. Did Hank win?"

Josie looked down and plucked her shirt away from her body with a laugh. "Looks that way. That was my first dog bath." And hopefully, her last.

Alice patted her arm. "It's a skill. One that develops over time."

"Mmm." She sighed. "I think he knew I was a novice." They both looked at Hank, who was sprawled on his back in the sun, looking for all the world as if the bath had worn him out. She had to laugh.

"It's a dog's life," Alice said fondly, and Josie couldn't disagree.

Josie hurried down the hall to her room, where she washed up and changed quickly into dry underthings, jeans and a hot pink T-shirt. She hung her wet things in the bathroom, since she didn't have time to do laundry right now. She'd prefer to wait until later, when the place wasn't quite so busy. The last thing she wanted to do was run into Luke with her underwear in her hands. That was way too personal. It seemed as if they danced around some kind of unspoken thing, as though if they didn't acknowledge the thing between them, maybe they could pretend it wasn't there.

She was willing to give it a shot.

That night, Josie lay on her bed, the full moon shining through her window. It bathed the mountains in an unearthly light, a cold glow, even though the night was comfortable enough to have the window open. It had cooled down significantly as the sun had dipped down lower and lower.

But the low fire in her belly jumped every time she thought of Luke.

She had her TV on, and a police drama played that she wasn't paying any attention to. To get her mind off Luke, she called her aunt to see how she was doing in Arizona. She'd gotten an email saying Aunt Rosa had arrived just fine but had wanted to give her a few days to get settled before she checked in.

Her aunt answered on the second ring. "Josie! How is everything up there?"

"Just fine," she assured her aunt. "It's been really easy to settle in here. How was your trip? How's Kelly?"

After asking about Alice, Rosa filled her in on all the details of her daughter's final few days of pregnancy, and Josie was content to let her talk away. When Rosa finished up and asked again about the ranch and how Josie was faring, she cheerfully reassured Rosa all was well and she was managing just fine.

"Are you getting along better with Luke?"

Josie held back a sigh. "Yes. Of course. He's a nice guy. They all are," she added.

"The best," Rosa agreed. Josie was tempted to head her off at the pass, in case her aunt wanted to press the issue. But she feared that could be misconstrued as pro-testing too much, so she said nothing. "Luke got dealt a raw hand. It'd be wonderful to see him come out of that shell." Before Josie could do much more than open her mouth, shocked, Rosa continued on as if she hadn't said anything of import. "I've been very fortunate to work for them. I'm glad you were able to do this, Josie. Thanks so much."

"It is my pleasure," Josie said. After asking her aunt to call as soon as the baby was born—which should be at any moment—they said goodbye and hung up.

Dealt a raw hand. Josie turned off the cordless phone and padded out to the office to return it to the charger base. Was that how Luke looked at it? She had no idea. She hadn't asked. Wouldn't ask, as it was none of her business. He'd been burned. She knew that for sure. But she had no idea if he'd be open to trying with someone new—not that she was volunteering for the position.

Far from it.

There was definitely a little chemistry with her and Luke. But it would be the height of foolishness to get involved in any way when she had to leave—and while she was all for the idea of two consenting adults going into something with eyes wide-open, she wasn't a fling sort of girl.

No, she was a committed kind of girl.

So she'd leave the idea of Luke to fantasy. In her experience, men didn't measure up in real life anyway. Her ex certainly hadn't.

But the memories of Luke's hand on her face and the look in his eyes made her shiver. In a good way. She wasn't sure she'd ever been looked at like that. As if he really saw her. All the way into her.

The next morning, Luke saddled two horses after breakfast, his usual mount, Kipper, and a paint gelding named Zippy—because he was anything but—for Josie. She'd told him at breakfast she'd be down there today, and while he had no reason to doubt her word, it wouldn't have shocked him if she'd bailed. Mandy would have. She'd been all show—and to be fair, she'd never pretended to be anything but what she had turned out to be. It was his own projections onto her that had gotten them in a mess.

He tightened the cinch on Zippy's girth, then walked him a few steps before tightening it again. This guy was known to hold his breath when being cinched up, and the last thing Luke wanted was for Josie to end up on the ground when the saddle slipped.

Then he looked up and saw her walking toward him. His first thought was, *Holy cow!*

She wore jeans that hugged her curves and her long legs, and disappeared into beat-up old boots she must have found in the mudroom. Her V-neck T-shirt didn't plunge nearly enough, stopping just low enough to give him an enticing peek of what it hugged. She carried a zip-up hoodie. Her hair was in a ponytail, and her face was clear of makeup. This was just Josie, and he was shocked to realize he'd never seen a more beautiful woman.

A small bubble of panic lodged in his throat. He didn't want to see her at all. Maybe he should cancel this ride. Maybe she would have done him a favor by bailing. He still wasn't sure what had made him offer.

She carried box lunches and had a tentative smile. Well, hell, no wonder. He was no doubt scaring her, staring at her as if he'd lost his mind.

"Hi," he said. "Um, you found boots." Then he just wanted to shut his eyes and bang his head on Zippy's saddle. Awesome. Show him a pretty woman and he turned into a master of the obvious.

But she just smiled as she came to a stop in front of him and looked down at her feet. She turned one of her legs to look at the back of the boot. His eye followed the length of her leg. Lord help him. "I did. Aunt Rosa's. Alice had me pack a little newspaper in the toes so they wouldn't slide around, but otherwise they work just fine."

"Good." He reached for the lunches. "Here, let me take those." Packing them in the saddlebags would give him something to do and give him a minute to redirect his wayward thoughts.

She handed them over and slipped her arms in her sweatshirt. He wasn't sure if he was relieved or not that she'd covered up the view he didn't want to enjoy. He could almost feel her nerves so he started talking.

"This is Kipper. He was born and bred here, and I trained him. One of the first ones. He's a great horse. You get this guy." He finished putting the lunches away and turned to place a hand on Zippy's flank. The horse turned his head and blew out a breath that sounded an awful lot like a resigned sigh. "This is Zippy. Don't worry, his name is a joke. He's not zippy at all. Since I don't know your level of experience or comfort with a horse or trail riding, I thought he'd be a good mount for you." He hadn't wanted to overwhelm her, and despite his laziness, Zippy was calm and dependable. A good trail horse.

Josie walked up and touched Zippy's neck, then stroked her hand down the chestnut's silky coat. "Okay.

That sounds good. It's been years, like I said, and I've never been on an actual trail ride."

"Then we'll make this one good. Ready?" Luke took Zippy's head. Not that the gelding was going anywhere. "Go ahead up."

Josie mounted the horse in one fluid motion and settled fairly easily into the saddle. He handed her the reins and Zippy stood still, other than to turn his head and look back at Josie with a small whicker. It made her smile. Luke quickly adjusted her stirrups a bit, then mounted Kipper. He turned to check on her. She looked pretty solid in the saddle, sitting as if she knew what she was doing. That was good. "If you're all set, let's get going." Then a thought occurred to him. "Are you nervous?"

She started to shake her head, then sighed. "Yes. A little. It's been a while and I'm not—" She stopped.

"Not comfortable out here?" It didn't surprise him.

"Not really. Not yet," she admitted.

He appreciated her honesty. "There's nothing out here right now that is going to bother us."

Her brow ached at that. "Right now?"

He gave her a grin, hoping to tease her out of it. "After dark is another story."

She shook her head at him, but there was the glimmer of a smile. She probably didn't know if he was kidding or not. He wasn't, but she didn't need to hear that right now.

They were able to ride side by side through the meadow, and he noted that she had a great seat and light hands. She said it'd been a while, but clearly it was coming back to her. Zippy plodded steadily along, head down. Kipper was steady as well, but alert and ready to go at a moment's notice. He patted the black horse's sleek neck.

"Where are we going today?" she asked. "And what are you doing up there?"

They talked as they went, about nothing in particular. She asked questions about the ranch and daily life there. He was happy to answer because she seemed actually interested in what he had to say. It was more than Mandy had ever done. He wasn't sure what it was about Josie that was bringing out the comparisons. This wasn't anything he'd thought about in ages. Mandy would never have ridden out with him, even on a gentle horse. He'd been unable to get her on a horse, period, even in the confines of the ring, because she was scared, which he could work with, but she hated the animals because they were too big and she thought they were smelly, which he couldn't work with. So he hadn't pressed it, but he had wondered how they'd make a go of life on a ranch if she wasn't willing to make an effort.

With good reason, as it turned out—she'd had no intention of staying.

Neither did Josie. But Josie wasn't Mandy. They weren't involved, much less married, and Josie had planned to leave from the start. She was here temporarily.

He could work with that, too.

Noticing that her expression was looking a little tight and her back was definitely stiffer, and mindful of the fact it had been a long time since she'd ridden, he suggested, "Why don't we walk the last little bit? Give you a chance to stretch out your muscles."

She gave him a grateful look. "That sounds good. Thanks."

They dismounted, and she held up a hand. "Give me a second while I make sure my legs still work."

He couldn't help but laugh as he reached for Zippy's reins. "They do. If you ride enough when you're here, you'll adjust pretty quickly." Would she? Or would this be it?

She walked around in a little circle, then took the horse's reins back. They walked together through the meadow. A little farther and they'd have to leave the horses. The last section was too narrow and rocky for the horses to navigate safely.

"Okay," he said. "Here's where we leave these guys." He nodded toward the trail. "Better if we go on foot."

"Oh. Okay." She frowned at the horses. "We can just leave them here?"

"Yep. They'll be ground tied, and they'll just stay here and graze or doze. They'll be fine."

He took out the lunches and the blanket and they started down the trail. The trees weren't that thick, and the underbrush was pretty scant. She must have been looking at the ground, watching her feet, because when they came out into the clearing it took a moment before he heard her gasp.

"Gorgeous, isn't it?" he said. It was. The mountains were spread in front of them, with the rolling valleys at their feet. They weren't really close, but they still felt majestic and imposing. The ridge they stood on was big enough to be comfortably back from the edge, and he looked at her, with her wide eyes and her ponytail blowing in the wind, and he wanted nothing more than to kiss her right there, under the blue, blue Montana sky.

Instead, he spread out the blanket while she took pictures with her phone. She gave him a wry smile and held it up. "No service, but I can at least use the camera."

"Something to be said for that," he agreed.

"Is any of this yours?" She gestured out at the scene in front of them. "Your mom said you own three thousand acres. I'm having a hard time wrapping my mind around that."

He came up next to her and caught a whiff of her scent, which was mixed with fresh air and sunshine in an almost irresistible combination. He knew he should move away so he didn't keep brushing against her, so he could quell this almost insatiable urge to kiss her, but he couldn't do it. "Yeah. From here you can't really see the fence lines, but that road right there?" He leaned around her to point to a narrow snake of gray in the green landscape. The wind blew a few silky strands of her ponytail against his face. Now he was just torturing himself. That was all there was to it. "That's the division between us and the neighbor to the east. We're not at the right angle to see any of the rest from here."

"Wow," she said, and looked up at him with a smile, and he couldn't help himself. He brushed a few of the loose hairs that were blowing in her face out of the way with his fingers. Her eyes widened, and then her tongue slipped out to run over her upper lip.

That was all Luke needed. He lowered his head to hers, slowly, giving her time to step away because

God knew, he wasn't going to be able to. He heard her breath hitch, and then his mouth was on hers and the world fell away.

Chapter 6

Josie laid her hands on his chest and leaned into the kiss, which Luke tried to keep light, but she tasted so damn good and was so responsive it all too quickly went from a slow exploration to a hot, urgent claiming. He gripped her hips and pulled her snug against him, and she wound her arms around his neck, giving as good as she got. Her mouth was hot and mobile under his.

Then a bird screeched as it wheeled overhead and the spell snapped. She leaped back, her hands still on his arms, her breath uneven, her cheeks flushed. She looked at him, then away, then backed away.

What had she just done? Holy cow, she'd kissed Luke. And more, she'd nearly climbed up his body to get closer to him. Practically crawled inside him. Nothing civilized about that. It was as if he'd ignited something inside her that had been dormant for years—she'd never felt anything like that before.

Luke's face was impassive. She couldn't read him. A little seed of doubt planted in her mind. Maybe she'd misread him, projected her attraction to him onto him? Imagined that he'd kissed her as if he'd been starving and she was the only thing that could satiate him? The whole idea that it could have been one-sided made her feel a little ill.

He cleared his throat, and before he could do something like apologize, which she really didn't want to hear, she blurted out, "What kind of bird was that?"

He blinked at her for a second, then rubbed his hand over his face and looked up at the sky. All of the ease he'd had with her earlier was gone. She felt its absence keenly. "Ah. A falcon, I think."

She edged away from him and toward the blanket. She tried not to think about other uses for that blanket, and the fact they were in the middle of nowhere, where no one but the falcons would see. Goodness. What was wrong with her?

Deciding to meet this head-on, she asked, "Are we going to be able to be normal?"

He smiled at her, but it didn't reach his eyes. There were tension lines around his eyes and mouth now. "We're adults. We'll manage."

It wasn't the best answer, but she wasn't going to push.

She'd thought kissing him would diffuse the tension building in her, building between them. Instead, she was dismayed to realize it may have done the exact opposite—stoked a fire she'd had no intention of seeing through. Far from being sated, the wanting was coiled even more tightly within her.

Nuts.

He pulled out the lunches, and she sat on the opposite corner of the blanket from him. He raised a brow. "Don't trust me?"

Flustered, she shook her head. "Of course not." When he laughed, she blushed even harder. "That's not what I meant." It was herself she didn't trust, not so much him. Something rustled in the bushes, and her pulse jumped as she whipped her head around in the direction of the sound. "What was that?"

He hadn't even moved from his laid-back position on the blanket. She couldn't help but stare for a moment at his prone form, completely relaxed. She wanted to crawl across the blanket and kiss him again. Infuriating man. "Squirrel, most likely."

Right. A squirrel. She took a bite of her sandwich and kept an eye out just in case…what? It tried to charge them? The idea made her feel a little stupid.

"We'd know if it were a bear," Luke said calmly. He didn't look up from his sandwich even when her head jerked up and she stared at him. "They smell bad and would make a fair sight more noise." She made a little strangled sound, trying to decide if he was messing with her or not. She settled for not. He held up the last bite of the sandwich. "Thanks for this, by the way. It was awesome."

She smiled a little, guessing that was his intent. "Thanks."

"When you're ready, we'll go back to the horses.

There's a broken latch on a gate down the way that I'm going to replace. You still okay with that?"

She gathered the leftovers and packed them back up. "Of course." No way was she going to allow a squirrel to spook her. Or a kiss to derail her.

"No attack squirrels. I promise."

She sent him a look and got caught for a minute by the grin on his face. "Ha-ha. The ones at the park near my condo are probably more likely to attack than any you have around here. They get a little pushy."

He smiled and his eyes crinkled at the corners. *Oh, my Lord.* The man needed to stop smiling. "There you go."

She fell in behind him as he started back toward the horses. "We don't have bears, though."

"You have muggers," he pointed out, holding a branch for her. "We don't."

"True," she said thoughtfully, letting her gaze rest on his fantastic rear end as he walked in front of her. Might as well enjoy the view. She'd never been such a fan of jeans as she was today. "But they don't generally eat you."

"Is that what you're afraid of?"

She shrugged even though he couldn't see her. "Kind of. I guess." Might as well be honest.

He stopped at the end of the trail. She could see the horses around him, in the clearing. He settled his hands on her shoulders, and she looked up, startled, into those incredible blue eyes. "I won't let anything happen to you." His tone was dead serious, all teasing gone.

She swallowed and gripped the bag tighter. "Okay. Thanks." For a heartbeat she thought he might kiss her again, but instead he squeezed her shoulders gently and stepped back. Swallowing her disappointment, she followed him out to the horses.

They spent the rest of the time in a companionable, if not fully comfortable, manner. The little currents flared occasionally, and it seemed to Josie the air hummed if they got too close to each other.

It was a new experience for her, and she wasn't sure if she enjoyed it or not.

She watched him fix the latch, noting the black dots of the cattle way out in the pasture. There weren't any nearby, which was just as well—she was still a little surprised by how big they were up close.

But it was hard to tear her eyes off the play of muscles under his T-shirt. He'd stripped off his long-sleeved shirt, and she was captivated by his back. Zippy shifted underneath her, catching her attention for a second, his head dropped low. She was pretty sure he'd gone to sleep.

Luke strode back toward her, his eyes shaded by his hat, his stride over the uneven ground long and confident. Not unlike his animals, she realized. He belonged here, and moved over this land with a sure-footedness she didn't think she'd ever match. He was completely comfortable in his skin, and that was incredibly sexy.

He smiled at her, but it was a little remote around the edges. While that tugged at her a little bit, she knew it was for the best. He'd had time to process what had happened with them and, like her, had clearly decided to let it go.

"Ready to go back?"

Josie looked out over the huge expanse of land and mountains and felt small. "Yeah."

"How'd it go?" Alice said when she returned to the house. Luke had declined to come back up. She'd helped unsaddle the horses, and the other hands had showed her where things went. Luke had been polite but distant, really no different than he'd been before they'd gone on their ride. She had been able to actually see him withdraw deeper and deeper into himself the closer they got to the barns. No one could probably tell the difference, but she could. It stung a little.

A little shiver ran through her at the memory of Luke's mouth, hot on hers, and his body, hard against her. Heat shot through her.

Oh, goodness.

There was no way she could say any of that to Alice. "It was beautiful," she said instead, because it was true. "A really amazing view."

"Yes. It is gorgeous out here. A little sore?" Alice asked, clearly noting Josie's wince when she sat on a bar stool.

She laughed. "A little." Then she paused, took stock of her aching lower half and amended her answer. "Okay, a lot. But I'll be fine."

"Take a hot bath later," Alice advised her. "That'll help. Or sit in the whirlpool tub tonight. That would work wonders."

Well, since she hadn't brought a bathing suit, the regular tub would have to suffice. In fact, the idea of soaking in hot water was heavenly. "The bath is a good idea. Thanks."

She moved stiffly around the kitchen as she prepared dinner that afternoon, but she wouldn't have traded the soreness for a minute less of the time she'd spent out on the horses today. Nerves built a little as it approached time for Luke to come in for dinner. Would he act as if nothing had happened? Could she keep from letting his family know what had happened with them?

She certainly hoped so. She had a feeling he didn't want them to know he was attracted to her, much less that he'd kissed her.

Luke came in and gave her the same nod he always did, the most restrained of his brothers' greetings. She almost sighed. They'd play this as though nothing had happened, then. Fair enough.

He paused before he went in the dining room, concern on his face. "You doing okay? Mom said you're pretty sore."

"Yes, I am," she told him cheerfully, to hide the awkwardness. "Your mom suggested a bath or the whirlpool tub because hot water can do wonders. But since I have no bathing suit, I'll take the bath when I'm done here."

Was it her imagination or did his eyes get hot? Her fingers curled around the platter she held like a shield. But all he said was, "That'll help."

She nodded and he stood there for another awkward second, then left the kitchen.

She watched him go, unsure if she wanted to laugh or scream. Instead, she lightly banged the platter on her forehead, then set it on the counter. It was too bad they couldn't explore this thing between them. She had friends who had casual relationships all the time. But Josie needed more than a man who blew hot and cold, depending on the day of the week, his mood or what she'd worn that day. She'd been there, done that and wasn't going to repeat the experience, especially for something that would have to be a fling.

She'd never had a fling.

She moved the platter into the sink and considered it. It wasn't because she was against flings—she had friends, both male and female, who had them regularly and moved on when it was over, usually with minimal regrets or drama. But Josie had always been a relationship girl, and even those had been few and far between. She was just too busy. Okay, possibly too picky, as she'd been teased more than once.

But she wasn't starting now. Luke wasn't the guy for her, in any sense, no matter how incredibly he kissed or how he made her toes curl. It was too bad, really. It just wasn't a risk she was comfortable taking.

Luke heard the water running in Josie's room shortly after dinner. He knew that usually she sat in the living room with his mom, watching TV and talking, but tonight she'd gone straight there. She'd admitted she was sore from their ride—she'd been moving pretty stiffly by the time she was cleaning up from dinner. She hadn't complained, though. Her smile had been uncertain when he'd come in. Yeah, he'd sent some weird signals out, and had gotten them back in return.

He needed to back off.

When the water stopped, he wanted to bang his head on the wall. He didn't know how to stop the parade of images that ran through his mind like an X-rated reel. Now she'd be peeling off her clothes and slipping into the water. Her face would be flushed from the steam, and maybe she'd moan a little bit when she sank into the water, like she had in his arms earlier when she'd kissed him. Her full breasts would bob gently in the water, her nipples playing peekaboo if she'd added bubbles...

And hell, he was as hard as a rock and aching for her like he hadn't been with a woman in years. This wasn't a situation that was likely to change.

While she soaked in a hot bath, it'd be a cold shower for him. But, hey. At least they'd be naked at the same time.

As he headed into his bathroom, stripping as he went, he couldn't help but think as far as consolation prizes went, it wasn't much.

After a night spent dreaming about her, Luke couldn't help but notice that Josie did her best to avoid him the next day. If she'd known the role she'd played in his dreams last night, she'd run screaming for the hills. He supposed he should clear the air, and say... what? He wasn't sorry he'd kissed her. He was sorry for the extra stress it was going to cause her. But still, she was perfectly polite, poised and friendly as she had been every morning so far, and he doubted anyone but him noticed the difference.

"What did you do to Josie?" Cade asked as they walked to the barns after breakfast.

Luke winced. So much for that hope. Cade, who was completely clueless about a certain other woman, noticed what was going on with Josie? That was rich. "Nothing."

Cade stopped and glared at him. "Nothing? You took

her up to the ridge yesterday. Today, she didn't come near you all morning, and the two of you kept looking at each other when you thought the other wouldn't notice. And let's face it. If I noticed, it must have been pretty damn bad."

Luke rubbed a hand over his face. He could see his breath on the crisp morning air. Fall was on the way. "Nothing happened, Cade. Drop it, okay?" He wasn't going to confess to his brother. He doubted she wanted anyone to know about the kiss, and he sure as hell didn't. He'd never hear the end of it. Not to mention people might get ideas he didn't want them to have.

Cade started walking again. "She's a nice woman. She deserves better than a cowboy who won't leave the ranch unless it's under extreme duress."

"Hey. That's not true," Luke started, but Cade held up a hand.

"Yeah, it is. It is. You'll go to Kalispell, but that's as far as you'll go. And that's only been the past couple of years. For the longest time you wouldn't even do that. For a guy who lived in a bus on the road for weeks at a time—"

"Stop," Luke growled. "Everything changed. You know that." Mandy had left him and he'd been played for a fool in front of millions of people. Many of them happened to live in Montana.

Cade sighed. "Yeah. I do. But that doesn't mean it can't change again." He shook his head and walked away, leaving a completely flummoxed Luke standing there, staring after him. What the hell did that even mean?

Trying to set it all aside, Luke lost himself in the

duties of the morning. Ranching took all his time and energy, and he was fine with that. They had a great group of hands who were loyal and hardworking, and he knew he did far more than he needed to, but it kept him busy. And truly, after all these years, he didn't miss Mandy. He knew how badly they'd been suited and how unhappy she'd been here. So he knew better than to act any further on the flash of attraction with him and Josie, no matter how powerful it was.

He also knew he was ten years older and no longer under the influence of hormones and the meteoric rise of his career. Who he'd been then wasn't who he was now. He'd thought he had it all figured out. What he'd actually been was foolish and stupid. Reckless. He wasn't any of those things now.

But he wanted to do more than kiss her. There was no point in denying that fact to himself. To feel her under his hands, under his body. She'd clearly freaked out about it, too, which was actually a good thing. Not that he thought she was after him for his name. She hadn't even asked him anything about his career. No money comments—not that either one of those meant she was a gold digger, of course, but he was primed to look for certain triggers, and those were two for him. Too many people had looked at him with dollar signs in their eyes and never actually saw *him*.

It made him wary and somewhat cynical about others' motivations. So no, Cade wasn't wrong. He did tend to avoid new people unless he had no choice, allowing his family and friends to do the vetting for him. He'd been gone from the country music scene long enough it was pretty safe for him to venture out. No one in Powder

Keg looked at him as anything but Luke Ryder, John Ryder's eldest boy.

He was okay with that.

He wasn't lonely. Alone, yes, but not lonely. There was a difference, and if that was starting to pull at him, well, he just needed to remind himself he had everything he needed here in this small part of Montana.

Didn't he?

He looked up at the sound of running feet and saw Larry, one of the hands, coming toward him, his face tight. "Boss, we've got a problem."

Chapter 7

"Uh-oh. I wonder what's going on?" Alice leaned forward and peered out the window. "That's Mike's truck."

Josie looked up from the dough she was kneading for rolls for dinner. The concern in Alice's voice caught her attention. "Who's Mike?"

"The vet." Alice frowned. "He's out here often, of course, but I don't remember any of the guys saying they had anything scheduled. I hope nothing's wrong."

Dinnertime came and went.

Josie packed up the meal and kept the meat warm—rule number one, according to Rosa, was to make sure whatever she made could be kept warm, since you never knew when someone would get held up—and she waited in the living room with Alice and Patty, the wife of the ranch foreman.

Both ladies were knitting and attempting to show

Josie how to do it. While they made it look simple, their needles clicking along and the rows unfurling, Josie was having a tough time finishing one single row without swearing.

But they were patient and she was determined. It was a good combination. They'd assured her with practice she'd get better at knitting—she just needed to stick with it. Truthfully, it wasn't anything she thought she'd enjoy. But maybe if she could figure it out, she would.

Alice and Patty were clearly worried. She gathered from them this kind of thing often indicated a serious problem, though they didn't say much, not wanting to borrow trouble.

So when they heard the men come in, all three women looked up sharply, then at each other. Josie caught the look the other two women exchanged, then all three of them rose.

"I guess that's my cue," she murmured, and set her pitiful little knitting aside.

When she went in the kitchen and saw their faces, her heart sank. "What happened?"

"Rough day," Cade said. His face was grim, and he looked tired, but her gaze settled on Luke like a homing beacon. There was a furrow in his brow, and she saw the tension in his body.

"Not over yet," Luke added. "We'll eat quick and go back out. Jake is still there. He'll come in when we get back. We've got some sick cattle. We've already lost four." His voice was flat.

"Oh." Josie lifted her eyes to his, saw the pain there. "I'm sorry." What did you say to that?

Luke managed a small smile, but there was no humor in it. "It's life on a ranch."

She didn't know what to say, so she just hurried and put together plates for each of them. They stood at the counter and basically wolfed it down. They talked to Alice about things that were beyond Josie's scope. Before they left, Alice added, "Send Mike up here for a few minutes if you can spare him. If it's going to be a long night, I'm sure he could use some fuel, too."

After dinner they all trooped back out. Josie didn't say anything, just watched as they each snagged a handful of the cookies she'd left on the end of the counter. These guys were dealing with life or death and all she could offer were cookies. It didn't seem right.

"They'll sleep out there, most likely," said Alice, her tone sad. She sighed and a faraway look crossed her face. "In shifts. Just like their father, looking after the animals as though they are children."

Josie couldn't imagine where there was to sleep in a barn. Even though she'd seen it, and had to admit that as far as barns went, it was clean and neat, she still had no idea where one would crash in it. Seemed as if it'd be loud and dirty, but she kept her thoughts to herself.

She went out and sat with the older women for another hour—they'd DVR'd Alice's favorite show—but both of them seemed a little distracted, and when they packed up for the evening, so did she.

She took her sad little knitting project—it couldn't yet be called a scarf when it was just a few inches long—and retired to her room. When she stood at the window she could see the moon hanging in the sky and the peaks bathed in its cool light. Somewhere out there

Luke was trying to save his cattle. She hoped he would be successful.

They did come in for breakfast, which Alice had told her last night they would. She was ready when they came in, with strong coffee and hot food. They were, to a man, dirty and exhausted looking, but slightly more optimistic than the night before.

"They made it through the night," Luke said before she could ask. "Should be out of the woods now."

"That's good," Josie said quietly. "Just lucky you found them?"

"Jake and Charlie, one of the hands, found them by the creek. We can't check on all of them every day, but we do it regularly. It was just luck we happened on them when we did or we could have lost more." He answered her next question, "The other herds have been checked. This was the only one affected."

"That's good," she said. "What did you do with the rest of them?"

He shrugged as he took a plate and loaded it up. "We moved all the rest of the cows and we'll keep them out of there until we can get rid of all traces of greasewood, which is a plant that can be fatal to cows. We check for it, but apparently we missed this patch. It was just unfortunate it happened when it did. We'll keep an eye on them for a bit longer, but the effects are fast. If any of the rest of them ate it, it'd have shown up by now."

They took a lot of care with the animals and other details. She couldn't help but compare that to her ex and his inability to care about anyone other than himself, much less his employees.

He took a plate loaded with food and followed his brothers into the dining room, and she hurried around putting things away. Alice wasn't up yet. She'd cook a fresh batch of eggs, even though Alice told her not to go to any trouble. Everything else would keep.

She ate her own breakfast and checked her email on the office computer. There was one from her best friend back home, with a link to an article she couldn't open. Allie had promised to send her anything that came up, and from the tone of the email she knew it wasn't a positive article. It was with no small amount of nerves that she fired off a request to cut and paste it into an email.

There was another from a restaurant wondering if she was looking for a new job. Those always gave her pause. She looked at it but just wasn't sure she wanted to work in the same town as Russ again. While LA was huge, the community they'd occupied was relatively small. An awful lot of people had sided with Russ, although part of that could have been that he was simply way more public than she. Still, if she took another job in LA they'd be sure to run into each other. The whole idea made her wary. Just too many memories of things she'd rather put behind her and forget.

Silly, but there it was.

She saved the job offer to an email folder and was about to close out when a new email pinged in. Allie again.

She opened it, a little curl of dread in her stomach.

Thought you should see this. Do you want me to do anything on my end?

She skimmed the article, which had run in that morning's LA newspaper. The curl of dread turned into a rock, and when she was done, she dropped her head in her hands, tears of anger pressing on her eyelids.

Damn Russ anyway. Was he trying to call her out? Why the hell would he even care?

The article was on the restaurant, on him as the sole owner now. On the changes he'd made, since the previous model hadn't worked well. Due to creative differences, he'd let his partner go and the business was booming.

He didn't mention her by name, of course, but she'd been the partner. She'd been his fiancée. And he hadn't "let her go," he'd ripped the whole thing away from her. It had been her baby. Simple cooking with fresh, local ingredients, lots of which had been grown around the area in inner-city gardens. It had been more of a café than a restaurant, and not the kind of place Russ would have ever started on his own. Which he'd let her know at every turn, even after encouraging her to open it—he'd apparently thought he could control the menu. She'd laughed at him, but he had been the one who laughed last, unfortunately.

"Are you okay?"

Alice's concerned voice broke into her thoughts, and she looked up quickly and sharply, closing out of the email as though it was illicit. "I don't mean to pry," Alice added quietly. "But you didn't hear me come in or greet you."

"Ah." Josie tried to focus on the computer screen she couldn't really see through the sting of angry tears. It would do her no good to cry over it. She'd decided a while ago he wasn't worth it. But this apparent choice to jab at her when she couldn't retaliate—even though she wouldn't—was frustrating. She took a quick breath and tried to get her composure back. "I'm sorry. I'm okay, yes. Just an unwelcome blast from my past, you could say." She'd need to contact her lawyer, see if this was a problem, if it mattered in the pending court case. Russ was arrogant enough to push this as far as he could.

Alice's hand settled on her shoulder and she gave a little squeeze. "I understand. I'll leave you alone. Let me know if I can help."

Josie pushed the office chair back and stood, determined to let it go for now. There was nothing she could do from here anyway. She smiled at Alice. "It'll be fine. Let me fix you breakfast."

Alice laughed and followed Josie back into the kitchen. "I see you and I are continuing the same tradition as your aunt and I. I can make my own breakfast."

Josie smiled as she fetched the jar of berry preserves from the fridge. "I know. I guess you're right." She set it on the counter as Alice fetched a plate and a butter knife. Hoping to keep the subject off her issues with Russ, she asked, "Did you make this here?"

"The preserves? Yes. Some of the berries grow wild on the property, some of them I grow in my garden. It's something I've always enjoyed doing." Alice spread some on her toasted bagel. "There are a few jars in the freezer, but they tend not to last long."

"I'm sure," Josie said. "It's delicious." Exactly the kind of thing she'd have served in her restaurant.

"Well, thank you," Alice said cheerfully. "Now, did they say anything more about the cattle?"

Josie filled her in on what Luke had told her and Alice listened with a small frown. She shook her head. "They take this so hard. They don't like to lose any of them, and something like this, a poisonous plant that they check for, is even worse because it can be prevented." She sighed. "Though really, over thousands of acres, you can't find every single harmful thing. It's impossible."

"I can see that," Josie said. She could also see that Luke would do everything he could to keep this from happening again.

Josie studied the fridge after Alice had left the room. Clearly, it was time for a trip into Powder Keg for some supplies. While she could send a list with someone else who was running into town, she rather thought she'd like to make this trip. Luke had told her she could use his truck. She went to the window and eyed the ranch trucks doubtfully. She'd never driven anything that big before. Not that she couldn't do it. But back home her car was more on the sporty side, not utilitarian. Luke had told her if she needed to drive to take his truck, and showed her where the keys were. She'd listened politely at the time, with no intention of ever taking him up on it.

It almost made her laugh. A month ago, she'd been in LA. Now she was way up north, staring down a huge pickup truck, the likes of which she'd never dealt with. She already knew from riding in this one that she couldn't see over the hood real well.

That could be an issue.

When Luke came in she asked him, "Is it still okay if I borrow your truck?"

He looked at her with surprise for a second. "Sure. You need to go into town?"

"I do. I have some things I need and I'd just like to get them myself." She would also like the opportunity to get a cup of coffee in a café, but didn't say that out loud.

He looked thoughtful. "I was heading that way myself. Want to ride along?"

Part of her wanted to beg off and go another day without him. But the more practical side of her knew it was a waste of gas to go on her own, especially when she was so unfamiliar with the area. Even though it could be a little awkward in the intimate confines of the truck's cab, with the memory of the kiss hanging between them.

"I won't bite," he said, clearly reading her hesitation. She flushed, because it wasn't a bite she was worried about. To cover her embarrassment, she shrugged and smiled.

"That's fine. When are you going?"

He glanced at the clock. "Now. I was just going to check with you and Mom to see if you needed anything."

For a second she was tempted to give him her list and hide here in the kitchen. But there was no real way to back out now. "Okay. Just let me grab my purse." Before he could answer, she hurried from the room. She closed her door and leaned on it, taking a deep breath to settle her nerves. To kill a few more minutes she went into the bathroom and examined her reflection, which was silly, because it really didn't matter what she looked like. She wore skinny jeans and a slim pink T-shirt with a palm tree on the front. Not fancy, and most definitely not very Western. It'd have to do. She smoothed her ponytail, added a touch more lip gloss because she couldn't help herself, then grabbed her purse and went back to the kitchen.

Luke was waiting, a paper in hand.

"Alice need anything?"

He held up the paper. "Yep. And she knows me well enough to write it all down or I'll forget. Ready?"

"Sure." She slipped her feet into flats—also not great footwear, but way better than heels—and followed him out the door.

The atmosphere in the truck was as intimate as it had been the trip home from Kalispell. Luckily this time the trip to town was significantly shorter.

They rode in silence most of the way. Luke had a satellite talk radio channel on, and they were discussing ranching-related business. She didn't understand any of it, talk of grain prices and such, so she tuned it out. She focused instead on the incredible scenery and tried to think of spices in alphabetical order. She also tried with less success not to be tuned in to every move Luke made on the other side of the cab. His long fingers wrapped around the steering wheel, and with every inhale she breathed in his scent. It was making her more than a little crazy, as if she was a teenage girl on a first date with her dream guy.

She wasn't a teenager or on a date, of course. She also knew there were no dream guys.

She was more than a little relieved when they got to Powder Keg. Like before, there were several trucks parked along the main drag, and there were people on the street who waved at Luke as they rolled by. She wondered if they caught sight of her and wondered who she was. She didn't want to start any gossip that might make things uncomfortable for Luke. She'd been so conditioned to fly under the radar, and it was hard to break the habit.

When he parked in front of the store, she got out and went to stand on the sidewalk. An older man winked at her as he walked by. Luke came to join her. She followed him inside and blinked at the way the place was packed from top to bottom.

A woman let out a squeal.

"Well, look who we have here. Long time no see, Luke." There was a definite purr and familiarity in her tone. Because of the layout of the store, Josie was still behind Luke in the entry, and the woman had them both penned in. "Perfect timing. You busy tonight? A group of us are going to the Hole."

Josie could smell the woman's overpowering perfume and coughed.

Luke managed to move forward enough that Josie could step around him. She gave both of them a toothy smile. The woman, a petite bottle-blonde with large breasts that strained at her shirt, frowned.

"If you'll just point me toward where I need to go, I'll get out of your way," she said pleasantly as the other woman looked her over from top to bottom and clearly found her lacking. Josie spotted the grocery section and grabbed a cart from near the door. "Never mind, I see it." She walked away, pushing the cart over the uneven floor, her chin up, her steps deliberate, a sour feeling in her stomach.

"Another city girl, huh, Luke?" Her voice was loud,

a little shrill, a little mocking, and it followed Josie as she went down the first aisle she saw. Luke's voice was too low for her to hear his response, and Josie disappeared into the freezer section, her face burning. Her scorn shouldn't matter, since the woman was clearly jealous, and that wasn't Josie's problem. The woman wasn't wrong. Josie already knew she didn't look anything like a local with her designer flats and city clothes. And it shouldn't matter. But she didn't want to cause problems for Luke. Though frankly, if that woman was any indication of the type he preferred, no wonder he'd pushed her away after their kiss.

She stopped to examine a display of snack foods, disturbed by the direction of her thoughts. Why should his type matter? She should be grateful it wasn't her. It'd save her a lot of grief down the line.

Chapter 8

Luke found Josie studying two different kinds of frozen corn. He cleared his throat and she turned slightly. Her gaze was cool. Impersonal. Which he deserved. He knew how that had looked, and he'd kissed Josie. It made him look bad.

"I'm sorry about Candy," he said quietly. He wasn't quite sure how to explain his relationship with her—or rather, lack of relationship. He'd had a drunken fling with her years ago after his marriage had imploded, and she'd been on a mission ever since to have a repeat. She had various boyfriends at various times, but she'd made no secret she'd drop them all for him. He suspected that had more to do with his status as a former country star than for him personally. After all, they'd both lived around Powder Keg for their whole lives, and it wasn't until he'd gone to Nashville that she'd shown an interest in him.

"She has some ideas about me that I haven't been able to get her to drop," he explained, even though it was obvious.

Josie set one of the boxes in her cart and met his gaze. "You don't have to explain," she told him. He took his hat off and shoved his hand through his hair, exasperated with himself more than her.

"Yeah, I kinda do. I need you to understand I'm not stringing anyone along, and if I was involved with someone, I'd never have kissed you." This was delivered in a fierce whisper in deference to the fact he never could be sure who was lurking around the next aisle. Everyone meant well, but every one of them talked, or lived with someone who talked. It was the way of a small town, especially one you'd grown up in, where people felt they not only knew you but actually owned part of you. It wasn't something he normally minded—it was part and parcel of a small town and the life he'd chosen. But he didn't want Josie getting tangled up in it all somehow.

She nodded. "I get it. I do. I never thought you were a player, Luke. It was just a weak moment on both our ends."

He wasn't sure if that was a relief or not. He figured either way it was better to move on while he was ahead.

"Did you get everything?" He took in the contents of the cart as she nodded.

"Enough. They've got a lot here. This place is bigger than it looks from the outside."

He smiled. "It is. They use every square inch."

Clothes, hardware, tack, even toys as well as groceries filled the space, literally to the ceiling. Outside, there was the feed area, and big things like galvanized water tubs and fencing material. Schaffer's did a brisk and solid business, and had been here as long as Luke could remember. It'd been owned by the same family as well for decades, like a lot of the businesses in town and the surrounding ranches, too. Deep roots. It was amazing how many people stayed or came back.

He left her to gather the things his mom had asked for, then followed Josie to the registers, his mom's items in a basket. Would Josie be willing to put down roots here? Or were hers in Los Angeles? Or did she not have any at all? He wasn't sure what bothered him more, that she might not want to put down roots or that he was even wondering about the damn thing in the first place.

The latter, for sure. He had no business going there. At all.

They each paid for their purchases and loaded everything up into the truck, including the cold items in a battered cooler that Josie looked at askance.

"What do you keep in here?" she asked, eyeing it.

"Food," he said carefully. What else? He opened it up and showed her the inside, which was clean. "It's just beat-up because it slides around in the back of a truck. We use it because typically the trips into town take some time, and that way nothing spoils."

"Okay," she said, and sorted the groceries quickly, pulling out the ones that needed to be kept cold. When she started around to the cab of the truck he asked, "You want to grab a quick bite? Donna's Diner's good and fast. Not on the same level as the burger place," he said with a small smile, "but really good home cooking."

Why had he asked her? She'd say no, for sure, and he'd look stupid. Or, worse, she'd go and just be polite. He opened his mouth to tell her to never mind, but she nodded.

"I'd like that. I like to sample other restaurants."

He didn't point out that this wasn't at the same level as what she'd cooked at. She already knew that, and he knew that she wasn't a food snob. He liked that she was game to give it a try.

They walked in the diner and the place was packed, which wasn't a shock, considering it was lunchtime in the ranching world. They snagged a booth near the entrance. He'd have preferred to be closer to the back, but it couldn't be helped. He didn't know if Josie was aware of the eyes following them, but he sure was. People would look at her because she was young and gorgeous and make assumptions that he couldn't help.

They sat down, and she gave him a weary smile. "Does it bother you?"

"Does what bother me?" he asked, looking up as the waitress popped up to drop off menus and plunk down silverware. After taking drink orders and telling them the specials, she hurried off.

"Being watched like that," she said.

He didn't pretend he didn't know what she was talking about. "It doesn't happen very often here. Besides, it's you they're looking at, not me."

She fussed with her silverware. "Why me?"

He shrugged. "You're new." He didn't add "gorgeous and sexy." That was over-the-top, even if true.

She shrugged. "I imagine that'll wear off soon enough."

He heard what she didn't say—she'd be gone soon enough anyway. Even unsaid, those were the most important words. The ones he needed to focus on when he got the crazy urge to kiss the hell out of her.

Josie was used to the stares, but usually they were directed at the man she was with. This time she was the subject, and it made her uncomfortable. This was a much smaller town, and a whole new world. But these people were looking at the city woman with Luke Ryder, not the woman who was engaged to a high-profile and popular TV chef. With Russ, she'd faded to the background, like she'd preferred.

Like *he'd* preferred, she realized. She was pretty enough to be on his arm, but not so much that she'd overshadow him or distract from him. Anytime the cameras started clicking, he'd started preening, and she'd be relegated to the back. At the time she'd been okay with it. But now, understanding the reasons for it, it made her feel a little ill. How had she been so blind? How could she make sure it didn't happen again?

Luke tapped on her menu. "You okay over there?"

His concern snapped her back to the present, and she realized she'd been staring at the same page for a few minutes. She smiled at him. "Just hungry. Any suggestions?"

"The chicken potpie on special is a popular choice," he said. "And you can't go wrong with the beef stew, either."

She chose the potpie because she was planning to

make one herself. He ordered the beef stew. The waitress was friendly and prompt, bringing them coffee and then their meals. Josie had to smile as she looked at the steaming potpie in the huge bowl in front of her. "Everything out here is cowboy-size portions, isn't it?"

He raised a brow at her as he tucked into his stew. "You mean regular size?"

She picked up her fork and thought of the small, perfectly arranged portions they'd served at Aloha's, the restaurant she'd first worked at with Russ. More for art than consumption. Two extremes. "I'm pretty sure this is more than regular."

He grinned and shrugged. "You can get a box to take it home, I'm sure."

Now she had to laugh. "I'm guessing you've never had that problem." She took a bite and closed her eyes. The flavors exploded in her mouth. She tasted tarragon, maybe some lemon and paprika, too. The broth was perfectly done, not too thick, and not runny. The crust was clearly homemade, and no doubt with lard. When she opened her eyes, Luke was looking at her, his fork in the air, his gaze a little intense.

"This is amazing," she said, and he gave her a wry grin as he scooped up more of his stew.

"Is that how you eat everything?" he asked and his voice was a little strangled. "You looked as though you were experiencing it, not just chewing it."

She took a sip of her water. "Not everything, no. But yeah, food should be an experience. Good food should make you stop and savor it. There are different levels of flavors as it moves across your palate." She took another bite, enjoyed it. It'd be a challenge to top it, even if she wanted to. "The cook here knows exactly what he or she is doing."

"You can tell her yourself," he said. "Donna is here every day. These are her own recipes. She's a great lady. I'm sure you can talk to her. She'd be tickled to have a real chef in her kitchen."

She rolled her eyes. "She's as much of a chef as I am, clearly. Maybe more."

They finished eating, and she noticed the stares had stopped. She hoped it had been more of a new-person-in-town stare than a who's-with-Luke stare. When the waitress returned to their table, Josie asked for a box and Luke added, "Is Donna too busy for a quick visit?"

The waitress, whose name was Annie, smiled. "I'll check."

She returned a minute later with her boss in tow. Donna was a tall woman, with a kind face and a ready smile. She gave Luke a hug. "Well, Luke Ryder. Wonderful to see you out here." Then she turned to Josie, her hand extended. "Donna Jones."

Josie shook her hand and introduced herself. Luke added, "She's filling in for Rosa, Donna."

"Ah," Donna said, and her gaze sharpened. "Rosa talked a lot about you. You're the chef, correct?"

"I am," Josie confirmed. "And I'm blown away by your chicken potpie. Was that tarragon and lemon I tasted in there?"

Donna brightened right up. "Yes. So you know your stuff."

They spent a few minutes talking shop, and Luke slipped away to talk to another rancher. Henry Parker eyed Luke when he came over. "Who's the woman? You got something you need to tell me? Because I'd say it's about damn time if you do."

Luke shook his head and sat down across from Henry. "Nope. She's my cook. Temporary cook," he corrected himself. "Rosa's niece."

"Quite a looker," Henry observed, but there was nothing inappropriate in his tone, so Luke didn't jump down his throat. Henry's gaze flicked to Luke's. "And a city girl to boot." The last was said quietly, with a concern that Luke understood.

Luke held his gaze. "That she is," he said mildly. "Like I said, temporary cook." Henry wasn't a talker, but he'd tell Brenda, his wife, and she'd set people straight. He liked the Parkers. They were good people.

He steered the conversation toward the ranching question he had, and Henry didn't say anything else about Josie. When Henry looked up with a smile, Luke realized Josie was standing there. He rose and did the introductions. Josie was friendly and open, and he could see that Henry was taken with her quickly. He'd tell Brenda that, too. That was okay. People would be wary of Josie, from the city, after what happened with Mandy. Henry and Brenda vouching for her would go a long way. They were well liked around Powder Keg.

Josie chatted with Henry for a few moments, and Luke could tell the older rancher liked her very much. He didn't blame the guy for being a little dazzled.

As they left the diner, he asked her, "Do you need to go anywhere else?"

"Do we have time to stop in the bakery?" she asked.

"Sure." He led the way and opened the door for her. An old high school friend of his owned it. Katie'd been divorced for going on five years now, and had had quite a time of it getting the place going. She'd stuck with it, and now Sugar was a favorite stop in Powder Keg. She greeted him from behind the counter with a big smile.

"Luke! Good to see you. And who's this?" She came around the counter, her hand outstretched, her smile warm.

"Katie, this is Josie. She's the cook at the ranch." To Josie, as Katie took her hand, he added with pride on her behalf, "Katie has made this place work from scratch."

"Lots of sweat and tears," she said cheerfully as if it hadn't taken her years to get it up and running. "Nice to meet you, Josie."

"You, too," Josie answered, her smile warm. Luke had often wished that he could settle down with someone like Katie, who was sweet and solid and always had a smile, but the sparks just weren't there. No, instead, he just made mistakes.

"So what can I get you today?"

Luke watched as the women walked back to the cases. There were a good amount of cookies and cupcakes and various other pastries left in the cases. On weekends it was critical to get here early—things sold out fast. Josie chose an assortment of items and paid. She and Katie chatted for a few moments and as Josie turned to go, Katie mouthed, "I like her" and gave him a thumbs-up. He gave her a small smile and shook his head, then followed Josie out the door. He didn't want Katie to get the wrong impression. Or anyone to get the wrong idea. Least of all himself.

In the truck, she opened the bakery bag, took out a

big frosted sugar cookie, then held the bag out to him. "Want one?"

"What if I wanted that one?" he teased as she took a bite. She shook her head at him.

"This one was mine. I figured you weren't the pink frosted type." She arched a brow. "Perhaps I was wrong?"

"Busted. You'd be right." He selected a white frosted one. It had sprinkles, but he couldn't win them all. He took a big bite and looked over at Josie. She had a smudge of frosting on her cheek, and a couple random crumbs. He couldn't stop himself. He reached over and brushed the crumbs off. Her eyes got wide when his gaze snagged on her full, sexy mouth. Her breath whispered out and he nearly leaned in, over the console, over the bakery bag, and kissed her.

She must have read his intent, because alarm filled her eyes. She shook her head. "Luke." That one word managed to convey both a plea and regret. He sat back and took a frustrated bite of the cookie instead and looked up to see Mrs. Mitty, one of the town's biggest talkers, smiling broadly at him from the sidewalk in front of the truck.

Fact was, he'd nearly kissed Josie right in the middle of town. And they'd been caught.

He heard a strangled little sound from Josie and knew she'd read Mrs. Mitty's expression, as well. The bright smile on her face gave it away, pride in the fact that she'd been the one to catch the moment.

A moment that shouldn't have happened at all.

He put the truck in gear and backed out of the spot.

* * *

There was no mistaking the fact it had been building all day, in the little bumps and touches and glances. He knew what was happening here, and it seemed to be happening despite their best efforts to avoid it. They rode the rest of the way, small talk filling the space between them, and she finally asked the question he'd been wondering if he'd hear.

"Do you miss it? Performing?"

There was the standard answer he gave everyone, and then there was the truth. Josie had been nothing but open with him. So she deserved the truth. "I do. I miss it a lot. I miss connecting with people through music. I don't miss the grind of touring, that's for sure." He gave a half laugh. "It was a rush at the beginning. But after a while, you forget where you are. You stop all these places, but you can't ever really see them. It's tough to just run out and grab a burger, or go for a run, or catch a movie. All of a sudden, you belong to all these people and you've traded your privacy for their loyalty." He stopped, realizing he'd said more than he'd meant to. Somehow he'd bottled it all up and convinced himself it didn't matter. Yet once he'd started talking about it, it had fizzed out of him like soda out of a shaken bottle.

He glanced at her and cleared his throat. Her face was soft, pensive. "So, yeah. I miss it."

She reached over and touched his leg. He felt the heat of it through his jeans. "Have you ever thought about going back?"

That was an easy one. "No."

"No?" He heard the skepticism in her tone and shook his head. He understood, after what he'd just said—it sounded as though he wanted nothing more than to get back to that life.

"No. I haven't. I don't want to get back under the fishbowl of that life. Be scrutinized like that. Or put my family back in it, either." Right there was a huge issue—they'd been caught in the glare of his life, even all the way out here.

She nodded. "I can understand that. Do you still write songs?"

He hesitated. "Not really, no. I haven't picked up my guitar in ages." That wasn't entirely true. He'd written snatches of songs over the years, but couldn't bring himself to play the guitar. Not because he hadn't wanted to. He did. He missed it. But he'd come to view it as part of his past life and bringing it out, reminding people— his family—he'd left, then come back too late, didn't feel right. Even if there was a hole that the songwriting had filled for him. He'd never done it for the fame. He'd done it for the love of the music. The fame had surprised him completely.

"That's too bad," she said quietly after a moment. There was no judgment in her tone, and he was absurdly grateful for it. "I can't imagine not cooking anymore. It's not the same, of course, in terms of the fame and the performing you did—but it's still a huge creative outlet, and I need it to keep me grounded."

He couldn't swallow around the weird lump in his throat. That was it exactly, and he'd cut himself off from it.

Chapter 9

Josie left her window open for a while in the evenings, even though the night air was cool. It wasn't real quiet here, and she found she didn't miss the noises of the city anymore. She'd gotten accustomed to the sounds of nature instead.

A chorus of otherworldly howls rose on the night and came in through her window. Josie froze, goose bumps rising on her skin as the sound rose and fell, followed by a high-pitched yipping. Slightly freaked out, she left her room and went out in the living room, where Luke stood. He turned when she got close, and gave her a half smile.

"What is that?" The sound rose again, fell. The hairs rose on her arms. She rubbed them, the chill she felt much more primal than the coolness of the air.

"Coyotes. Look at Hank."

Hank was as still as a statue, his body tight and his hackles up. A low growl rumbled in his throat. Josie wrapped her arms around her torso.

"Cold?"

She looked down at herself, in her yoga pants and long-sleeved T-shirt. "Not really. Just— I've never heard them before. Or seen Hank like that." Suddenly, LA seemed really far away. It was at night that this place seemed most wild. There was a complete, velvety darkness that she'd never experienced in Southern California. And in it, things howled and prowled that didn't live in the city.

The room was dark but for one small lamp in the corner that gave off more of a glow than any real light. The moon was full, though, and thin clouds scuttled in front of it. It was enough light that she could see Luke standing by the sliding door, which was open. His pose was deceptively relaxed. He was on alert, too, she realized.

She came and stood beside him, breathing in the scent of his aftershave and the scent that was just— him. A slight breeze blew in.

"Will we see them?" Even her hushed tones seemed loud in this darkness.

"Probably not." Luke's gaze was trained outside, much like Hank's. She peered, too, but didn't see anything. There was more yipping and howling, and then Hank dropped to his haunches and let out a howl of his own. Startled, Josie stepped back quickly. Luke grabbed her elbow and she was pressed against his chest. He hadn't moved when she'd jumped. She could feel his heat and the beat of his heart through the thin undershirt he wore. For a moment, it was all she could concentrate on.

The side of his face brushed her hair as she turned her head slightly. "Um. Thanks. Sorry, I still get a little spooked out here."

He let go of her elbow and she felt the loss of contact keenly, but he didn't move away from her. "I know. It's not for everyone. You don't have coyotes in Los Angeles?" His tone was hushed.

She moved away just slightly. "I don't know. I don't think so. I've never heard them. But we don't have this—quietness that you do out here. There are different sounds here."

"Bugs, frogs, big and small night creatures," he filled in.

"Exactly." She wanted him to understand. "Where I live, I can hear the sound of the 405 freeway. It's not real close, but it's a constant background noise. I hear dogs barking, people talking, doors slamming, whatever. I look out my living room doors, like these, and I see an absolute sea of lights. It's never fully dark, the way it is here, and never fully quiet the way it is here." She'd been disconnected from nature, she could see now. Maybe it was inevitable with the life she led. She never would have noticed or missed it, but being here had opened her eyes.

"Here you look out and can see the stars," he said softly. "All of them. You can see far more than you could ever see down there. The light washes them out."

"Yes." She'd noticed that right away, the first clear night she'd been here. Tonight, as well. So many stars, the night sky looked like a glittery celestial pincushion. "It's amazing. I never knew what was out there."

"It's not all bad here, is it?" His voice was joking, but there was something under it, some tone that she couldn't quite understand or define. She wondered at it.

"No. Of course not. Just a lot different than what I'm used to." She couldn't say she'd be sorry to get back to the city, but this place had grown on her. It pulled at her in a way that surprised her. She'd never expected to feel a connection out here, to nature and the people who lived here. To feel, oddly, as if she belonged here. They were quiet for a few moments and the sounds were farther away, then gone. The silence between them wasn't awkward, but it was a little heavy. Josie was very aware of the man next to her.

"They've moved on for now," Luke said finally, his voice loud in the quiet room. Hank still sat at attention, but he was more alert than tense and his hackles were down. That had to be a good sign. She figured he knew what was going on.

She rubbed her arms and moved away from the door. "That's good, right?"

He shrugged. "They are out of earshot, but they're out there somewhere. Unlike wolves, they are pretty adaptable. Which is why I wondered if you'd ever heard them down there."

She shook her head. "Nope." Aware of the sudden change in the air between them, she murmured, "Well, I guess I'll go back to bed."

She looked up at him and caught her breath at her thoughtless comment. His gaze was intense on her. Suddenly she was very aware of the fact she was braless under her shirt. It was loose enough it didn't cling, but she crossed her arms over her chest, hoping to hide the evidence of her sudden reaction. From the chill of the air through the doors or his suddenly hot gaze, she didn't know.

From the heat pooling between her thighs, she could guess.

He moved a little closer, and she didn't move. Not only because the dog was behind her, but because she didn't want to. She wanted, more than anything, to feel his mouth on hers again and feel his arms around her. When he moved in and slid his hands up her arms, she didn't resist, caught in the spell, and tipped her head back. He lowered his mouth to hers slowly.

"Tell me this is a bad idea," he murmured, his breath whispering over her mouth. She couldn't, for the life of her, say the words. Not with her body humming and her toes curling in anticipation.

In reply, she lifted on her toes and pressed her mouth to his.

He opened to her right away with a groan, and wrapped his arms around her and pulled her in close. She felt the hardness of his chest, the pound of his heart that matched her own, the heat of his skin that seeped through the thin fabric of her own shirt. The pressure of his chest on her breasts was exquisite. When his hands came up, slid under her shirt and cupped her breasts, she moaned and arched into his hands. He brushed her nipples with his thumbs and she nipped his lower lip with her teeth. He gave a startled laugh, then a growl. "That how you want to play?"

He walked her back against the wall, away from the

door, kissing her the whole way, then lifted her shirt and took one nipple in his mouth. He tugged and played with it, his free hand doing the same to the other breast, and she buried her hands in his hair. The pleasure shot straight to her core, and the flash of heat was intense, more than anything she'd ever felt.

"Luke," she gasped, her head rolling back and forth on the wall. She wanted—more. So much more. For this fire to consume her, consume them both.

But he stood back up and tugged her shirt down, taking her mouth in a crushing kiss instead that had her head spinning even more than it had before. She felt his hardness on her belly and she ached for him. When they came up for air, he rested his forehead on hers and she laid her hands on his chest, feeling the unevenness of breath that matched her own. Josie fought for some semblance of control over her feelings. There were so many, too many, and she'd had no idea pleasure was such a razor's edge. She wasn't a virgin, and her earlier experiences had been pleasant enough, but nothing like this. Like this fire that roared through her and threatened to burn from the inside out. She wondered what he'd be like in bed. Wondered if she'd be able to find out. The heat that already was searing her body kicked up another notch.

Then she wondered why the hell she was wanting things she couldn't have.

She pushed him away gently so she could duck away, where she could breathe air that didn't smell like him and her hormones had a chance to settle back down. She couldn't think when she was basking in his body heat and all she wanted to do was curl into him and hold on.

What was happening to her? She was so good at being in control. What was it about Luke that made all that evaporate?

He let her go and turned slowly to face her. "Did I scare you?"

His voice was low and rough and sent exciting little chills down her spine. She turned and took quick small steps back to him. Shook her head as she laid her hand on his face. His cheek was deliciously rough under her palm. "No. Oh, no. You couldn't do that."

Not in the way he meant anyway.

"That's good. I'm not real sure what to think about this." He shoved his hands into his pockets and rocked back a little on his heels. She dropped her hand and moved away again. Hank had given up on staring outside at some point when they were—um, busy—and had wandered off.

That made two of them. "Me, either."

She stood there for another moment, staring at him. Then she said, "I guess I'll go to bed." Even from her vantage point she saw his eyes flare. "Alone," she amended weakly. She wasn't sure if she said it to remind him, or herself.

He came toward her and she didn't move, just tilted her head back when he stopped in front of her. He lowered his head and kissed her again, a softer, searching kiss this time, slow and deep. She gripped his strong arms to keep from melting into a puddle right at his feet.

When he released her mouth, he ran his thumb lightly over her lips. She knew if she sucked it into her mouth the way she wanted to, they'd end up in her bed. And she wasn't ready for that. He whispered, "Good night. Sweet dreams."

"You, too," she murmured, and fled to her room.

There was no point in pretending there wasn't something going on with her and Luke. And no point in pretending the whole ranch didn't know it. It was a close-knit community and word traveled fast—even though far less had happened than many of them thought, no doubt. The connection between them was almost a living thing. She thought of it as a shiny band she couldn't seem to slip...and wasn't sure she wanted to.

Josie recognized a losing battle when she saw one. So though she had told Nikki, whom she had come to consider a friend, that no, she hadn't slept with Luke, she kept her mouth shut with everyone else. The idea of his family wondering about their relationship was mortifying. She wondered if she needed to say something, then realized Luke would have to deal with that end of it. Thankfully, none of them ever said a word to her.

But that didn't stop the knowing looks and the teasing grins. And in some cases, suspicion. This was from the older employees, the ones who remembered his marriage and divorce to a woman who'd been an avowed city girl. Like Raphael, the hand who helped her with Zippy's tack that morning. She was going riding with Nikki, who was taking her current charge out for some experience on the trail.

Raphael had been polite and helpful, but distant and cool, too. She might have written it off as simply his personality, except she got the same treatment from a few others, as well. Never disrespectful or rude, just wary, no doubt of her and her motives. Looking out for their boss, to whom many of them were devoted.

She understood and respected it.

All she could do was make a point of being friendly and warm. Why it mattered to her if they accepted her or not was a mystery. She wasn't staying. She supposed she didn't want to be lumped in with Luke's ex-wife any more than she already was.

There'd be no broken hearts when she left.

She led Zippy to the corral after thanking Raphael and waited for Nikki. She wasn't far behind. "All set?" she asked as she walked up with Firefly.

"All set," Josie replied. They mounted the horses and started out. They'd planned an easy ride. Nikki figured it'd be about two and a half hours, which was plenty of time for Josie to get back to the house to start making dinner. They'd become friends over their shared love of shoes and food. Nikki was a horsewoman all the way through, but she'd grown up in her family's Greek restaurant. She had some family recipes she'd offered to share with Josie, and Josie was looking forward to giving them a try—after a trip to Kalispell to get the ingredients she needed.

Josie had, in fact, noticed some tension with Nikki and Cade. She hadn't asked about it, mindful of her own issue with a Ryder brother, but Nikki had known she'd seen. There had been sparks and definite heat, but Nikki said there was nothing going on with them.

Later, she'd admitted that she'd shared a hot night with Cade a year or so ago, and ever since then, it had been awkward. He wouldn't commit, but he wouldn't just sleep with her, either. It was frustrating, and if it wasn't for the fact she loved this job and they took such good care of her as an employee, she'd leave.

Josie understood, but she also thought it was a long time to be caught in that kind of limbo. She was ready to combust and she had only been around Luke barely two weeks. Nikki had explained they were pretty good at avoiding each other. But still. They lived a stone's throw away from each other on an isolated ranch. It couldn't be easy.

Today, though it didn't take long for the conversation to turn to Luke.

"Was Raphael rude to you?"

Surprised, Josie shook her head. They rode side by side through the field. "No. Why?"

She sighed. "They are worried for him because you're leaving."

Josie shut her eyes for just a moment, felt Zippy underneath her. "I know. I understand. But I've never been anything but open about it. I don't think I should be punished for that."

Nikki nodded. "I agree. But I guess it was really bad here after she left. You'll need to ask him the details, if it gets that far, but they were really worried about him."

Josie thought of all she knew about Luke's marriage. It really wasn't much. She'd been sympathetic at the time, but only in a fleeting way as she'd seen it on the tabloid front pages, in the way you were as a fellow human, but not someone you actually knew. She also understood, having been in a few tabloids herself, that what was printed wasn't necessarily true, or in some cases, even based in truth. "I don't know everything that happened. But I understand people being protective of him. I think that's a good thing."

"Yeah," Nikki said. "You don't think you'll stay?"

Josie looked around at the gorgeous scenery and thought of how different from home it was. "No. But it's not because I can't hack it out here. It's because my life is elsewhere and I have to get back to it." Of course, her life outside the Silver River Ranch was in ruins, but there was no point in bringing that up.

Nikki gave her a grin. "You've done well, city girl." Then she sobered. "Not that you had to prove anything to anybody."

Josie shook her head. "I did. This was way different than I thought it'd be. Even talking to Aunt Rosa over the years, I didn't really grasp what it's like out here."

Nikki nodded. "It took me a while to adjust, too. Plus being female creates some issues. I'm outnumbered quite a lot. I had to earn the respect of each of them, more than if I'd been another guy with the same skills. That took time. If it helps, Luke would be a hell of a catch."

Josie shook her head. "You know it doesn't."

Nikki's smile was wry. "I know. I just thought I'd point it out."

A while later, Nikki frowned at the sky. Clouds were gathering and they were dark. But they were still an hour from the ranch. Josie looked up and asked, "Is that rain only?"

"I'm not sure," Nikki said. Flashes of light answered that question—lightning. She swore and immediately wheeled Firefly around, and Josie followed suit with Zippy. "Let's go. We'll get as far as we can before the storm hits. I knew this was coming, but it wasn't supposed to be here until after our ride."

Josie didn't answer as Nikki urged her horse into a canter and she followed suit. She dropped low in the saddle as they went across the field. Soon enough, there was a bit of a rocky point in the trail that would mean they needed to slow down. The wind rushed past her ears and she felt the change in the wind—it got a little cooler, and as they slowed the horses to a walk for the rocky part of the trail, Josie didn't dare look up at the sky. Nikki's worried face when she turned in her saddle was enough.

"You okay?" she shouted, and Josie nodded, giving her a thumbs-up. Tree branches swayed and thrashed around them, but by the thunder and lightning count that even Josie knew, the storm was still a few miles off, even though the rain was starting to pelt them. Zippy tossed his head, but stayed steady under her, and Josie pretty much just gave him his head. He knew where he was going better than she did.

By the time they came out the other side, the rain was a downpour and Josie had lost her sunglasses somewhere. She'd put them on the top of her head and they'd fallen off either from the wind or the rain. They'd been expensive but she didn't even care. Right now she wanted to be sure she got Zippy back where it was safe.

Now the thunder rolled and shook the ground and both horses were clearly spooked. Nikki's mount was dancing a bit under her steady hand, but kept her head pretty well. The count was much closer—the storm would be on them in a matter of moments.

It was then she realized that they weren't going to make it.

Chapter 10

"Luke." Raphael's face was tight with tension and worry. "Nikki and Josie aren't back yet."

Luke rounded on the man. "Back? From where?"

"They went for a ride. Took Firefly and Zippy. But the storm—"

Luke ran to the barn entrance and stared out at the rain and the thunder that shook the barn. He swore and shoved his hat back on his head. "Where did they go, Raphael?"

The man told him. "Nikki knows to stick to the plan. She knew the storm was coming, but we thought they had an extra couple hours. They would have been an hour out." There was agony in the other man's tone. There were various shelters out there. It was anyone's guess if they'd made it to one in time, or which one Nikki had chosen.

Cade and Jake came in the barn. "Everything okay?"

Luke was blunt. "Nikki and Josie are out in this." Even in his own worry and fear he saw the same expression cross both of his brothers' faces.

"Where?" Jake asked.

Luke told him what Raphael knew. "We can each take a truck and find them." Even as he said it he knew it was impractical. Some of those places weren't accessible by any type of vehicle larger than a four-wheeler. Some were on foot or horseback. So even if they drove out, there wasn't any way, in this storm, to get to them.

Jake spoke, his voice calm. "Nikki knows her stuff. She knows this ranch as well as we do. She'll have found shelter for them and the horses."

While Luke knew his brother was right, he still thought he might crawl up the walls waiting.

Cade blew out a breath. "That's true. She does." He looked at Luke. "Hey, man. Jake is right. And as soon as it's clear, we'll take four-wheelers and go looking. Though I'm going to guess that as soon as it's safe, Nikki will move out. Again, she knows what she's doing."

"I know." He didn't doubt her, or Cade's words. But he couldn't suppress the panicky feeling that pressed on his chest and made it tough to take a full breath. He scanned the sheet of rain, so heavy that visibility was nearly zero. He couldn't see the house, much less fifty feet out.

Josie was out there, and Josie didn't know what the hell she was doing. She wasn't the strongest rider and she was still somewhat fearful, though brave, about the outdoors. Some of those shelters weren't more than shacks with leaky roofs and no doubt rodents or some other animal in residence.

He stood in the door of the barn, sheltered from the rain, with his brothers, who were equally tense and quiet for different reasons, and watched it pour down, and the lightning put on quite a show for what felt like forever. When they deemed it far enough away to start the ride out, the three men went and got the four-wheelers out and each took a slightly different route, not too far off the original one Nikki had planned. There were four possible shelters in the area, depending on which way they'd decided to go, but one of them was a cave, and they agreed that she'd most likely avoid that one unless absolutely necessary as there was no place for the horses.

Luke split off at his designated spot, pushing the four-wheeler as fast as it would comfortably go on this terrain—which wasn't nearly fast enough. The wind rushed past his helmet and the noise of the engine made it hard to think about anything but where he was going. He wasn't going to examine his fear for Josie. He tried to tell himself that it was equaled by his concern for Nikki, but that just wasn't true. He was worried about them both, yes. But he was half-insane over Josie.

The shack in front of him was empty. He could tell as soon as he came over the small ridge. There were no hoofprints in the mud, no sign they'd been anywhere near here. His heart sank and he ground out a curse that he couldn't hear over the roar of the ATV.

His radio crackled right before he'd reached the shack and Jake's voice came over it. "Found them. They're fine." The relief he felt was more than he could have imagined. More than he wanted to feel.

He turned around and went back.

It wasn't until he saw her, wet and muddy and with Cade's arms around her, that he could take a full breath. And then with the next one he wanted to punch the hell out of his brother. But she turned from Cade and looked at him and gave him, improbably, a small smile.

He wanted to run and pull her in his arms, then carry her inside and check every inch of her to make sure she was okay. He forced himself to walk, albeit quickly, over to where she stood. He could see Raphael and another groom disappearing into the barn with the horses.

"Are you okay?" Some of the intensity of what he was feeling must have shown on his face, because Josie took a small step back.

"Yes." It was one word, just one word, but it eased something coiled inside him.

"She's a tough one," Nikki said, and gave her friend a weary smile. Josie returned it. "Let her tell you about it on the way to the house. I'm sure she wants out of her wet clothes as much as I do." She gave Josie a hug. "You did good."

"Thanks. You don't have to come with me," she said quietly when Luke turned and started toward the house with her. "I'm fine."

He still wasn't convinced of that. She was awfully pale. "That's good. What happened?"

She took a deep breath, then started the story. In the house, they toed off their boots and he caught her arm before they left the mudroom. "Can I come with you?"

He wondered exactly what he was asking. Wondered exactly what she was going to answer. But she lifted solemn eyes to his and nodded.

So he went in her room and she closed the door. Before he even really knew what he was doing he kissed her, hot and hard and deep and with all of the urgency and all of the fear he'd had inside him while she'd been out there. She leaned into him and kissed him right back. He stepped back and lifted her shirt at the hem, then looked into her eyes. She took the hem from him and lifted the shirt over her head. Her nipples beaded against the black lace of her bra, which was low cut over the tops of her breasts. He groaned and freed both nipples for his mouth and hands, getting some of the lace in his mouth as he laved her nipple and she arched against him.

"Luke," she whispered, and it was a plea, a demand. He lifted his head, and she reached around and unhooked the bra. She let it slide down her arms, and he filled his hands with her before it even hit the ground. Her breasts were round and soft, and he wanted to bury himself in them for days. Her skin was cold, a reminder of what she'd just been through.

"Josie. God." He kissed her, his hands on her breasts still when she slid her hand between them and cupped him. He groaned and pressed against her hand.

It only took a few more minutes—her jeans were wet and took a little extra effort to get off—but they were naked soon enough, and she was pressed against him, her nipples brushing his chest, his hard length firm against her belly. As they sort of fell onto the bed, he shifted to avoid landing on her. His fingers brushed her thigh and she thought she'd combust if he didn't touch her, if he didn't move his hand over just a little bit…

Then he did, and his fingers sank inside her. She bucked and reached for his length, but he pinned her with a kiss. "If you touch me, I'll lose it." He pulled away, his hand stilled and she whimpered. "Condoms. I don't—"

"I'm protected," she told him. "And I was careful, always." With Russ, they'd always used a condom, which in retrospect was a good idea.

"I was, too," he said, and positioned himself over her, and she was touched that he trusted her. She opened her thighs wider and he sank in, inch by inch, the tight set of his jaw telling her just how hard he was holding on to control.

"Josie," he groaned, and she lifted up to meet him.

The rhythm was hard and fast, and she thought she'd fly apart all too soon. The pressure built and when she couldn't hold it back, at his urging, "Let it go, Josie, so I can go with you," she did, and even as she shattered she knew from his hoarse cry that he'd gone over the edge with her.

Whoa.

Josie lay there, under Luke, feeling the pounding of his heart and the unsteadiness of his breathing, both of which matched her own. He shifted slightly and rested next to her. It was then that she realized they'd barely made it to the bed and were sideways across it. She was still wearing her wet socks. As a bonus, she was no longer cold.

"Wow," he said after a moment. "Josie." He turned his head to look at her, and she saw warmth in his blue,

blue eyes and something else, something that looked a lot like regret. But he leaned in and kissed her, a soft kiss. "Let me start a shower for you."

What she wanted to do was curl up in his warmth and soak it in. But that wasn't an option. Instead, she got up and gathered clean, dry clothes from her dresser and peeled out of her socks as she picked up her wet and scattered things from the floor. Luke came out of the bathroom and steered her toward it gently, where he'd started the shower on hot. The room was full of steam. When he kissed her again, she pulled him toward it with her. "Shower with me?"

He hesitated, then shook his head. "I don't think that's a good idea."

Josie's face flamed. Just like that, all the warm feelings she'd been enjoying crashed to the floor. Not wanting him to see it, she simply said, "Okay," and walked into the bathroom. And shut the door in his face.

She wouldn't cry. Goodness, it wasn't worth that. But she was more than a little embarrassed to have been so bold only to be shut down.

Obviously, making love hadn't meant the same thing to him as it did to her.

Lesson learned.

Josie knew she should have walked away. She'd allowed herself to be swayed by a look, by what she'd wanted to be true and real and bright. But then Alice had bustled in, all concern, and she'd found herself trying to hide her feelings while telling her the story.

She and Nikki had taken shelter in a building that was little more than a shack. It had three sides and was deep enough they could stand back from the worst of the splashing as the rain ran off the roof. However, the roof had leaked almost as much as it had kept out and the rain had driven in through the gaping cracks in the sides of it, but it had kept them and the horses out of the worst of the weather. It had quickly smelled of wet horse and leather, as well as the scent of the rain itself. She'd been waiting for it to come down on their heads, with the way it had creaked in the wind.

Nikki had explained that there were a couple small cabins on the property that were weather tight and had things like blankets and canned goods, and were checked fairly regularly to make sure there were no animals living in them, but none of them were more than an hour's ride of the main buildings.

The worst of the storm had gone through pretty quickly, and as soon as Nikki had deemed it safe, they'd headed back out.

The whine of the four-wheeler had reached them about ten minutes in, and Josie had been very glad to see Jake.

"Ladies," he'd greeted them, his smile not masking the concern in his eyes as he'd looked them over, and the horses, too. "Everything okay?"

"We're fine," Nikki had assured him. "We stayed at the lean-to back over the hill. Damp and chilly, but out of the weather."

"All right. Good." The relief in his voice had been clear. He'd radioed Luke and Cade and let them know they were safe. "Been pretty worried about you."

"It came up fast," Nikki had admitted. "I thought we should have had more time."

"It happens to all of us." He'd gone on back and they'd followed.

Cade had been there right away, and he'd given her a hug. Luke had shown up only a couple minutes later.

The intense way he'd looked at her had heated her from the inside out. Of course, she'd left the part about what had happened after out of the version she'd told Alice.

Which brought her right back to the fact he'd bolted from her room as if his hair was on fire. After she'd asked him to stay. Her face burned, and she was grateful Alice had left the room.

Josie took one of the trucks into town that afternoon—not Luke's. It was her first solo trip, because there was a rumor she could get real, actual cell phone service if she parked behind the Laundromat.

Plus, she could avoid Luke. That was a bonus right about now.

So here she was, on a few errands, but the most important one was to call Allie.

"Josie! How are you, up there in the wilds of Montana?"

It was so good to hear her voice. A wave of homesickness washed over Josie. "I'm making the best of it. You know me."

"Yeah." Allie's voice softened. "Did you call your lawyer?"

"Yes." She sighed, even though right now it all seemed very far away. "I'm not there to defend myself, and he's trying to make himself the victim. Annoying, but not a surprise."

"And he has the new girlfriend," Allie said quietly.

Josie shook her head even though Allie couldn't see her. "Not new. She was one of the ones on the side. His favorite one." A few weeks ago that would have burned Josie, made her angry and sad and sick. Now? She was disgusted with him, but detached. It was a wonderful step.

Allie huffed out a half laugh. "God. Well, he'll get what's coming to him, Jo. Men like him always do."

Maybe. But it wouldn't be from Bree, the current honey. As far as she could tell, neither of them cared enough about the other to be able to cause any real or lasting damage. That had been her mistake—actually caring for Russ and thinking he cared for her.

Luke flashed in her mind. He had more integrity in his left eyebrow than Russ had in his whole body. Even if he confused her.

"I hope so," she said finally.

"So what's it like working for Luke Ryder? Can you tell me anything about him without violating his privacy?"

Josie nearly choked. Allie had no idea what a loaded question that was. She settled for a half answer and hoped Allie wouldn't pick up on it. She didn't want to go into how he'd kissed her and had made love to her that morning. Allie would never let her hear the end of it. "He's just a normal guy. Nice. They all are. It's different working in a private kitchen, but they're open to anything as long as it's hearty."

"So a nice change from the pressure cooker of your old job and good fit for you, then," Allie said. "Even though it's temporary."

"Yes," Josie agreed, ignoring the little pang the word *temporary* gave her. Though after what had happened earlier, it was just as well. "Even though."

They chatted a bit longer, and Josie assured her friend she missed plenty about California and she had no plans to stay in Montana. When she disconnected, she knew she hadn't been fully honest. She wasn't sure she would be returning to Cali for good. But she did know she wouldn't be staying in Powder Keg, Montana, on the Silver River Ranch, either.

Chapter 11

Luke felt like an ass. No. He was an ass. Damn it. Not only had he broken his promise to himself, he'd made Josie feel bad. He couldn't get the hurt look in her eyes out of his mind. She hadn't deserved him running away.

Thwack! He buried the ax right in the middle of the log and split it cleanly in two. There was a growing pile nearby, but he hadn't succeeded in wiping out the image of her pained expression.

She deserved a hell of a lot more than he could offer her. But that was already a given.

Cade strolled up, brow cocked. "Is it working?"

Luke didn't even pretend. He was too tired. "Does it look like it's working?"

Cade shoved his hands in his pockets. "No. Have you tried just talking to her?"

Luke stared at him like he was mad. "Why would I do that?" What could he say? "Sorry" wasn't exactly right. He was sorry for hurting her, but not for the time spent with her, and he knew himself well enough to know he'd blow it if he tried to make the distinction.

"Oh, I don't know. Maybe because you're both adults? And I don't want her to leave because you've screwed something up."

"She's not going to leave," Luke mumbled as he lined the next log up. He hoped she wouldn't anyway. *Thwack!*

"Right. Fix it, damn it. She's as grumpy as you are. Whatever you did, you did it wrong."

Luke's head came up and his hand tightened on the ax handle. "What are you saying, Cade?"

Cade met his gaze squarely. "I'm saying you messed up and you need to fix it. That's all." His footsteps crunched on the gravel as he walked away.

Luke let out a breath. He'd heard a criticism that wasn't there. Cade had only been talking about the here and now, about how he'd hurt Josie. He tossed the wood into the pile and spent the next hour transporting it to the rest of the pile, where it'd wait until winter. He also tried to work out exactly what he'd say to make sure he didn't diminish what they'd shared.

It had been more than he'd expected. She was more than he'd expected. Way more. And it was wrong to make her feel bad just because he had some issues.

He snagged his shirt off the ground. Cade was right, as much as he hated to admit it. He'd go apologize for being an ass. Hopefully, she'd accept it.

* * *

He came in the kitchen and realized, when Josie looked at him with a little frown between her brows, that he was maybe not dressed for groveling. He was sweaty and dirty and probably smelled bad. But it was now or never. He doffed his hat and wished he hadn't put that cautious look in her beautiful eyes. Or earned that blank look on her face.

"I'm sorry," he blurted, and winced as soon as the words were out and her expression went cool. "I'm an ass," he added. When she simply stared at him, he wondered how he could write song lyrics that affected millions, but when it came to an apology to a woman who mattered he couldn't manage to keep his foot out of his mouth. He took a deep breath and started over, since she didn't seem inclined to say anything. "I'm not remotely sorry for what happened between us. I am sorry I freaked out and left you like that. I'm an ass," he repeated, and waited. For whatever she wanted to throw at him. He'd take it because he'd earned it.

Because she mattered and she deserved more than he'd given her.

Josie came around the island and approached him slowly. He was filthy, sweaty and dirty. "What have you been doing?" He didn't normally look as if he'd been through the wringer when he came in.

"Chopping wood." His gaze was cautious and level.

"You made me feel crappy." She managed to keep the hurt out of her tone, but she felt he should hear the truth.

His gaze softened with regret, and he shifted in place, his fingers kneading the brim of his hat. "I know. It wasn't my intention."

His clear discomfort, as much as his words, softened her. "I can't say the way you handled it was okay. It is fine that you didn't want—to stay. It was—it was pretty intense." She'd been ridiculously hurt. Shunted aside, not good enough. So it meant a lot that he would make sure she knew—clumsily, at that—that it hadn't been her.

"I wanted to stay." He reached out one hand, then stopped before he touched her. "More than you know. I just— I panicked, I guess."

She understood that. For two people who hadn't been looking for anything, they'd sure fallen into something. "I know."

"Am I forgiven? I don't want you to leave. Or be uncomfortable around me."

He sounded so earnest, if he hadn't been such a mess she'd have gone up and kissed him. "Yes. Of course."

Now they were at a crossroads. There was so much she wanted that she wasn't going to get. But still, she took a deep breath and looked him in the eye. In for a penny...

"What do you want, Luke? Where do you want to go with this?" She gestured between them. Might as well get this out in the open, where no one could hear them. It needed to be dealt with, one way or another.

He stepped closer and she saw his eyes go hot. "What do I want?" he repeated. "I want the chance to show you that I'm not going to leave you like that." His voice got a little rough. "I want a chance to do it right."

Josie's mind went blank. *Do it right?* Her whole body hummed to life at his words. When she recovered enough she managed to say, "I do, too. But—it'd be good to set the lines now, so we don't—make any mistakes."

His eyes flared. "You think we'd be a mistake?"

She shook her head. A mistake implied there was something wrong with them together. She didn't think that, not at all. "Oh, no. No, I don't." Her voice was nearly a whisper.

He moved closer and set his hat aside so he could lay his hands on her shoulders. "Josie." Her name, full of wonderment and confusion. He was as torn up as she was. Which way to go? Did she dare to take the risk that might ultimately cost her her heart?

She cleared her throat. "I have to leave. There is a very set end here. I'm not sure I'm the fling type, Luke." She needed to lay that down before this went any further.

His gaze was intense on hers. "I'm not asking you for a fling."

"What do you want from me? Are you willing to see where it goes? To just keep things casual?" Her boldness took her by surprise. If he turned her down, it'd be awkward. *More* awkward, rather. At least she'd know where she stood. There was power in that, too.

He was quiet for a moment, and her heart pounded and her face started to heat. When she opened her mouth to tell him to forget it, he spoke. There was heat in his eyes and a wariness, too, that she wished he would let her help him erase. There wasn't time for that, of course.

"Are you sure, Josie?"

She had no intention of falling in love. None whatsoever. She liked Luke, and enjoyed the fact they were so attracted to each other. He made her burn in ways she never had, made her want in a way she never had. It was a little scary, but she was pretty sure her heart was safe. If it wasn't, she'd find a way to heal and move on. Luke had been nothing but clear on his intent to stay single and live on this ranch. That wasn't going to work for her long-term. She had a life in another state, another city, hundreds of miles away. There was no real way to meet in the middle. Which was too bad, since she thought they'd be good together. But could she let this chance, possibly her only chance at something like this, slip away because it might hurt her?

She swallowed hard and lifted her gaze to meet his serious ice-blue one. "I'm sure." Her voice was low, but steady. And with those two words, she changed everything.

A pleasant week passed, with Josie feeling a little like a college girl in the throes of her first real romance. Sadly enough, it sort of was. Her previous relationship hadn't had any romance to speak of. Luke was sweetly romantic.

It was killing her, in a good way.

"You free tomorrow morning?" Luke's question was posed as he set his dinner dishes on the counter. She looked up, momentarily distracted by his nearness. She gave a quick mental run-through of her menu for the next day.

"Yes, I can spare a couple hours," she said. "I need to be back by three, if that'll work."

"That's not a problem." He leaned one hip on the counter and crossed his arms. "If we leave right after breakfast, we'll be back in time."

Josie made some mental adjustments to breakfast. "All right. Where are we going?"

"Kalispell. That's all you need to know right now." He gave her a lazy smile and her heart turned over.

"Mmm. A surprise, huh?" She'd never been big on surprises. They'd often ended up being more about the giver than her, and many of them had been flat-out unpleasant.

Luke must have heard the doubtful tone in her voice because he tipped her chin up with one finger. "Hey. Do you trust me?"

He wasn't joking now. His expression was completely serious, and she realized he was asking about more than just a trip into town. So her answer was about more than that, too.

"Yes, Luke. I trust you."

A smile quirked the corners of his mouth. "Good. Then we'll head out as soon as you're ready in the morning." He settled a light kiss on her mouth, just a promise of what could be later, when Cade walked in the room.

"Whoa. I didn't see anything," he said loudly as he crossed the room. Josie's first instinct was to jump away from Luke, but he settled a light hand on her shoulder and squeezed.

"There's a woman out there who would let you kiss her. After she kicked your ass for being—well, for being an ass," Luke said, and Cade's face darkened.

"That's not the same," Cade mumbled. "You know that."

Luke shook his head but didn't say anything else. Cade gave them both a cocky smile, but now Josie could see the pain underneath it. He hid it well, but the better she got to know him, the more she realized there was far more to him than the carefree-cowboy front he so carefully nurtured.

"You kids have a good night," he said, and waggled his eyebrows at them. "Don't do anything I wouldn't do."

"That doesn't narrow it down very much," Luke said, and Cade just laughed as he left the room.

Josie looked at Luke. "Nikki?"

He nodded. "Yeah. They've been dancing around this for a long time. I don't see either of them changing. Too damn stubborn."

She thought of the story Nikki had told her. She wasn't going to share her friend's confidence, but she did think it was too bad they couldn't see their way to each other. But all she said was "I think stubbornness runs in the Ryder family." Then she gave him a big smile.

Luke grunted what could have been assent, then took his leave, as well. She finished up in the kitchen and prepared the coffeepot for the morning—she set the timer to start it ten minutes before her alarm went off, so when she came into the kitchen, the wonderful aroma was already filling the room. It was a little trick she'd used at home, too.

She hurried up to her room. They'd developed a system over the past week, she and Luke. He'd come to her in a bit, and stay with her—they'd make love, then he'd leave before they could fall asleep.

He never spent the night.

On the one hand, she understood. There were other family members in this house, although she didn't think any of them were fooled by what was going on under their noses. And other than Cade tonight, no one said anything.

On the other hand, she didn't think it had anything to do with family. She suspected it was deeper than that. That it was a way for him to hold back from her, to keep himself separate from the deeper intimacy of sleeping together. If he stayed all night, it would signal a level of commitment neither one of them was comfortable with.

She didn't let it bother her. Well, she tried not to let it bother her. It wasn't worth it, wanting more, asking for more, when she already knew she was leaving in two weeks. There was no point in getting emotionally involved—more so than they already were. It would make her leaving a messy thing, and she was all about avoiding an emotional mess.

But she was kind of worried there already would be one. On her end, at least.

She darted into the bathroom to brush her teeth. Just as she was dropping the toothbrush back in the holder, the knock came. Soft, but she'd been waiting for it, her whole body vibrating like a tuning fork.

She opened her door and stepped back to let him in. "Hi," she said, trying to hide the giddiness, as if she hadn't just seen him fifteen minutes ago.

He gave her a slow grin. "Hi yourself."

She closed the door and locked it, then turned into his arms and gave herself over to the feelings.

Luke lay awake, Josie's breathing steady and deep beside him. She was so beautiful. The moonlight streamed in the room, just enough that he could see her. The sheet was still bunched around her waist, but dipped low enough he could see the shadow of hair between her legs. Her breasts were plumped against the mattress, the rosy nipples calling his name. Her hair fanned on the pillow, and he touched it lightly. He laid a hand on the curve of her waist, then pulled the sheet and blankets up over her as he carefully got out of bed. The mattress dipped as he did so, and he held his breath as she stirred slightly, but didn't wake up.

He pulled his pants on and just stood for another minute, wanting to stay, wanting to curl up behind her, to wake with her in the morning. But he couldn't. He needed some kind of distance, and this was it. It was understood between them, even if they didn't ever mention it.

Regretful it couldn't be more, he slipped out and pulled her door shut, only to see his mother standing there. Shock, then disapproval crossed her face.

Hell. He had no shirt on, but thank God he'd put his pants on. "Mom."

She tilted her head. "Luke Jackson Ryder, what do you think you're doing?"

There were a lot of answers to that question, but none of them were probably what she wanted to hear. "I don't think I need to explain, Mom. We know what we're doing." Then he attempted to change the subject. "Are you okay? Why are you up?"

She poked him in the chest, hard. "I'm fine. Went in the kitchen for a drink. We are not talking about me. You can't even stay the night with her?" She gave her head a firm shake.

He shut his eyes. "Mom. It's just best I don't." So

that Josie didn't think there was more here than there actually was? So *he* didn't think there was more than there actually was? He wasn't sure.

"Don't break her heart," she said sharply. "Because you and I both know if you didn't care about her—a lot—you wouldn't be in her bed."

Luke scrubbed his hand over his face. "Mom. We're not going to talk about this." Of course he cared about her. He wasn't a total heel.

His mother harrumphed and walked off into her room and shut the door. He was left in the hallway, feeling chastised—rightly or not, he wasn't sure—and embarrassed. Then he shook his head and returned to his room.

Yes, he and Josie made love. No, he couldn't wait to get naked with her. But it was more than that. They talked, they watched TV, they laughed. They had a relationship—a friendship—and it was based on more than mutual attraction. No, they weren't in love. But that had never been on the table anyway. He thought she was gorgeous and sexy. He liked her a lot. Liked her company a lot. Liked that she didn't push him, that she just accepted him for—well, for him. For who he really was, not as the country star.

Which was good, because it'd been a long damn time since he'd been a star. He'd been out of the business far longer than he'd been in it. But lately he was getting the itch to write songs again. So he'd started jotting some lines down, listening to the music in his head. He hadn't tried to get the guitar out and do any actual composing, because that made it too real. He still hadn't gone down to the recording studio in the basement. He wasn't ready to visit that part of his past yet.

He did not miss performing and touring. Well, maybe a little bit. He missed singing and the energy of the crowd and the music and the band. When it all merged together properly, it was an almost holy experience.

Okay, yeah, he missed it. And he wasn't sure why it was surfacing now.

He could already tell sleep was going to be hard for him. So he got out his notebook and worked on the song.

Chapter 12

Josie was ready the next morning, dressed in jeans and a light sweater—it was going to be a cool day, but sunny. Luke gave her a smile and a kiss on the temple, but he seemed tired and distracted.

"You okay?"

He nodded. "Just tired. Nothing new there. Bring a pair of regular socks, too."

She went and grabbed a pair of argyle knee socks and shoved them in her purse, then joined him in the kitchen. Alice had told her not to worry about dinner; if they were a little late, she'd start things for Josie. Josie had thanked her, but hoped she'd be back in time.

She started the dishwasher and followed Luke out the door. He opened the passenger door of the red truck for her and she hopped in smoothly.

She felt a little bloom of pride. It was true—she'd

gotten much better at entering and exiting the truck over the weeks she'd been here. In fact, she'd garnered lots of new skills she'd never thought she'd need. Like dog washing and caring for horses.

Luke got in and started the truck. Even though he'd said he was fine, his jaw was a little tight. She'd thought things had seemed a little strained with him and Alice this morning, but she wasn't completely sure. Nor would she ask. It wasn't her business.

"Can you tell me now what we're going for? Why do I need socks?" She did trust he wouldn't pull any kind of crap with her but she was still a little leery. She'd had plenty of surprises foisted on her over her life. *What do you mean you want an open relationship, Russ?* Yeah, that had been one of the nastier ones.

He gave her a grin. "No. You'll see. You trust me, remember?" When she nodded, he added, "It's nothing bad or unpleasant. Just something I want to do for you, as a thank-you for all you've done for us. Okay?"

She exhaled. Put that way… "Okay. Fair enough. Even though you don't owe me anything," she added.

He reached over and laced his fingers in hers. "More than you know."

They talked on the trip, and she was surprised again at how comfortable she was with him, and how much he'd opened up to her. It was such a change from the beginning. A little thread of regret snaked through her. To think they'd found this kind of ease with each other, and she had to leave.

But she knew that bringing up the future would only ruin the moment, when they'd been very clear on the fact there was no future. It just wouldn't work. And maybe the ease was only there because there was a time limit on this and it was fast approaching the end. Maybe it allowed him to relax, when he knew she wouldn't be around much longer.

She hoped that wasn't it. She didn't think that was the truth. But it was hard to tell and she couldn't imagine asking. What if it ended things earlier than expected? She wanted every moment they could get.

In Kalispell, he found a parking spot just off the main drag and rubbed his hands together. "Ready?"

She smiled at him. She couldn't help it. He was excited—almost giddy—about whatever this was. Like a kid. "I'm ready."

"Good." He leaned toward her and she met him halfway, and he kissed her quick and hard and thoroughly. She lost her breath for a moment and he touched her face. There was a tenderness in his touch that spoke to something deep inside her. "Let's go."

She grabbed her purse and met him on the sidewalk. He didn't take her hand, but they did walk close enough their arms brushed, and he rested his hand on the small of her back as they navigated the pedestrian traffic on the main drag. She stopped in front of a boutique Western store with an incredible display of gorgeous Western boots that made her stop for a second. These, with their intricate scrollwork and details, were far from the beat-up old boots of Aunt Rosa's she'd been wearing. These were works of art.

"Oh, wow," she said, awed.

Luke bent close, and his breath feathered over her ear. "Lucky for you, this is where we're going."

She twisted to look up at him, delight blooming in her chest. "Really?"

He dropped a quick kiss on her forehead and reached past her for the door handle. "Really."

The bell jangled over the door and a gorgeous woman, probably in her late twenties, looked up with a smile that quickly grew more genuine when she saw Luke. Josie heaved an internal sigh. Not much of a shock here.

She came around the end of the counter, her long black hair in a thick braid down her back. "Luke. So good to see you. And you must be Josie."

She held out her hand and her friendliness didn't dim at all. This wasn't a woman who was out for Luke. Josie relaxed a little.

Not because it really mattered—Josie was leaving, and if Luke could have a woman nearby, that'd be better anyway. Right? Her stomach immediately clenched. Okay, so she had a little work to do on convincing herself.

She took her hand. "I am."

"Nice to meet you. I'm Skye Howard. This is my shop. Luke said you're in the market for new boots?"

"Ah." She glanced at Luke, who looked a little bit as if he was up to something. "I don't own any."

Luke stepped in. "Skye makes them herself. She's a master craftswoman. And this is my treat. Like I told you in the truck, I just wanted to thank you for all the work you've done for us."

"Oh." Josie was touched, and she caught Skye's avid expression. No doubt she could see there was...something between her and Luke. "Wow. Are you sure?" Because she was willing to bet Skye's handiwork didn't come cheap. Even for a friend.

He brushed his hand down her arm, lightly, then nudged her forward toward Skye. "I am." He told her he had another errand to run and left them to it.

Skye smiled at her. "Are you ready?"

"Oh, yes." Josie followed her over to a chair where Skye indicated she should sit and slipped off her shoes, understanding now why Luke had told her to bring regular socks. She pulled them on. "Are all these your work?" she asked, looking around the shop.

"No." Skye fitted her foot in to the measuring device and made a note on a pad. "I do this mostly on commission. The ones in the window are mine, and I have a few pairs in here, but mostly I carry other brands. Not everyone wants or can afford custom-made boots. I do a pretty solid online business, as well."

Josie examined the top of Skye's head as she crouched at her feet. Her hair was jet black and long. The braid came nearly to her waist. Her skin was a golden brown and her eyes were a sparkling brown. She was small and slender, but her quick fingers were long and nimble. Skye took a tablet and set it up on the table between them. "Here are some samples of my work. See what works for you, if there's anything you like or don't like. Some are more everyday, some are more special occasion, but I make them all to withstand real use, not just for show."

There was pride in her voice, and Josie could quickly see that it was well deserved. As she swiped through the album, she was more and more impressed. Some of the detail work, with flowers and vines, was truly amazing. "Skye. Wow. You do all this yourself?"

"Right now I do. If the business keeps growing, I'll need to bring in others to help, but I'll keep a close eye on it and stick with the designing. That's what I love, and what makes each pair individual, even if someone chooses the same design as someone else. They'll never be identical."

Josie decided to go simple. She chose black leather with a rambling rose in deep pink and green vines. It would twine up the side of the boot on the outside and over the toes. Skye drew it freehand out for her quickly so she could see, and then made a copy of it for Josie.

"I know you're leaving soon, so I'll put a rush on this. If you have to leave before I get them done, I'll mail them to you, but I'd really like to have your feet in the store if possible, to make sure that they fit you properly."

Josie smiled. "Thanks, Skye. I can come back, just let me know when."

Skye hesitated, then said, "This is none of my business and I know it, but are you and Luke an item? He looks at you— Well, he looks at you. I've gotten to know him and his family over the past couple of years and I've never seen him look at someone like he does at you."

Josie hesitated. She didn't know Skye, not really. She liked her, but wasn't sure how much to say. So she just smiled at her. "It's fine. I like him a lot, but I'm leaving." She gave a little shrug that was not nearly as carefree as she'd have liked it to be. "So no, there's not really anything there."

Skye studied her for a second. "Fair enough." Then

her gaze drifted behind Josie. "Hey, Luke. You're just in time."

Luke was polite to her, but when they left the store, Josie wondered if he'd overheard and misconstrued her shot at being nonchalant about them. Because in reality, it wasn't nearly as casual as she'd made it sound. She was trying to pretend it was, but deep down she knew better. To test the waters, she said, "Thanks for doing that for me. They're going to be beautiful. And Skye is awesome."

He nodded, his jaw still seeming a little tense. "She is. She's been a great addition to the city. Her work is in high demand. And you're welcome."

Luke didn't know why her comment had bothered him so much. They'd been pretty much operating on the assumption that it was going to be over soon, but to hear her classify it as "not really anything" had hit him oddly hard. It didn't do him any good to want it to be more. Or her either, for that matter.

But she mattered to him. He wanted to think he mattered to her. That *they* mattered.

He had no idea how to even say that, so he kept it to himself. Better to keep it that way than run the risk of making things awkward and weird for both of them.

"I can't wait to see them," Josie was saying. Her smile was wide and a little worried, so he smiled back and made himself relax. It was okay. They were okay. He wasn't going to push her.

"She'll get them done as soon as she can. She knows you're on a tight schedule."

"Yes," Josie agreed. "I just hope she's not putting a lot of other things to the side to accommodate me."

Skye had assured him it would be no problem to make the boots for Josie. She'd been excited to do it. "I think she would have said if she couldn't get them done in time. She's a good businesswoman on top of being a design genius. She's not going to do anything to risk her reputation." And Luke already knew her reputation had been built with care. She didn't say much about her past, of course, but he'd heard that she came from a rough family. More power to her if she was able to rise above that and make her own way.

"That's good," she said with a sigh. "I don't want to put her out."

Again, he was struck by the difference between her and Mandy—it wouldn't have occurred to his ex-wife that Skye might be inconvenienced by what she wanted. Mandy wouldn't have been mean about it, it just simply never would have crossed her mind to ask. She'd spent so much time being told how it was all about her that she'd wholeheartedly believed it. It had made things difficult when Luke had finally realized she wasn't ever going to change. She'd wanted him more as a satellite than as a partner, which was not his view of marriage.

They stopped for a quick lunch—not the burger place or the diner this time, not enough time—and headed back to the ranch.

He did pull over, down a remote road, and leaned over for a hot kiss. It nearly led to more, right there in the truck, but she eased back and smiled at him. "Something to look forward to?"

He half laughed, half groaned. "Yeah. Okay." Not

for the first time he wished there would be no one in his house so he could have his way with her as soon as they walked in the door.

She laughed at him as she eased back into her seat. "You'll be fine. Let's just get there, shall we?"

"Did you have a good time in Kalispell?" Alice asked her a little later. Josie smiled at her.

"I did. It was so sweet of Luke to think of that for me. I can't wait until they're done."

Alice smiled back. "He's a good man. A very good one. And you make him smile."

This was the most direct Alice had been about her and Luke yet, though she'd been dropping hints for days. Josie decided to respond in kind. "It's mutual, Alice. You raised good boys."

Her smile turned a little sad around the edges. "Yes. No thanks to their mother."

Confused, Josie set the knife on the counter. "What? Aren't you their mother?"

Alice eased herself on a chair at the island. She folded her hands on the counter and lifted her somber gaze to Josie's. "I'm going to tell you something that I'm not even sure his ex-wife knew. Luke never talks about it—I don't know if any of them do. But their mother left when they were young. Really young. Luke was four, so he has some hazy memories of her. The other two don't remember her at all."

Josie sucked in a breath. "Oh. Oh, Alice." Her heart broke a little for the small boys who'd lost their mom— who'd left them behind.

Alice ran her hands over the cool stone of the counter, her pensive gaze on her hands. "She wasn't ready to be a mother, much less ready to be a wife. John loved her madly but she didn't feel the same. She tried, but she was just too selfish to make it work." There was no trace of bitterness in her voice. Just sadness and maybe a bit of bewilderment.

Josie wondered at "loved her madly." Why had he remarried if he was so in love with the woman who'd left him? Maybe the question was written on her face, because Alice gave her a sad smile. "He married me a few months later. He wanted a mother for his boys, whom he loved but was in way over his head with, and I—" She stopped, then took a deep breath. "I wanted what my sister had, what she threw away like it was no more than trash. A family."

"Your sister," Josie said slowly, and then it dawned on her. "You're their biological aunt." It explained the family resemblance. She never would have guessed Alice wasn't their mom. They all shared the same smile.

Alice nodded. "I am. But I'm also their mother in every way that counts." There was a bit of fierceness in her tone.

Josie didn't doubt that. "What happened to—to your sister?"

Alice sighed. "She was an addict, as well. She died five years after she left. In New York City, of all places. And I only found that out by accident."

Sympathy flooded her. "Oh, Alice." Saying she was sorry didn't seem like enough, but her heart ached for Luke, Cade and Jake, who would never get the chance to make amends with their mother.

"I know. It— I know it left a hole. But it has to be

said, John and I had a good marriage. He was a loving husband, a good father. He and Luke butted heads a lot, but that was because they were very similar in a lot of ways. At the time you couldn't convince Luke of that." There was a faint smile on her lips now. "We make a good family. I'm so grateful I got to be their mom."

Josie realized, after Alice had left, that the older woman had another point. The women in Luke's life left him. His mother, his wife. She was going to leave him, too, but of course she wasn't a part of his life the way they had been, or should have been. But it probably only validated what he felt—that he was somehow unworthy. This broke her heart a little. She wasn't leaving because she wanted to. Not now. She was leaving because she'd never pretended any different. Nothing had changed in that respect. She hadn't come in here with any intentions other than to cook for the family. But she was going to be leaving a lot behind. Friends, to be sure, and possibly her heart, as well.

She wasn't going to dwell on that last point. There was no reason to. Nothing was going to change, no matter how much she wished it.

Chapter 13

"Help me move back to my house, please?"

Luke frowned as he surveyed the packed bags lined up neatly on the bed behind his mother. "Are you sure you're ready? Maybe you should give it another week." What if she fell?

She reached up and patted his cheek. "Of course I'm ready. I would have been just fine weeks ago. I only stayed up here because I knew if I didn't, the three of you would be trekking your way down to check on me at all hours of the day and night. But you need your own space back. And I think it's time for Cade and Jake to look into building their own places."

Startled, Luke looked at her. "What? Why?" They'd lived like this for years. There was no reason for him to be in that big house all by himself. Was it really okay for her to leave?

Alice sighed and turned to lift the smaller of the duffels off the bed and set it on the floor. "Luke. At some point you're going to want the place to yourself. You and Josie—"

He held up a hand. "There is no me and Josie—"

She gave him a look and kept on talking. "You and Josie together got me to thinking. You're not going to be single your whole life. None of you are. None of you should be."

Numbly, he repeated, "There is no me and Josie." Even though, yes, there was a relationship there. It wasn't going anywhere.

The other two bags joined the first on the floor. Alice started to strip the sheets off the bed, and he jumped in to help.

"Well, there should be. There's something between you, more than just the physical, it's crystal clear to everyone here. It'd be a damn shame to let her go, don't you think?" Before he could answer, she kept right on talking. "But if you do, you might find another woman to marry. Such a shame to keep letting Mandy win."

Luke stood there, completely poleaxed, the sheets balled up in his hands, not sure where to start to respond. Or if he even should try. She'd said an awful lot in just a few words.

She lifted the duffel, and Luke immediately dropped the sheets and took it from her. "I'll carry this and I'll take care of the rest of the room later."

His mind reeling, he followed his mother over to her house. He noted her pace was slow but her steps were steady. No limping or sign of pain. He wondered if she'd told Cade and Jake they should think about moving out. They each had their own lots on the ranch. Neither had opted to build on them yet because they were all single, so it made more sense to just bunk in the same house, where they shared a cook. But if they wanted to do their own thing, obviously there wasn't anything he could do about it.

What had she meant about letting Mandy win?

He followed his mother into her little house and set the bags on the bed where she directed him to. She pulled him in for a hug. "Thanks for the help. I love you. I just want you to be happy, but you seem to think that's not in the cards for you. That you had only one shot at it with a woman you weren't a good match with to begin with. Don't write it off. Don't just let Josie go because Rosa is coming back. Please."

Those weren't promises he could make, because he knew most of them couldn't be kept. So all he said was, "I love you, too, Mom."

After she assured him she was fine and would let them know if she had any issues, he left her little cabin. Down the lane another half mile or so was the lot Cade owned. It wouldn't be within eyeshot, but close enough. They'd all been given parcels that would allow them privacy, but yet be close enough that working on the ranch wouldn't be an issue. It had been his mother's idea, he suspected. And he knew she was right. If Cade and Jake were ready to build, he wasn't going to stop them. Sure, he'd rattle around that big house all by himself, but when his brothers married there'd be wives and kids and plenty of people. Or maybe he'd offer the house to them, and take one of the parcels and build himself a little cabin, like his mother's.

* * *

Josie frowned at the ball of sheets in the hall in front of Alice's room. She wasn't anywhere to be found. So when Luke came in the back door, she met him in the mudroom. "What's going on with your mom? Is she okay?"

"She's fine." Luke toed off his boots. "She moved out."

"Alice moved back out?" Shocked, Josie could only stare at Luke. Alice hadn't said anything to her. "Why? Oh, gosh. Should I take her a plate? Will she come up here for meals?"

Luke settled his hands on her shoulders and squeezed gently. "Josie. Relax. I said that wrong. She didn't move out, she went back home. She'll cook for herself, but come up here often for meals."

"Oh. Why?"

Luke shrugged, but there was something in his posture that made her think there was more to the situation than he was telling her. "Luke. What happened?"

He sighed and rubbed his hand over his face. "She thinks I need space. My own space," he clarified. "I ran into her the other night after I left your room. Apparently that was enough to make her decide to go home. She insists she was ready anyway."

Josie's face burned. "She saw you leave?" This was new, as Alice hadn't given her any indication she was aware of an actual relationship with Josie and Luke. But— Oh, my. How to face her now? *Yes, Alice, I'm having excellent sex with your son.* Oh, God. No.

"Yeah. She didn't say much—we're both adults

after all, and it's no one's business but ours, but yeah. It wasn't my favorite mother-son moment."

Josie cringed. "Oh, God." Adults or not, there was something mortifying about being caught like that, and him leaving made it seem as if he wasn't willing to spend the night with her, as if he was hiding something. Hiding her.

He pulled her in and kissed her, hard. She held on and kissed him right back. He pulled away lightly and nuzzled her cheek. "Are you going to tell me not to come to your bed anymore?" His breath feathered on her cheek.

She sighed and leaned on him, her cheek now on his chest. "Sadly, no."

A chuckle rumbled through him and she had to smile. She wasn't willing to give him up. These next two weeks would be priceless for her. She'd already accepted that she'd be leaving and he'd be staying—no shock there. But she was determined to get everything out of this experience since it was unlikely she'd connect with another man the same way. It just didn't seem possible. If she'd been wondering if she'd been in love with Russ before, she had her answer now—no. She didn't know exactly what she felt for Luke, didn't want to dig too hard into it, but she knew it was far more than she'd ever felt for Russ. And that alone was a win in her book.

Luke gave her another kiss and went back outside, and Josie returned to her work.

When he walked into the kitchen the first thing he saw—the first thing he always saw lately—was Josie. She gave him a quick smile as she looked over her shoulder from the stove, where she was stirring something that smelled wonderful. He washed his hands and came up behind her, wrapping his arms around her lightly and kissing her neck. She went perfectly still, spoon in hand.

"What was that for?" she asked, her tone light, but her eyes were serious. Luke knew he'd just advanced them another step, past the point they'd been toeing for a while now, that they seemed to have tacitly agreed they wouldn't cross. But his mother's words had shaken something loose in him.

"No reason other than you looked like you needed it," he said lightly, and she smiled at him, then returned to her pan. "What is that?"

"Gravy. My bugaboo." She gave a little laugh and pushed her hair back with her free hand. "If I blink too many times it gets lumpy. Or thick. Or doesn't come together."

"You're a professional and it still happens?"

She shrugged and sent him a little look. "Oh, all the time. In fact, it was one of the things—" She stopped and hunched her shoulders a little bit. As if she'd gone too far.

"One of the things what?" he prompted, curious since this was the most she'd referenced her past. He'd figured there was a good reason she wasn't at her restaurant anymore, but since she hadn't said anything he hadn't wanted to push.

She gave her head a quick shake. "Nothing."

But he wasn't in the mood to be brushed off. Not today. "Josie. Please don't shut me out."

She took the pan off the stove and turned to face

him. She took a deep breath. "It was one of the things my relationship broke up over. I didn't do it his way."

Luke went very, very still. *His way.* So there was a guy mixed up in all this. "Over gravy?" He couldn't help his incredulous tone.

She gave a little laugh and a half shrug. "Yes. And no. It was more that I didn't do things the way he considered the right way. His way, which as it turned out was the only way."

Luke's hands fisted. He forced them to relax. "And who is that?"

Josie went to the sink to fiddle with the dirty pans she'd put there. If she was going to tell this story, she needed to keep busy. "It's a long story. But I met Russ Crosby at a party hosted by mutual friends. I know you're not a big TV watcher, but he's big on the Cook's Network and often appears on talk shows and things. So really well-known. He took me under his wing, you could say, even though I was not interested in a career in television. He also owns three restaurants—two in LA and one in New York City. I worked for him for a while in LA and things kind of—kind of developed." She'd been flattered he'd taken the time to notice her, to compliment her and eventually to ask her out. "We dated for nearly three years. He did a lot of travel and I started my own place, which he eventually took over. Only it was by little increments. I didn't even really realize what was happening until one day, when I thought we were going to get married, I found out he'd been unfaithful. Very unfaithful."

Luke made a sound that could have been a growl. She looked over her shoulder, then grabbed the dish towel and turned to face him, wiping her hands on the towel. "Oh, yes. All the way along. And he'd inserted himself neatly in my restaurant so that when I left him, I had to leave that behind, too. He'd loaned me the money and it was all set up so that if I left, he'd get it." She shut her eyes. This was the part that made her the most angry. She'd been so stupid. So blind. "I missed it, Luke. I didn't know—I knew I had to pay him back, but he'd been undermining me the whole time."

Luke got up and came around the counter, wrapping his arms around her when he got there. She didn't cry— she had no tears for Russ—but she did lean on Luke and let him just hold her. "So that's why you came here?"

She nodded her head against his chest, enjoying the solid feel of him. "Yes. It'd been about three months since it all went down and I needed to get away." She also needed the money from a paycheck, since their very public breakup had been engineered by Russ to look as if he was the injured party, just helping his struggling fiancée out, and look how she repaid him by leaving him, blah, blah, blah. "I also—I also couldn't get a job at that same level. No one in the city or nearby wanted to hire me. Not because I wasn't any good, but because Russ is so very much larger-than-life that no one wants to mess with him." There was bitterness in her words and she knew it. Could taste it. Luke's arms tightened around her. "There were signs all the way along. Like I said, little things like how I made gravy. Or plated an entrée. Or whatever. He'd come in and correct me or tease me—now I can see how very controlling he was, but he was so subtle about it, at the time I just couldn't."

She hadn't listened to those who had tried to warn

her. She hadn't wanted to believe it, or believe that she could be such a fool. And in the end, she'd been a far bigger fool than she'd ever imagined.

"So what happened with your restaurant? How did he get it?"

Josie explained the loan he'd given her had had a clause written in by his lawyer—and she'd trusted him enough not to hire her own, a mistake she'd not make again—that the whole thing reverted to him if business struggled according to the stringent terms he'd set. It had struggled in the beginning, as new places were likely to do, but he hadn't given her all his support like he'd promised. And if she'd realized how it was all set up, she would have done things a little differently. She hadn't needed him to make her a success, and that had completely burned him. But it was too late now.

"Wow. What a bastard."

Josie rose up on her tiptoes and kissed his cheek. He made her feel better, as weird as it sounded. Having someone completely on her side, with no knowledge of Russ, was wonderful. "Thank you. Yes, he is."

"So you can't go back?"

She shrugged. "To work at my place? No. I can't. I have a lawsuit against him, but it won't give me the restaurant back. People's memories are short, you know?" Still, she didn't know how short, or if she wanted to risk it. And the more she thought about it, the more she thought that maybe it was time for a change. "I spent ten years there. That's a long time. I have a condo. I have friends there. I have other options that I'm considering." She'd had a life, such as it was, but it was run by her career. Another mistake she wasn't going to make.

He ran his hand down her hair. "It's not easy."

She supposed he'd know, having been through something similar. Though hers wasn't nearly as high-profile as his breakup. She'd been a nobody all the way along. "No. It's not. But I'm looking at options. I love to cook. It's what I want to do. Now I just have to figure out where I'm going to do it."

It was time she put some of those irons in the fire. Russ had knocked her down, but she wasn't out of the game. Not yet. Not unless and until she wanted to be.

Josie felt better for telling Luke her story. She hadn't really told anyone all the details, other than Allie, because she'd been embarrassed to have been so thoroughly duped. Luke hadn't judged her. He hadn't laughed at her or asked her how she hadn't seen it coming. He'd just listened.

She valued that beyond measure.

She'd spent a lot of time beating herself up over this. How had she not seen it, how could she have trusted Russ, etc. But she'd come to realize that though the signs were all there, in the context of their relationship they simply hadn't been warning signs. She hadn't liked being treated in the kitchen the way he'd treated her, and she'd told him so. He'd apologized, improved and eventually they'd fall back into the same pattern. She hadn't been a doormat, and that was important.

But still.

So Luke's unquestioning support felt good. She'd never really had anyone who sat solidly in her corner before. Not her parents, who had insinuated that she'd screwed this up on her own, and not her coworkers, who'd known where their bread was buttered—by Russ's hand. He was petty enough that he would have used their support against her, or worse, as reason to fire someone and make it hard for them to find a new job. She wasn't going to hold any of that against them. They'd done what they could and they all needed the work.

Taking out her phone, Josie pulled up her list of potential places. She called her former mentor, who had a few suggestions for her, as well. She'd never really considered being a personal chef, for example. She'd gotten used to being in the pressure-cooker atmosphere of a commercial kitchen in a popular, world-renowned restaurant. Her experience here at the Silver River, though, was reminding her how much she loved food. How much she just loved to cook. So maybe it was an option after all.

Her mentor promised to put out feelers and let her know if anything came up. It was exciting to realize there were a lot of prospects out there for her that were beyond Russ's reach.

She was ready to find them.

Chapter 14

Josie heard it as soon as she stepped in the house, returning from a trip to town the next afternoon. The notes of a guitar, muffled slightly by what probably was a closed door, but there was no mistaking the music.

Luke was playing.

She shut the door behind her softly, not that he'd hear it. But she didn't want to risk him sensing her arrival and stopping. The song was melancholy, and he kept stopping and starting, as though he was trying to work out the exact notes. She set the groceries and the mail on the counter and listened. The guitar was an extension of his soul. To hear it now, when he'd said himself that he'd given it up for years, was a gift.

Far too soon, the music stopped and she heard the door open. She held her breath, feeling as if she'd intruded when all she'd done was return from town early.

He came in the kitchen and stopped. Discomfort crossed his face. She preempted him from making any excuses by smiling at him, keeping her tone casual. The last thing he'd want was her to make a big deal of it. "That was lovely, Luke. New song?"

He shoved his hand through his hair. "I— Yeah. Listen, Josie—"

She held up a hand. "I won't say anything. But I have to ask—why do you want to hide it?"

He shook his head. "It's just not a good idea. That's all."

"Oh, Luke." But there was no more for her to say, nothing that would matter. She didn't know how to help him heal the wound left too long ago. Maybe, by playing today, he'd started down that road himself.

He shrugged. "Water under the bridge now," he said as he left the kitchen. She heard him in the mudroom, and then the back door opened and closed.

She watched him walk down the path toward the barns, her heart aching. Music and the guitar were part of him. A part of him he'd cut off. It had to have felt like he'd given up something vital and critical to his well-being. There was a recording studio in the basement. She'd found it one of the first days she'd been here, when she was down there to visit the root cellar. The door had a window in it, and she'd glanced in. It looked as if it hadn't been touched in years. At the time she hadn't thought too much about it. But now, knowing what she did, she wondered if it ever had been used— his marriage had been short and he'd left the industry right after that. From what Alice had told her, the house hadn't been all the way completed at that time. So she figured it was a good bet the recording studio had always been empty.

She turned from the window and started taking items from the bags on the counter. Whatever Luke was punishing himself for, it seemed as though it went a lot deeper than a marriage that had been ill-fated from the start.

Luke mentally cursed himself for getting the guitar out. He'd come in the house to take care of some paperwork in the office and had realized that the house was empty. He'd been unable to stop himself from going upstairs and taking the instrument out of his closet.

Lately it had been calling to him. Every time he opened the doors, it had been the first thing he'd looked at. As if it was done being ignored. It was all coming back, the songwriting, the need to play—he'd locked it all away for so long that to have it come back now was disconcerting at best.

The beat-up old Gibson felt like coming home in his hands. He could tell the story behind almost every ding and scratch. He could still feel the guitar in his hands. All he'd had to do was close his eyes and his fingers…and the music…took over. He'd plucked out a few bars of the melody he'd envisioned to go with the song he'd written, played with it, and felt the rush he'd been missing.

He stared at the hay bales in front of him, barely seeing them. Then he'd come in the kitchen and realized he'd been caught. By Josie, who looked at him with soft eyes and a knowing smile. He'd panicked, as though he'd accidentally let her in deeper than he'd intended.

Which was silly. But he had the feeling that she had seen and understood what it had meant for him to play again. He wasn't sure how he felt about that.

Movement caught his eye, and he turned to smile at Nikki as she approached him, the phone clutched in her hand. The he noticed her face was set in tense lines. His smile faded. "Nikki. What's going on?"

"I need to go home. My mom just called. My father had a stroke. It's not— They don't know—" Her voice trailed off as she took a gulping breath and Luke caught her arm.

"I'm so sorry, Nikki. We'll get you right out of here. Did you make flight reservations yet?"

Cade strode over and his gaze zeroed right in on Nikki. "Nik. Are you okay? What happened?" To Luke he repeated, "What the hell happened?"

Nikki spoke before Luke could. "I'm going home. I've got a flight out of Kalispell at six."

"I'll drive you," Luke said. "You packed?" He checked the time. "We'll need to leave in about fifteen minutes to make it."

She looked at him gratefully, and Cade's mouth tightened. "I'll be ready. Thanks, Luke."

As she hurried off, Cade turned to him. "I'll drive her."

Luke wasn't going to get in the middle of whatever was between Cade and Nikki. "She going to be okay with that?"

Cade looked after her, his jaw set. "We'll find out. If she won't get in the truck with me, you can drive her."

Luke studied his brother for a minute but didn't ask

what had gone wrong. He figured he knew. Nikki and Cade and been very flirty a while back.

Cade strode off in the same direction Nikki had gone without another word, and Luke figured if Nikki turned Cade down flat, he'd hear about it soon enough. So he stuck close to the barn until he saw Cade's truck, with Nikki in the passenger seat, drive by.

That was going to be a tense ride for both of them.

Then he saddled Kipper and headed out to catch up with another crew. Keeping busy had the added benefit of keeping his mind off Josie, but truthfully, she wasn't far from his mind at any given point. This was an issue. And he was worried about Nikki, too.

Cade came in late that evening. Josie had left a plate for him, just in case, ready to be warmed up. Luke hadn't known much, only that Nikki's father had a stroke and she'd needed to get home right away. Josie had waited for Cade, hoping to get more information on how Nikki's father was faring.

"I don't know if you ate already, but there's a plate in the fridge," she said when he came in. "How's Nikki doing?"

He gave a harsh laugh. "I don't know. She won't talk to me. She's very close to her family so I'd guess this is very hard on her. Being so far away."

Josie held up the plate and he nodded, helping himself to a beer from the fridge. "Thanks." He popped the top off and the metal cap danced on the counter. The bottle made a clinking sound on the granite when he set it down. The only other noise was the hum of the microwave. Josie leaned on the counter and said nothing. Cade was in his own world, and she wasn't going to try to break in. She already knew Nikki had feelings for him, even if he didn't realize it, but Josie wasn't going to say anything. They'd have to figure it out themselves. God knew she wasn't in any position to hand out romantic advice.

"She said she didn't know when or if she'd be back," Cade said. When he fell silent, she pulled the plate out of the microwave, set it in front of him and added silverware. "Said she wasn't sure if it was worth it to come back. Thanks," he added.

"You're welcome." She studied him for a minute. He looked bewildered. She stifled a sigh. Unless Nikki gave her the go-ahead, there wasn't anything she could really do here. Neither of them wanted to admit their feelings.

Maybe like someone else she knew. She got protecting yourself. She really did. But she also wondered—why couldn't they all have a shot at a happy ending? Or at least, a happy right now? Why were all of them unable to take those steps?

Since she had no answers, she let it go.

"I'm sure she's feeling awful over her father," she said. "When she has a chance to see how things are there, she'll be able to make that decision easier. Her job is here. She loves it here. You know she does." Because that was true. She knew Nikki did. The other woman had told her so.

Cade forked up a mouthful of beef she was willing to bet he didn't really taste. "Yeah. She does." Then he looked at her and actually focused on her. "You going to leave Luke?"

Josie floundered for a moment at the change in subject. "What? I'm not leaving Luke. I'm going home, like I'd planned from the start."

He shrugged. "Looks the same from here. He wants you to stay."

Those words tugged at her heart. He hadn't said that to her and she hadn't said anything about it to him. They didn't go there. "Oh, Cade. Don't say that, okay? Don't make this any harder than it already is." It was as honest as she could be.

He looked at her intensely for a minute, then mopped up gravy with a roll. "Going to suck for both of you. I wish there was another way."

Yeah, me, too. But Josie just said nothing. His blunt statement was true. There wasn't another way. Wanting it to be different wasn't going to change anything. All she said was, "If you hear from Nikki, will you tell me?"

"Yeah. But I won't. She'll let Luke know what's going on."

He sounded sad, mad and resigned all in one, and she just said, "Okay," and let it drop.

What a pair she and Cade were, she thought as she trekked off to bed after Cade had left the kitchen. Wanting something they couldn't have, for very different reasons. Or maybe all four of them were like that—wanting what couldn't be, and not knowing how to change it. If they should even try to change it. In the case of her and Luke, she couldn't stay, and there was no way Luke was going to leave the ranch he'd dedicated so much time to, the place he'd spent nearly his entire life. She'd never ask him to do so.

And that, right there, about summed it up.

Cade's statement had been spot-on. It was going to suck. And she wished like crazy she knew a way to change it.

Josie spent a restless night—Luke hadn't come to her room last night, and she wasn't sure why. It shouldn't matter.

Plus, her dreams had been the sort that she couldn't remember after waking up, but they left her feeling discontent and slightly out of sorts. So she was very happy to get her morning cup of coffee in her hands. She knew all too well the signs of a day that would end up being fueled by caffeine.

Maybe all those years of running in high gear had finally caught up to her. Though she hadn't realized it at the time, she'd been in a constant state of stress from one thing or another. Since coming here, that had all faded into the background. There were still things she needed to take care of back in Los Angeles. But she wasn't overcome with it anymore.

It was as if being here gave her the space to breathe. Space she hadn't even known she'd needed.

She stepped outside on the back deck and heard the noises from the barns. The workday started long before daybreak down there, though the sunrise was hitting the peaks of the mountains and turning them pink, the rest of the area was still the grayish dark of early dawn. Hank trotted around, not straying too far from her, but checking out what had come through his territory overnight. She took a deep breath of the crisp air, feeling it clear her head of the leftover muzzies from her night. Maybe she wouldn't need all that caffeine after all.

Of course, in LA she wouldn't step outside and take a nice deep lungful of smoggy air. It wasn't really the same.

So maybe she wouldn't go back to LA.

That thought kept circling in her head as she prepared and served breakfast, and accepted a quick kiss from Luke before he went out the door. He didn't say why he hadn't come last night, and she wasn't going to ask.

"You want to take a ride with me this afternoon?" he asked her quietly, after letting her know Nikki had made it back to Minnesota okay and her father was stable. "There's something I'd like to show you."

"Sure," she said, far too pleased by the prospect of time with him. "I'd like that."

"All right. I'll be back up here around eleven, so any time after that is good."

She said she'd be ready and watched him go out the door, allowing herself for just a moment to dream that this was their life. That she was a part of this, that they came down together in the mornings from his room and in the other room, their kids still slept, little versions of Luke with his gorgeous eyes. It was so much the opposite of what she'd ever wanted—or ever thought she'd wanted—that she slumped against the counter for a moment because she wanted it so badly it took her a few heartbeats to find her breath.

She'd never wanted anything like this with Russ and she'd been going to marry him. She'd thought their life would go on much as it was, just as an official team. But this—with Luke—was entirely different. And it made leaving very important, because she was sure that he didn't want the same thing. He'd never given her any reason to hope, despite the nagging feeling of belonging that had dogged her since she'd arrived. It felt as if she'd come home.

Right. Home. To a place that was about as opposite from the life she'd led as she could get.

How could that be possible?

She got ready for her ride—her new boots wouldn't be done until just before she left Silver River. That was a bittersweet thought, but they were going to be so pretty she wasn't sure she'd have worn them out on the trail anyway, even though Skye had assured her she could.

She'd bought jeans at Schaffer's last time she'd been in Powder Keg. Because the wind was a little cool today, she put on a long-sleeved T-shirt—also purchased in Powder Keg—and grabbed the hat Luke had bought for her on the trip. Looking at herself in the mirror, she almost didn't recognize herself. This woman looked happy and relaxed. Josie stared at herself for a moment longer. There were no shadows under her eyes. No tension lines around her eyes or mouth. Her skin was clear and almost glowed. She wore no makeup other than a touch of mascara, and hadn't in a month. The changes she'd undergone here were startling. She hadn't realized how pale and wan and tense she'd been for years.

She gave herself a final quick once-over and hurried downstairs, slipped on her aunt's boots and headed out. She put Zippy in the cross ties and saddled him herself, remembering that he would hold his breath when she tightened the girth. She gave him an affectionate pat, and he turned his head as far as he could in the ties.

"We're friends now, right, big guy?"

Zippy's answering chuff could have meant anything, but she chose to take it as an affirmation of his affection.

She got him all ready to go, then led him out to the yard, where Luke and a group of other cowboys were just coming into sight. He greeted her with a grin when he got close enough.

"Give me ten. I'm going to take out a different horse today. Kipper can take the afternoon off."

"Is he okay?" she asked, reaching out to stroke the horse's neck.

"Yep. Just need to work out one of Nikki's horses a little bit, and this is a good way to do it."

He took care of Kipper and saddled a new horse, this one a splashy paint named Zeke, then they set off.

"Where are we going today?" she asked as Zippy plodded along next to Zeke. She enjoyed these opportunities to see the ranch from horseback. And okay, to spend time with Luke. She was running out of chances for both.

"You'll see," he said, and slanted her a grin. "I can tell you it was one of my favorite places as a kid."

She was touched he'd share something like that with her. "All right. I can't wait."

They rode in companionable silence, with Luke occasionally pointing out this and that, and Josie just basking in the sun and his company. She was happy right now. Just—happy. On the back of a horse, in what to her was the wilderness. Funny how life worked.

Chapter 15

It was a good hour or so on horseback, but Josie's body had acclimated to riding and she wasn't sore when they dismounted and ground tied the horses. She planned to pick up riding again wherever she ended up. He pulled a blanket and some lunches out of the saddlebags and they set off a little way on foot. Josie could hear water, and she looked at Luke quizzically. "There's a river out here?"

He laughed and dropped a kiss on her cheek. "Silver River Ranch, remember? But here it's more of a creek. It widens farther downstream."

She shook her head and mimed slapping her forehead. "Of course."

They came through the trees to a clearing as the sound grew louder. "And here there's a bit of a waterfall."

Josie stepped around him and her eyes widened. It was a waterfall, all right. It fell maybe twenty feet below to where the rest of the river wended its way off the ranch. "How pretty! Look at the rainbows." The water caught the light as it fell and the resulting rainbows flashed in the sunlight.

"It is. We've come here for years. As kids, not sure about as adults." No real reason to as adults, unless maybe his brothers brought girlfriends here. He hadn't brought anyone here until Josie. It was secluded and quiet and beautiful and the one place that represented the ranch to him. "I'm sure there are other places my brothers went. We all had secret places we liked to hide or hang out in. Just the way of kids, I guess."

"I guess," Josie murmured, her gaze still on the waterfall.

"Did you?"

She looked at him, surprised. "Did I what?"

"Have a place like this. Not like this exactly," he said, gesturing at the water, "but a place you could go to get away when you were a kid?"

She stared at him for a long moment, her expression changing from thoughtful to sad. Then she shook her head. "No. No, I guess I didn't. We moved around kind of a lot when I was a kid. It seemed as if I'd just settle in and we'd have to go."

Luke spread the blanket on a soft patch of grass, and she sank down on it and played with the grass with her fingers. "Did you have a parent in the military?"

"No." Her smile was a little twisted. She looked at him, then away. "My dad was— Well, he was a con artist. Not only that, but a bad one. I didn't know that at the time, of course. Eventually he went to jail and my mom divorced him, but I was almost in my teens by then. She'd had plenty of issues of her own."

That hadn't been what he expected. Somehow he'd assumed she'd been raised in the same affluence she'd appeared to have had in Los Angeles, since she wore it so naturally. Anger flashed through him. Selfish adults. "I'm sorry to hear that."

She sighed and lifted a brow. "Which part?"

"All of it. No kid should have to go through that."

She smiled at him. "I survived. And I'd say that I did have a place I went. I cooked, even then. Someone had to, and I didn't mind it."

He tucked a piece of her hair behind her ear and smoothed her cheek with the back of a finger. Her skin was so soft and smooth. A sharp, sweet contrast to the roughness of his hands. "You've come pretty far since then."

She shrugged. "We all have. My dad's out of jail and works for a construction company. He's remarried. My mom is a manager at a bank. She got her degree. I'm actually very proud of them both. They just—they just weren't any good together. I don't think either of them had really grown up before they got married."

Still. The adults had put her through the wringer, and that wasn't fair to a kid. "I'm sure they are proud of you."

She smiled at him but didn't answer, then pressed her lips to his for a slow, sweet kiss. He wanted to lay her back on the blanket right then, but managed to hold on to ask another question. "Josie. Are they proud of you?"

She sighed and shut her eyes. "Yes. But they don't

understand why I didn't marry Russ. He'd charmed the hell out of them. So it was just easier not to go into all the details."

He understood that. He'd done much the same. But still. He stroked his hand down her face and under her chin, and when she lifted up he kissed her again. Before it could go further he pulled away and had to smile at her little huff of frustration.

"I want to show you something."

He stood, and she took his outstretched hand. He tugged her a little harder than necessary and she stumbled into him. He kissed her again and she laughed into his mouth.

"What?" he asked.

"We were doing that pretty well down there," she teased, pointing to the blanket.

He stole another quick one. He had every intention of having her naked on that blanket as soon as possible. "Yep. But first come see this."

He took her hand and led her toward a well-worn but overgrown path. She had to walk behind him, and she kept her free hand on his back. He loved the feeling.

They came out next to the waterfall.

"Luke, what is this?" she asked from behind him, loudly, to be heard over the rushing water, as she peered over the edge. He squeezed her hand lightly and led her under the waterfall, into a cave of sorts. She gasped.

"Are we under the river?" she asked, looking up and then out the curtain of swiftly falling water. "Oh, my gosh, Luke. I've never seen anything like this."

The expression on her face was one of pure wonder. It was loud in the cave, a bit of an echo from the noise of the water, so he put his mouth close to her ear. "Yes. We are. Pretty cool, huh?"

The cave was maybe ten feet wide and ten feet tall and probably twenty feet deep. At some point the river above would wear through the ceiling, but that was a long way off. The rock was pretty durable. It was also cold and damp, so he led her back out and up the trail to the blanket.

"That was so cool," she said, her eyes bright. "Did you go there as a kid?"

He grinned and lay back on the blanket, hands behind his head. "Yeah. We weren't supposed to. And we were expressly forbidden to jump. The currents at the base are strong, and it's not really that deep for the height of the jump. So we didn't do that. There are better places along the river for that."

She stared at him. "I don't think I'd jump in the river," she said solemnly, and he laughed as he tugged her down to him.

"No?" he whispered into her mouth and tugged her shirt up and over her head and reached for her bra clasp so fast it made her laugh. "Will you get naked next to one instead?"

Her response was a moan as her breasts fell free of the bra, and he had his hands and mouth on them, teasing, flicking, sucking. When they were naked and she was poised above him, the dappled sunlight slanting on her sleek body, a goddess all his own, she looked down at him and said, "I've never done this outside." There was wonderment in her tone.

He gripped her hips and let out a half laugh, half guttural groan as she slid down his length. Slowly, slowly, inch by hot, wet inch. "Josie. Now's a great time to start."

And she did.

Back at the ranch later, Josie thought this was the best time she'd had with Luke yet. Their lovemaking was phenomenal and hot, and something about it touched her on a soul level, not just the physical. She'd told him about her unconventional upbringing and he hadn't run away or flinched. The part about her dad being a con man, and ex-convict to boot, was often a bit of a relationship killer. In fact, she'd never told Russ, though he'd found out anyway, no doubt through a private investigator. In retrospect, if she'd hired one first she could have saved herself a lot of trouble.

Anyway.

They'd just been together, in an easy way she wasn't used to but enjoyed. Just Josie and Luke. No cameras, no rushing off to put out some kind of fire at a restaurant. No using the moment to make someone else look good. Just the two of them, together. It made her feel wonderful and valued in a way she wasn't used to. As thought there was more to her than her career—and even that had taken a backseat to Russ's. Somehow she'd lost sight of her own life and been enfolded in his.

That wouldn't happen again.

As soon as they got in the barn, Luke headed back to a stall in the far corner that was in the partial light. He turned with a grin and reached for her hand.

"Look." Luke tugged her to the open stall. Inside, lying on the clean straw was a pretty dog. She was snapping at her sides a little and whimpering, but she gave a little wag of her plumy tail when she saw them.

"Is she okay?" Josie asked, worried.

"Yes. She's in labor. We'll keep an eye out. This isn't her first time. Her first labors were smooth. Her name is Taffy."

Josie stood outside the stall and watched, rapt, as the puppies entered the world and Taffy licked and nudged each one, her warm tongue rolling them around in the clean hay. Luke had grabbed some clean towels. But the littlest one wasn't moving. "Luke," she started, but he was already in motion. Taffy nudged the baby and looked at Luke, who picked up the little brown puppy. It was so tiny and delicate in his big hands, and he handled it with such infinite care that Josie's eyes watered.

"Can you help him?" she whispered and Luke sent her a worried look.

"I don't know. Sometimes you can, sometimes not. We'll know in a few seconds, though." He held the puppy upside down and rubbed firmly with one of the towels.

Josie held her breath and let it out in a rush as the puppy started to struggle a little in his hands, and he carefully set it back down, where Taffy started to lick it and nuzzle it, clearly as relieved as a dog could be.

And Josie realized, watching him with the dog and puppies, that she'd gone and fallen head over heels in love with this man. Her heart both ached and wanted to fly. She was leaving in just a week, and there was no way for her to stay. She had to be back for the court hearing, and her whole life was in California. But seeing him with the puppy, the gentle way he treated Taffy and helped her, just made her melt inside. Somehow, despite her best efforts not to, she'd managed to fall for him. Wholeheartedly.

And, she feared, foolishly.

Luke gave her a little bump with his elbow. "We did it."

She hoped her mix of emotions didn't show on her face as she looked up at him with a smile. "We? I didn't do anything. Well, except pray."

He smiled back, and the sweetness of the moment wove around them. She wanted to capture and hold these fragile moments as if they were butterflies landing on her hand. Savor them, so when she left, she had something to look back on.

Taffy made a little whiffing noise, not a bark exactly, and Luke reached over to rub her head. "You did good, girl," he said softly. "Real good."

Josie wanted to cry. She also wanted to lean into his side, to say those little words that were swelling in her heart, but she knew once they'd been said, she couldn't take them back. She didn't want to make the last of their time awkward, or worse, find out that he absolutely didn't feel the same way and therefore she'd humiliated herself. He took her arm and steered her away from Taffy and her new puppies in the quiet, warm stall, and gave her a quick kiss. As he headed out and she went back to the house, she wished again, for just a moment, that all of this could be real and lasting. That the sense of belonging she experienced here was for real. It was a foolish fantasy, not to mention a dangerous one.

For now, she was determined to stay in the moments

as they came to her and Luke. She sort of tucked them away like little jewels to savor after she'd gone.

A short while later, Josie stood in front of the window and looked out at the jagged mountains and the wide expanse of green that spread at their feet. She was putting together dough for rolls for that evening's dinner. The longer she stayed at the Silver River, the more she grew to love it. It was so peaceful here.

Alice smiled at her when she came in the kitchen from the back door. "Well. You look happy."

"I had a good afternoon," Josie said cheerfully, which was true, and she couldn't of course go into all the pieces that had made her afternoon so wonderful. Her relationship with Luke wasn't something she wanted to talk about with his mother, no matter how much she liked the older woman.

"That's good to hear," Alice said, and didn't ask any further, for which Josie was grateful. "I made a pie this afternoon and thought I'd drop it off for dinner."

Josie peeked under the tin foil covering the fragrant plate Alice handed her. "Mmm. What kind? Apple?"

"Yes, apple raspberry. Jim picked a bunch for me. Usually I do it myself, but this year I can't be out on the uneven ground like that. I made pies for them, too. And I made a little tart for myself," she said with a laugh. "So no, I don't need any of this, before you ask. The boys will decimate this anyway, so make sure you get a piece before they get to it if you want some."

"Believe me, I will." The pie looked lovely, like something from a magazine, which told Josie that Alice had probably been baking them for decades. "Maybe I'd better hide it in the pantry until after dinner."

Alice laughed. "Maybe." She turned toward the door, her cane light on the floor. She was moving better, Josie noted.

"How are you doing in your house?"

Alice turned back and smiled a little. "Wonderful. I love this house, have always loved it, but that little place is mine, and I really missed my own space and my own things. I really have the best of both worlds here. My kids nearby and my own place. I'm very blessed."

Josie smiled at her. She knew so many people who just ran through life without really looking at what was passing them by. It was possible she'd been one herself. Out here, you were kind of forced to slow down and look. That was a good thing. "Yes. You are."

Alice left, and Josie made a mental note to tell Luke she was moving well and he could relax a little bit about her health. She doubted he would, but it was worth a try.

She looked outside and saw clouds gathering on the horizon. It was still sunny here, so the clouds looked especially ominous and dark in the bright light. Someone had mentioned snow on the peaks this morning. This must be the storm that was bringing it. She tied her apron on and got to work, only to be interrupted by a knock at the door. With a frown, she went to answer it. No one out here knocked. They just walked in. And more likely, they bypassed the house altogether and went down to the barns.

She left the dough for the rolls on the counter and hurried to the door. She yanked it open to see Russ standing there. He opened his mouth, and she blinked at him.

What the heck?

She shut the door right back in his face, pressed her hands to her mouth, and stared at the door like maybe she could vaporize him. Her pulse pounded in her ears. This couldn't be right. Russ? How could he have found her? More important, why would he care? He'd made it perfectly clear he didn't want to see her anymore, and she'd been very clear it was mutual. Plus there was the court case she had against him. He wasn't supposed to be contacting her, except through her lawyer.

There was another knock, harder this time, and she yanked it back open. "What do you want?" No point in pleasantries.

He arched a brow. "That's not a very friendly greeting for your lover."

She couldn't help it. She laughed, and saw his face flush. Good. He was getting annoyed. "That's because you're not. What do you want?"

He gestured at the door. "May I come in?"

She hesitated. It wasn't her home, and she didn't want him, even as a guest. So she shook her head and stepped outside. Annoyance flashed across his face, but he moved aside. She shut the door firmly behind her and crossed her arms. "Make it quick, please."

He stared at her and she simply stared back. Now she wondered what she'd seen in him. He possessed none of Luke's quiet authority or sincerity. He was good-looking, but now he looked pale and weak, and far too smooth in comparison to Luke's rugged good looks.

How could she have been so blind to what this man really was?

He couldn't hold a candle to Luke.

His expression was too smooth and she knew it well, bracing herself for the usual onslaught of flattery mixed with insults. "Josie. You're looking gorgeous as always. The cowgirl look works for you. Being out here in the backwater appears to agree with you."

She couldn't help it. She laughed, again. Hard. So hard, in fact, the tears came and she doubled over, her hands on her jeans-clad thighs. Miffed and clearly confused, Russ stared at her. "Josie. For God's sake, what is wrong with you?"

She leaned on the door and wiped her eyes. "You. God, Russ, you'll never change. If only I'd realized that way sooner." Like *way sooner*. Like before she'd started dating him. She was much, much wiser now. "Why are you here?"

His eyes were hard now. "I came here to offer you your job back."

Chapter 16

All laughter fled and a kind of rage filled Josie. "What?"

He tipped his head at the door. "Can we take this inside?"

Josie turned and walked in, not bothering to see if he followed. She didn't want her job back. There was no way to get her restaurant back unless he handed it over to her, and she knew that wasn't going to happen.

Russ sat at the counter and looked around the room. "Nicely set up for a home kitchen," he said. "But of course, Ryder has money to burn. Can I get a drink?"

Josie took a glass from the cupboard and willed herself not to throw it at him. Instead, she filled it with water and set it in front of him with a *thunk*. "I wouldn't know about that. But yes, my aunt knows her way around a kitchen. She designed this one years ago."

What, did he think Luke had suddenly remodeled his kitchen to suit her?

He took a drink and winced. Plain old water. That was another thing. His drinking had gotten worse as they'd been together. He was good at hiding it. Too good.

"Do you have anything stronger? That drive was hell."

"No," she said coolly. "Nothing I'm going to waste on you."

He set the glass down and smiled at her, but it was hard around the edges. "When did you get so disagreeable, love? Is it all this time in the sticks?"

She shook her head, then tapped her finger on her lips. "Let me think. I think it was when I got lied to, cheated on and stolen from by my fiancé."

"Josie—"

She interrupted him. "What do you want from me, Russ?" He wanted something. That much was sure. He wouldn't have come all this way otherwise. "You already took everything I had."

He didn't even have the grace to look chagrined at her quiet accusation. "Now, Josie. That's not true. You couldn't make a go of it on your own, remember? That's why I helped you out."

Right. Helped her right out of thousands of dollars and her reputation.

When she said nothing, just stood there with her arms crossed and her gaze level, he sighed. "I want to give you a thirty-percent stake in the restaurant in exchange for you dropping the lawsuit."

Josie's jaw dropped. "Thirty percent?" she repeated.

Was he kidding? After all he'd put her through, he thought a measly 30 percent stake in her own restaurant would make her drop everything and come back? He clearly thought even less of her than she'd thought.

He beamed at her. "Yes. And you drop the lawsuit."

"No."

He frowned. "Josie, it's fair. You couldn't make it work."

She advanced on him and saw him fidget on the bar stool. "No, Russ. I made it work just fine. Which you hated so much you came in and ruined it for me, because you couldn't have me be successful on my own. There is no way in any hell that I'd work for you again. Now get out of here, and rest assured I'm calling my lawyer to tell her about this visit."

He cursed and started toward her. "Be reasonable—"

Before Josie even knew what happened, Hank was there, all hackles and teeth. His low growl and sharp barks had Russ throwing his hands up. "Call that mutt off, Josie!"

Josie crossed her arms. "I don't think so. He's a good judge of character."

The back door banged opened and Luke strode in just as the front door slammed. Hank had run to the door and was still barking hard. "Josie! Are you okay? What's wrong with Hank?"

"Nothing," she said as the dog trotted back in and licked her hand. She patted his head and his tail wagged, all happy now. "Russ was here. Still is in your driveway, I think."

"Did he hurt you? Do you want him arrested?"

She shook her head. "When he raised his voice, Hank took exception. And no, I just want him to leave." Forever.

Luke made a quick call. "Jim will escort him off the property and all the way out to the main road to make sure he leaves." He reached for her, and she went willingly into his arms. He smelled like fresh hay and the sun and the scent that was just Luke. "What did he want?"

"To offer me a small stake in the restaurant I founded in exchange for me dropping the lawsuit." She pulled away. "That reminds me. I need to call my lawyer and fill her in."

"Guy's got some nerve," Luke muttered. He bent and patted Hank, too. "Good dog," he said. "You got rid of the bad guy."

Josie laughed. "Yes, he did. Russ couldn't get out of here fast enough." Then she sobered. "I'm sorry he came here. I know how much you value your privacy."

He caught her chin and kissed her softly. "It's not your fault. Anyone with a computer can look up where I live. It's not a secret." He straightened up. "I doubt he'll be back."

"Probably not," she agreed, and went into the office to make the call to her lawyer. Still. She felt bad that she'd brought him to Luke's house.

The lawyer took serious exception to Russ's visit and promised to make a heap of trouble about it. Josie hung up, satisfied. It was why she'd hired her. She needed someone to force him to pay attention. It did shame her, though, to realize that Russ thought so little of her— and so much of himself—that he could make a paltry offer like that and think she'd come running back like a puppy.

He'd had no respect for her, then or now.

Luke stalked to the barn, anger fueling every step. If only he'd been there. If he'd intercepted the guy, he wouldn't have gotten anywhere near Josie. She'd been upset, even though she'd tried to pass it off. It had shaken her.

He wasn't a violent guy, but he would have loved the chance to run the asshole off himself. Better yet, land him in a small-town jail where no one cared who he was or how much money he had. Be good for him.

Luke's phone buzzed, and he slowed as he pulled it out, recognizing the number as his agent in Nashville. Rob called him every few months to try to bring Luke back to the stage. Luke always said no. It was a dance they did each and every phone call, yet neither of them terminated the agreement. He wasn't sure why. Probably because Rob ran interference for him, dealt with things like offers so Luke didn't have to. Plus, he liked the guy.

"Luke," Rob said. "How're things in Montana?"

They spent a few minutes on the obligatory small talk. Rob did his job well and he protected Luke's privacy, even if he didn't fully understand how Luke could just walk away from his career like he had. The reason Luke kept him on? He wouldn't find another agent who would do the same.

"So what's up?" Luke asked, bringing Rob around to the reason for his call.

"Hear me out before you say no. Okay?"

"I always do," Luke pointed out, both amused and ashamed by the observation.

"Yeah. That's because you're too polite to hang up on me. But you don't really listen. So I'm telling you, listen to this. Okay?"

"Okay," Luke said and moved to stand under the maple tree that was just beginning to change color.

Rob detailed a concert series that was medium-size venues with a couple other bands. He would be a guest performer, not the main draw—though Luke wasn't sure anyone would pay to see him anymore anyway—and it would be released as a new album. The band wanted him to guest on a new single.

"This is a way for you to get back out there and boost your sales. You still sell pretty strong, and you get a lot of airplay. But this will be like the icing on the cake. And if you wanted it, maybe a way back into Nashville."

A way back into Nashville.

Luke just stood there. A few weeks ago, he'd have turned Rob down flat. But now—he thought of the songs he'd written over the past few weeks, how they just seemed to come out of nowhere, pour out of him like a part of him had been unlocked and set free. Having the guitar in his hands again was like being reunited with an old friend. "When do you need an answer by?"

There was the tiniest of pauses, but Rob was enough of a professional and knew Luke well enough to keep his response low-key. "End of the week. I'll email you the details."

"Thanks, Rob. I'll let you know." He disconnected and stared at the phone in his hand, not quite sure why he hadn't said straight-up no like he had all those times before over the years. Then he looked up and saw Josie walking toward him, her hair in the braid she'd taken to wearing and her hat on her head. She looked like a cowgirl now, not the city girl he'd feared she'd be when she arrived. Except for the tennis shoes on her feet, but even they were more practical than the three-inch-heeled boots she'd had on when he met her, if not as sexy. He did miss those damn boots.

Hell, who was he kidding? Everything about this woman was sexy. Whatever she did or didn't wear. When she was smudged with flour from the kitchen or dirt from a ride. When she talked and laughed with the ranch hands, or his family, or him. He wanted her with every breath he took.

Not just physically. He wanted her in his life, every day, from here until forever. The realization rocked him to his core.

She stopped in front of him and gave him a slightly quizzical smile. It was then he realized he'd been staring at her. So he gave her a little smile and quick kiss on the mouth to cover his suddenly roiling emotions. "Hey. Everything okay?"

"Everything's fine. I talked to my lawyer." She recounted the conversation quickly. "Russ will regret he bothered to come here."

"Good. You deserve so much better than him, Josie." And better than himself, as well. "Are you sure you don't want me to call the cops?"

She touched his arm lightly. "I'm sure. He's made enough trouble for himself just by showing up here. I looked out the window and saw you over here on the phone. Everything okay?"

He looked down at his phone and slipped it back in his pocket. "Yeah. Just had a call from my agent." Without really knowing why, he shared the details with her and watched her eyes grow larger. He never told anyone when Rob called, though he imagined they knew he did. He never wanted to justify why he'd decided to turn down yet another gig.

She clapped her hands. "Luke! That's so exciting. Wow. Are you going to do it?"

Her excitement was contagious. But he was still cautious. "I'm not sure. I need to think about it." To talk himself into it? Or out of it? He wasn't sure.

She lifted to her toes and kissed his cheek lightly. Another first, given they were outside, where anyone could see. "I know my opinion doesn't matter, but I think it'd be a wonderful opportunity for you."

He caught her hand and looked into her eyes. "What do you mean, your opinion doesn't matter?" Because it did. A lot. More than it should, considering she was leaving soon. She'd come to matter to him. Really matter.

She gave him a little smile that was tinged with sadness and shrugged. "You know what I mean. I'm leaving. This doesn't have anything to do with me. It's your life and career we're talking about here." Her voice faltered a little bit, and then she brightened up. "What are you thinking?"

Her words and her sad expression hit him in the gut. No, she wouldn't be here to see him off. To greet him when he came home. It seemed as if she might be feeling that loss as keenly as he was. He tried to bring his thoughts around. He didn't want to go down that path right now.

"I'm not sure," he admitted. "I've always said no before, and I think it shocked the hell out of Rob I didn't do it this time, too." He had to grin. Rob's startled pause after Luke's agreement to think about it had been priceless. Years of turning the other man down had clearly taken its toll.

"So why didn't you? What's changed?"

Josie's quiet questions gave him pause. He didn't have an answer. Things had changed somehow since she'd been at the Silver River. He couldn't really put his finger on it, but it was there, hovering under the surface. As if somehow she'd woken something in him that he didn't know he needed or missed. She'd shown him how to be comfortable with himself in a way he hadn't been in years. Maybe ever.

"I'm not sure," he repeated, and rubbed a hand over his face. "It just— Maybe it's time." He could hardly believe what he was saying.

She leaned on his arm, and the soft press of her breasts against him distracted him for a moment. "I think that's great, Luke. I think people will be thrilled to see you again."

He laughed. "You think they'll remember me?" Then the memories welled up of his divorce, the awful ending, the headlines. The prying. Would the press show up here? Russ had found it easily enough. He didn't want to go through the whole thing again. "On second thought—"

She laid a hand on his arm and squeezed. "No. Don't

talk yourself out of it. Talk to your brothers. Your friends here. I think you'll find they all support you."

Her words warmed him. "You think?"

She shrugged. "Why wouldn't they?"

He could think of several reasons. He'd been gone when his father had died and they'd needed him the most. He'd brought Mandy here and they'd had to deal with all the associated wreckage that decision had caused. The parade of people who had wanted a piece of him, or to use his family to get to him. But he was touched that she was so solidly in his corner.

He rubbed his hand over his face. "I don't know, Josie. It didn't go so well the last time."

She touched his arm. "That was a long time ago. Talk to them, Luke. You might be surprised."

Luke did as Josie suggested that night at dinner. He asked her and his mother to eat with them, too. He looked at them and wondered again if he was doing the right thing even considering this gig.

"I had a phone call today," he said casually into a conversational lull, and Josie started to rise, murmuring something about the kitchen. He laid a hand on her arm, as close as he'd been to her in front of his family. "Stay. Please."

She sat back down as Cade said curiously, "What kind of phone call?"

He took a deep breath and set his fork down. "From Rob. He had an offer for me." He filled them in on the details, since he'd had a chance to run into the ranch office and check his email. They all listened quietly, and Josie's eyes never left his face. He drew strength from her quiet presence. "So it'd mean I'd be gone for a lot of next summer," he finished. "And I'd have to head out to Nashville to meet with everyone and do the single before that."

"Oh, Luke," his mom said, and he winced. Of course she wouldn't want him to do this, after how badly it had gone the first time around.

He shook his head. "It's okay, Mom, I won't do it. I'm not even sure why I was considering it."

She slapped her hand on the table and he actually jumped. "Oh, for God's sake, Luke, I wasn't going to tell you not to go! I was going to say it's about damn time!" When Luke's mouth fell open at both the sentiment and the mild profanity, she leaned over and laid a hand on his arm. "Honey. You've been hidden away here for a long time. You have a great talent and shouldn't hide it. There are people out there who would love to see you, have you share your music with them. I hope you decide to do it. It's not our decision. It's yours."

Cade and Jake nodded, and Josie gave him a little grin. Not quite an "I told you so" but close enough.

He cleared his throat. "What about the press? The stories? Everything that happened the first time coming back out?"

Cade shrugged. "We'll deal. It's too remote out here for anyone to really be bothered to stick around for long. As far as the rest goes, well, that's your call. It's your past. Nothing happened in there that looks bad on you."

He thought back through those years. He hadn't been a bad husband, sure. An overwhelmed one, maybe, with his crazy wife and unexpected success.

"You were young and out of your depth," his mother

said quietly, echoing his thoughts. "No one's going to hold that against you. What do you think, Josie?"

Her head came up, surprise in her eyes. "Oh, this isn't about me."

"Of course it is. Luke values your opinion, don't you, Luke?"

He nodded, and realized again it was her opinion that mattered the most, and she wasn't even going to be here. She was clearly uncomfortable pitching in but she said quietly, "I think it's a great idea."

To Josie, this felt a lot like a family meeting—which it was—and she was out of place here. She wasn't family, as much as she liked them, all of them, and as much as she loved it here, it wasn't her home. Wouldn't be her home. She rose and grabbed a few plates, shaking her head when they tried to rise to help her.

She took them in the kitchen and loaded the dishwasher, trying to clear her mind. She was in far too deep here. It was much too easy to pretend she was a part of this, that she had a say in Luke's life because he valued her, because they were a couple—when in reality, they were just a temporary item, bound to end when one of them left in a week.

A week. Almost at the point it could be counted in hours.

Chapter 17

She swallowed hard and started when Luke's strong arms came around her from behind. He held her close, his chin on her head, and she could see their reflection in the window as she lifted her dry hand to press on his hands. They made a good couple, but it was every bit as transient as the reflection in the glass. Tears burned her eyes, and she willed them away. Moments like this were gold. She didn't want to lose them. Enveloped in his arms, in his scent, she was safe and warm and as close to loved as she'd ever been.

"Thank you," he whispered in her ear, and she turned in his arms to look up at him. He loosened the circle of his arms but didn't let go of her.

"For what?"

He kissed her nose. "For making me talk to them."

Now she laughed. "I didn't make you do anything, Luke. You know that."

He was completely serious. "No. But you didn't let me talk myself out of it."

She thought if he'd been against the idea, no one would have been able to talk him into it. But she didn't point that out. "Are you going to call Rob tonight?"

He shook his head. "I want to sleep on it. Or not," he added, his voice low and sexy.

She laughed even as his tone set off heat inside her. "You're insatiable."

"It's you, Josie. Something about you that just makes me crave you all the time." He said it with a note of wonderment in his voice. She felt the same way but didn't think it would be a good idea to tell him so. She needed to start pulling away, to protect herself as best she could. Still, she couldn't bring herself to withdraw when he leaned in and kissed her.

In the end, he helped her in the kitchen, then went to her room with her. When they came together in the dark, her heart ached just a little. The words she so badly wanted to say were trapped in her throat. It would change everything in a way that wasn't fair to either of them. So she said them in her head and carried them in her heart. *I love you, Luke.* She turned her head to press a kiss to his bare shoulder, grateful for the dark that masked the tears threatening to fall.

It wasn't until later, when the bed dipped as he rose and her door opened and closed ever so quietly behind him, that she let the tears come.

* * *

When she talked to Allie the next morning, her friend picked up at once that something was amiss. "Spill," she demanded, and Josie stifled a sigh. She didn't want to share her feelings. To put them into words would make it too real, might make the pain later too much to bear. She wouldn't want Allie watching her too closely when she went home, monitoring her for signs of heartbreak.

"There's nothing to spill," she assured her friend, keeping her tone light. "Unless you count Russ showing up here."

"What?" Allie asked, incredulous, and Josie filled her in on the details of Russ's unannounced little visit. When she finished, Allie breathed, "Wow. The nerve. He's something else."

"Yeah. You know, the thing is, a few weeks ago I'd have negotiated something to get my restaurant back, even if it was only part ownership. But now—" She stopped.

"But now..." Allie prompted softly.

"Now I wouldn't settle. He'll never sell it, and I won't get it in the court case." It still made her sad, but somewhere along the line she'd decided she deserved better than the scraps Russ decided to toss her way. If only she'd realized it far sooner. "I've let it go. I'm ready to move forward." It was liberating to say the words.

"I'm so happy to hear that, Josie. I was really worried about you. So. How's that handsome cowboy you're working for?"

Josie tucked the phone on her shoulder and reached for a dish towel. She chose to keep her answer evasive.

"They're all fine. They work hard. They're nice men, Allie."

"I'm sure they are, but I was asking only about Luke," she said bluntly. "When you talk about him your voice changes. You mention the others, but not in the same way. Are you falling for him, Josie?"

"No, of course not," Josie said with a laugh that was a teeny bit forced. Darn it, Allie knew her too well for Josie to keep this kind of thing from her. Hoping her friend didn't catch it, she hurried on. "It'd be the dumbest thing I could do. You know that. I'm leaving here soon. It's not as if anything could ever work." She winced and slapped her hand on her forehead. And that was too much of a protest right there. She'd flung open the door. Allie was far too astute to not barge straight through it.

"Who are you trying to convince? Me? Or yourself, Josie?" Allie's voice softened with worry. "Maybe it's too soon after Russ? I mean, it ended so badly."

Josie gave a little laugh. "You know what it was like," she said. "I know now it wasn't really a relationship. I didn't love him. I thought I did, but I didn't." And she knew this thanks to Luke. The depth of her feelings for him were far beyond anything she'd ever felt for Russ. She wasn't going to say that, though. "I never think about him. I don't miss him. I don't miss what could have been. He never would have changed, Allie. He proved that when he showed up here. I'm better off without him." That was all true, right there. She wished it had all ended differently, where she hadn't ended up losing so much and being played for a fool, but she was very grateful Russ was out of her life before she'd made the horrible mistake of marrying him. Of believing love was something far less than it was, and settling for it. She'd make sure she didn't make that kind of mistake again. Ever.

Luke, though—Luke had shown her what it could be. And, oh. The sense of loss spilled over her. Luke, she'd miss with all her heart. She pressed the towel to her eyes. She didn't want to break down on the phone and give herself away.

Allie's sigh carried clearly through the connection. "Well, that's good. I just don't want to see you go through that kind of thing again. It was awful."

"It was," she agreed. It had been humiliating and horrible, but it was only her pride that had suffered, not her heart. But still. "I'm not going there again." She was smarter now.

They chatted a little bit longer about far more neutral topics, and when Allie got another call, they hung up. Josie tried not to promise she'd tell Allie if things went anywhere with Luke. They already had.

Josie put the phone back on its base and looked out the office window. The day was sunny, but there were streaks of clouds. Something Allie said nagged at her. That Josie sounded different when she talked about Luke. She didn't want to sound different. She wanted to sound exactly the same no matter who she was talking about. Because it might be too late not to be in love with him, but she needed to keep it to herself.

Luke took a break midmorning to call Rob back. Since he'd made up his mind, it seemed pointless to wait to get things rolling. Rob was thoroughly shocked but thrilled. They talked awhile longer, and Rob promised to get back to him in the next day or two on all the dates once he'd informed the band. He told Luke it might be a quick exit on his end, so to be prepared to leave on short notice. They'd send a plane for him.

That alone made him shake his head as he disconnected the call. Send a plane. He rested his foot on the bottom rung of the corral and watched Jim work the horses. Never would he have thought he'd be the kind of guy who rated a plane, even when he had been. Now it was starting all over. The whole thing felt surreal. It had changed so fast. This time, though, his eyes were wide-open. He was in full control of his career.

But—Josie.

He shut his eyes just for a moment. He hoped he could be here for the rest of her stay. There was an odd ache in his chest when he thought of her leaving. He'd been trying to ignore it but it was stronger now, that the end was in view and coming up fast. Too fast.

He realized Jim had said something to him. "What was that?"

Jim inclined his head toward the horse. "I said, what do you think?"

To be truthful, Luke had barely noticed the horse even as he'd been tracking its movement around the ring. His thoughts were far away. "He looks good, Jim. Really good." He knew it was true because he'd seen this particular horse worked before.

Jim came over with a small frown. "You okay, boss?"

I'm about to lose Josie for good. Hell no, I'm not okay. But he couldn't say that. "Just fine." The lie stuck in his throat. If Jim had noticed and commented, he must really be in bad shape. Since he was leaving— even though it wouldn't be for all that long—he threw himself into the chores with renewed vigor. This place wouldn't miss him. It ran like a machine, with everything in its place and by people who knew exactly what they were doing. He and his brothers were damn lucky.

But there was something missing, something he hadn't wanted to acknowledge he was missing until Josie came into his life. All too soon, it'd be missing again. This time, though, he wasn't sure how he'd go back to life being the same as before. Because it wouldn't be, without Josie.

He shut his eyes on the revelation. Hell. He'd fallen in love with her, let her into his life and his heart and she couldn't—wouldn't—stay. It wasn't her fault. It was his. But when she went home, he'd be left behind once more.

He'd vowed never to let that happen again.

A clean break would be easier for both of them. A phone call to Rob, and that plane would be on its way within the hour. He could clear out and save both of them the trouble of a prolonged goodbye. It seemed like the best idea. Plus, the sooner he got away from her, the sooner he could get over her.

Swallowing the suddenly sour taste in his mouth, he pulled out his phone.

Josie knew the moment Luke walked in the door something wasn't right. She could see it in his posture and his closed expression. So instead of going to him, she moved casually to the coffeemaker to pour a cup she didn't really want, hoping to cover up the sinking feeling in her stomach.

"Is everything okay?" Her tone was normal but her hand was shaking a bit, so the coffee splashed out of the mug. When he didn't answer, she gave up the pretense of coffee and turned. "Luke?"

He had his hat in his hands, and she knew from the look on his face that whatever he had to say, it was bad. "Are there more problems with the cattle?"

He shook his head. "No. I'm leaving, Josie. In an hour and a half, I'm heading to Kalispell to catch a plane to Nashville."

Josie's mouth fell open. Now? He was leaving now? She gave her head a little shake. "I don't understand. I thought that was still a week or so away."

His face was impassive now. "I decided it was best if I went today. No point in waiting, you know?"

She stood very still and looked at him. He met her gaze, and she saw none of the tenderness and heat she usually did. Had the whole thing been a mirage? Had she just imagined that maybe he felt for her what she felt for him?

But then, she caught just a hint of remorse and realized what was going on. A little bit of hope popped up. "You're running away." Running away meant he had feelings for her, even if he was handling them badly.

He shook his head. "No. What would I be running from?"

She moved closer and heard him take a sharp breath when she stopped right in front of him. "Me. Us."

He looked at her, and his eyes were the cool icy blue they'd been when she'd met him for the first time. "There is no us, Josie. It was great while it lasted, but it's over now. You're a city girl. You don't belong here."

You don't belong here. The words hit her harder than a slap. She'd felt as if she belonged, for the first time, when she'd come to the Silver River Ranch. And now this man—whom she loved—had just told her she was mistaken. That none of it mattered.

She took a shaky breath as first pain and then anger washed over her, sharp and hot, and she welcomed the sting of it. "I see. Well, how lucky for you I won't be here when you get back. Good luck, Luke. You'll need it."

She turned and walked out of the room, her back straight and her steps measured, not willing to let him see the tears that had already begun to fall.

By the next morning, she was dry-eyed. She'd cried half the night and was in some sort of a lovely welcome fog that insulated her from her pain. At some point it'd wear off. She knew this. In the meantime, she'd work damn hard to not feel.

She'd heard Luke leave yesterday. Heard him pause at the base of the stairs, but he hadn't come to her door. Not that she would have answered it. At least, she was pretty sure she wouldn't have.

She'd also packed her bags. She had decided to leave today. There was no point in her staying and prolonging the agony any longer. There were plenty of meals in the freezer, and her aunt would be back in less than a week.

She changed her flight and asked Cade, when he came in, for a ride to Powder Keg. She could call a cab from Kalispell to pick her up. Pricey, yes, but worth it.

He shoved his hat back. "Of course I'll take you. I'll take you all the way to Kalispell, there's no need for you to take a cab. My idiot brother— I'm sorry." He shook his head. "We all thought you guys would get married."

Cade's words nearly knocked Josie to the floor. They made an unfortunate hole in her fog, and some of the pain seeped in. She swallowed hard. "Well, you thought wrong." While an extreme understatement, it was all she could think of to say.

Alice came in the door and came straight to Josie and wrapped her arms around her. Josie squeezed her eyes shut tight, trying to hold against the torrent of emotion she could barely contain. Too many holes had been punched in her fog. "Please don't apologize," she rasped. She wouldn't be able to bear it. "Please."

Alice squeezed her, then stepped back. "Then, I won't. But I will say he's running, Josie. From what he feels and what he's afraid of. I hope the two of you can work it out."

The ache in Josie's chest sharpened. "There's no chance of that. We're too different and live in completely different worlds. Now, about the meals—" She changed the subject, and after exchanging a look with Cade, Alice went with it, for which Josie was grateful.

She'd miss them like crazy. All of them. When it came time to leave that afternoon, she didn't let herself look back, just focused hard on her hands in her lap, as if maybe somehow they held the answers she needed. But all the same, it seemed as though she'd left a significant portion of her heart behind in a place she would never belong.

Chapter 18

Josie stood on her balcony and overlooked her view. She'd bought this condo because she could see the ocean in the distance on a clear day, and those were rare. She could see the 405 freeway, congested as usual, and the sea of roofs and parking lots lined with palm trees and stretches of green here and there, dotted with the sparkle of pools. The heat shimmered over the pavement.

She couldn't help but compare it to another view she'd grown to love, one that involved cowboys and cattle and horses and green pastures and huge mountains. It was all tied up with the one man she couldn't get out of her head.

She shut her eyes for a moment. It had only been ten days. Ten days since she'd left Montana. Eleven since she'd seen Luke. She'd used the time to begin a job search in earnest. She was moving on with her life, as hollow as she felt without Luke in it.

It would pass.

She turned and went back inside, leaving the slider open. It was October in Los Angeles, but it was far warmer than it had been in Montana. She wore capris and a tank top. Casual outfit, after the suit she'd worn earlier to court.

Russ had agreed to pay her for damages in exchange for her to drop all charges. After his little visit to her at the Silver River, he'd pretty much tied his own hands. The money would be welcome, but she couldn't muster up much more than a deep-seated relief it was over. He was out of her life for good. She'd wanted to call Luke, but of course, she couldn't. Forcing down her disappointment, she'd called Allie instead.

"Meet me at The Cantina at three," Allie said. "I'll buy you a drink. You need to celebrate this!"

Josie had agreed, but her heart wasn't in it. Still, she had to keep moving forward, so she changed clothes again and headed out to the little café.

Allie showed up in a whirl and gave her a huge hug and a squeal, then pulled away and looked hard at Josie. She frowned. "Josie. You look like hell. What is going on?"

Josie burst into tears right there in the café.

The waiter, drawn over by Allie's bright bubbliness, paused uncertainly. Allie gave him a smile. "I think we need some more napkins."

"Sure. Be right back." He hurried off and Josie shook her head, sniffling.

"I'm sorry. God. I'm a mess."

"Yes," Allie agreed. "You are. Now spill. Is this about Russ?"

Horrified, Josie looked up and actually managed a laugh. "God, no."

Allie patted her hand. "Good."

The waiter placed two glasses of water and a stack of napkins on the table, then withdrew. Josie made a note to tip him handsomely even if they didn't order anything. She grabbed one of the napkins and patted it on her face.

"Josie?"

She sighed. "It's all good with Russ. I accepted a settlement in exchange for dropping the charges. It was fair. He's made a lot of trouble for himself and I just want to be done with him. Now I can move on free and clear." But to what? That was the problem. Everything she wanted was in Montana. But how was she going to make a living there? Not to mention Luke hadn't asked her to stay. In fact, he'd left so fast, as if he couldn't wait to get away from her.

"But," Allie prompted gently.

Josie took a deep breath. "But there's Luke. I just— I fell in love with him. And he didn't feel the same way."

"Oh, honey." Allie covered Josie's hand with hers. She couldn't help but notice her friend's sparkly gold manicure on top of her own nonexistent one. "Are you sure?"

She thought back to the moment he'd told her she didn't belong. "Yes. I am sure."

Allie narrowed her eyes. "So he's an ass."

Josie choked on a laugh. "No. He's not. That's the

thing. If he were, this would be so much easier." Because she wouldn't have fallen for him in the first place.

Allie squeezed her hands and sat back. "I'm sorry, honey. What can I do to help?"

Alcohol and ice cream weren't the answers, and she'd already tried both. Plus, she wasn't sleeping well again. She hadn't taken any of her sleep meds the night she'd had too much wine, but she had the night she'd had too much ice cream. She took a deep breath and let it out slowly. "Nothing. I'll be okay. I've been looking for other opportunities. I'm thinking personal chef. My mentor from culinary school offered to set me up with an interview. I'm going to take her up on it."

Moving forward was her only choice. Sometime, the pain would lessen. It hadn't even been two weeks yet.

"If you need anything, you call me. Promise."

"I promise." She hugged Allie. "It'll take some time, but I'll be okay." She had to believe it. If she could convince herself, then maybe she could make it happen.

Josie got in her car and drove the three miles home in about an hour. Lots of traffic, lots of lights, lots of congestion. And the time of day didn't help, either. She hadn't missed this at all. She could have most likely walked it faster, even in her heeled boots.

She hadn't taken the ones Luke had ordered for her out of the box other than to try them on. They'd arrived three days ago. They were gorgeous and fit beautifully. She'd written Skye a heartfelt thank-you note, but they made her unbearably sad. She'd put them away in her closet. If only it were that easy to deal with the rest of the memories—pack them away in a neat box in the closet. Done.

She parked in her carport and made her way inside the glass-walled lobby of her building. A cowboy hat across the vast room immediately caught her attention, but she willed herself to ignore the silly leap of hope. Those hats were all over, even in this area. She'd never really paid attention before, but now she saw them everywhere she looked. It was foolish to get all quivery and then let down every time one caught her eye. So she turned toward the elevator, her mind skipping ahead to her evening. Takeout again? Allie was right—she should celebrate her victory over Russ. It wasn't too late to call her mentor, who was in New York. She'd get that interview set up.

"Excuse me, ma'am," came an all-too-familiar and low voice behind her. Josie froze, her hand outstretched to push the button on the elevator, then pivoted slowly to see that the cowboy hat did, indeed, belong to Luke. Her mind went completely blank even as that crazy little flare of hope spiked.

She took a deep shuddery breath as the elevator opened behind her. He motioned toward the door and she got on. He followed her. The door slid closed, and she wished like crazy she wasn't stuck in the small space with him, enveloped in his scent. Her hand shook as she pressed the button for her floor. All she wanted was to throw herself at him and hang on. Instead, she focused on the floor numbers that seemed to be going by very slowly. "What are you doing here?"

Dang it, her voice wobbled. She swallowed hard.

He cleared his throat. "It was brought to my attention that I was an idiot."

"Oh?" That little flare of hope leaped higher in her chest, but she didn't dare take her eyes off the numbers slowly ticking off as the elevator rose. Because she didn't want to look at him and see something that would break her heart.

He shifted beside her. "Yeah, *oh.* I owe you an apology, Josie."

The elevator stopped at her floor and the doors slid open. She stepped out, not looking to see if he followed. Her hands were shaking so badly that she could barely get her keys out, much less the right one in the lock when she stopped at her door.

She felt him come up behind her before his big hand closed over hers. The warmth and roughness of his palm on hers made her shiver. "This one?"

She nodded, unable to speak.

Inside, he pushed the door closed and set the keys on the table near the door. She heard the clank. She walked to the other side of the room, which was as far as she could go and still be in the same room, and finally faced him. "What kind of apology, Luke?" Because she really couldn't take it if he came all this way to say he was sorry for not loving her. No, that would crush her.

He stood there, looking big and sad and out of place in her modern condo. She missed him. Missed everything about him. "For not telling you how I really feel."

She shut her eyes. Oh, God. "It was pretty clear, Luke. You didn't have to come all this way to make sure I understood. I got it." She turned, intending to lock herself in her bedroom. Or the bathroom. Anywhere she could fall apart. This wasn't going to help her move forward, darn it. But he crossed the room with that impossibly long stride and laid his hands on her shoulders.

Then he kissed her. A sweet, gentle kiss that quickly turned hot. He pressed his lips to her forehead. "Josie. I didn't get to tell you I love you."

She went stiff. Surely she hadn't heard that right. "I'm sorry, what?"

He ran his hand down her cheek. She loved the roughness of his palms, the workingman's hands. "I love you," he repeated. "I was too afraid I'd screw it all up if I admitted it to myself, much less you."

Hope bloomed into something much sweeter as she searched his eyes and saw nothing but sincerity. And anxiety. "So—you ran away?"

He took her hands. She looked down at them, her smaller ones engulfed in his larger ones. "Yeah. It seemed easier. As if I'd spare you some kind of pain by running away."

She arched a brow. "Spare me?"

"And myself," he admitted with a wince. "I guess I thought if I loved you and I left first, it would somehow make me feel better." His hands tightened on hers. "I was wrong. And my family made sure I knew what an idiot I am."

She couldn't help but smile at his chagrined tone. "Really?"

"Really. I'm sorry. I didn't want to screw up."

Unable to stand that close to him and not touch him, she burrowed into his chest and felt his arms close tightly around her. Oh, yes. This was home, right here, wherever her cowboy was. "Luke. I love you. How could you screw up saying 'I love you'?"

He laughed and pressed his cheek to her hair. "I did, clearly." Then he squeezed her a little tighter. "Josie. I love you. So much. I was too afraid to take the chance that you wouldn't stay."

She understood. She did. "You never asked me to stay, Luke."

"I didn't think it was fair," he explained. "It's the middle of nowhere. I didn't want you to be miserable. That wasn't fair."

She'd been miserable without him. She stepped back, but not out of the circle of his arms. She tipped her head up to look at him. "That was a choice for us to make together, though. Not you to make for me." It was important that he understood that—Russ never had. She couldn't take the chance of being run over again.

"I know. I guess I thought I was trying to protect you, but really I was worried about putting myself out there." He took a deep, shuddering breath and rested his forehead on hers. "Holy hell. These have been the longest days of my life."

She rose on her toes and pressed her mouth to his lightly. "Mine, too."

His hands already starting to roam, she took his hand and led him to her bedroom, where she proceeded to show him just how sweet forever would be.

Nine months later

Luke came offstage after his first appearance performing in public in too many years. He'd just done an encore. Amid all the people backstage who congratulated him and pumped his hand stood Josie. She wore a T-shirt with his name in sparkles across the chest—he'd been a bit stunned by it—and the boots Skye had made for her with jeans. She threw herself into his arms as soon as he cleared the crush of people. He was sweaty and hot and pumped. It had felt good—so good to be out there, to feel the crowd's energy and excitement.

"You did it," she said into his ear—it was hard to hear, what with the roar of the crowd in the background—and he kissed her quick and hard.

"I did." He threw back his head and laughed. "Thanks to you." Thanks to Josie and her quiet dedication, he'd settled right back into the life he'd thought he'd left behind. This time was different, though. She was along for the ride as both his fiancée and his personal chef. It made for a calmer experience for him.

She smiled up at him as she looped her arm around him. He accepted a bottle of water and took a long drink. "Feel good?"

"I do." He dropped a kiss on her head. They were due to say those words at the end of the month. He couldn't wait. When the tour was over, they'd return to the ranch, where Josie would take over the diner in Powder Keg. Donna was ready to retire and had been more than happy to hand the reins over to another cook she trusted as much as herself.

The noise of the concert muffled as they went behind the venue. "It was amazing to hear you perform," she said. "They love you."

He shook his head, still amazed. "It's been a hell of a ride. I never thought— But I'm grateful beyond words."

She laced her hand in his as they walked through the humid night air toward his bus. He could clearly see their lives rolled out before him, all the way up to rocking chairs on the porch and grandkids at their feet. There was no one he'd rather spend forever with than Josie.

* * * * *

Joanna Sims is proud to pen contemporary romance for Harlequin Special Edition. Joanna's series, The Brands of Montana, features hardworking characters with hometown values. You are cordially invited to join the Brands of Montana as they wrangle their own happily-ever-afters. And, as always, Joanna welcomes you to visit her at her website, joannasimsromance.com.

Books by Joanna Sims

Harlequin Special Edition

The Brands of Montana

A Match Made in Montana
High Country Christmas
High Country Baby
Meet Me at the Chapel
Thankful for You
A Wedding to Remember
A Bride for Liam Brand
High Country Cowgirl
The Sergeant's Christmas Mission

The Montana Mavericks: Six Brides for Six Brothers

The Maverick's Wedding Wager
A Baby for Christmas
The One He's Been Looking For
Marry Me, Mackenzie!

Visit the Author Profile page at Harlequin.com for more titles.

A MATCH MADE IN MONTANA

Joanna Sims

This book is dedicated, with love,
to my dad.

In the whole entire world,
you are the best dad for me!

Chapter 1

"Man…" Lieutenant Wolf checked his watch. "I can't believe I got stuck working overtime the day I'm supposed to start my leave."

"Don't worry about it… I've got this. Why don't you take off?" Officer Cook asked.

"I appreciate it, but I don't feel right cutting out early. I'll just give my friends a call and let them know that…" Logan stopped midsentence, his attention was drawn to a silver car speeding their way. "Wait a minute…wait a minute…how fast are *they* going?"

Logan stepped closer to the side of the road, aimed his radar gun at the car, and clocked it breaking the speed limit by twenty-one miles per hour. Logan acted on pure instinct, sprang into action. He jumped onto the road, jerked his arm to the left, finger pointed at the side of the road.

"Pull over! *Now!*" Logan yelled at the driver. He stood his ground with his feet planted on the black asphalt until he saw the driver slow down and turn on their signal.

"That's reckless, right there…" Cook came up beside him.

"Sure is." Logan nodded.

Logan handed the radar gun off to his partner, grabbed his clipboard and pen, and then headed across the two lanes separating him from the car he had just flagged down. Giving this driver a well-deserved ticket was the last thing he was going to do before he went on leave.

Josephine Brand glanced over her shoulder to see the motorcycle cop striding across the lanes in her direction. She went back to frantically riffling through her glove box to find her most current insurance and registration information. She *always* kept everything together neatly in a labeled envelope in the glove box on top of the car manual. But…it wasn't *there*!

"I can't believe this is *happening*…" Josephine shut the glove box and went back to searching in her wallet.

She was already late, and she *hated* to be late so she made it a point never to *be* late. But she had gotten into an argument with her boyfriend, Brice, the night before and their disagreement had followed them into the next morning. They rarely fought, but when they did fight, it was usually a knock-down, drag-out affair. She was exhausted from lack of sleep, emotionally drained from fighting, and now she was going to get her first speeding ticket in years.

"Great…" she muttered. "Just *great*."

When the second search through her wallet was unfruitful, Josephine let out a quick, frustrated sigh and shoved the wallet back into her purse. License out and ready to be handed over, Josephine rested her head in her hand and waited for her inevitable ticket.

"Afternoon, miss." Logan had already surveyed the car and the driver as he crossed the street. Nothing looked suspicious, so he intended to treat this like a routine traffic stop.

"Good afternoon, Officer," she said respectfully and extended her license to him.

Logan positioned himself by the side-view mirror, his body facing oncoming traffic, his feet out of the line of the tires. He accepted her license, clipped it to the clipboard.

"Do you know how fast you were going?"

"No." Josephine slipped her sunglasses to the top of her head so he could see her eyes. "I'm sorry... I don't."

She had been stressed out about being late to the airport, and her mind had still been distracted by the fight with Brice, so she just hadn't been paying attention.

From the beginning, Logan had noticed that the driver was an attractive woman, much in the same way he had noticed the model of car she was driving. It was his job to notice everything about his stops. And taking inventory of drivers and passengers was routine. So, yes, he noticed that her hair was long and golden-brown, that the hair framed her oval face, and that her frowning lips were naturally pink. But when she lifted her sunglasses and looked up at him, he was temporarily captivated by her stunning aqua-blue eyes.

Annoyed that he had allowed himself to be distracted

from his purpose, Logan shifted his weight and refocused his mind on the task at hand. He had a job to do and he needed to get it done.

"The posted speed limit here is thirty-five. I clocked you at fifty-six miles per hour," Logan said. "Twenty miles over the posted speed limit is considered reckless driving."

Josephine's eyes widened, her lips parted slightly. "*Reckless driving?* No. That can't be right. I swear to you, Officer, I wasn't speeding intentionally," Josephine explained quickly. "I haven't had a ticket in *ten years*. When you look me up, you'll see. I have a perfect driving record…"

She could tell by the lack of expression on the officer's face that he wasn't remotely swayed by her explanation. He waited quietly for her to finish, then he asked for her proof of insurance and registration.

"I don't have them…" Josephine admitted. "I always keep them right there in my glove box…" She gestured to her glove box. "I just received my new registration. I think I must have just forgotten to put the envelope back in the car. But, I promise you, I have a current registration and valid insurance."

The officer gave one slight nod of his head, wrote something down on his clipboard, then walked to the front of her car to write down her tag number.

"I'll be back," he said to her before he headed back to his motorcycle parked in the median.

Josephine hit the steering wheel with the palms of her hands and dropped her head back. Now she was *really* late, and if this cop wanted to be a real jerk, he could easily cite her with reckless driving! Why couldn't she flirt her way out of stuff like some of her friends did? She'd never been good at flirting or using her femininity to get her way. She always felt stupid when she tried to flirt and it usually backfired anyway. So she didn't bother to try anymore.

While she waited for the cop to return, she called her twin sister, Jordan.

"I'm running a little late, Jordy." She didn't offer a reason why and she was glad when Jordan didn't ask.

"Don't worry about it. The plane can't leave without you." Unlike her, Jordan had never been uptight about sticking to a schedule.

Josephine noticed the cop heading her way and tried to rush off the phone. "I've got to go, okay? But, I should be there in fifteen or twenty minutes."

"It's all good," Jordan said before they hung up the phone. For once, her sister's cavalier attitude about being on time came in handy.

"I'm going to have to give you three citations today, Ms. Brand. One for lack of proof of insurance, one for failing to produce your vehicle registration, and one for speeding." Logan handed her the clipboard and a pen. "I'll need to get your signature on the bottom of all three citations."

Josephine felt the blood drain from her face; her heart beat faster. She'd *never* gotten that many tickets at one time! She had a spotless driving record, and yet this cop couldn't show her even one little ounce of mercy? All of her internal frustration flowed into her tense fingers; she gripped the pen so tightly that her knuckles turned white. The lines of her signatures were heavy, dark and smudgy.

When she was finished, she slapped the pen onto the top of the first citation, handed the clipboard back to the officer and then slid her sunglasses back down over her eyes. Since she couldn't, at the moment, look at the officer with the respect she felt his uniform deserved, she didn't want him to be able to see her eyes at all.

Logan quickly finished the transaction, separated her copy of the citations from his, handed them to her with her driver's license.

"You'll note that I didn't cite you with reckless driving," the officer said. "And, once you show proof of insurance and current vehicle registration, the other two citations will be dropped."

Well, that was something at least; he'd dropped the reckless driving charge. Josephine folded the tickets neatly in half and tucked them into her purse. It sounded, to her ears, that the officer sounded almost... *sorry*...that he'd had to give her that many tickets. But it certainly hadn't stopped him from throwing the book at her!

When she turned her face back to the officer, she noticed that he had taken his sunglasses off. She was immediately drawn, naturally drawn, to his eyes. They were such a dark, rich brown that they were very nearly as black as his pupils. His gaze was direct, and there was a moment, a flash second, when she thought that she had caught a glimpse of this man's soul.

"On a personal note, are you related to Jordan Brand?" the officer surprised her by asking.

"She's my sister." Josephine replied stiffly. "You know her?"

"I actually pulled her over downtown about a year ago," Logan explained.

"I'm not surprised." Josephine retorted. "Unlike me, Jordy speeds all the time."

"Well…" Logan hadn't missed the sarcasm. "All I can say is that I'm sorry that we met under these circumstances and it's actually ironic because…"

"Look…" Josephine cut him off. Was this guy *really* going to try to pick her up when he'd just written her *three* tickets? "Am I free to go? I'm really late…"

"Yes. You're free to go." The officer put his sunglasses back on and stepped away from her car. "Drive safely, Ms. Brand."

Josephine ran through the private airport, lugging two overstuffed carry-on bags on each shoulder, and dragging one oversize rolling suitcase behind her. She had never been to Montgomery Airport in San Diego before, but she had printed out a map of the facility the night before and highlighted the quickest route to her destination. She had been raised on a Montana ranch, but she had learned how to run in high heels years ago. Up on the ball of the foot and full steam ahead!

"I'm so sorry I'm late!" Josephine called out to her sister, Jordan. Jordan was standing in front of her fiancé's private jet, occupied with her phone.

Jordan looked up, spotted her, and smiled brightly. Her sister jogged over to greet her with a warm hug.

"Relax, sis!" Jordan said. "You know that nothing's set in stone for me."

Jordan slipped one of the bags off her shoulder, and

the bag dropped to the ground with a dull thud. "Uh…
wow, Jo. What in the heck did you pack?"

"Textbooks." She would be a third-year law student
in the fall and the suggested summer reading list had
been *pages* long. "I hope I brought enough."

"Trust me, you brought enough," Jordan said teasingly. "I just hope your bags don't put us over our weight
restriction. We might have to make a tough choice between you and your books."

"Haha, very funny." Jordan had always picked on
her about her overachieving ways. They were more than
twins, more than sisters; they were best friends. But
they were complete opposites. Jordan was a professional
artist, a painter, who had dropped out of graduate school
to pursue her passion. Josephine, on the other hand,
could never stop something before she finished it. She
finished everything she started, and she finished it *well*.

Together, they walked the short distance to Ian's jet.

"I can't believe that this is the start of your wedding
trip, Jordy." Both sisters stopped walking and talking
at the same time; they looked at each other, and easily
read each other's thoughts.

"Holy crap, Jo! I'm getting *married*!" Jordan shook
her head in disbelief.

"You're getting married." Josephine smiled, her eyes
starting to tear from a mixture of happiness for her sister and sadness for the changes that would inevitably
follow. Nothing ever stayed the same.

"OMG, don't start crying already!" Jordan hugged
her again. "I swear, between Mom and you, there's not
gonna be one tissue left in the entire state of Montana."

Josephine laughed and brushed the tears out of her

eyelashes. "I'll do my best to keep the waterworks to a minimum…at least until the ceremony. After that, no deal."

"Well, of course you have to cry at the ceremony," her twin said as Josephine rolled her large suitcase over to the cargo area for the pilot to load.

"Hey, you got my message that Brice won't be joining us, right?" Josephine asked.

"Yeah, what's up with that?" Jordan put her hands on her slender hips. "Is everything okay with the two of you?"

"Well, actually, that's why I was…" Josephine started to say.

Jordan got distracted by a man walking through the airplane hangar.

"Captain Stern!" her sister yelled and waved her hand in the air. To her, she said, "Hold that thought, Jo. That's our pilot and I need to tell him something before I forget."

"Okay." Maybe she shouldn't tell her sister about the fight with Brice anyway. Her family, especially Jordan, had never really been fond of him.

Jordan started the walk over to the waiting pilot; she turned around and walked backward for a few steps.

"Why don't you go get settled?" her sister suggested. "Ian'll tell you where to find the booze. He only stocks the best."

Josephine lugged the carry-on bag loaded with textbooks up the small flight of stairs that led up to the main cabin of the jet. She'd seen pictures of the jet, of course, but to see it in person was an entirely different experience. The cabin was decked out in sophisticated grays and blacks and accented with polished mahogany. There was a long leather couch on one side, while the other had two separate seating areas with oversize recliners and a small table in between. In the back, there was a narrow hallway that led back to a bedroom and en-suite bathroom.

Ian Sterling, Jordan's fiancé, was sitting on the couch. Next to Ian's left leg sat a muscular black Labrador retriever.

"It's me, Ian," Josephine said to her soon-to-be brother-in-law.

"I thought I heard your voice." Ian stood up to greet her. He was a model-handsome man and world-famous for his photography. But a rare eye disease had recently destroyed his central vision, rendering him legally blind and sidetracking his career as a professional photographer.

Josephine hugged Ian; it made her feel really good that Jordan had found her perfect match in Ian Sterling. She had never seen two people as crazy for each other as they were.

"And who's your friend?" Jordan had finally managed, after nearly a year of trying, to convince Ian to get a service dog.

"Shadow." Ian rested his hand proudly on the dog's head.

"Is it okay if I pet him?"

"At ease, Shadow," Ian commanded gently.

Shadow's body language changed on the command and he started to wag his tail.

"Shake, Shadow." Ian gave the Lab a second command.

Shadow immediately extended his right paw to her. Josephine took the paw, smiled, and gave it a shake.

"It's very nice to meet you, Shadow."

Josephine had already set up her computer and unloaded her books in the short time it took for her sister to appear. Jordan plopped down next to her fiancé, tucked her long legs to the side of her body, and frowned at her.

"I hope it's not going to be like this our entire trip, Jo," Jordan complained.

"I'm not going to spend all of my time studying, but I can't just pretend like I'm not in school for two months. The third year is a make-it-or-break-it year. That's when they really try to thin out the herd."

"You always say that about everything and then you always end up on top." Jordan rolled her eyes.

"Quit bugging her about it." Ian put his arm around Jordan's shoulder and pulled her tightly to his side. "Not everyone waits to the last minute to get things done like you do, beautiful."

Josephine smiled triumphantly at Jordan. She finished arranging her collection of items in an orderly and precise way: a book stand held a thick constitutional law book upright, her laptop and tablet were both charging, three differently colored highlighter pens were situated in a perfectly even row.

"There…" She surveyed her work. "This is perfect."

"I need a drink." Jordan stood up. "Anyone care to join me?"

"I'm good." Josephine sat down in the large recliner and used the controls to adjust it perfectly to her body. "Shouldn't we be getting ready to take off soon?"

"We'll leave as soon as our fourth arrives," Ian told her.

Josephine glanced at her sister. "Didn't Jordy tell you that Brice couldn't make it?"

"I told him." Jordan poured herself a scotch on the rocks.

"Then who are we waiting for?" she asked.

"My best man is catching a ride with us," Ian explained.

Josephine turned the swiveling recliner toward the couch. "Wait a minute. Dylan is coming with us? I can't believe he agreed to come without Mackenzie and Hope."

"Oh! That's right! You don't know…" Jordan returned to her spot next to Ian.

"Know what?"

"Mackenzie has been having some issues with her pregnancy and her doctors don't want her to fly."

"I didn't know that," Josephine said, concerned.

Ian's best friend, Dylan Axel, was married to their cousin, Mackenzie, and they were expecting their second child together.

"So, Dylan had to beg off being Ian's best man."

"I'm so sorry to hear that. I had no idea that Mackenzie was having a rough pregnancy."

Sometimes law school was like living in a bubble. There were a lot of times that she just didn't have contact with the world outside of school. She would turn off her phone, ignore all forms of social media, and she would focus all of her energy on studying.

"I'll have to call her," Josephine said aloud to herself before she asked, "Who's going to stand in for Dylan?"

"One of my old friends from high school," Ian said.

Jordan smiled brightly. "You're gonna love him, Jo! He's such a cool guy. And what's really funny is that he was actually there the day that Ian and I first met…"

"I think I hear him now." Ian nodded toward the direction of the door.

Josephine heard two animated male voices coming from just outside of the jet. Then, she heard the sound of heavy, decisive footsteps heading up the metal stairs to the jet's cabin.

Josephine looked at the doorway curiously; both Ian and Jordan stood up.

"It's real nice of you to finally show up, Logan!" Jordan called out to the best man teasingly.

Logan Wolf, still in his uniform, stepped into the jet's cabin.

"Hey…" Logan smiled charmingly at Jordan. "Don't blame me, blame the San Diego PD."

Jordan hugged Logan in greeting before he shook hands with Ian.

"I'm glad you could make it, man," Ian said.

"I appreciate the invitation," Logan replied. He could feel Josephine's eyes on him, but he'd deliberately waited to look her way.

"Logan, I'd like you to meet my sister, Josephine."

Josephine stood up and extended her hand.

"Oh…" Her eyes locked onto Logan's. "Trust me… we've already met."

Chapter 2

"Wait, *what*?" Jordan asked, her expression a mixture of surprise and intrigue.

"Officer... Wolf, is it?" Josephine slipped her fingers free of his.

Logan rested the duffel bag on the seat next to him and smiled warmly at her. "Lieutenant, actually, but I think it's all right for you to call me Logan now, Josephine."

"Hell-*o*?" Her sister was impatient for details.

"As it turns out..." Josephine paused, looked skyward with a little shake of her head, before she continued. "Logan is the reason why I was late."

Logan told Jordan and Ian, "I pulled her over for speeding."

And here it comes, Josephine thought.

Jordan's eyes lit up, as did her face. First, she smiled

broadly like a Cheshire cat, and then she tipped her head back to laugh out loud.

"You got a *ticket*?" Jordan gleefully exclaimed. "Holy *crap*! Miss 'I haven't gotten a ticket in ten years' *actually* got a *ticket*?"

Logan said, "She shared that fact with me during the stop."

"Of course she did," her sister chirped. "Trying to worm her way out of the ticket, no doubt."

"Don't you think that you're just a little too happy about this, Jordy? I mean, really." Josephine had her arms crossed over her chest, not enjoying this conversation nearly as much as Jordan.

Ian had taken his seat and Jordan flopped down next to him. "Oh, please, you know exactly why I'm enjoying this so much!" To Logan, her sister said, "You have to understand, Jo has been harassing me about my driving for *years*!"

"In my defense," Josephine explained to Logan, "Jordy has had her license revoked *twice*."

"Irrelevant!" her sister exclaimed. "Because *now* you can't wear your perfect driving record like a badge of honor when you're lecturing me about *my* driving."

"You are a menace to drivers everywhere." Josephine had relaxed her arms as she relaxed into the conversation. "You ride that Ducati of yours like you're a bat out of hell."

"I'm a great driver." Jordan put her hand on Ian's leg to get his attention. "You trust me when I drive, don't you?"

"Absolutely not," Ian replied with a deadpan expression. "I am grateful every day that I can afford a driver."

"That's a horrible thing to say, GQ!" Jordan punched her fiancé lightly on the arm. "Now do you see what I have to put up with, Logan?"

"I do see," Logan nodded thoughtfully, playing along.

"That is why you are officially my hero for the day." Jordan pointed at Logan.

"But let's be clear," Josephine said. "He's not a hero for putting on a uniform every day and risking his life. You're saying he's a hero for giving me a ticket so I can't harass you about your terrible driving anymore. Right?"

"What's your point?" Jordan asked with a shrug.

Josephine looked at Logan. "Do you see what *I* have to put up with?"

"You're in a no-win situation, buddy," Ian warned his longtime friend.

"I see that, too," Logan laughed good-naturedly, then lifted the duffel bag off the seat. "Hey, before we take off, I'd like to change out of this monkey suit into some street clothes."

"Straight back to the bedroom." Ian pointed in the direction of the back of the jet. "You can change in there."

"If you'll excuse me, then. I came here straight from work and I'd really like to feel like I've started my vacation." Logan's arm brushed Josephine's when he walked past her to get to the back of the jet.

It wasn't long before Logan returned carrying the duffel bag in one hand and a garment bag in his other.

"Is there some place I can hang up my uniform?" he asked.

"Closet's right there." Jordan pointed. "You can put your bag in there, too, if you want. While you were in the back, the pilot said that we're about ready to taxi out to the runway, so grab a seat and make yourself comfortable."

Logan did just that. After he hung up his uniform and stowed his bag, he took the seat across from Josephine's recliner. Logan Wolf had been noticeably handsome in his uniform, and he was just as attractive in his crisp jeans, tucked-in short-sleeved green polo and San Diego Padres baseball cap. She was in a long-term relationship, yes, but she still had eyes and could see if a man was good-looking or not. Logan was a good-looking man. But then again, so was her Brice.

Thinking of Brice, Josephine checked her phone to see if he had called her. When she left for the airport, things were still *messy* between them. Normally, he would have called her by now; he would have tried to smooth things over before her flight. But this time, he hadn't. What did that mean?

Not wanting to spend the beginning of her sister's wedding trip dwelling on her problems with Brice, Josephine turned off her phone and prompted Jordan to tell her all about the latest wedding plans. Ever since she was a young girl, she had loved all things wedding, and hearing about all of the latest details of her twin's upcoming nuptials would be the exact distraction she needed.

While Jordan excitedly shared the latest details of her wedding with her, the pilot taxied the jet out to the runway and they took off for Helena, Montana, soon after. Jordan, who had always been a nervous flier, had stopped talking and held on tightly to Ian's arm while the jet quickly ascended to the level of the clouds. Once the jet leveled off, Jordan opened her eyes again.

"You're much better than you used to be, that's for sure," Josephine complimented her sister.

Jordan hugged her fiancé's arm more tightly and smiled at him. "Being with Ian has really helped me."

"Not as much as being with you has helped me." Ian brought her hand up to his lips and kissed it.

Josephine was so happy for her sister. But she felt a twinge of jealousy whenever she saw Jordan with Ian. He loved her so much; it was plain to see in the way he spoke to her, the way he spoke about her and in the way he touched her. She knew that Brice loved her, but he wasn't, by nature, a demonstrative person. And even though she had accepted that part of Brice's personality, she couldn't stop herself from *craving* what her sister had found.

Ian tried, unsuccessfully, to stifle a yawn. "I'm sorry, guys… I promise it's not the company."

"You do look tired, Ian." Josephine had noticed that earlier.

"He didn't sleep well last night," Jordan explained, holding his hand. "Why don't you go lie down, baby?"

"I'm not just going to leave all of you out here while I sleep." Ian shook his head.

But both Logan and Josephine assured him that it would be okay with them, and Ian appeared to be so tired that it didn't take much convincing. He kissed Jordan and stood up.

"Bedroom, Shadow." He gave the black Lab the command, which Shadow immediately followed.

When Ian disappeared into the bedroom, out of earshot, Jordan confided in them.

"Ian's been having a really hard time sleeping. The specialist says that it's not uncommon for people with Stargardt to have a sleep disorder. He's been on melatonin, but it's not really helping all the much. Honestly, we were both up all night last night."

"Then you need to go back and get some rest, too," Josephine told her.

"What about you guys?" Jordan rubbed her eyes tiredly.

"I've got plenty of reading to do," Josephine assured her.

Logan nodded his agreement and held up his earbuds. "And I'm going to kick back and listen to music. Don't worry about us. We'll be fine. Go get some rest."

Like Ian, Jordan didn't take much convincing. When they were alone together, Logan said jokingly, "And then there were two…"

Josephine smiled faintly; she hoped that he really was going to listen to music and didn't expect her to entertain him now that they were the only two left in the main cabin. She had so much summer reading to do that until she got started with it and finished it, it felt like a giant albatross around her neck.

"I really do have a lot of reading to do." She tried to remind him politely that she needed to concentrate.

"And I really am going to listen to music," he countered easily; he put his earbuds in his ears, fiddled with his phone, leaned back his head, and closed his eyes.

Josephine couldn't hear any sound coming from his earbuds over the noise of the jet. There wasn't one excuse left not to open the first textbook and get to work. She took in a deep breath, let it out and relaxed her shoulders at the same time, and then took the book off the stand and set it down on the table directly in front of her. The spine of the thick book was stiff as she cracked it open for the first time. Josephine took the cap off a fresh, yellow highlighter pen, grabbed a black ballpoint pen, and held them together in her right hand. When she studied, she had her own system of highlighting, underlining information, and tabbing pages. Armed with her study utensils, she began the daunting task of wading through the first few pages of her textbook.

After trudging valiantly through the first, tedious chapter, Josephine leaned back in her chair, closed her eyes, and tried to rub the soreness out of her neck. She wished she could just throw all of her textbooks out the window so she could enjoy her first trip home in years, but there was just too much to do. There was still way too much information that she didn't know or understand. And unfortunately, at the moment, her brain was repelling all new information. Josephine breathed in deeply through her nose and then let it out on a long, tired sigh. She gathered up her cache of studying devices and neatly put them back into their proper places. The one thing that had led to her success above all else was her determination to stay organized. That was her lifeline to sanity, as well as success.

Lounging across from her, Logan had been impatiently waiting for Josephine to stop studying. He didn't really want to listen to music alone at the very beginning of his first real vacation in years. He wanted to celebrate, but he also respected that Josephine was dedicated to her studies. Periodically, he would open his eyes to see if she was done reading. He checked five times throughout the hour, but it wasn't until the sixth time that he caught Josephine rubbing her eyes. The minute he saw Josephine start to pack up her books and computer, Logan switched off his music and pulled the earbuds out of his ears.

"Taking a break?" he asked hopefully.

Josephine nodded, yawned, and carefully wound the cord of her computer neatly and secured it properly with the provided Velcro.

"I'm trying to get ready for my last year, but I'm afraid that my brain has hit its saturation level." Josephine slipped the computer into its designated spot and then zipped the bag shut.

Logan stood up and stretched. "I was thinking about raiding the liquor cabinet. Care to join me?"

"You know what? I think I would." Josephine's first thought was "no," but her verbal answer switched to a "yes." "You'll find the liquor right across from the closet."

"Jackpot!" Logan opened the cabinet with a smile. "What's your poison?"

"You don't happen to see any gin in there, do you?"

Logan pulled out a black bottle and held it up for her to see. "Hendricks okay?"

Josephine gave a slight nod, a small smile. "Have you ever made a martini?"

"Before I was a cop? Bartender..." Logan found two martini glasses, vermouth, and olives.

"Um, I usually like just a hint of vermouth and two olives." Josephine leaned forward a bit. "Please."

"Why don't you let me make you a martini my way? I don't want to brag, but I was pretty well-known for my martini."

Josephine wasn't really adventurous with her food or her drinks. She knew what she liked, she liked what she liked, and she stuck to what she liked. If she didn't like Logan's martini, she wouldn't be able to grin and bear it quietly.

"Okay, give this a try. I hope you don't mind your martinis dirty." Logan carefully handed her the martini glass and then sat down across from her.

"To Ian and Jordan." Logan held his glass out to her.

"Jordan and Ian." Josephine touched her glass to his with a tired smile.

Josephine knew Logan was watching her as she took a small sip of the martini. She never drank her martinis dirty and she typically preferred the taste of Tanqueray. Logan's martini was different, the tangy taste unusual, but it was surprisingly...

"Mmm." Josephine's eyes widened with pleasure. "This is really good..."

"I have a 100 percent satisfaction-guaranteed record with my martini..." Logan slid the two olives off the toothpick into his mouth.

"But, you don't want to brag," Josephine teased him before she took a slightly bigger sip. "I have to be honest. I wasn't expecting to like it. Normally, I only like the way my boyfriend makes a martini."

Logan stopped chewing the olives for a second when he heard the word "boyfriend." Up until now, Josephine hadn't mentioned a significant other, so Logan was starting to believe that he might have a shot of taking her out on a date while they were in Montana together. From the moment he looked into Josephine's eyes, he'd wanted to ask her out. He was really attracted to Jordan's beautiful sister, more so than he had been to any woman for a really long time, and it was just his rotten luck that she was taken. Of course, she was taken…why wouldn't she be?

Disappointed, Logan raised his glass up in the air a little. "I respect any man who can make a decent martini."

Josephine laughed. "I think Brice was probably weaned on martinis."

"Is that right?" he asked out of politeness, but he really didn't want to hear about the guy who was currently seeing the woman he wanted to date.

"I'm going to have another." Logan finished his drink, stood up. "Are you still good with that one?"

Josephine nodded and showed him that she still had some left in her glass. She wasn't much of a drinker and the last thing she wanted to do was arrive home for the first time in years tipsy.

"Come to think of it," she added, half thinking aloud, "I never drank martinis until I met Brice. We met in college and then we ended up deciding to go to law school together. He's a couple of years ahead of me, so he's already graduated, passed the California Bar, and taken a job with a firm in Van Nuys." She paused to take another small sip of her drink. "He practices environmental law, which is why he can't come join me in Montana until right before the wedding… He was just given a really big case."

Wanting to bring the conversation back to his point

of interest, which was *her*, he asked, "What kind of law do you want to practice?"

"Oh!" Josephine's face lit up. "Well, my dream ever since I was in high school has been to work for the Southern Poverty Law Center. Have you ever heard of them?"

Logan shook his head "no."

"They've been fighting for the civil rights of marginalized and poor communities for years. And I know I would love to do that work."

"But?" He heard a definite *but* at the end of her sentence.

Josephine sighed and shrugged, thought for a second or two before she answered him. "But I don't think that it's practical to think that I'll work for them one day."

"Why not?"

"Because, for one thing, they need experienced litigators for the types of cases that they handle, so I'd have to get that experience first."

"That shouldn't be a problem for someone like you, and we have plenty of people in our state who need defending." He smiled at her. "I arrest 'em, you defend 'em."

That made her laugh, before she said, "But they really only operate out of the South, so…"

"That's what moving vans are for."

Josephine finished off her drink, and placed the empty glass carefully on the table. "Brice will never move down South. He grew up in California. He's never wanted to live anywhere else."

Logan wanted to ask her the question: *Not even for you?* But he drank from his glass instead.

"And…" Josephine felt bad for making Brice seem like her dream-killer. "I can certainly practice civil rights law in California…immigration law."

Josephine looked out the window at the clouds for a minute and then nodded as if she had just convinced herself.

"Why don't you talk for a while?" She smiled at Logan. "I've been just babbling away over here."

"Well, I think you know by now that I'm a cop," Logan said with a deadpan expression.

"Yes." She frowned playfully at him. "That much I do know."

"Hey." Logan leaned his forearms on the table between them. "All kidding aside, you aren't going to hold a grudge against me for giving you those tickets, are you?"

"No, I've never been much of a grudge holder."

"That's good…because as maid of honor and best man, I think we're going to be spending a lot of time together."

"I'm sure we will," she agreed. The thought of spending time with Logan made her want to turn on her phone and check to see if Brice had called.

No messages, no missed calls.

She couldn't believe it. He *still* hadn't called or so much as sent a text. But she kept her phone turned on this time, just in case he tried.

Logan didn't want Josephine's attention to be distracted from him or their conversation. After she checked her phone, the expression on her pretty face changed. The muscles along her jawline tightened; her lips became tense. Perhaps a less casual observer wouldn't notice these almost imperceptible changes, but he did. He noticed.

"Well, I'm glad you're a forgiving woman, or this trip could've been a real bust."

Josephine looked up from her phone. "I could really say the same about you."

"I'm not sure I follow."

"I was kind of rude to you after you gave me the tickets. You were trying to tell me who you were and probably that you were heading to the same place I was, but I cut you off."

"Trust me, I'm used to it. Nobody's happy when I hand them a ticket."

"I'm still sorry. I was just…"

"Mad at me."

"Mad at you…mad at me…mad at…" *Brice.* "…the stupid clock that said I was late!" She laughed at herself, and then asked him, "But did you really have to give me *three* tickets? I mean, come on! I really think that someone with my driving record deserved a warning."

"Your driving record is the reason I dropped the charge down from reckless driving."

Josephine frowned. "Would you have still given me all of those tickets if you knew I was Jordan's sister right away?"

"Of course."

"Seriously?"

"Enforcing the law isn't personal for me. It's my job. Most people just don't get that."

Josephine's phone rang and interrupted their conversation. "It's Brice!"

"Hi, honey. Hold on, okay?" Josephine stood up,

moved out of Logan's earshot, and sat down in the last seat at the very back of the jet.

"Okay, are you there?" she asked in a lowered voice. "I'm so glad that you called…"

Head down, Josephine listened carefully to what her boyfriend called to say. After a couple of minutes, she asked in a harsh whisper, "What do you *mean* you aren't coming to the wedding?"

Chapter 3

Josephine didn't really think that Brice had deliberately tried to spoil her first homecoming in years. But that's what it *felt* like on her end. He had called specifically to tell her that he thought it was best if they took a break from their relationship. He had basically broken up with her, and left her dateless for her own twin's wedding in the span of five minutes. Brice had said what he called to say and then got off the phone. He had been between appointments when he called.

After they'd hung up, she had stared at the phone for a while, wondering what to do next. Pretty quickly, she decided it would be best if she pretended, for a while at least, that the phone call had never happened. What if this whole thing blew over in the next couple of days and she had been bemoaning their breakup to her family the entire time? Her family didn't need one extra piece of ammo against Brice. So, pretend she did…

She smiled all the way through their mini family reunion at the Helena airport. She smiled her way through the long ride home to Bent Tree, the family ranch. And she smiled and laughed her way to the end of dinner and clearing the table and loading the dishwasher. And she didn't stop smiling and pretending until she could retreat to her third-floor bedroom. This was the bedroom of her adolescence, the bedroom that she had shared with Jordan. She switched on the antique Tiffany lamp next to the door and gently pushed the door shut. The room smelled of cedar and cinnamon, and the nostalgia for her uncomplicated youth made her start to tear up.

She wiped the tears out of her eyes and said sternly to herself, "Stop that!"

Josephine worked very hard not to cry while she unpacked her suitcase and carefully hung up her clothing in the small closet. Undergarments and jeans were neatly folded into a dresser drawer, a nice variety of shoe options was neatly lined up in the closet, and toiletries were put away in the small en-suite bathroom. Josephine had stowed her empty suitcase beneath the bed and began to unpack her books.

A quick, loud knock on the door startled her. Before she could react, the door swung open, and Jordan barreled into the bedroom with the family cat, Ranger, flung over her shoulder.

"Okay if we come in?" Jordan asked.

"I think you're already in, aren't you?"

"Good point." Barefoot, her sister sat cross-legged on the bed and gently put Ranger down on the mattress.

Ranger, a big coal-black cat with bright golden eyes, immediately flopped onto his side and began to wash his long, black whiskers.

"So...what's wrong, Jo?"

Josephine looked over at her sister, gave her a weak smile. She knew she had to tell her twin about Brice now; lying to Jordan was a waste of time. They had never been able to keep secrets from each other.

"Brice and I are...going through a rough patch."

Jordan moved over to one side of the bed and patted the spot next to her. "That's what I figured."

Josephine kicked off her shoes and joined her sister and Ranger on the bed. She sat cross-legged, facing her sister with Ranger sprawled out between them, belly up.

"This is just like old times, isn't it?" she asked Jordan. "Except we had two single beds in here instead of this queen-size bed."

"I had a picture of Ian from his modeling days hanging up right there." Jordan pointed to the spot just above the rolltop desk.

"And now you're marrying him, Jordy...the man of your dreams." Josephine smiled right before she felt new rash of tears starting to form.

Jordan saw the tears swimming in her eyes. "Tell me what's going on, Jo."

Josephine pressed her lips together tightly, looked away for a moment to gather her emotions before she said, "Brice called and told me that he isn't coming to the wedding. He thinks we should use our time apart this summer to reflect on our relationship in order to make a prudent decision about our future"

"Wait a minute...he *dumped* you?" Jordan's eyebrows collapsed together. "The *knuckle dragger* dumped *you*?"

"He didn't *dump* me exactly. He just wants us to re-flect…"

"Oh, my *God*, Jo! Don't *defend* him!" Jordan nearly yelled those words.

Josephine jumped off the bed and shut the door. "Could you keep your voice down, please? I don't want anyone else to know! This whole thing could just blow over tomorrow."

"Why would you even *want* it to blow over?"

Josephine sat back down on the bed. "Because I love him, that's why. We've been together for over five years. I'm not just going to throw that all away just because there's a little bump in the road."

"This isn't a tiny little bump, Jo, this is a ginormous frickin' crater!"

Josephine scratched Ranger beneath his chin and on the top of his silky head. "I know you've never liked Brice, Jordy."

"I never once said that I didn't like him."

Josephine looked up at her sister. "You call him 'the knuckle dragger' more than you call him Brice."

"Fine, so I don't like him. But that's just because he thinks he's better than us, Jo. He thinks he's better than *you*, with his family money and country club and connections to *Beverly Hills*, like any of us could give a rat's behind."

"I know that's how he seems to you, to all of you, but do you really think that I'd be with him for five years if he wasn't a good guy?" Josephine said point-edly. "There's a lot more to Brice than any of you really know because none of you have given him an honest chance. Dad's always so *stiff* around him and Mom has refused to warm up to him just because I decided…" She put her hand on her heart. "*I decided* to spend the Christmas after Daniel died with his family instead of coming home."

"Well, Brice knew your brother had just died. It was stupid of him to even invite you to his parents' *La Jolla beach house* in the first place."

Josephine sighed from frustration. "Just promise you won't tell anyone. Okay? If they need to know, I'll tell everyone myself."

Jordan pretended to lock her lips and toss the key over her shoulder. Her sister stood up, wrapped her arms around her shoulders, and gave her a tight squeeze.

"Now, come on, let's go downstairs. There's no sense in you sitting up here by yourself moping, especially if you don't want anyone to pick up on the fact that something's wrong," Jordan said. "Besides, nothing's better for heartbreak than family."

As it turned out, Jordan was right. Spending time with her family had helped get her mind off Brice's sudden, and unexpected, desire to end their relationship. And the plans for Jordan's wedding were the best kind of distraction for her. Her mom had turned the family library into "Wedding Central," and once she went back downstairs, she spent hours in the library with Jordan and her mom looking through all of the wedding regalia. She was blissfully surrounded by cake toppers and invitations, seating charts and stacks of RSVPs that needed to be answered. There were scrapbooks filled with all of the selections that had been made for the wedding and Josephine immersed herself in looking through each and every one. She spent hours, laughing and talking with her sister and her mother, and she was stunned when she realized that Brice had barely crossed her mind.

But afterward, when she was alone in bed, in the dark, all she could think of *was* Brice. Her mind just kept on going over the last several months of her relationship over and over again. Had there been signs that she hadn't seen? Red flags that she had willfully ignored? Yes, he had been distant and unavailable, but he had just been handed the biggest case of his young career. This case could make or break his career in the field of environmental law. He needed to be focused and she had understood. But now that he had suggested that they take a "break" from their relationship and left her without a wedding date, the idea that his withdrawal from their relationship was only work-related was no longer a plausible explanation. So, what was it?

"Another woman?" Josephine queried quietly aloud. *It feels like another woman.*

That's what her head was saying. That was what her gut was saying. But her heart just couldn't accept it just yet. Another woman meant that everything that they had been working toward together for years was over. Done. A horrible waste of time for the both of them.

Knowing that she wasn't going to be able to go to sleep with all of these questions buzzing around in her brain, Josephine got out of bed and quickly pulled on some sweatpants and matching sweatshirt. Josephine tiptoed down the wooden stairs and she was careful to avoid the creaky boards. Life on the ranch started before dawn, so bedtime was early. Chances were, she'd have the downstairs to herself, which was exactly what she wanted. At the bottom of the stairwell, by the dim light streaming in from the library lamp that was always left on, Josephine stopped to straighten the picture of her brother, Daniel, in his Army uniform. She had three older brothers, but everyone knew that Daniel had been her favorite. After he was killed in Iraq, it was hard for her to imagine the ranch without him. It still was.

After one last look at her brother's portrait, Josephine continued her quiet route to the front door. The front door was always unlocked, so she slowly turned the knob, and pulled the door free from the frame. Once that was accomplished, she carefully pushed the squeaky screen door open a crack, slipped through, and stepped out onto the front porch. She'd started suffering from insomnia when she was in high school, and when she couldn't sleep, she had always found her way to the giant rocking chairs on the front porch. Still holding the screen door open, she closed her eyes and breathed in the cool, fresh Montana air. She had missed that smell; it was clean and crisp.

"You're not out here alone." A male voice in the dark made her jump.

Startled, Josephine let go of the screen door handle and it slammed back into place. Her heart gave one hard thud in her chest; she placed her hand over her heart.

"Sorry," Logan said in a loud whisper. "I didn't want to scare you."

"Your attempt to not scare me *scared* me," Josephine whispered back.

"Sorry," he repeated.

Crossing her arms over her chest, Josephine hesitated for a second before she decided to join him. It wasn't ideal; she wanted to be alone. But she wanted to sit outside in her favorite rocking chair more than she wanted to go back upstairs. She sat down in the rocking chair, glad that Logan wasn't occupying it, and sighed more loudly than she had intended.

"Taking a break from your studies?" Logan asked.

Obviously, he's going to insist on talking.

"Insomnia. Chronic."

"It takes me a while to get comfortable in a strange bed."

Josephine nodded silently.

"I wanted to get to bed early so I could get up early to hike. I suppose I'm going to have to plan on covering less ground tomorrow."

For the first time since she had joined him, Josephine turned her head his way. "You like to hike?"

Logan moved over to the rocking chair next to her so he could talk to her in a quiet voice. "Hiking, mountain climbing, rock climbing, anything outdoors…if you can name it, I'm probably into it. How about you? Growing up in a place like this, you must love to hike."

"I used to hike all over these mountains when I was a kid. No matter how old I get, I think I'll always love these mountains the most."

"Well…" Logan stood up. "I think I'm gonna give sleep another try. But if you want to join me, I'm thinking about heading out around seven, seven-thirty."

"There's so much to do around here with the wedding. But thank you, though."

"Sure." Logan headed down the porch stairs, using the light of the moon to light his footing. At the bottom of the steps, Logan paused to look back at her.

"If you change your mind, I wouldn't mind the company."

"I'll let you know. Good night, Logan."

"Good night." Hands in his pockets, Logan strolled in the moonlight the short distance back to Tyler's bachelor cabin.

She had wanted him to go; she had been relieved when he got up to leave. But now that she was alone on the porch, and alone with her thoughts, Josephine suddenly regretted that Logan had left. He had distracted her, temporarily, from her melancholy and now it was back. Instead of staying on the porch, as she intended, she crept back inside, popped some over-the-counter sleeping aids, and took a steaming hot bath. If she could just get herself to sleep, if she could just *demand* that her body go to sleep, things would most likely appear less crappy in the morning. Josephine got into bed with that hope. She punched her pillows, kicked at her sheets and blanket, and finally, stiffly, flopped onto her back, hugged one of her pillows to her chest, and closed her eyes. She had already made up her mind that she was going to stay right where she was until she fell asleep. Even if it took all night.

The next morning, Josephine wasn't surprised when she awakened before the alarm went off. Even with insomnia, she had always been an early riser. Ranger had meowed at her bedroom door until she had finally relented and let him in. Why he had picked her, she couldn't be sure, but he had curled his body around the top of her head and she had fallen asleep to the rhythmic sound of his loud purring. After she rubbed the sleep out of her eyes, Josephine sat up slowly, scooped Ranger into her arms, and hugged him. He started to purr again, and she kissed him on the head before she set him gently on the bed. She could hear her family already stirring downstairs and she wanted to join them.

"Let's go see what everyone is up to," she said to Ranger.

Josephine got dressed quickly and headed downstairs.

"Good morning." Josephine walked into the kitchen with Ranger trotting along beside her.

The smell of homemade biscuits, sizzling butter, sweet bacon, and eggs permeated the kitchen. Mom was at the industrial-grade stove, frying up more eggs. Her father, Hank, was in his usual seat at the head of the long rectangular table that could seat up to twenty ranch workers if necessary. The family dog, a German shepherd named Ilsa, was sitting to Hank's left, patiently waiting for her father to sneak her a piece of bacon. Tyler was at his father's right hand, guzzling down a large mug of coffee loaded with cream and sugar. Logan sat to Tyler's right, quietly eating his breakfast. It was strange for her to see someone else occupying what had been Daniel's favored seat at the table. Logan nodded his head and smiled at her; she gave him a quick smile in return.

"Good morning, sweetheart, did you sleep well?" Barbara Brand tilted her head a bit so her daughter could give her their customary kiss.

"Once I finally fell asleep, I slept like a rock." Josephine wrapped her arms around her mom's shoulders from behind, gave her a quick hug, and a kiss on the cheek.

No matter what time in the morning, Barbara was always put together. Her mom smelled faintly of her signature perfume; her hair, blond streaked with silver, was pulled back off her classically pretty face into a chignon, and her makeup was light and flawlessly applied. The woman never gave up. She had lived with dirty cowboys and cows for over forty years, but she had refused to let go of her sophisticated, big-city Chicago roots. Her mottos were Simplicity Is Elegance and A Woman Can Be Stylish Anywhere. And she lived those mottos on a daily basis.

"Orange juice is on the table. Scrambled or fried?" Barbara pointed to the eggs with her spatula.

"I think I'm just going to grab coffee and a banana." Josephine put her hands lightly on her mom's shoulders. "Can I help?"

"No, honey, I'm just doing my thing. Go spend some time with Dad before he disappears for the day." Barbara started to flip the eggs over one by one.

Next, Josephine greeted her father with a hug and a kiss.

"Mornin', Princess. You're up with the rooster." Her father squeezed her hand affectionately.

Henry "Hank" Brand had Montana ranching in his blood. His family had owned the Bent Tree Cattle Ranch for four generations. Raising cattle was what Hank loved to do; he was in his early sixties, but he was tall and lean and could still sit straight in the saddle with the youngest ranch hands. He had thick silver hair, usually hidden beneath a cowboy hat, and he had bright blue trademark Brand eyes, deeply set, that stood out in contrast to the tanned skin of his narrow face.

"Sit right here next to me." Hank leaned over and pulled the chair out for his daughter to join him.

Josephine grabbed a cup of coffee and then headed back to the table. Before she sat down, she hugged Ilsa around the neck; the shepherd was definitely starting to show her age. Ilsa was graying around her muzzle and eyes. Josephine took the seat next to her father and reached for a large ripe banana from a bowl of fruit. Tyler stopped chewing for a second to smile at her with closed lips; he nodded to the pitcher of fresh-squeezed orange juice. She held out her glass for Tyler to fill it for her.

"So what you were saying, Logan, is that we might be able to relocate the chapel?" Hank pushed his plate forward and reached for his mug full of steaming black coffee.

"I don't know why we're even discussing this." Barbara walked back over to the table, her hands resting firmly on her hips. "We aren't changing the venue for the wedding. I've been killing myself for over a year with all of these arrangements. We've paid the deposit, the invitations have been sent out…" Everyone in the kitchen, including the dog, was focused on Barbara now. "St. Peter's is where all of my children were baptized, St. Peter's is where Dan is buried, and St. Peter's is where the wedding is going to be held!"

Hank reached for his wife's hand. "Barb, we're just

talking about relocating the chapel. Jordan knows that the chapel is out of the question for the wedding."

"Oh, I missed that part." Before Barb turned back to the stove, she pointed to her son. "Tyler, how many times have I asked you to *not* to feed Ranger at the table?"

Josephine looked across the table at her brother; Ranger was sitting on Tyler's lap waiting for a morsel to come his way. Tyler winked at her and smiled, but didn't move Ranger.

"I haven't been up to the chapel in years." Josephine remembered playing wedding there with Jordan when they were girls. "Are you really thinking about moving the chapel, Dad? How? And where would you put it?"

Great-grandpa Brand had been a full-time rancher and a part-time preacher. He'd built a small chapel on the ranch with his own hands, and had a small congregation that would come on Sunday morning to hear him preach. It had sat abandoned, unused, for decades.

"I don't really know." Hank snuck Ilsa a full strip of bacon from his plate. "I haven't been up there in years. I couldn't tell you if it's even still standing."

"It's standing," Tyler said. "But it's rough. Real rough."

"I'd be willing to take a look at it for you, sir," Logan offered. "My uncle's a contractor. He had me framing houses before I could drive. I could take some pictures and get my uncle take a look at them."

Hank stood up and grabbed his hat off the back of his chair. "I'd appreciate that."

Ranger hopped down to the ground when Tyler stood

up and grabbed his hat as well. "I can take him up there so he can get a look around."

"No, I need you supervising the work on the north fence today." Hank grabbed his plate and utensils, stacked them in the sink, and then kissed his wife.

It hit her out of the blue, but the only thing Josephine wanted to do with her morning was see the chapel. She didn't want to spend the morning cooped up with a bunch of textbooks. She wanted to get out in the fresh air, get out into the sunlight, and get her blood pumping by hiking her way up to the ninety-year-old chapel.

"Mom? Jordan's not going to be ready to tackle wedding stuff until after noon. If you don't need me, I could take Logan up to see the chapel."

"That's fine, honey. Just make sure you take plenty of water and bug spray." Her mother never took a break from being her mother.

Josephine looked at Logan. "If you don't mind… I'll take you to the chapel."

Logan had been sitting across the table from Josephine, trying not to stare at her. There was just something about her that got his attention and *held* it. Would he *mind* spending the morning hiking in the mountains with the most beautiful woman he'd seen in a long time?

Heck, no!

Logan did his best *not* to look like a kid who had just been handed the keys to the candy store when he casually said to Josephine, "No, I don't mind."

Chapter 4

Josephine quickly changed into a pair of denim cutoff shorts and hiking boots, and layered a sweatshirt over a Berkeley Law T-shirt. She grabbed sunglasses, a baseball cap, and raced down the stairs. She deliberately left her cell phone behind. This was her time to take a break from her worries over her relationship with Brice. This was her first full day home at the ranch and it seemed sacrilegious *not* to at least make the attempt to enjoy it.

"Ready?" Logan was waiting for her.

"Ready." Josephine hopped down the porch stairs to meet him.

Logan liked the way Josephine's face was lit up with excitement. He had no doubt that the excitement was related to the hike and seeing the chapel, but he couldn't stop himself from hoping that perhaps spending time with him factored into that equation.

"Lead the way, boss." Logan lifted his heavy ruck-sack onto his shoulders.

They walked along a well-worn dirt road that would lead them up the mountain to her great-grandfather's chapel. Before they reached the tree line at the base of the mountain, the early morning sun was heating up the bright blue, cloudless sky. By the time they reached tree line, Josephine was ready to shed her outer layer of clothing.

"This road will take us about three-quarters of the way up this mountain." She wrapped her sweatshirt around her hips and put her hat back on. "There's an incredible view of the continental divide once you reach the peak. You've got to be sure to check that out while you're here, but you'll have to get there on foot or on horseback. Do you ride?"

Logan nodded. "All my life."

"Well…" Josephine slid the sunglasses back into place. "Anytime you want to ride, just let London know. She's the intern working in the foaling barn. She'll make sure there's a horse saddled up for you."

Together, side by side, they walked along the gravel and dirt road that followed a winding stream up the mountain. Although she had known him for only a very short time, it wasn't awkward hiking alone with Logan. Out of his uniform, he wasn't uptight. Their conversation was easy, and right when a lull was about to occur, Logan would ask her another question about the history of the ranch. She couldn't stop herself from thinking that Brice had never shown this much inter-est in her family's history. Even though she hadn't re-ally paid much attention to that before today. But with

Logan's genuine interest as a comparison, it was pretty hard to ignore.

"Do you mind if we take a quick break?" she asked when they reached the halfway point.

Josephine found a large boulder near the stream embankment and sat down. She closed her eyes for a minute to enjoy fully the sounds of the mountains. It seemed so quiet when they were walking and talking, but right now she could hear how loud the water flowing over the rocks in the stream sounded.

"Thirsty?" Logan, kneeling nearby, had opened his rucksack. He held out a bottle of water to her, which she accepted.

She drank the water slowly, taking some time to catch her breath. Logan downed his water, stuffed the empty bottle back into his bag, and then stripped his T-shirt off. Beneath it was a ribbed tank top that clung to his chest and stomach. For a second, Josephine found herself mindlessly staring at Logan. He wasn't tall; she typically dated tall men. In fact, when she stood next to him in heels, she was a little taller than he was.

But on the other hand, he was built like Michelangelo's *David*. His body was incredible. She'd never seen anything like it in real life. His shoulders, his biceps, his chest, were covered with thick, defined muscle. His waist was tapered and she could actually see the ripples of his abdominal muscles through the ribbed material. Logan didn't have a six-pack—he had an *eight*-pack. In particular, she was fascinated by the large tattoo of a dark gray wolf that covered a large portion of his upper left arm and chest. Part of the tattoo was obscured by his tank top, and Josephine wished she could move the material over and take a closer look at the design. It looked like beautiful work. Knowing that she needed to stop staring at the man, she looked at the stream instead. But, she could still see him out of the corner of her eye as he wiped the sweat off his face, neck, and arms with his T-shirt.

After a minute, she stood up and brushed the dirt off the seat of her shorts. "I'm over here huffing and puffing and you've barely broken a sweat."

Logan rolled up his T-shirt and packed it back into the rucksack. "I spend a lot of time indoor rock climbing."

"It shows." This was blurted out without thought. Josephine inwardly cringed as she extended her empty bottle to him.

He smiled at her as he held out his hand for her bottle. She was genuinely relieved when he didn't latch on to her comment and run with it. He just zipped up his bag, slung it back onto his shoulders, and adjusted the straps for comfort.

"Ready?" he asked.

"Yep." Now that she had caught her breath, she was eager to reach the chapel. So many years had passed by since she had laid eyes on her childhood haunt. What would it be like to see it now, through the eyes of an adult?

"There's a fork in the road up ahead," she told him. "If you take this road to the right, it will take you to a cave that my grandfather found."

"A cave?"

She sidestepped a dip in the road. "It's incredible. But it's hard to get into. You basically have to crawl on your back along this narrow tunnel that leads to the main chamber. The main chamber is huge—completely dark. Archaeologists have studied our cave for years. There are areas all along the sides of the main area where they believe that prehistoric humans lived. And they ended up finding a lot of artifacts in the main chamber and some of the smaller chambers."

"I'll have to check it out."

"I don't like the crawling part so much… It's a little claustrophobic. But once you get inside, you feel like you've been transported back in time. I haven't been there in ages, but I can still remember how cold it was inside the cave."

At the top of a hill, they reached the fork in the road. She stopped for a minute to catch her breath; she had put in hundreds of hours on the elliptical machine, and the climb was still tough. The change in altitude, the thinner air, impacted her mild case of asthma. Next time she came up here, she'd have to remember her inhaler.

"Up that way is the cave…" She pointed to the right.

"I suppose this isn't the day for that?"

"I really need to get back before noon. There's still a lot that needs to get done for the wedding. But, you can head up there after we see the chapel, if you want."

Logan shifted his rucksack on his back to a more comfortable position. "We'll see."

In actuality, he didn't intend to separate from her. This was her ranch, and she knew the territory better than he did, but he had a protective nature. He wouldn't feel right not seeing her safely back to the house.

"It's not too far now," Josephine said as they started up a new hill. Her thigh muscles were burning from the hike and she couldn't believe how much protesting her body was doing. When she had been a little girl, she could run up and down these hills without any trouble at all. Now, it was taking all of her strength, physical and mental, to hike to the chapel without taking a ton of minibreaks. If Logan hadn't been with her, she would have taken several breaks already. But since he was pressing on, she was pressing on.

At the bottom of another steep hill, the final hill that would lead them to the plateau where her great-grandfather had built his chapel, Josephine paused. Her face felt hot and wet with perspiration. She used the sleeve of her sweatshirt to wipe the sweat from her face and then prepared to tackle the last leg of this impromptu hike.

"Doing okay?" Logan stood beside her patiently.

She nodded. "The altitude is getting to me."

"You've been setting a really tough pace for this hike," he said. "Why don't we slow it down a bit?"

Hands on her hips, bending forward slightly, trying to catch her breath again, Josephine looked at him, surprised. "I've been setting the pace?"

He nodded his head "yes."

Josephine laughed a breathy laugh, and then coughed. "And here I've been blaming it on you!"

Logan laughed with her. "No. I've had to work to keep up."

"You're kidding?" Josephine laughed again with a shake of her head. "Do you mean that I feel a little like I'm going to pass out and I've done it to myself?"

Logan's smiled faded as he took a step toward her. "You feel light-headed?"

"A little. It's no big deal. Asthma."

"Here…" He pointed to a flat boulder on the side of the road. "I think you should sit down."

"The chapel is right up that hill. I'll rest when I get up there."

"How long has the chapel been there?"

"A hundred years."

Logan put his hand on her shoulder to guide her toward the boulder. "Then, chances are it'll still be there thirty minutes from now."

It was a point that she couldn't argue, so she walked over to the boulder and let him help her down to a sitting position. She crossed her legs and gave herself permission to rest.

One knee on the ground, Logan knelt in front of her and opened his rucksack. He held out two high-energy protein bars for her to see.

"Take your pick."

She chose the peanut-butter bar and gratefully accepted another bottle of water.

"What else do you have in that thing?" she asked when he joined her on the boulder. "It's like you're carrying a mini convenience store on your back."

He opened the wrapper of his bar with his teeth. "Did you see the movie *127 Hours*?"

"Uh-uh…" She wished she had time for movies, but she didn't.

"It was about a rock climber who had to cut off his own arm."

"Oh!" She nodded. "I remember that—the guy in Utah, right?"

"As a rock climber, first, it kind of scared the crap out of me, to be honest. But second, it reminded me that

I have to be prepared because, if a freak accident like that could happen to that guy, a freak accident could happen to me."

Then he asked, "Feeling better?"

"Much." After eating the protein bar and taking a moment to rest, the light-headed feeling had passed.

"Ready to get back to it?"

Josephine nodded. "Sure."

Logan stood up and offered her his hand, which she accepted.

"Thank you for talking me into taking a break—and feeding me."

"Anytime." He hoisted the heavy backpack onto his shoulders.

She had enjoyed it, as well. Sitting with Logan on that boulder, without another soul in sight, had been perfectly comfortable. It had taken her months to feel comfortable around Brice; he had always made her feel so nervous because he was so brilliant with the law. If she were to be honest with herself, sometimes Brice still made her feel a little anxious whenever they got into a conversation about California statutes or federal law. But with Logan, she was at total ease—not a single nerve in sight.

What did that mean?

Josephine forced her brain to stop trying to unravel meaningless life riddles, and refocus on finishing her trek up the steep hill. She leaned slightly forward, bent her knees, ignored the burning in her thighs and lungs, and willed her body to finish the last half of the hill quickly. At the top of the hill, Josephine threw back her head and let out a loud whoop to celebrate her accomplishment.

"I made it!" she exclaimed happily.

Logan joined her at the top of the final hill. She was glad to see that he was finally winded, too.

"Now, that felt good…" He wiped the sweat off his brow with the back of his forearm. He smiled at her. "You're a maniac."

Pleased, she asked, "I am?" No one had ever called her that before. Cautious and tenacious, yes. Maniac? Never.

"I nearly had to sprint up that hill just to keep up with you." He was impressed with her. "I'd really love to take you rock climbing one day."

For a moment, they both considered what he had just said. It sounded like he had asked her out on a date.

Knowing that she had a serious boyfriend, Logan added, "You and Brice…"

"I think I can safely say that it would be a definite 'no' for Brice." Brice was an avid sportsman. And he was very skilled at many things: fencing, sailing, golfing. But rock climbing? That wouldn't turn out well for anyone involved.

"It's not for everyone," he agreed, walking beside her through a small clearing to the edge of a patch of trees and overgrown brush.

"There it is!" Josephine pushed some branches out of her path and stepped over a fallen log. "See?"

"That is too cool." Logan looked through the branches of the trees and spotted the old chapel, tucked away in the hillside.

He pulled a small machete out of his rucksack. "Let me get in front of you so I can cut a path for us."

She shook her head, an amused smile on her face. "Really? You brought a machete?"

"Like I told you, I need to be prepared. I never know when I might have to perform an emergency amputation." He stepped in front of her and started whacking away at the branches.

"We'll have none of that, sir." She hung back, far away from the sharp blade.

Logan seemed to relish clearing a path for them, and in no time at all, they were standing in front of the chapel. They stood together, silently and reverently, in front of the structure that her ancestor had built a hundred years before. It was a small building—much smaller than she remembered. But, she supposed, everything looked smaller when you looked at it again as an adult. And yet, it was just as magical as she remembered.

"It looks like a little hobbit house, doesn't it?" She asked him quietly. She didn't know why she was whispering—it just felt right.

Logan put away the machete. "The construction is incredible. It still looks solid as a rock."

The chapel was the size of a modern day one-car garage, with a steeple roof, stone foundation, and a curved, heavy wooden door. The shallow stone steps leading up to the chapel door were covered in moss, decomposing leaves, and twigs.

Josephine ran her hand over the pitted wood of the chapel door. "I always loved this door—I can't really believe that it's still here…still on its hinges."

Logan checked the hinges. "They're rusted through.

If you want to go inside, it's going to take some brute force."

"I'm going in." There wasn't any scenario in the equation that didn't include her going inside the chapel.

Together, they used their body weight and strength to force the door open. Logan slammed the side of his body into the wood, while she used her hands to push. Finally, after several attempts of prying the hinges free, there was a loud sound and the door cracked open.

"Keep pushing!" Logan leaned harder into the door, using his feet to brace himself in place.

The top door hinge broke under the pressure, popped off, and flew over her shoulder.

"Whoa!" She ducked to the side. "That was close!"

"You all right?"

"Yeah…it just missed me. Can we get in?"

"Almost." He gave the door one last hard shove with his body and pushed it open wide enough for them to squeeze through.

Logan stepped inside the dusty, cobweb-laden chapel first. It was dirty, and there were signs that animals had been inside of the structure, but it appeared to be safe.

When she stepped inside of the chapel, it was like stepping back in time. Her heart felt it…her brain felt it…for just a split-second, she was transported to her childhood. This was the enchanted place where she had played and dreamed with her twin. They would spend from sunrise to sunset up on this mountain, perfectly content acting out every fantasy they could imagine.

"Look—only one of the stained glass windows broke." Josephine slowly walked along the narrow aisle that led up to a pulpit hand-carved by her father's grandfather.

On either side of the aisle, roughly hewn benches were tipped onto their sides. Originally, there had been four benches on either side of the aisle. Now, there were only five benches left. Birds had flown through the broken window and had made nests up in the rafters. Much like the chapel itself, the nests seemed to have been abandoned long ago.

"What do you think?" she asked him.

"I love this place," Logan said immediately. His eyes were taking inventory. He'd spent a lot of time on jobs with his uncle and he had been personally involved with moving older structures.

The moment she reached the pulpit, she started to brush the dirt and leaves off of it. She could see herself, so clear was the memory, standing behind the pulpit pretending to preach to an enthralled congregation.

Her fingers found what they were searching for: her initials, carved into the top of the pulpit. "Can it be moved?"

On the other side of the pulpit, he looked up at the tin roof and the beams holding it in place. He nodded slowly, thoughtfully. "Yes. It can."

"You're serious."

"It can be done," Logan said definitively.

Her mind started to whirl with ideas. "If we moved it closer to the ranch, we could actually restore it!"

"Absolutely." He would love to have a hand in restoring the chapel.

Face-to-face, with only the pulpit between them, they stood smiling at each other as if they had just uncov-

ered a buried treasure. Josephine, exactly at that moment, noticed Logan's eyes. Yes, she had seen his eyes
before. But, she hadn't really noticed how incredibly
beautiful they were—such a dark, rich brown that they
reminded her of expensive black satin.

"What?" He asked her, in a half curious, half amused
manner.

His single-word question snapped her out of it—she
had been unintentionally staring into his eyes. Once
she realized that she had been mindlessly ogling him,
she started to laugh.

"Sorry—I was just thinking about something from
when I was a kid."

"What's that?"

"When I was…oh, I don't know…seven or eight…"
Josephine walked out from behind the pulpit and joined
Logan where he was standing.

"I used to stand in this exact spot and pretend that
I was getting married. Jordan and I took turns offici-
ating the wedding and being the bride…" Josephine
laughed softly and looked over at him. "You standing
here just reminded me of that. I haven't thought of that
in years. And, of course, that was before I discovered
Gloria Steinem when I was thirteen and swore off marriage entirely."

"But, Gloria Steinem did eventually get married,"
Logan said thoughtfully.

Brow wrinkled, Josephine asked, "How do you even
know that?"

"Hey, I'll have you know I'm more than just a pretty
face. I'm current with the cause, equal pay for equal
work. The Lilly Ledbetter Law."

Josephine laughed. "I hate to say this out loud, but I wouldn't take you for a feminist sympathizer."

"That's okay. I know that I don't exactly fit the image of a typical feminist. I'm a cop who looks like a muscle-head. But my mom was raised on *Ms.* magazine—so I pretty much had the chauvinist trained out of me at an early age." Logan smiled at the thought and pulled out a professional-grade Nikon camera from his bag. "Let's grab these shots so we can get you back by noon."

"Sure." Josephine checked her watch with a nod. "Where do you want to start?"

Chapter 5

They both had similar work styles—slow, methodical, and thorough. Together, they captured detailed shots of the interior of the chapel, as well as the exterior and surrounding landscape. She had helped Logan take measurements before they started their hike down the mountain. Both of them were so excited about the prospect of moving the chapel that they discussed it nonstop all the way back down the mountain. By the time that they reached the gate, which signaled that the final leg of the journey was complete, it seemed to Josephine that the two of them had bonded. On the round trip to and from the chapel, she had unexpectedly made a connection with Logan. He felt like a friend.

"Well..." Logan paused at the end of the path that led to her brother's cabin. "I'm going to send my uncle these pictures and measurements so I can report back to Hank."

Josephine nodded toward her sister, who had set up her easels and paints on the porch and was painting a new picture for her next gallery show. "It looks like Jordan is waiting for me."

They parted ways. After he had taken a few steps away from her, Logan stopped and turned to look at her.

"Hey…" he called out to her.

Josephine slowed down and glanced back at him.

"Thanks for being my guide today."

She smiled a small smile. "I enjoyed it."

For a second time, they parted ways and Josephine had an odd feeling in the pit of her stomach as she approached her sister. Jordan looked tense and irritated, when she normally looked happy when she painted. She was also, Josephine noted, biting on her lower lip, which was what she did whenever she was upset or ticked off.

"Hey." Josephine slowly climbed the stairs to the front porch.

"Hey…" Jordan put down her paintbrush and moved to the porch swing. "How'd the chapel look?"

Josephine perched on the porch railing opposite the swing. "It's pretty rough on the inside, but salvageable. Logan believes the structure's sound—you know, Dad has it in his head to move it."

"Mom told me. Cool idea."

"Logan's pretty certain that it can be moved." Josephine wrapped her arm around the wooden post to keep her balance.

"He's a great guy, right? He's been a huge part of our support system."

Her sister was stalling. Whatever was on her mind, it had to be bad. Outspoken Jordan didn't often beat around the bush.

"So, have we done enough small talking yet?" Josephine asked her twin pointedly.

Her sister stared at her and they didn't need words between them. A couple of seconds later, Jordan frowned, shook her head, and pulled her phone out of the front pocket of her shorts. Silently, Jordan looked down at the phone before she looked at her.

"I saw something on Instagram this morning."

Josephine wasn't sure where this was heading, but her stomach already didn't like it. There was an uncomfortable, unusual, anxious quivering in her belly. It was if her body knew something that her mind hadn't yet figured out.

"I didn't know if I should show it to you or not, but here…" Jordan uncurled her long, pale legs, stood up, and held out her phone to her.

Josephine met her sister's angry eyes and then took the phone from her. When she saw the picture on Jordan's phone, her arm tightened around the post. She hugged the post so tightly, in fact, that the wood dug painfully into her skin.

"Where was this taken? Do you know?"

"At a charity event."

She had been with Brice when he had been measured for that tuxedo, but this photograph was the first time she had seen him wear it. It fit beautifully. But then again, everything fit Brice beautifully. Nature had been very kind to him—he was tall with nice shoulders and golden-boy good looks. The woman beside him—her arm linked with his, her hand on his sleeve, her body leaned intimately into his—was stunning. She had shoulder-length dark hair, flawless olive skin, and full red lips. Josephine wished she could put her into the "bimbo" category, but this woman had intelligent eyes and a classic, elegant style.

She handed the phone back to Jordan. "Well, I suppose we know why he's not coming to the wedding."

"That's it?" Jordan slipped the phone back into her pocket.

Josephine slid off the railing and tugged the legs of her shorts down. "That's it."

"I was right to tell you, I think," her sister said defensively.

"Of course you were." She hugged Jordan to reassure her. "I'm going to go freshen up and then we'll work on the wedding, okay?"

"Wait a minute, Jo. Why are you acting like a Stepford Wife?" her sister asked with a shake of her head. "You should be really pissed right now, and the fact that you're not is kind of freakin' me out…"

"I'm not going to let Brice ruin the only summer I've had off in years," Josephine replied. "He apparently wants someone else. Me being angry won't change that, will it?"

"Well, then I'll be pissed off for the both of us." Jordan scowled. "If he was here right now, I'd sock him right in his stupid aristocratic beak!"

Jordan ran interference for her with their mom while she escaped to the sanctuary of her third-floor bedroom. Once inside of her room, she went to the bathroom and closed that door, too. She needed as much of a barrier between her and the world as she could muster. She sat down on the edge of the claw-footed tub and just sat there, staring at a hairline crack in the porcelain pedestal sink. It was strange—she didn't really feel angry or sad or jealous. There was a burning in her stomach and a burning behind her eyes, but she didn't need to cry.

Was she in shock? Was that it? Or had she known, at some primordial level, that he had recently lost interest in her?

"That's more like it…" she said aloud.

And who was this woman who had taken her spot at Brice's side?

Not seeing any sense in speculating about the picture when she could just call him and ask, Josephine left the bathroom, turned on her phone, and sat down at the desk. His cell phone went straight to voicemail; his secretary took a message. So, she called his private office number. She never called that number, respecting Brice's wishes that she would only use it if there were an emergency. This qualified, in her opinion.

"Hello?" He sounded good. Happy.

"It's me, Brice."

There was a long pause, followed by a chair squeak. Josephine imagined him spinning his chair around so the back of his chair was facing the people who were undoubtedly sitting on the other side of his desk.

"Josie…"

She hated it when he called her that. He was the only one who did.

"Are you okay?"

The burning in her stomach became hotter, more intense. "I'm fine."

Another pause, then he said. "I'm in the middle of something here. Let me call you back in a bit."

"Oh, sure." It was work to keep her tone light. "But, before you go, I just wanted to tell you how handsome you looked in your tuxedo last night."

She was being snarky and sarcastic and it felt...*great*.

The chair squeaked again and she heard Brice say to whomever was in his office, "I need to take this call. Let me catch up with you in fifteen."

Brice waited a second or two before he said, "I was afraid this was going to happen. I wanted to wait until you got back to tell you about Caroline."

"I think you should tell me now."

Caroline Santiago, he explained, had recently joined the firm. She was an environmental lawyer who was working on the same case. Meetings turned into lunches, which turned into dinners, and dinners turned into interest on both of their parts. But Caroline refused to date him because she knew he was involved. So, Brice decided to become uninvolved with her.

"Do you...love her?" She couldn't believe how rapidly her heart was beating. It was pumping hard like she had just sprinted for a quarter mile.

"I don't know. Maybe."

Maybe? *Maybe?* The first flush of anger broke through the numbness.

"You haven't been sleeping with the both of us, have you? I think I have the right to know if I need to make an appointment with my doctor for an STD screen."

"No. God. *No*, Josie. You know me better than that. We haven't slept together…"

There was an unspoken "yet" at the end of his sentence. They both knew it, and she couldn't allow herself to ignore it.

"You know…" she said much more calmly than she felt inside. "I've known you for five years, Brice. *Five years*. And, for the first time in all of those years, the only thing I can think to say to you is 'goodbye.'"

"Josephine… I didn't plan this. Lightning struck. But, I always want to be able to count you as one of my friends."

"Goodbye, Brice."

"Hey, Mom, how's it going?" Josephine emerged from her room as night was falling.

"Hi, sweetheart. Everyone missed you at dinner." Barb was sitting in the study, opening a new stack of RSVPs. "Did you get all of your studying done?"

She actually had gotten quite a bit of studying done. She had always had the ability to concentrate in a crisis. "It put a dent in it, at least. Where is everybody?"

"They're all out at the campfire toasting marshmallows and smoking your father's cigars." Her mom picked up her reading glasses and slipped them on.

"You aren't supposed to know about the cigars."

Her mom looked at her over the rim of her glasses. "I've been married to your father for four decades, sweetie. There isn't anything that man does that I don't know about. But when you're married, sometimes you just have to let the other person breathe. Even if it means that the breathing they're doing includes cigar smoke."

Josephine laughed before she asked, "Do you need help?"

"No, honey, I've got this all under control. Why don't you go out there and show those boys how a real pro toasts marshmallows?"

Josephine strolled along the gravel drive that led to the permanent fire pit. All of her life, and as far back as she could remember, her family had gathered around a campfire. More than anything, she had looked forward to spending time with Brice and her family by the bonfire. But that just wasn't meant to be. He didn't love her anymore. He didn't want her anymore. And she had spent the last several hours trying to adjust to a new normal. Brice had been her first love—her first lover—and she had believed that he was her future. It was difficult to be so wrong.

"Hey! Sissy!" Tyler shouted from across the fire. "Where the heck have you been?"

"Studying." She smiled at the sight of her family gathered at the fire.

Josephine sat down on one of the tree stumps that her father had fashioned into rustic chairs years ago. Her sister handed her a roasting stick and the bag of marshmallows; she carefully put two large marshmallows on to the end of the stick before she picked the perfect spot above the fire to start browning them.

"Mine always catch on fire," Logan told her.

"It takes patience." She slowly turned the stick as one side of the marshmallows began to turn golden brown and bubble.

"Here." Josephine extended the two perfectly cooked marshmallows out to Logan.

"You sure?"

She nodded. Logan pulled the gooey, hot marshmallows off the stick and popped them into his mouth. She watched his face and waited.

"Mmm." He smiled at her. "The best I've ever had. Thank you."

"Well, don't get too impressed. This is the only thing I know how to cook."

There was a moment, when she was cooking marshmallows to share with Logan and listening to Tyler strum the guitar, that she did feel normal. Perhaps most people wouldn't like the smell of campfire and cigar smoke, but for her, it represented home. She enjoyed hearing her sister and Ian talk about their wedding and their business plans and the remodeling of their downtown San Diego penthouse. She enjoyed hearing her father and Tyler discuss the day-to-day operations of the ranch. They talked and she listened. When there was finally a lull in the conversation, Josephine set the agenda for the next topic: the chapel.

"Have you heard back from your uncle?" she asked Logan.

Logan, who was pouring some water from his bottle onto his fingers to wash off the sticky residue left by the marshmallows, nodded his head.

"I filled Hank in before you got here," he said.

"So…" she asked expectantly. "What's the verdict? Can it be moved?"

Hank stubbed out his cigar and held the unsmoked part of the cigar between his thumb and forefinger. "We can move it by rigging it up and hauling it down. But we're going to have to rustle up the right equipment and that's gonna take some time."

"Don't you think that you should at least get another opinion, Dad? No offense, Logan."

"When people want a second opinion, they go to Logan's uncle," Ian said. "If someone wants an expert opinion right off the bat, they go to Logan's uncle. He's the gold standard when it comes to moving old structures. If he says that it can be done, then it can be done."

Everyone around the campfire was quite for a moment, contemplating Ian's words. Then her father spoke.

"I believe Logan wouldn't lead us astray on this. You've seen the chapel—you've seen the terrain. What do you think, son? Can the chapel be moved or should we just scrap the idea?"

Josephine couldn't stop herself from frowning. It was an immediate, unavoidable response.

Son?

She quickly looked between Logan and her father. Her father was a cautious man. He didn't just embrace people wholeheartedly without their proving their worth, and he certainly didn't trust them with decisions about the ranch on a whim. Hank had only met Logan *yesterday* and he'd already taken him into his confidence and was calling him *son*?

What the heck?

"It can be done," Logan responded. "It's going to cost a pretty penny, but it can be done."

"Money's not a problem," Hank told Logan. "But, I think we are going to need your help to get the job done."

"Uh…*wow*! Are you really going to do it, Dad?" Jordan asked.

"If Logan's willing to take time away from his vacation, this might just be the best time to finally get it done." This was her father's answer.

"I've got no problem helping out," Logan said. "I'm used to working. I need to keep busy."

"Then, let's get it done." Tyler strummed a couple of chords on his guitar. "You know I'm in."

As the campfire died down, the conversation also ebbed. The events of the last two days with Brice, and the effort it took to pretend like nothing was wrong, suddenly made her feel bone tired. She stifled a yawn behind her hand.

"Well, family, I think it's time for me to go to bed." She stood up.

After kissing her father on the cheek and saying good-night to everyone, Josephine headed back to the house. She was a short distance from the fire pit when she heard Jordan call her name. She slowed down and waited for her twin to catch up to her, and then once they were out of earshot of the rest of the family, Jordan said, "I've been worried about you. How are you holding up?"

"I actually feel pretty numb right now." Josephine crossed her arms in front of her body. "It's not the end of the world, right? It just seems like it is."

"Did you talk to Brice?"

"Sure did."

"I figured you would. Was he straight with you, or did he try to weasel out of it?"

Josephine stopped walking, and Jordan did, as well.

They stood together in a shadowy stretch of the driveway, where the light of the fire and the lights of the house didn't reach. Under the wide, blue-black, starless sky, Josephine tried to think of a way to quickly recap her conversation with Brice, but couldn't.

"Do you mind if…" She started the sentence and Jordan finished it.

"…we talk about it tomorrow?"

In the dark, Josephine nodded.

Her twin hugged her. "We don't have to talk about it at all, if you don't want to, Jo. I just want you to know that I'm here for you. I love you."

"I love you, too." Josephine returned the hug, glad for her sister's support.

After the hug ended, she said to her sister, "I'll tell everyone tomorrow—there's no sense waiting anymore. I'm sure they'll all be happy to hear it."

"No one's going to happy that you're in pain, Jo."

Josephine breathed in deeply and then let it out quickly. "No. You're right. I know you're right. Good night."

"Okay, get some rest," Jordan agreed. "But, if you need anything, you know where to find me."

Jordan headed back to the fire and her fiancé, while she returned to the farmhouse. She had almost reached to porch steps when she heard the sound of heavy footsteps on the gravel. Someone was running toward her in the dark.

"Hey, Josephine!" Logan jogged toward her. "Hold up!"

The only thing she wanted to do at the exact moment was to go to bed. She needed to wash her face, brush her teeth, get into her comfy pajamas, crawl under the covers, and be left alone. And, for some reason, she couldn't seem to make a clean getaway.

"I was just talking to your dad and Tyler about the cave and they said that you are the resident spelunker."

"I suppose that's true," she said as she stepped onto the first porch step—one step closer to her bed.

"I'm going to head up to the cave tomorrow before plans to move the chapel get under way." Logan had followed her onto the first step. "And I wanted to know if you wanted to go with me."

The first word that came to mind was "no." And it was also the first word that tried to pop out of her mouth. But she refused to speak the word. She needed to resist the urge to retreat and force herself to forge ahead.

"What time?" she asked.

"Seven?" He seemed surprised that she said yes. That made two of them.

"Seven's good," she agreed. "If I don't see you in the kitchen, I'll meet you at the gate."

Chapter 6

The next morning, Logan greeted her at the fence and they made their way back up the mountain. She wanted to be quiet on the hike—she felt like she needed it. Normally, she would ignore her needs in favor of her companion's needs, but she felt comfortable enough with Logan to speak her truth. He didn't ask her why; he just respected her wishes and only spoke when she spoke first. At the fork in the road, they traveled to the right in order to reach the cave.

"It looks like it's trying to rain," Josephine noted. The sky was a muddy gray and there were heavy storm clouds gathering in the distance.

Logan surveyed the sky. "We should get back before it starts. I've got a couple of ponchos just in case."

After that brief exchange, Josephine turned inward again. She had awakened feeling odd. She wasn't sad—

she didn't feel angry. She felt—out of sorts. Her head ached, all of her joints burned for no apparent reason. Behind her sunglasses, her eyes were tender from crying herself to sleep. This was her first real breakup with a man she still loved, and she wasn't exactly sure *how* to work through that.

Twenty more minutes along the winding mountain path, and then Josephine pointed straight ahead.

"There's the entrance, right there in that rock face."

Logan had been happy to be spending a second morning hiking with Josephine. He knew he was in permanent friend zone, no-man's-land, but he didn't see any reason why he couldn't enjoy the company of a beautiful, intelligent woman when crossing the line was already off the table. He liked her as a person, and during their second hike together, the silences between them weren't uncomfortable at all.

"I've gotta confess, I've been thinking about this place ever since you told me about it," he replied. He'd had this cave on the brain since yesterday. The idea of being able to visit an archaeological site intrigued him. He was about to enter a place where prehistoric man, and woman, had made their homes.

"I don't blame you. It's an amazing place. I remember when a crew from *National Geographic* arrived to photograph our cave. I was convinced that we were famous."

Logan noticed that she smiled, just a little, for the first time that day. He sensed that something was bothering her—there was a change in her from their trip to the chapel—but he didn't know her well enough to inquire. The best he could do was to respect her wish to hike in relative silence.

"Is that a lock?" he asked, concerned.

Josephine pulled her key chain out of her front pocket, held up an old brass key. "I never took the key off my key chain."

Long fingers of tall, dried weeds brushed against the bare skin of her legs as she forged a path to the small opening of the cave. She knelt down in front of the cave entrance, which was secured with a heavy door made from thick steel bars. To her, it had always resembled a jail cell for gnomes. She slipped the key into the rusted lock and tried to turn it.

"I think it's too rusted to open." Josephine twisted the key back and forth. "It's not opening."

Logan slipped his backpack off his shoulders, dropped it on the ground, and joined her. He knelt down beside her and studied the lock.

"Careful—if you don't handle it gently, the key will snap in two."

He was close to her—closer than he'd ever been before. His golden-brown skin was hot and sweaty from their hike, and there was something appealing about his natural scent. Her senses were stimulated in a completely unexpected way. She had always liked the way Brice smelled after he had applied cologne, but she couldn't really remember physically responding to the scent of his skin.

"Do you want to give it a try?"

She stood up and stepped back to give him room. Logan, she noticed, was a focused worker. All of his attention was aimed at coaxing the lock open. For a man

with such developed arms—truly spectacular arms—
he seemed to have a very light touch with his hands.

"Any luck?" she asked.

"We're close." He kept his eyes on the lock.

Then she heard a small click and when Logan smiled
at her triumphantly, she knew that he had managed to
finagle the lock open.

"Bingo," he said. The key chain was handed to her
so Logan could twist the lock free of the gate.

Once the gate was unlocked, he sat down on the
ground, braced his feet on the rock face, and used the
strength of his arms and the leverage created by his
legs to wrench the door open. At first, the steel door
wouldn't budge.

"It's frozen, but good." Logan took a short break
and used the back of his forearm to wipe the sweat off
his forehead.

"Do you want me to help?"

"Maybe." He wrapped his fingers around the bars
and repositioned his feet. "Let me give it one more try."

He didn't need a third go at the gate. Logan lowered
his head, closed his eyes, and grunted from the force
he was exerting to force the gate from its frozen position. The muscles in his arms, the biceps and triceps,
hardened and bulged beneath his skin; the veins in his
neck popped to the surface and she was about to tell
him just to forget it. But then, she heard a loud cracking sound, followed by a long, low creak.

"You did it!" she exclaimed. "That's amazing!"

Logan yanked the door all the way open before
he stopped. The look on Josephine's face made him
smile. Her face, such a pretty face, was transformed.

Her cheeks were flushed and her sweet lips were smiling. The fact that he was able to make her smile the way she was smiling now made him feel like he'd accomplished something pretty major.

"Sorry that was so hard." She saw him flexing his fingers, undoubtedly to work out the stiffness from gripping the steel bars.

He stood up and brushed the dirt and gravel from his cutoff khaki shorts. "No need to apologize. I consider stuff like that to be fun."

The look of a younger Logan flashed across his face in his excitement. That's how he must have looked when he was a boy.

"If you thought that was fun, you're going to love this next part." Her smile grew. She was starting to feel the excitement, the anticipation, of going down into the cave. Like the chapel, it had been years.

"I'm ready, if you're ready."

After a short discussion, they opted to leave Logan's backpack behind. The opening to the cave became smaller and narrower as it descended quickly into the massive main chamber. Josephine led the way with Logan following behind. At the beginning of the cave, the tunnel was large enough for them to walk crouched over. When it became too tight to stand, they both sat down and used their feet to propel themselves forward.

"It's much tighter than I remember," Josephine said. Her legs were already covered with a fine coating of dust and she knew that the sharp-edged shards of rock had scraped the skin of the backs of her thighs. It would have been wise to wear long pants.

She paused for a moment to switch the flashlight to

her left hand, so she could use her right hand to help push her body forward.

"Are you okay?" Logan asked her.

She couldn't turn her head around to look at him. The tunnel had become very narrow and cramped. They were nearly lying on their backs, unable to sit upright, surrounded by walls of sediment and granite. The light from the flashlights was the only light available.

"I'm okay. We're coming up to the slide. It's a really sharp drop, FYI."

The "slide," as her family had dubbed it, was the reason why it was inadvisable to crawl on your hands and knees into the cave. It was a drastic drop that could send a person tumbling headfirst into the jagged boulders down below.

"I'll hang back so we have some leeway between us."

The flashlight she kept on her key chain was small enough to clench between her teeth. With both hands free, Josephine cautiously scooted forward to the entrance of the slide. Her feet pushed loose rocks down the incline and she could hear them rolling and rolling and rolling.

She closed her eyes, for just a minute, and then took a deep, calming breath. This was always the only part of the tunnel that made her nervous. Luckily, the tunnel widened at the opening of the slide and she was able to sit up without hitting her head. Bracing her feet on either side of the tunnel wall, she used her hands to push herself slowly onto the slide. The sharp incline of the tunnel was pulling her body forward, and she had to use the strength of her arms and her legs to slow her descent.

"How're you doing?" she called back to him.

"This is awesome!" he said. "How are you doing?"

"So far, so good—the main chamber is at the end of this section of the tunnel."

"Roger that."

The closer they got to the main chamber, the cooler the temperature felt. It would be at least thirty degrees colder in the main chamber than it was aboveground. Her bare legs and arms were covered with goose bumps as she negotiated the last section of the tunnel into the cave. Able to stand upright, she stepped off the side, careful of her footing, while Logan finished his climb down the slide.

Some loose rocks, and the light from his flashlight, preceded Logan as he made his final descent into the chamber. Soon he was standing next to her, his body throwing off heat in contrast to the frigid air of the cave.

"This is frickin' unbelievable." He moved the beam of his flashlight to different spots around the cave.

She was already starting to feel uncomfortable in the cold. She should have thought to bring a lightweight jacket, but she wasn't really herself this morning. She crossed one arm over her body so she could still maneuver her flashlight.

"This main chamber is the size of two Olympic swimming pools." Her words echoed back to them from the other side of the cave. "And if you look up there…" She shined a light to a ledge on the cave wall. "That's one of the places that the archaeologists believe the prehistoric Americans made their home."

"Incredible," he said in a reverent voice.

She loved the cave and it always made her feel good

to find someone else who shared that love and appreciation. It was awesome, and humbling, to stand in the presence of a place that had been home to ancient Native Americans two thousand years before.

"Is there a way to get to the other side?" he asked.

"There is. But it's too dark to be safe today. If you want, we can ask Tyler to help us set up the right equipment." She added, "And there's another tunnel on the other side that leads to several smaller chambers. Archaeologists found a cache of arrowheads there—I'll have to ask Dad if he still has some of them for you to see."

Even though Logan couldn't cross the cave today, he could at least survey the cave landscape for a future exploration. And Josephine didn't seem to be in a hurry. She perched herself on a small natural rock ledge nearby and seemed content to spend some time shining her flashlight at various spots along the far wall. The floor of the main chamber was packed solid with enormous, jagged boulders that didn't appear to be as dangerous as Logan knew them to be from his rock climbing experience. The boulders were uneven and could be very slippery, and the crevasses between the individual boulders could be deadly. Before he would dare cross to the other side, he would have to figure out a way to bring the proper equipment through the narrow tunnel.

"Shoot," he heard Josephine say. "My battery is dying."

"Do you want to use mine?"

"No. My phone has a flashlight. Thanks, though."

He saw the light on her phone turn on and he heard

her make a childlike sound of pleasure when her phone flashlight worked, which meant she was back in business. She stood up and walked to over to a flat, elongated boulder nearby. He wasn't expecting her to walk onto the boulder, but that's what she did.

"Where're you heading?" He worked to keep his question light—she didn't seem like the type of woman who appreciated a man even *sounding* like he was trying to boss her around.

"Over to that spot right there. I can't see the right side of the cave from here."

He wanted to tell her to wait. He wanted to tell her to be careful. But, instead, he only said, "Do you mind if I join you?"

"You're welcome to join me. There's enough room. And you get a 180-degree view of the space."

He shined the light from his flashlight directly in front of his next footstep, and occasionally moved the light ahead to mark out his path. Josephine, quickly and with less caution than he would have liked, walked across the first boulder and then made the small jump onto the next boulder beside it. Once he made it to the second long, flat boulder, Logan made it a point to stand close enough to Josephine to catch her if she lost her balance. The darkness and the enormity of the space threw off his equilibrium. He had to imagine that it was doing the same to her.

He heard her sigh, he imagined from contentment of being back in the cave. And he understood why she wanted to risk venturing out onto these flat boulders. Standing there next to Josephine, surrounded by a sea of boulders, Logan was awestruck by the majesty of this dark, cool, underground world. This was a special moment he was sharing with Josephine, a moment that he didn't believe either of them would soon forget.

"Oh! *No!*"

His reverie was interrupted by Josephine's exclamation. His eyes naturally followed the light of her phone as it slipped out of her fingers and falling toward a deep, black crevice. Before he could react, she lunged for the phone and slipped off the side of the boulder. He heard a cracking sound, the sound of bone hitting granite, and he heard her cry out in pain.

His law enforcement training and rock climbing instincts kicked in. Something had thankfully stopped her from falling all the way down into the crevice. With the light of the flashlight, he could see that her position was temporarily stabilized. Her arms were hugging the top of the boulder near where he was crouching.

"What's hurt?" he asked.

He had seen the pinched, pain-stricken expression on her face when he moved the light past her torso to examine her position in the crevice.

"My knee." He heard the distress in her voice. "I hit it on a rock on the way down."

"Does anything feel broken?"

Her thigh was scraped and bloody; from his angle, he couldn't see her knees or her feet.

"No. I don't think so." She gasped. "But I can't move my foot, Logan. It's stuck under this rock."

That was the last thing he wanted to hear. Getting a limb trapped was always a concern for a rock climber. Once trapped, it could be extremely tricky to free a person's limb. If her foot wasn't broken, he could break it while trying to move the rock. And, after assessing the situation, moving the heavy rock was the only choice. Her right foot was pinned beneath it, and there wasn't any wiggle room.

He made certain her position was still secure before he began to execute his plan to move the rock. He silently cursed his decision to leave his backpack full of supplies behind, and knew that he may be making the trip up the tunnel to retrieve it if his first plan wasn't successful.

Three attempts at budging the rock and Logan knew that he needed more leverage than the strength of his arms and legs alone. He knelt down beside Josephine to deliver the news.

"I need my backpack."

"I know." Her voice had a weak quality that put him on alert for shock.

"I'm going to leave you the flashlight, but I need you to shine the light on my path back to the tunnel. Can you do that?"

Josephine took the flashlight and nodded.

It worked in both of their favors that Josephine had managed to remain calm. How long that calm would last—Logan couldn't be certain.

He used a quick and steady approach to climbing through the tunnel to the surface to get his supplies. He used the same approach to get back to Josephine. He knew he needed to remain calm for her sake, but he wasn't completely confident that he could free her without hurting her. The moment he cleared the tunnel, he called out to her, his voice echoing loudly in the chamber.

"Josephine! Shine the light on the path for me!"

He grabbed the tools he intended to use in an attempt to dislodge the large rock and left his backpack near the tunnel entrance. Sure, steady, cautious steps brought him back to Josephine. Once by her side, he knelt down beside her.

"I need your help, Josephine. Are you still with me?"

In the low light, he saw her nod her head.

"Reach down and feel around the side of the rock. Look for a place where I can thread the rope through."

"I… I think there's a place—but it's too small. I can't even put my finger through past my knuckle."

"That's okay," Logan reassured her. "That's okay. We can work with that."

While she held the flashlight, he started the chore of digging around the rock. It was a tedious, laborious task and it had to work in a tight space without causing Josephine further harm.

"I think I got it," he said to her.

He grabbed his strong climbing rope and threaded it through the space he had just created.

"Talk to me," he commanded gently. Her breathing sounded shallow.

"I'm okay."

"Hang in there with me just a little bit longer, Jo." Logan quickly wrapped the rope around his waist several times, climbed down between the boulders, and found a spot where he could brace his legs and feet.

"I'm going to count to three, Jo. When you hear me say 'three,' you need to push the rock. Let me know you can hear me."

"I hear you."

Logan wound the rope around his hands and prepared himself to pull. "This may hurt, Jo."

"Just do it!" she yelled at him.

"One. Two. Three!"

It took all of his strength to pull the rock forward. He groaned loudly from exertion and he heard her scream when the rock moved.

"It's off!" The two words he was waiting to hear pinged around the cold cave walls.

"Can you get your foot free?" He didn't release the tension on the rope. They still weren't out of the woods yet.

"No!" she yelled back. "No!"

Her ability to stay calm was deteriorating. He needed to get her out, and he need to get her out now. He needed to make sure that the rock couldn't roll back onto her foot. He closed his eyes, mustered all of his strength, and with a loud battle cry, he pulled on the rope to move the rock farther away from Josephine. Once he was sure the rock wasn't a threat to her, he crawled back onto the boulder and went back to her side.

"My boot won't budge!"

On his stomach, he leaned down and loosened her shoelaces so she could work her foot free. Then he slipped his arms under her armpits and around her chest and hauled her up onto the boulder.

"I can't feel my foot." Josephine reached down to touch her right foot. "I can't feel my *foot*!"

Logan squatted down next to her. "Put your arms around my neck, Jo."

This was a no-nonsense command that she followed without question. Once her arms were around his neck,

Logan used his strong thigh muscles to pick her up carefully. With Josephine in his arms, and the flashlight in his hand to light his way, Logan took one cautious step after another until he had brought them both to safety.

Chapter 7

Josephine held on to Logan's neck as tightly as she could. All of her bravery, all of her stoicism, had evaporated. In their place now were anxiety and pain. Her foot, which she hadn't been able to feel moments ago, was starting to throb. She was starting to notice, for the first time, that her knees hurt and her upper thighs felt raw. She had banged her body up nicely and she was lucky that Logan could remain calm in a crisis.

"I'm going to put you down right here, okay?" he told her.

"Okay." She looked down where he was planning on setting her, straining in the dark to see.

Gently, slowly, he set her down on the cold floor. He opened his backpack to find what he needed. First, he helped her into a lightweight jacket. She had been cold since they entered the main chamber, and had been shivering for a while. The jacket felt like much-needed relief.

"I'm going to wrap your foot over the sock to help protect it, alright?"

He was using a very calm, soothing voice to keep her in the loop. And she found that she liked the sound of his voice—it was quiet, which limited the echo, and confident.

But the minute he touched her foot, her pain level intensified and she jerked her leg back instinctively.

"I'm sorry. I'm sorry," she said, her teeth grit hard together. "I can't do that. It hurts too much."

"I have to wrap it, Jo. If I don't, you're going to be one hurting puppy going through the tunnel."

She had been in such distress that she hadn't given much thought to the trip up the tunnel. Now, after she couldn't have Logan touch her foot, a suffocating feeling of dread swept over her body. How was she going to get back up to the surface? *How?*

Logan must have noticed that her breathing had changed. She was starting to hyperventilate. Her foot was throbbing and felt like someone had smashed it with a meat cleaver. She could not go up that tunnel. She just couldn't do it.

"Jo, what do you do when you need to calm down?"

In a choppy, breathy voice, she said, "Listen—to—music."

"Well, I don't have a radio. But I can sing for you."

"Are—you—any—good?"

Logan's laugh—a deep, rich laugh—sounded good to her ears; Logan's steadying hand on her calf, a warm, strong hand, felt good on her skin.

"Karaoke champion two years in a row."

"That's…impressive."

He laughed again. "Do you have any requests, madam?"

"Surprise—me."

"Okay. I'll sing you one of my favorites," he said. "Now, Jo, when I start wrapping your foot, focus on my voice. Don't think about anything but my voice. Okay? Are you with me?"

"I'm—with you."

And then he started to sing for her. He couldn't have known it, but the song he chose, Bill Withers's "Lean on Me," was one of her favorite songs, too.

He had a million-dollar singing voice. Smooth and deep—it cut through her anxiety and her pain. The acoustics of the cave made it seem that his voice was swirling around her, enveloping her. It wasn't hard to focus on his voice, because it was everywhere. And it was beautiful.

"Ow!" Her concentration broke when he started to wrap her instep. "That's too tight. It's too tight!"

"It has to be this tight." He insisted. "You're doing great, Jo. Almost done."

Her breathing was already steadier and even though the throbbing from her swollen foot was creeping up her leg, she didn't feel as panicked. She just needed to brace herself against the pain.

Logan continued with his song before he continued wrapping her foot. She squeezed her eyes shut and forced herself to focus on his voice.

She smiled right before she grimaced when Logan wrapped the bandage around the ball of her foot. And

then she smiled again, in relief, when he announced
that he was done.

"How's that feel?"

"Better." The compression helped the throbbing and
his singing had helped her calm down. She had managed to get a hold of herself, which could only make
things easier for the both of them.

"You're going to have to crawl out on your hands
and knees, Jo. It's the only way. I'm going to follow
up the rear, so you're not alone in this. I'll catch you
if you fall."

Logan bandaged her knees, put on his backpack,
and then lifted her into the tunnel. She had already determined that she wasn't going to complain or cry or
even so much as make one whimper. She was going to
be tough and strong and stoic. She had already "lost it"
in front of Logan—she refused to let it happen again.

Slowly, painfully, she crawled upward on her hands
and knees. She tried, but she couldn't always keep her
injured foot elevated. Whenever she accidentally let it
drop and it came in contact with the unforgiving surface of the tunnel floor, she had to clamp down on her
lip to stop herself from crying out. At those times, she
had to stop. She had to take a break and regroup. Logan
stayed close, but not too close. He was encouraging
and supportive without rushing her. She appreciated
that. She *needed* that. At one point, he told her that he
needed to take a break. She knew that the break was
for her. He had her lie down on her side to take pressure off her knees and hands. When she was ready,
she started again. Together, inch by inch, foot by foot,

they climbed to the surface. It wasn't until the warm, late-morning sun touched her face and she smelled the pine in the air that she felt like she was out of danger.

Just outside of the cave entrance, she collapsed onto her back, arm over her arms, and tried to catch her breath. Jagged rocks dug into her back, but she didn't care.

"Lie still for a moment," Logan said.

"No problem." She kept her eyes closed—they needed time to adjust from the dark of the cave to the light of the day.

He was respectful during his examination, always letting her know where and when he was going to touch her. She was dirty and grimy, and she could detect the pungent scent of stress sweat overtaking the barrier of her clinical-strength deodorant. Under normal circumstances, she would have been horrified to have a man, other than Brice, touch her while she was in this condition. But Logan was a professional. He was a cop and trained to handle emergencies. The only thing she felt right now was relieved that he was here to help her.

"I'm not finding any other obvious injuries." Logan sat back on his heels. "That's the good news."

Josephine opened her eyes and blinked several times rapidly until her eyes adjusted to the sunlight. "And the bad news?"

"Your phone is in the cave and I left mine back at the ranch." He pulled a bottle of water from his sack. "I'm going to have to carry you out of here."

"Let's sit you up." Logan held out his arm, clasped her elbow with his hand, and eased her gently into the seated position.

Josephine took a couple of small sips of the water. She already felt like she needed to relieve her bladder. She handed the bottle back to him.

"Can you do that?" she asked him. With all of that muscle, he outweighed her for sure. But they were nearly the same height. How was he going to carry her all the way back to the ranch? It seemed like an unlikely plan.

He gave her a sharp look. "I can do it."

"I just meant—maybe I could stay here while you go get help."

"Negative." He stuffed the water bottle back into the pack and zipped it close. "I'm not leaving you behind." His attention returned to her. "When I start carrying you, it's going to put a lot of pressure on you. It's going to be a bumpy ride. If you think you need to relieve yourself, let's do it now."

Blunt, to the point. She wasn't used to that approach. But she could respect it. He was focused on getting her home safely. And her bladder did feel full and she imagined that the jostling was only going to make that worse.

"Yes." She nodded. "Thank you."

Logan picked her up in his arms and carried her to a spot, not too far away, but completely private for her to take care of business. When she was finished, he caught her hopping on one foot and was by her side. Once he had her situated on a flat boulder nearby, he disappeared into the woods for a moment himself. He returned quickly, split the last of the water with her, and then left his backpack near the entrance of the cave. Before he returned to her side, he closed the door to the cave and relocked it.

Josephine watched him silently. She had caused all of this mess because she had strayed away from the security of the walls of the cave. If she had been more cautious, they wouldn't be in this situation.

"I'm sorry about all of this," she thought to say.

"I don't want you to worry about that right now." He dried his palms off on his shorts. "We've got another challenge we need to manage together. Let's focus on that."

Logan helped her stand and then knelt down, his back facing her. He instructed her to climb aboard, yet she hesitated. Because she was tall, she was heavier than she looked. Yes, he outweighed her—but, by how much?

"Josephine." Firm and commanding, that was the tone he used. "I'm going to get you out of here, but I need you to cooperate. You've got to trust me."

Josephine knew she had to relinquish control. It was difficult, but it had to be done. As he had directed, she climbed onto his back and wrapped her arms around his neck. He hooked his arms beneath her thighs and then told her to "hold on and stay straight" while he stood up. He had thickly muscled thighs, but she was still surprised when he was able to stand with the weight of her body on his back.

"We're movin' out, Jo. Are you ready?" he asked.

She hadn't ridden on someone's back since she was a teenager. Back then, it had only been for a short distance and had been fun. This piggyback ride, on the other hand, wasn't any fun at all. Besides the expected pain from her injured foot and her scraped-up knees, her arms felt like they were being wrenched from her arm sockets and her shoulder muscles had started to burn soon after Logan started walking. It also seemed like they had to stop frequently so he could reposition her on his back. She had unintentionally choked him a couple of times, and because she wanted to watch where they were going, he had to remind her time and again, not to lean to one side or the other and throw them off balance.

"Need another break?" Logan's question broke the silence.

"Yes." The word was pushed out of her body as he shifted her into a more secure position.

They found a spot to rest near the stream. Logan took a folded, clean handkerchief out of his pocket and saturated it with the cold stream water. He brought if over to Josephine for her to cool off her face and neck.

"Thank you." She handed it back to him after she wiped off her face, neck, and the front of her chest.

While he rinsed the handkerchief in the stream for his use, she rubbed her sore shoulders.

"We've made some good progress." He stood in front of her, wiping the sweat off of his face and arms and chest, seemingly unaffected by the fact that he had just carried her for nearly half a mile. He was a little winded, and there was a flushed undertone to the tanned skin of his face, but other than that, carrying her didn't appear to have sapped much of his strength.

A couple more minutes and Logan insisted that they hit the trail once again. He was concerned about the swelling that had traveled past her ankle and into her calf. In silence, they traveled, along the shaded path that wound down the mountain. Exhausted, Josephine turned her head to the side and rested it on Logan's shoulder. She closed her eyes, and tried, *tried*, to ignore all of the places on her body that hurt while Logan pressed on. He was a determined, goal-oriented man—this much she had discovered about him. He was taking her safe return back to the ranch very personally.

"Hey!" Logan yelled.

Josephine's eyes snapped open. She lifted up her head and saw what had caught Logan's attention. Through the trees, she spotted a truck driving across the small pasture at the bottom of the mountain.

"Hold on to me tight, Jo!" Logan's big voice boomed in her ear. "I'm going to try to catch them!"

She clamped her thighs harder around his waist and forced herself to find a reserve of strength in her arms to hold on without strangling him. Logan leaned forward just a little bit more and started to half jog, half shuffle down the gradual incline to the bottom of the mountain. Once they cleared the tree line, they both screamed at the truck. Logan's breathing was labored now and her arms were wet with the sweat that was pouring off his face and neck. He didn't give up. She felt his legs give way, but he caught them and kept moving forward. He didn't stop until he heard her say to him excitedly, "They saw us!"

Logan stumbled again and he landed on his knees. "I've got to put you down. I'm sorry. I've got to put you down."

She rolled off his back and landed in the grass. Logan was kneeling beside her, head back, eyes closed as if he were in pain. He was breathing like he'd just run a marathon, his face was bright red, and his entire torso was drenched in sweat.

It was instinctive for her to reach out and touch his hand. "Are you okay?"

"Leg cramped up on me," he finally said. Then he opened his eyes to look at her. "I dropped you. I'm sorry."

"Please don't…" Her words were cut off by the sound of the truck door slamming and the sound of her brother's voice calling her name.

"Jo!" Tyler ran to her side. "What happened?"

"I slipped in the cave." Josephine explained in a rush. "Logan saved me."

There was a silent moment of gratitude that passed from her brother to Logan.

"She needs to have that foot x-rayed." Logan nodded to her bandaged foot.

Tyler nodded his understanding as he picked her up and carried her to the truck. Clint, one of the workers on the ranch, had dropped the bed of the truck down.

"Clint, grab that blanket, man. It's scorchin' back here."

Clint ran to the front of the truck, grabbed the blanket, and then fumbled his way through unfolding it. Once the blanket was in place, Tyler set her down on it. Tyler climbed in the back of the truck with her, while Clint got behind the wheel.

"Hop in, buddy!" Tyler waved his hand at Logan.

Logan was standing now, hands on his hips, still a little winded from the exertion he had used to bring her to safety.

"You go on and get Jo some help." He shook his head. "I left my pack back at the cave. I'm gonna go get it."

Tyler nodded and knocked on the glass so Clint

would know that they were ready to head back to the ranch. Clint drove in a semicircle onto the road. For a moment, Josephine couldn't see Logan. She twisted her head around. It was inexplicable—she didn't like the idea of losing sight of him. When was able to see him again, she experienced the oddest sense of relief.

Their eyes met, as if for the first time. The man, who had carried her down the mountain, stood on the road, his hands resting on his hips. Strong, sweaty, and sexier than any man she had ever seen. No words passed between them, but it seemed like the air was filled with silent words. Never taking his eyes off her, Logan trailed behind the slow moving truck with a noticeable limp. When he stopped moving, he lifted his hand up and waved it one single time. She waved back and continued to stare after him until the truck rounded the corner and he disappeared from view.

Later that evening, Josephine was stretched out on the couch in "wedding central" with her foot elevated. It was a severe sprain, not a fracture, which was a relief. She wouldn't have to hobble down the church aisle with a cast on her foot. It wasn't the best outcome, but it certainly wasn't the worst either. Much worse could have happened to her if it weren't for Logan's quick thinking.

Logan.

He had been on her mind. She had hoped to see him at the dinner table, but he didn't join the family for dinner. Tyler mentioned that he had returned to the cabin, so at least she knew that he had returned from the mountain safely.

"Your brother told me that it's not fractured. That's good news, right?"

Josephine looked up from the pile of RSVPs she was cataloging. She had been so completely focused in her own world, and perhaps a bit foggy from the Tylenol 3, that she didn't hear his footsteps on the hardwood floors.

She put down the RSVP on her lap and smiled at him. "Hey. We missed you at dinner."

"I was beat." Logan was still standing in the doorway. "I fell asleep and just woke up a while ago."

"I bet." She nodded. "Do you want to sit down?"

"I don't want to wear you out," he said.

"You won't." She wanted him to stay. "I need company."

Logan sat down on the ottoman that was just across from the couch. She could tell that he was fresh out of the shower—the air had the clean, crisp scent of soap and shampoo.

She smiled at him affectionately. "I really need to thank you for what you did for me today."

He leaned forward, forearms resting on his thighs, hands clasped together. "You don't need to thank me. I was just doing my job."

He had such a nice mouth.

"I know," she said. "But, I still need to thank you. So—thank you."

"You're welcome." He smiled briefly with a slight nod. "Did you have a chance to talk to Brice?"

Josephine felt her chest tighten when Logan mentioned Brice's name. She still felt sick to her stomach when she heard it, and he was the last person she wanted to talk about.

"Why do you ask?" She tried, very hard, to keep her voice as normal as possible.

He was a cop, so he was trained to notice small details. There was a slight shift in his dark brown eyes— she was sure certain he had detected something odd in her voice and her question.

He responded. "You were out hiking alone with a guy he doesn't know. Some people still don't believe that men and women can be friends."

"Oh." She had a frown etched into her brow that she couldn't control. "Well, you don't have to worry about that. Brice and I aren't together anymore."

It took him a second to process her statement. He had been worried, for Josephine's sake, about Brice's reaction. He had also been worried that a bad reaction from Brice would taint his budding friendship with Josephine.

There was a moment when he looked directly into her bright, aqua-blue eyes and she didn't look away. And that's when he read the hurt in her eyes that wasn't a result of her sprained ankle—it was a direct result of her broken heart.

"I'm sorry to hear that…" he finally said. It was the standard answer that was given in a situation like this and his delivery had sounded sincere. But, was it true? Was he really *sorry to hear* that Brice had done a truly stupid thing by letting Josephine Brand slip through his fingers?

No. He wasn't. Not one bit.

Chapter 8

That first visit rolled into the next, and soon Logan was coming to check on her every afternoon after he had finished working on the relocation of the chapel. She had begun to count on those visits. She had begun to look forward to them. In fact, she had started to look at the clock, anticipating his arrival. And if he was late, she felt disappointed. Yes, she had plenty of things to keep her busy while she let her foot heal—she was getting a ton of schoolwork done and she loved immersing herself in the wedding with her mom and Jordan. But, her daily visit from Logan was what she looked forward to the most.

"Jo." Her sister's voice interrupted her internal dialogue. *"Jo!"*

Josephine shifted her eyes from the window to her

sister, who was now standing in front of her wearing her wedding dress.

"Oh, Jordy—it's beyond." She set her laptop off to the side and swung her legs off the couch.

Her sister had chosen an Eve of Milady wedding gown from the couture line. The sweetheart bodice was hand-beaded and the fit-and-flare long skirt was made of fine silk organza. There was an edge to the gown, with its completely sheer back, that matched Jordan's personality perfectly.

She stood up. She need to get a closer look at the gown she had helped her sister select. When she eventually married, she wanted to wear a ball gown. But this sleek, sophisticated silhouette was her twin to a tee.

Her foot felt like it was almost healed when she walked the couple of steps over to where Jordan was standing.

"Have you seen yourself?" she asked her sister.

Jordan nodded. "Would you zip the back for me?"

Josephine raised the zipper carefully. "Where's Mom? She should be here for this."

She was about to call out for their mom, but Jordan stopped her.

"I want it to be just the two of us for a minute. Then we'll call Mom. Okay?"

"Okay," Josephine said with a question in her tone.

Her sister turned around to face her and they naturally reached for each other's hands. Quietly, Josephine admired her twin and the beauty of the dress.

"You are so stunning in this gown, Jordy—you take my breath away."

"Thanks, sis." Jordy hugged her before she asked, "Are you okay, though? I mean, *really* okay?"

Josephine glanced down at her ankle and moved it around. "I'm almost back to 100 percent."

"I didn't mean that. I meant, are you okay with the wedding? With what happened with Brice."

Whenever Brice's name came up, her stomach muscles tightened unpleasantly. Why did everyone insist on talking about him? When she was dating him, no one wanted to talk about him. Now that they were broken up—she couldn't get them to *stop*!

Josephine took a step back and said with a stiff smile. "Let's not ruin a perfectly wonderful moment by bringing up the *B* word. Okay?"

Ever since they were little girls, they could feel each other's pain. Josephine knew that Jordan could feel her pain now. The forced smile didn't fool her.

"You're right. I shouldn't've brought up the jerk. My bad. I'm just worried…the wedding is making you sad."

"*Sad?* What are you talking about? You know I love weddings. If anything, helping you and Mom with all of the planning has kept my mind occupied."

"No. I know you love weddings, Jo. It's just that both of us always thought that you'd get married first…"

"Well, that's how it turned out and that's okay." Josephine met her sister's eyes and held them to make certain Jordan understood that she was sincere. "Yes, I've been feeling a little sad. But, it doesn't have anything to do with your wedding. *That* only makes me feel happy."

Her sister's reply was waylaid by the sound of grinding gears and squealing brakes. Josephine and her sister's attention turned to the commotion outside.

"Looks like they're pouring the foundation today." Jordan moved closer to the window.

Josephine joined her. Her eyes searched the site up on the hill where the new chapel foundation was being poured; when she found Logan, her search was over. He had just jumped down from the cab of a large earth mover. It was easy to distinguish him from the other men. The size of the muscles of his bare arms and shoulders, the blackness of his hair—he stood out.

"Don't you just love a man with big equipment?" her sister asked her.

She could feel Jordan staring at her knowingly—she had been caught staring at Logan. There was no sense trying to deny it.

"Brice who, right?" Jordan asked, rhetorically.

"Quit bringing up Brice! I don't want to talk about him."

"An honest mistake," Jordan confessed. "Let's go show Mom my dress."

"Sounds like a plan. Let me grab this box of tissues. You know that waterworks are going to flow the minute Mom sees you."

After dinner, Josephine walked, for the first time without crutches, out to the campfire. She passed Jordan, Ian, and Shadow on their way to the guesthouse. When she reached the edge of the fire, Tyler stood up and handed Logan his guitar.

"Where are you going?" she asked her brother.

"Hittin' the hay." Tyler adjusted his hat on his head. "I'm plumb wore out, sissy."

Her father flicked the stub of his cigar into the fire

and stood up. "I suppose it's time for me to hit the hay, too."

"What? I show up and everyone clears out?" Josephine said, half teasing, half serious, as she hugged her father good-night.

She called after Hank. "I can smell the smoke on your shirt, Dad!"

She heard her father laugh before he called back to her, "It'll clear off before I get back to the house."

Josephine looked after her father and brother for a minute and then, arms crossed over her chest, she asked Logan in a playfully stern tone, "I suppose you're going in now, too?"

Logan looked up from the task of tuning her brother's old guitar. "Not me. I made the mistake of having two cups of coffee at dinner, so…sleep's going to be a long time comin'." He nodded to the seat next to him. "Keep me company."

Josephine didn't have to think about whether or not she wanted to join him. She did. Logan had an easy-going nature that she appreciated. It was in stark contrast to her personality, and it was certainly in contrast to Brice's conservative, rigid, type-A personality. She tried not to compare them, but found it almost impossible *not to* compare them. And, even though Brice's personality was so close to hers, and she was attracted to his serious, always-on-task persona, Logan's laid-back, devil-may-care attitude was a refreshing change. Was it a change that she wanted for the long term? She wasn't sure about that. Brice had always been the plan in her head and it was hard to imagine walking through life with another man—especially a man who was so dif-

ferent than Brice. But, for now, it felt…comfortable…
to be with Logan.

Josephine grabbed a nearby stick and poked the logs
in the fire pit to stoke the small flames. She was wearing a long-sleeved top made of thin cotton, and wished
now that she had grabbed her lightweight jacket before
she headed out of the house. But, she had been in a rush
to get down to the campfire. She had been cooped up
in the house healing her ankle all week and she felt a
little stir-crazy. And, if she were honest to herself, she
wanted to see Logan. He hadn't stopped by to see her,
as was usual, and he wasn't at dinner. Her brother mentioned that Logan was video chatting with his uncle,
making the final arrangements for relocating the chapel.

"Here, you look cold." Logan leaned toward her, his
arm extended, holding out a rolled flannel shirt.

"Don't you need it?" She took the shirt gratefully.

"Nah, I'm good." He strummed lightly on the guitar
strings. "Got any requests?"

She slipped her arms into the shirt and pulled it
tightly in front of her, then crossed her arms once again.
She rocked back and forth a little while she thought.

"Surprise me," she finally said.

"You like James Taylor?"

Surprised, she smiled at him. "Love him."

"Me, too…"

Tucked warmly inside of his shirt, a shirt that looked
like it had seen a lot of years and use, Logan began to
play her favorite James Taylor song, "Fire and Rain."
She had heard his singing voice when he sang to her in
the cave to keep her calm. He had a beautiful voice—
the kind of voice that made a woman stop and listen.

The kind of voice that sent chills popping up all over her body.

In the firelight, Josephine watched Logan as he played the guitar and sang. He was giving her a private concert, and the moment was—special. Intimate. It was the perfect setting, and the perfect moment, for lovers. Even though they weren't lovers, there was a connection there. She felt it, and she could tell that Logan felt it too.

She had always found him to be handsome, ever since the first day. It was undeniable. The dark hair, tanned skin, eyes the color of aged brandy. Not to mention his incredibly fit body. But when she first met him, she had been Brice's girl. His handsomeness hadn't mattered.

She wasn't Brice's girl anymore, was she? And Logan's handsomeness had become much more interesting to her lately.

At the end of the song, Logan looked over at Josephine. Her eyes were closed and the light from the fire was casting a beautiful array of yellow and gold across the delicate features of her face. Halfway through the song, she had started to sing with him. And their voices were a perfect complement. There had been only one other woman whose voice had complemented his voice, with whom he loved to sing duets, but he could hardly remember what it felt like to sing with her. This moment—this night—was all about lovely, sweet Josephine.

"You have a really good voice. I didn't know you sang." He smiled at her.

Josephine's aqua-blue eyes opened wide, in surprise. "I didn't realize I was singing out loud."

He could feel her embarrassment, as much as he could see it. "You should sing out loud all the time."

"Only in the shower."

"That's too bad. You've got a great voice."

She smiled at him, almost shyly. "I was a choir geek all through high school."

Logan stroked the strings, one by one, with his thumb. "I tried to date all the choir geeks in high school."

"Oh, yeah?" She leaned forward and rested her elbows on her legs. "Any luck?"

"Some." His answer was casual, but Josephine detected a deeper undercurrent beneath that one, simple word. "Give me another song—one that you like to sing. I might know it," he said.

"Um, let me think. You wouldn't happen to know any Judds' songs, would you?"

Logan played a couple of chords. "Do you know the lyrics to this one?"

"'Why Not Me,'" she said. Logan had an uncanny ability to pick her favorite songs. Brice hated country music, so she had stopped listening to it when he was around to be courteous. What was strange, and she hadn't really thought about it until just now, but she had stopped singing when Brice was around several years ago.

"You sing. I'll play."

"No way, Jose! If I sing, you sing."

"Alright," he agreed. "Do you want to be Mamma Judd or Wynonna?"

"Wynonna."

"I was afraid you were going to say that." Logan shook his head with a small smile.

Beneath the large expanse of the blue-black starless sky, they sang their first song together. She hadn't sung a duet since high school, and singing with Logan was as natural as walking or talking. They just fit. They were able to pick harmony together and anticipate what the other would do next. In singing, at least, they were a compatible pair.

By the end of the song, Josephine was laughing. She wasn't laughing because anything was funny—but because singing again had made her feel good inside.

"You're really good, Josephine." Logan rested his arm on the top of the guitar, which was resting on his thigh.

"No, you're good." Josephine beamed at him. "Who taught you to sing like that?"

"My mom, mainly—and singing in church." He slipped the guitar pick between two strings. "How 'bout you?"

"The same. You should hear my mom sing. She's really got some amazing pipes."

Logan stood up, stretched, and then held out his hand to her. "So do you."

She didn't argue with him—instead, she took his offered hand and stood up as well.

"Looks like your ankle's healing nicely," he said, looking down at her foot.

"Can't complain." She held out her foot a little. "Now, if only my replacement phone would get here, everything'll be copacetic. What a stupid move that was—my whole life was on that phone."

He walked beside her, keeping pace with her slow pace as they headed back toward the ranch house.

"Maybe you needed a break," he suggested quietly. "Maybe you needed to start over."

"Maybe," she agreed thoughtfully. "Maybe."

When her replacement phone arrived, she couldn't wait to get it out of the box. It had felt like she had been missing a vital appendage without her constant phone companion. However, once it was out of the box and she had it set up just like her "lost forever to the cave" phone, she had a serious lapse in judgment and checked social media.

She had actually thought that she was doing fine—that she was handling the sudden "dumping" from her first love pretty well. Yes, there had been a couple of nights that she had cried herself to sleep in the fetal position, but she wasn't thinking about Brice every minute of every day and she hadn't allowed herself to dwell on trying to create a mental picture in her head of the woman who had captivated him.

Once she checked social media, she was reminded again what the other woman looked like. Brice had put posted several pictures of himself, *at his parents' estate*, with a knock-out brunette with a Sofía Vergara–type body. All Josephine could do, for several long, painful seconds was to stare at the new woman in Brice's life. Brains, beauty, and a bangin' body—no wonder he'd defected.

Josephine slammed the phone facedown on her comforter and flopped back onto the pillows. She couldn't *un-see* those pictures—she only wished that she could.

Her hand moved to her chest. Brice had always told her that he didn't mind her size A cups. He'd given her the "brains over boobs" speech on several occasions. And yet, in the end, he'd traded her in for a shiny new floor model that came standard-equipped with brains *and* boobs.

She grabbed her pillow, covered her face, and screamed as loud as she could. Then she did it again. That picture triggered all of the jealousy and disappointment and anger she had suppressed. It was bubbling to the surface like magma pouring out of a volcano.

She wanted to hit something. She wanted to kick something. In all honesty, she really wanted to punch Brice in his stupid face!

Josephine pushed the pillow off her face and sat upright. She needed to go outside and clear her head. She had intended to study, but now she couldn't. She just *couldn't.*

She swung her long legs off the bed, yanked on her hiking boots, and headed downstairs. Her plan was to race past the kitchen, where her mom was sure to be, and get outside without talking to anyone. She hit the second floor landing and smelled the delicious scent of homemade root beer and sweet-potato pie. Since her daughters had arrived home, her mom had spent at least part of her day happily baking homemade goodies that she knew that they loved.

As she raced past the kitchen entrance, Josephine called to her mom, "I'll be outside if you need me."

Not waiting for her mom's answer, she shot out the door, slammed it behind her harder than she had intended, and then hurried down the porch steps. She needed a place where she could be alone—a place where she could unleash some of this newfound fury without an audience. And she was going to go there right now.

Logan pulled one of Bent Tree's trucks in a spot near the barn and turned off the engine. He noticed Josephine walking quickly toward a small structure that was farther away from the working barns. He didn't know what was in that building—from the looks of it, he'd assumed that it was an old storage barn. Josephine always caught his attention—he was always hoping to catch sight of her. Not only was she easy-on-the-eyes, but he liked her. He *really* liked her. He had started to know her mannerisms—the way she walked, the way she talked, the way her eyes twinkled when she smiled. Today, there was something different about her. Her shoulders were stiff, her hands were balled up, and she was looking down at the ground.

Perhaps it was the wrong thing to do, he acted on gut-instinct alone, but he followed her. He got out of the truck without giving it much thought and went after her. When he was close to the building, he could hear faint sounds drifting through the cracked-open door. It sounded like *grunting*, and he hoped he wasn't about to come upon something that he really didn't want to see.

Logan opened the door wide enough for him to look inside. In the middle of the small building, hanging from the rafters, was an old heavyweight punching bag. The only light that was coming into the building was from the areas of the walls where the wooden planks were missing. Josephine was standing in front of the bag, oblivious that he was watching from the doorway, intent on beating the bag with her small fist.

The expression on her face, in what he assumed to be an unmasked, private moment, could only be described as anguished. Sweat had darkened the hair around her face and long pieces were stuck to the side of her neck as she pounded the bag with the side of her hand. She hit the bag again and again. He thought she would notice him; when she didn't, he started to believe that perhaps it was best that she hadn't.

Logan took a step back from the door, and turned to leave. But when he heard her curse and yell "Ow," he changed his mind.

"You're hitting it wrong." He pushed the door to the building open wider to let the light in.

Winded and sweaty and disheveled, Josephine stared at him. She didn't bother to try to hide the raw pain in her eyes when he got closer to her. And she didn't tell him to leave.

"You're hitting like a girl."

"I *am* a girl."

"No, I meant that if you keep hitting it like that you're going to hurt your hand," he told her.

"Then show me the right way," she snapped.

She didn't apologize for snapping at him, and he didn't expect one. They both knew that he was the one invading her privacy.

"First we need to get your stance solid." Logan adopted a fighting stance, his right foot back, his left foot forward, his knees slightly bent. He waited for Josephine to copy him and then showed her the proper way to punch.

"Ball your fingers up firmly, with your thumb wrapped around your pointer finger—like this…" He instructed. "Now put both of your arms up to protect your face and your chest—like so—your elbows are in to protect your ribs. When you punch…" He demonstrated by showing her how to execute a forward jab. "Your arm comes out straight—at this point, your fingers should be relaxed, and right before your impact of your target, that's when you tighten your fist up."

Logan stepped closer to her, took the spot in front of the bag, and punched the bag hard.

The rusty chain holding up the bag creaked when it swung back toward them. Logan caught the dusty bag to stop it from swinging.

"Now you do it," he told her.

Josephine adopted the fighting stance, balled up her fist, and held up her arms, just like he had instructed. Then, with a straight arm and solid follow-through, she jabbed the dirty punching bag. To her ears, the bag made a satisfying "thud" sound when she hit it.

"That really felt good." She smiled at Logan with a natural, satisfied smile. "I'm doing that again."

Chapter 9

For the next hour, Josephine learned how to punch the bag properly. Logan taught her how to jab the bag, slow and steady, without hurting her hand. And then he showed her how to rapid punch using both hands. Once she had the hang of it, Logan stepped behind the bag and held it in place so she could hit the bag as many times as she wanted. He didn't say a word and she was glad he didn't. She wanted to focus on punching the bag, again and again and again.

Every time she hit the bag, she imagined that she was hitting Brice. In her mind, with every strike, she was yelling at him.

You stupid jerk! You pompous ass! I trusted you! I loved you! I wasted five years of my life on you! And you ruined everything!

She hit the bag and hit the bag and hit the bag until

her arms ached and her knuckles were red. When she was too tired to throw one more punch, she sat down on the ground and tried to catch her breath. She was completely spent physically, and she felt better mentally.

Logan joined her. "Feel better?"

Her head was lowered, her knees bent, her arms wrapped around her shins. She nodded "yes."

In silence, they sat on the dirt floor of the abandoned storage shed, while Josephine had a chance to recover. So much of her anger had been spent, but what was left, what remained, was a deep sense of loss. A deep sense of sadness. Brice had been a big part of her life—he had been more than her lover. He had been her confidant, her best friend. They had talked every day and he was the first one she called when something exciting happened to her. But now, all of that was gone. It felt like a death.

She couldn't stop what happened next. She couldn't help what happened next. The tears started to pour out of her eyes, as if they were flowing directly from her heart onto the cheeks of her face. She pressed her forehead hard onto her knees and bear-hugged her legs so tightly that her arm muscles shook from the strain.

Josephine felt Logan move closer, felt him put his arm around her shoulders for support. She didn't pull away, but she couldn't fully accept him, either. She stiffened beneath the weight of his arm and couldn't lean on him. Brice was the one who was supposed to give her comfort and support. Brice was The One. But he was gone. She knew that now. A picture speaks a thousand words, the saying goes, and seeing Brice at his parents' house with Caroline told her more than she wanted to know. He looked happy. Had he ever looked that happy in pictures with her?

"No!" She answered the question in her head out loud with a shake of her bent head.

She sniffed loudly, trying to get some air through her clogged nose. Unable to breathe through her nose at the moment, she took a breath in through her mouth and used her shirt to wipe the tears from her face. She pulled away from Logan, and he dropped his arm right away.

Josephine stood up, and Logan followed. She turned her face away from him, embarrassed.

"You must think I'm a real nut job," she said.

"No," he said, quietly. "I think you're grieving."

His response was intuitive and showed a sensitivity that surprised her. Arms crossed tightly in front of her body, Josephine glanced at him.

Logan saw the question in her eyes. "I've been in your shoes."

"Who did you lose?" she asked.

"My wife."

Josephine looked directly into his eyes—unshuttered eyes that let her glimpse the heart inside of the man.

"Did she die?" It was an inelegant question, but she wanted to know. She hadn't even known that he had been married.

"No," he said. "But it felt like she had."

"What happened?"

Logan didn't turn look away when he said, "I wasn't enough for her. She wanted something else. Someone else."

"I'm sorry," she said, and she meant it. She was sorry

for anyone who had felt the same kind of sharp pain she was feeling right now.

"It was a long time ago and I've moved on."

"Well…at least there's a little hope for me yet."

"There's hope—just don't let yourself get stuck."

She knew exactly what he meant. He was telling her not to wallow. Mourn and then move on, because Brice already had.

Logan pushed the door open wider and let her walk through first. The bright sun hurt her eyes, but the heat, which she normally liked, only made her feel hotter and stickier. A shower was the only solution.

On the walk back to the house, she asked, "Where'd you learn to box like that, anyway?"

"When you're the scrawniest, shortest little kid in the neighborhood, you either learn how to fight or you accept getting the crap beat out of you on a weekly basis. I figured I couldn't force myself to grow, but I knew I could learn how to fight. So, I did."

She looked at his profile. It was a strong profile. Not aristocratic, like Brice's profile—it was more rugged, more masculine.

"Did the bullies leave you alone?"

"Yeah, they figured out pretty quick not to mess with me anymore. I was little, but I had heart. That's what my uncle called it anyway. All I knew was that I was tired of getting my block knocked off every week."

They both stopped a few feet away from the porch, away from the kitchen windows. "You'll be okay, then, right?"

"Oh, sure." She tried to sound upbeat. "I feel better

already. I'm not going to tell any of my fellow pacifists this, but punching does have its perks."

"You're planning to go with us tonight, aren't you?"

Jordan, Ian, her brother, and Logan were all going into town for some dancing and drinking. She had intended to beg off, but now, after having seen Brice out having a great time with his new love interest, she knew that sitting home moping wasn't the answer. She needed to go out and have some fun.

"I'm going." She stopped a few feet away from the porch, away from the kitchen windows. "How do I look?"

"Like you've been crying." Logan examined her face with a critical eye. He slipped off his sunglasses and gave them to her. "Here—wear these."

Josephine put the sunglasses on and then looked at him. "How about now?"

"Beautiful."

She had already discovered that Logan was an honest man, sometimes to the point of being blunt. So she knew that he meant what he said. And, in that moment, perhaps even more so than any other moment, she needed a little ego boost. Being told by a good-looking cop that she was beautiful qualified as a definite ego boost in her book.

"You're a good friend, Logan."

"I try to be," he said. "So, I'll catch you later, then. I've got to get back to work. We're moving the chapel in one day."

"All you've done is work on your vacation," she noted. "When are you going to relax and have some fun?"

Logan smiled at her, walked backward a couple of steps, and lifted both of his hands to gesture to the ranch and the mountains.

"Are you kidding me?" He laughed. "This *is* my paradise."

After Josephine took a long shower, she lay on her bed with a cold washcloth over her eyes. Her eyes were puffy and they stung. And even after several cold washcloth sessions, her eyes still looked like she'd been crying. Her eyes were too sore to study, and she didn't feel like staying cooped up inside anyway. She wouldn't mind working on the wedding, but she didn't feel like explaining her appearance to her mom, which would only lead to yet another discussion about Brice and her "feelings." Instead, she decided to go for a ride.

"Hey. Where're all the horses?" Josephine looked around the empty stable.

London Davenport, an intern from Montana State University, answered her rhetorical question. "Your brother told me to turn them all out in the north pasture. So, that's what I did."

"Well, shoot." Josephine frowned, hands on her hips.

London shoveled a large pile of manure and hay into her cart before she closed the stall door. London loaded her pitchfork onto the cart and moved the cart to the next stall.

"You could always take Easy," the intern suggested.

Josephine grimaced at the thought. Easy Does It was the offspring of her grandfather's donkey Nomad and one of Bent Tree's purebred quarter horses. It was an accidental coupling that produced a mule that completely embodied the phrase "stubborn as a mule." Yet he was beloved by all of them and had become a Bent Tree mascot of sorts.

The mule seemed to recognize that they were talking about him, that they were suggesting that he participate in some sort of undesirable physical exertion, and he turned around so his narrow butt was facing them. It was all the challenge that Josephine needed. She had a rather unfortunate history with this mule, and even though he had outsmarted her before, she was certain that today redemption was within her grasp.

"He looks like he could use some fresh air," she said to London.

London looked at her like she was crazy, and she probably was. "That mule is so barn sour and stuffed full of hay that it's gonna take the two of us to get him out of that stall, you know."

"Are you up for it?"

London was a tall, Nordic-looking blonde who was one of the few women she'd ever met who was taller than she was. The intern had a ranch-wide reputation for being as strong, and as determined, as most of the men.

London gave her a nod. "Just give me a shout when you're ready."

Josephine groomed, saddled, and bridled the mule. And then, she couldn't get the mule out of the stall.

"Need help?" London came up behind her.

"I was hoping that I could convince him to follow me, seeing as we're old friends and all." Josephine frowned at the mule that refused to cross the threshold of the stall into the aisle. "But no such luck."

The intern held up a feed bucket. "This is the only way to get Easy out of the stall nowadays."

With a lot of patience and coaxing and sweet feed, Easy Does It finally put one hoof over the threshold.

"It's going to be dark by the time I get him out of the stall!" Josephine complained.

"He's counting on the fact that you're going to give up." London laughed as she shook the feed bucket just out of the reach of the mule's searching lips.

"Not a chance," Josephine vowed. "I'm going to win this round."

And she did. With London's help, they managed to convince Easy to walk, at a painstakingly slow pace, out of the stall and out of the stable. Josephine easily mounted the short-statured mule and then she squeezed her legs around Easy's hay-filled belly to signal that he should move forward. But he didn't budge.

"Darn it, Easy! Go!" She wiggled a little back and forth to encourage the mule to take one step forward.

She sat on the mule's back, in the same spot, not moving, for a good five minutes before London had mercy on her and came out of the stable carrying the trusty feed bucket. London got Easy moving, and then once he was moving forward, Josephine was able to keep the momentum going.

"Thank you, London!" she called over her shoulder. "Come on, Easy! You can do it!"

She decided to take the road that would eventually take her in the direction of the chapel. Once they made it through the gate, and Easy caught a glimpse of the field ahead, he started to jog. Easy's trot was a choppy, bone-jarring gait that was impossible to ride comfortably. She couldn't sit in the saddle for it, and she had to post at double pace—up, down, up, down, up, down, up!

Easy wasn't easy to get started, but as was fitting with his contrary personality, he was also hard to stop. His jog turned into a canter.

"Whoa! Easy does it, Easy!" She tightened the reins to slow him down.

Easy ignored her command and took off across the field. Josephine grabbed a chunk of his wiry mane, held on, and decided to let him run it out. This was how Easy Does It got his name after all—when her brother first tried to ride him, the entire family could hear him screaming, "Hey! Easy does it, mule! Easy does it!" at the mule when it bolted across the field.

Across the field, Easy's short legs churned until he was tired and then he halted out of the blue. Holding on to the mane stopped her from being catapulted over his head and onto the ground.

"Really, Easy?" She exclaimed loudly. "Really?"

It was a good thing that he had stopped. But getting him started again proved to be a chore. She had imagined herself galloping across the open fields of the ranch, the wind on her face and blowing through her hair. She had imagined a movie scene kind of moment. Instead, she got a Comedy Central kind of moment. She was stuck, in a field, astride an obese, spoiled mascot mule, hot *and* thirsty. She had forgotten to put on bug spray, so there were random bugs buzzing around her, harassing her, harassing Easy, and on top of everything, she seriously needed to pee after suffering the mule's torturous trot.

Josephine moved her hips back and forth. "Move, Easy! Come *on*! Move!"

But she knew he wasn't going to move. In fact, she knew that Easy could stand there for the rest of the day, not moving a muscle. He'd had his run and now he was done. He wasn't about to go one more step in the direction that was taking him away from his stall.

"Fine!" Josephine gave up and gave in. "Easy Does It, two. Josephine Brand, *zero*!"

She turned the mule to the left and Easy headed back to the barn with an animated, brisk walk. The longer she sat in the saddle, the more pain she was starting to feel in her bladder. There was no way she was making it back to the barn without making a pit stop first.

When she asked Easy to stop, and he *did*, she was pleasantly surprised. She tied his reins to a nearby tree and carefully stepped into the brush. She hadn't finished relieving herself when she heard the horrible sound of hooves pounding on dirt.

"Darn it, Easy! Don't you *dare*!" She yanked up her pants halfway and hopped over the brush onto the road.

The mule had managed to untie the reins and was running like a Kentucky Thoroughbred back to the barn. Josephine watched the mule's hind end get smaller and smaller, until he completely disappeared.

"This day sucks!" She threw up her hands. "This day *seriously* sucks!"

She couldn't believe that the mule had managed to leave her stranded *twice* in one lifetime. She quickly zipped up her pants and began the long schlep back to the ranch. Frustrated, annoyed, angry—more emotions sprang up unbidden. Tears, coming from a place of exasperation rather than sadness, ran down her cheeks while she marched forward.

At the halfway mark, Josephine heard the sound of a vehicle coming up the road behind her. She wiped the residual tears from her face onto her T-shirt, and then turned around to see who it was.

"Really?" She looked up at the sky.

It was Logan. How many times did he need to see her at her worst in one day?

"Need a ride?" Logan stopped the truck next to her.

"Yes," she said bitterly. "My mule left me stranded."

"What?" Logan laughed.

She hopped in next to him and slammed the door shut. "That stupid mule, Easy! He managed to untie the reins and then he just took off!"

Logan was still laughing as he shifted into Drive and pressed on the gas. "Why were you riding a mule in the first place?"

"Because Tyler told the intern to turn out all of the horses in north pasture—it was the mule or nothing. I chose the mule." Her social mask had slipped and she couldn't manage pleasantness at the moment.

"You're not having the best day, are you?"

"No." Josephine smashed a mosquito that had dared to land on the truck's dash. "I'm not."

"Well—at least you have tonight to look forward to. You'll dance, you'll drink a little…" Logan told her. "It'll be like today never happened…"

"I'm not going." She stared out the window. Her ability to "rally" and "press on" had vanished along with her mule.

"Oh, come on. You don't want to sit at home and mope…"

"Yes, I do."

He ignored her comment and continued. "I was counting on you to teach me how to do the two-step. I'm a pretty liberal guy, but I'm not going to ask Tyler to teach me."

She turned her head to look at him. "You really want to learn how to line dance? Why?"

"I want the complete cowboy experience while I'm here." Logan smiled at her. "So you've got to come out with us and show me how to dance like a real cowboy. Fair's fair…" He added. "I taught you how to punch, so you should teach me how to dance. One good turn deserves another, don't you think?"

Logan pulled the truck into an empty space in front of the barn and shifted into Park. Through the windshield, Josephine could see Easy was in the paddock attached to his stall and he was munching on a pad of hay. She had sent a text to London to let her know not to send search and rescue out, that she was "okay" and that Easy was heading her way. London offered to come pick her up, but she hadn't wanted the intern to see her crying. But Logan had already seen her cry—so she had taken the ride.

"Jo, what do you think?" Logan asked her.

"Why do you call me 'Jo'?" Hand on the door, Josephine told him, "Only my closest friends and family call me that."

"I don't know. Just seemed natural, I suppose." Logan stopped smiling. "Do you want me to stop?"

"No…" She shook her head. "I was just thinking out loud, really."

Josephine got out of the truck and shut the door behind her. Logan quickly followed her lead, got out, and met her at the back of the truck.

"Thanks for the ride, Logan," she said, walking toward the house. "I'll see you later."

Logan stopped walking, sensing that she needed to be alone. "As in, see you later tonight?"

She nodded. "I'll come. I wouldn't wish line dancing with my brother on my worst enemy, much less a friend."

Logan watched Josephine walk slowly to the house, her long, golden-brown ponytail swaying from one side to the other. He had been attracted to her physically from the beginning when he had pulled her over for speeding. Now that he had gotten to know her, as a woman, as a friend, he knew that there was much more to Josephine than just her pretty face. She was a kind woman—a generous woman, intelligent, humorous. Loyal. Yes, she was a little uptight and structured, but when it came to Josephine, those qualities were endearing to him. He wanted Brice's loss to be his gain. And he didn't know how he was going to manage it, but he fully intended to get the heck out of the "friend zone" ASAP.

Chapter 10

"Hi, sweetheart. Don't you look nice," her mom said to her when she stepped out onto the porch.

Even though they didn't get to see each other much during the day, it was a ritual for her parents to sit on the porch swing together after dinner. They had the kind of marriage that Josephine had always wanted for herself. Her father adored her mother, and her mother adored him right back. After more than forty years of marriage and raising five children, they still hugged and kissed and laughed together.

"Why don't the two of you come with?" Josephine gave her father a hug.

"No…" Her mother smiled with a shake of her head. "I'm going to spend a quiet night alone with your father for a change."

"Honey, I don't know how quiet of a night it's going

to be…looks like one of the mares is about to give birth," Hank said. "Tyler'll be staying behind tonight either way."

Josephine nodded her understanding. That's how life had always been on the ranch—plans were always tentative because the health of the animals came first.

"Good evening."

Josephine turned toward the sound of Logan's familiar voice. This time, when she heard his voice, something different happened—she felt a nervous excitement in the pit of her stomach.

"Evening, son." Hank smiled easily at Logan. "How are we set for tomorrow?"

It was still hard for her to adjust to Hank referring to Logan as "son." He hadn't started to refer to Ian with that title and he certainly never came close with Brice. But, whether she thought it was appropriate or not, she could see the respect in her father's clear, deeply set blue eyes whenever he interacted with the San Diego cop.

"We're set, sir." Logan rested his arms on the porch railing. "As long as it doesn't rain, we're bringing her down the mountain tomorrow."

Her father looked satisfied and her mother looked irritated. Barbara was displeased with her husband's decision to start such a major project with the June wedding on the horizon. Hank wouldn't be dissuaded. He was determined, as a wedding gift to Jordan, for the chapel to be relocated and presentable for wedding pictures. Her mom was used to getting her way with her father, but not this time.

Logan made it a point to chat with Josephine's parents. Yes, he liked them, but he also knew how close she was with her parents and he wanted her to see that they accepted him. It could only work in his favor.

"Well, we better get going. Are you ready?" he asked Josephine.

He had always thought she was a beauty, from first sight. Yet, tonight, unbelievably, she looked even more radiant to his eyes. She wore her golden-brown hair long and loose, and the little touches of makeup she had applied enhanced the brightness of her turquoise-blue eyes, the highness of her cheekbones, and the fullness of her lips. He had to remind himself not to stare at her face.

Josephine nodded and met him at the bottom of the porch stairs.

"You're dressed like a bona fide cowboy." She gave him a quick once-over.

He glanced down at his getup. The yoked cotton shirt and brown cowboy hat were loaners from Tyler's closet.

"When in Montana…" he said.

Now that she was standing next to him, he could smell the sweet honeysuckle fragrance that he had come to associate with Josephine.

"You look uncomfortable." She laughed gently.

"I feel kind of uncomfortable," he admitted and tugged at the borrowed belt. "Maybe I should change."

"No. Don't change. You look good." She reached up and unbuttoned the top button of his shirt. "You just need to loosen up a little bit, that's all. You aren't on duty right now, so you don't have to have everything tucked in so tight."

Logan tugged at his shirt to loosen it per her instructions. He was used to having his shirts tucked to regulation uniform standards and it was hard for him to leave a button-down shirt loosely tucked. But if that was how Josephine preferred it, he was willing to make the adjustment.

"How's that?"

"Good."

"Watch out for my girl, son." Hank had been watching them closely.

"And have a good time..." Barbara added.

They both said good-night to her parents before they met Jordan and Ian at the truck. Jordan got behind the wheel, Ian took shotgun, and Josephine climbed into the back of the cab with Logan.

Her sister put the key in the ignition. "Are you sure you don't want to drive, GQ?"

Josephine glanced over at Logan—he had noticed the unusual tension between Ian and Jordan, too.

"What's wrong?" Josephine asked her sister.

"Oh, nothing," Jordan said in a sarcastic, singsong tone. "Tyler thought it would be a good idea for Ian to drive the truck today when they were dropping hay for the cattle."

"Let it go." Ian used a low, stern tone with her sister that she had never heard before. It caught Josephine's attention—and like a child stuck in the middle of two parents, all she wanted to do was try to smooth things over between them.

"Come on, Jordy, don't spoil tonight over something petty."

"Petty?" Jordy retorted. "He *drove* the truck."

"He looks like he survived okay." Logan used his calm, even, de-escalation tone of voice.

"And Tyler wouldn't have done it if it wasn't safe," Josephine added on to what Logan had said.

Her sister's reflection in the rearview mirror was stony. "Tyler thinks everything's a joke. I don't think this is funny."

"Hey…beautiful." Ian used a more conciliatory tone this time. "I'm okay. I wasn't in any danger. We were way out in the middle of nowhere—I couldn't've hit something if I tried. And you and I agreed…we *agreed*…that I needed to live my life. Take some risks. Not let my eyes hold me back…"

Josephine knew, and so did Logan and Ian, that behind her sister's anger was fear. She was afraid of Ian getting hurt. She was afraid of losing him, because she loved him so much.

"I've got to live, beautiful," Ian added gently. "You're the one who convinced me of that."

At the end of the long drive from the ranch house to the road, Jordan stopped the truck and looked over at her fiancé. "At least promise me you'll only drive in the fields."

"I swear on my honor as a Webelo." Ian leaned over to kiss her sister.

After they shared a kiss, Jordan explained, "Ian was a Boy Scout and he used that fact as a part of his strategy to woo me."

"You wanted me right from the start," Ian quipped.

"No. You wanted *me* right from the start, GQ. *I* thought you were a downtown wing nut."

That made Ian laugh, which completely broke the tension.

"You were there when they met, weren't you?" Josephine asked Logan.

"He was writing me a ticket!" her sister confirmed.

"Yeah…" Josephine gave Logan a wry look. "He does that a lot."

Josephine had never really enjoyed the trek from the ranch to Helena, not even when she was a little girl. Driving over hills and curves always made her feel carsick. But sitting in the backseat with Logan, who smelled so good and looked so handsome and seemed to like talking to her so much, she wasn't bothered by the trip this time. In fact, it seemed like the trip went by too quickly. She had been deep in the middle of a conversation with Logan about the skewed negative impact that the drug policy had on lower income and minority communities. The man was sharp, no doubt about it. And she had to admit that she had judged him harshly. She had always figured that he was a blue-collar guy who wouldn't be able to keep up with her or her friends in a conversation about political policy or law. She was seriously mistaken.

It had been a long time since she had line danced or had a beer. The idea of it was surprisingly appealing. Perhaps she had had one too many martinis.

It was the weekend, so the bar was crowded. They found an empty table near a small stage off the dance floor. Josephine wondered how Ian was handling the noise and the people—he didn't like crowds. But he was sitting close to Jordan with his hand on her leg, and he was smiling.

"I'm going to grab the drinks. What does everyone want?" Logan hadn't joined them at the table.

Josephine stood up. "I'll go with you."

They managed to squeeze into a tight space at the bar. The front of his body was touching the back of hers. From their harrowing experience in the cave, when he had rescued her and carried her to safety, she remembered how his body felt. At the time, she had been too frightened, and in too much pain, to appreciate the sheer maleness of the man. But later, when she was alone, and had time to reflect, she had spent quite a bit of time thinking about how strong he was, how feminine he made her feel when she was next to him.

They grabbed four beers and headed back to the table. Logan pulled her chair out for her before he took the chair next to hers. They tapped their four bottles together and toasted the wedding.

"How long has it been?" her sister asked her.

In unison, they said, "Prom."

She hadn't line danced since she was in high school, but when she saw the dancers all lined up, laughing while they moved through the repetitive steps, she wanted to join them.

"Do you mind?" Jordan asked Ian, who shook his head "no."

Her sister grabbed her hand and they went out onto the dance floor together. They danced for one song, and then had so much fun that they danced two more. Josephine was flushed and laughing when they returned to the table. She grabbed her beer off the table before she sat down. Two beers later, she was feeling warm all over, her lips were a little numb, and she was ready to get back out on the dance floor.

She held out her hand to Logan. "Are you coming, Lieutenant Wolf?"

Surprised by her question, Logan put his glass of water down.

"I owe you a dance, remember?" His hesitation made her regret the question. But when he stood up and took her hand into his, her regret was forgotten.

"I remember," Logan said.

It felt strange to hold his hand. It wasn't the hand she was used to. It was smaller, rougher, and stronger. And yet, it felt like a key slipping into a lock. A perfect fit. Perhaps even a perfect match.

They found a small area on the crowded dance floor where they wouldn't be in the way of the other couples. The music was blaring and Josephine had to nearly shout her words.

"Have you ever danced the Texas Two-Step?"

Logan leaned his head down. "No. I don't really dance all that much in public."

"Oh. Okay. Um…is it going to bother you if I have to take the lead position at first?"

"Bother me?"

"Well…embarrass you."

Logan smiled with just his lips, and gave a quick shake of his head. "No. Why?"

"Just checking."

Most of the guys she grew up with wouldn't let a woman take the lead position on the dance floor. Maybe in private, but not in public where their buddies could see them. It was a macho thing, she supposed. She wasn't all that surprised that Logan would let her take the lead—he was a masculine man, yes, but he didn't have a macho persona.

Josephine took the lead position, one hand in his, the other on his waist.

"Okay—let me think this out—when I step forward with my left, you step back with your left—no! Wait." She laughed. "I step forward with my *right* and you step backward with your left."

"Like this?" He asked.

"Yeah. And then it's step, step, feet together. Step, step, feet together. See how they're doing it?"

Logan watched the feet of the couples dancing around them. He had a feeling that he was about to make a total fool out of himself in front of Josephine, but he wasn't going to back out now. This was an opportunity to get close to her, to touch her, and be near her. If he looked like an idiot, so be it. He was just happy to have the excuse to have her in his arms.

"Ready?"

"Sure. Step, step…"

"Feet together," she said in unison with him.

He watched the couple that danced by and then said, "I think I've got it."

He didn't have it. He moved the wrong foot back and then when he moved the correct foot back, he forgot to put his feet together. While the other couples whirled by them, they had only covered a short distance in a choppy, uncoordinated way. When he managed to trip the both of them and they nearly landed in a heap in the middle of the dance floor, they both stopped because they were laughing too hard.

"This stupid dance is harder than it looks." Logan tilted his hat back a bit on his head.

"Why don't you try taking the lead this time?" she suggested. "Maybe that'll help."

"Do you really think anything will help me at this point?" he asked, smiling.

"Honestly? Probably not. But, a deal's a deal."

Logan laughed at her blunt assessment of his dancing ability. "Hey, if you're willing to stick it out with me, then I'm going to give it another try."

Logan took her back into his arms and took the lead. In his head, he was thinking, *Step, step, feet together. Step, step, feet together.*

"Ow!"

"Oh, crap! I'm sorry, Jo!" Logan apologized when he stepped hard on her instep.

Josephine bent down and rubbed the top of her boot. It hurt. He had stepped down really hard on her foot, but instead of worrying about the pain, she was laughing. She had been laughing with Logan the entire time they had been on the dance floor. The man could not dance, but he was a lot of fun to be around.

"Are you okay?" he asked.

Still laughing, she nodded. "I'll be fine."

"I suck, don't I?" He was smiling now.

Josephine straightened upright, her foot still smarting a bit. "I'm sorry, but, yes, you really do…"

"Do you want to go back to the table?"

"Please."

He noticed that she was limping, just a little bit, when they walked back to the table.

"You're going to start thinking that I'm bad luck,"

he told her. "Every time I get near you, you end up getting hurt."

Josephine sat down. "Don't worry about it. I'll be fine."

"What happened out there?" Jordy asked them in good humor. "I told Ian that sometimes it's an advantage not to be able to see."

"Sucking that badly takes a lot out of you." Logan polished off the water left in his glass. "I thought I was going to have my John Travolta *Urban Cowboy* moment out there."

"From what Jordan told me, it was more like an urban train wreck out there," Ian said.

Josephine liked how easily Logan could laugh at himself. She had always appreciated that trait in other people, mostly because she didn't have that trait herself. She tended to be more self-conscious. She tended to be too much of a people-pleaser at times.

They had all discovered that Logan couldn't dance, but what he could do was sing. When the band took a break and the bar switched to karaoke, Logan put his name on the list. When he stepped onto the small stage, with his jeans and western-style shirt, and his charming smile, Josephine couldn't take her eyes off him. And she noticed she wasn't the only one. Like he was a country superstar, a small group of women gathered near the stage to hear him sing. Once the music started and he actually started to sing a popular country song, the crowd of women grew.

"Uh…*wow*!" Jordan swiveled her head around to look back at her. "Did you know that he could sing like that?"

Josephine didn't want to talk. She wanted to listen. She gave a quick nod of her head to her sister but kept her eyes on Logan.

"Did you know?" her sister asked Ian.

"Wolf was the lead singer for a band when we were in high school," Ian told them.

Logan's voice made chill-bumps pop up all over her body. His voice seemed to touch places *inside* of her body and made her feel the lyrics of the song as much as she heard them. Logan, with his stage presence, his looks, and his voice, could have been a professional singer. It made her curious about him. How had he ended up being a cop instead?

When he finished singing, everyone clapped. But the women near the stage clapped the loudest. One woman in particular, a pretty brunette wearing skin-tight jeans and tank top, approached Logan when he came off the stage. Josephine watched Logan bend down his head to talk to the petite woman. The uncomfortable, almost painful, sensation that shot through her body could only be described as good, old-fashioned jealousy.

Logan and the brunette actually looked good together as they walked together through the crowd toward the table. And she didn't like it. She didn't like how the woman reached out and touched Logan's arm now and again. She didn't like how overly friendly Logan was being.

"Everyone—this is Brandy. Brandy—everyone."

"Hi, y'all." Brandy gave a cute little wave. "Are you sure you don't want a shot? I'm buyin'."

"Thank you, Brandy. Maybe another time."

Maybe another time?

Logan should have given this Brandy chick the full-on boot.

"Okay, if you're sure." Brandy was staring up at Logan with open admiration. "I think you're an incredible singer. Are you coming back next weekend?"

"No," Josephine said this without thinking about it. "We're not."

Brandy looked at her as if she were noticing her for the first time. "Oh. Okay. Well…" Another cutesy wave. "See you around."

Logan said goodbye to his new fan and then moved his chair just a little closer to Josephine's chair before he sat down.

"Holy *crap*, Logan! You're frickin' amazing!" Jordy exclaimed.

"Thank you," he said humbly. "What did you think, Jo?"

When Josephine ran Brandy off, she gave him reason to hope. He had thought that this attraction was a one-sided affair. But now he was thinking that Josephine had started to think of him as more than just a friend.

"I think you're amazing," she told him. "I'd like to hear you sing again."

Logan signed up for another slot, but when his name was called a second time, Josephine heard her name called, too.

Logan stood up and held out his hand to her. "Come on, Jo. We're up."

"What?" Josephine asked, horrified. "No! I'm not going up there!"

Logan wouldn't take her "no" for an answer. He

grabbed her hand, tugged her out of her seat, and led her up to the stage.

The lights hurt her eyes, but at least she couldn't see past the first row of women huddled near the front of the stage. Right before the music started, she tried to exit the stage, but Logan held on to her hand.

"I can't do this," she whispered harshly.

"Sure you can," he whispered back. "I picked our song."

In the next moment, Josephine heard the music for her favorite Judds song begin to play.

"Come on, Jo." Logan squeezed her fingers. "Sing a duet with me."

Josephine looked into Logan's rich, black eyes and what she saw in his eyes made her want to never look away. No man in her life had ever looked at her the way Logan was looking at her right now. And that was when she decided to stay on the stage with him.

"Okay…" she finally agreed. "But I'm Wynonna."

Chapter 11

It was a quiet trip back to the ranch. Josephine couldn't remember the last time she'd laughed so hard or had so much fun. The last several years of her life hadn't been about having fun. They'd been about getting her education and becoming the type of attorney who could make a difference in people's lives. She had literally let her hair down tonight. She'd put on her boots, drank more than a few beers, danced, and even sung karaoke with Logan three times. The first, Logan had basically pushed her onstage. The second and third time, she didn't need any pushing.

Josephine hugged her sister and her brother-in-law-to-be and then she was alone with Logan. It was after midnight and the ranch was asleep. For weeks, as her friendship deepened with Logan, she had always felt comfortable whenever she was with him. But standing with him now, she felt something shift inside of her body. Tonight, and truly for the first time, Logan seemed much more like a man who had captured a piece of her heart than a man who was only a friend.

Logan was grateful that Ian and Jordan had given him a chance to be alone with Josephine. Standing beside her, with the dark Montana mountains in the background, and bright yellow stars splashed across the blue-black sky, he wanted to kiss her. To his eyes, she was more beautiful tonight than any woman he'd ever seen. The gentle night air was blowing the loose, long strands of her hair around her face and shoulders. This woman was so pretty, so soft and sweet. He knew now that he wanted more from this woman than he had ever wanted from another woman.

"Well, good night." Josephine turned away from him, arms now crossed protectively in front of her body.

"I'll walk you back." Logan had almost built up the nerve to kiss her when she turned away from him.

Josephine started to walk quickly toward the porch. "You don't have to…"

"Yes, I do." He fell in beside her.

Josephine had been giving him green lights all night, but now, her body language was throwing up a giant stop sign. It wasn't the right time for a first kiss.

She flew up the stairs and it made him think that, like him, she had felt something change between them tonight. Up until tonight, Josephine had always treated him like a good friend. But when she chased Brandy away at the bar…that gave him hope—hope that a new spot had opened in her heart. A spot that he'd like to fill.

"Jo…"

At the top of the steps, Josephine stopped. The soft moonlight made the long strands of her hair look like threads of gold blowing gently around her beautiful face. It was a face that he had grown to love.

"Look, I don't know where you are in your recovery, but do you want to go out on a date…with me?"

Josephine had felt in her gut that this question was coming. She had known, for a while, that Logan found her attractive—that he was interested—but until tonight, she had never encouraged him. She had always kept him a safe arm's length away. Her possessiveness at the bar, when she told Brandy to shove off, had surprised her. Yes, Logan was a nice-looking man. That was undeniable. But in most ways, he wasn't really her type. He was laid-back about life; he wasn't as driven to succeed in a career as she was. There were fundamental differences. Should she start something with a man that seemed destined to end? Or was a summer fling with a hot cop exactly what she needed?

"Okay." She agreed to the date. "When?"

"We're moving the chapel tomorrow, but I was planning on heading up to Flathead Lake for some snorkeling the day after next. Are you up for a little road trip?"

"Actually…" she said after a moment of hesitation, "I am up for it. Thank you."

"Then…it's a date?" Logan asked.

Standing on the porch stairs of her childhood home, with a full moon and the majestic mountains off in the distance, the romance of the moment didn't escape Josephine.

"Yes," she said quietly. "It is a date."

* * *

The day they moved the chapel down from the mountain was a crazy day at the ranch. Josephine's dress for the wedding, which should have arrived the week before, finally came. It seemed to be a day for arrivals, because her mom's horse, Rising Star, decided it was a good day to give birth to her foal. There was so much activity, with the extra men and equipment for the chapel move, and Josephine wanted to be out in the mix. Instead, she was inside of the house trying on the dress for the wedding. Normally, trying on a pretty dress would be a top priority, but today wasn't a normal day.

"It's too loose around the waist." Her mom clucked her tongue. "I told you that you looked like you were losing weight, Josephine. You're getting too thin."

"I'm not trying to lose weight." She spun around and looked at her reflection in the full-length mirror.

Her maid of honor dress was to-die-for. It was a floor-length gown with a straight silhouette and a completely sheer back. The fabric was dark purple, silk chiffon that made her look like she was floating when she walked.

"We're going to have to get it altered right away." Her mom pulled the fabric tighter around her waist to make it fit perfectly.

"What do you think, Jordy?" Josephine asked her sister.

"I think it's the perfect dress for you, Jo." Her twin nodded her approval. "You look like you just walked right off the catwalk."

Josephine twirled around in a small circle with a smile. She had intended to pass on this dress because it was so striking that she didn't want it to seem like she was trying to compete with the bride. But Jordan had insisted that this was the gown she would wear for the wedding.

"Why don't we plan on…" Her mom started to speak, but a loud booming sound outside startled her and interrupted her sentence.

Barbara shook her head, her expression tense and irritated. "I am so *annoyed* with your father about this chapel business. That chapel has been sitting there for a hundred years, and this is the time to move it?"

"This is Dad's wedding present to me, Mom." Jordan looked up from her phone. "You should really give Dad a break."

"Jordan?" their mom asked. "Don't you have a painting to finish?"

"So, that's my cue to buzz off." Her twin laughed easily. "By the way, sis, I posted the pics from last night on Instagram."

Josephine shrugged her shoulders and made a face. "I've broken up with social media."

"Well, most people haven't, if you catch my drift. Chances are, the dingle-berry will see them."

"I doubt he'll care one way or the other," she said.

"Jordan, really," Barbara piped up. "Do you have to be so crass? You're about to become the wife of a very well-known man."

Jordan kissed her mom quickly on the cheek. "Trust me, Ian knows how I am and he loves me anyway."

"Go!" Barbara pointed to the door, half playful, half serious. "Paint!"

"Fine, I'm going. Ian and I are going up to check out how far along they are with the chapel."

After Jordy left, Josephine got out of the gown as quickly as she could. She agreed to eat a few more carbs before the wedding and her mom agreed to hold off on calling the seamstress. Once she was back in her boots and jeans, Josephine ran out the front door and walked quickly up the driveway. Her father had decided to re-locate the chapel on top of a small hill that overlooked the farmhouse. Like a crown jewel, there would a bird's-eye view of Bent Tree Ranch from the chapel.

She could hear the voices of the men yelling back and forth, shouting instructions and words of caution as they moved the chapel up the hill to the new foundation. Josephine climbed up to the top of the hill and joined the crowd of people gathered there.

"Oh, my goodness…" She said to no one in particular. The sight of the chapel, now on the back of an enormous, specialized semitruck, was remarkable. She had thought it was an impossible task and would likely be the end of the chapel. But she was wrong. The truck with the intact chapel was creeping up the hill toward the spot where a foundation had been built.

"Pretty frickin' amazing, isn't it?" Jordan asked her.

"It's really something," she agreed.

Everyone was there. Tyler, Jordan, Ian, her dad. It didn't seem right that her mom wasn't here to witness this historic family event. But just as she was having that thought, her mom appeared from the other side of the hill. Josephine scanned all of the men who were working to find Logan. She didn't see him at first, but she heard his voice. When he appeared from the other side of the truck that was carrying the chapel, she smiled. That was her immediate, spontaneous reaction to seeing Logan again. A smile.

When Logan saw her, standing on the hill next to her parents, he smiled, broadly and freely. It was a brief, shared moment between them before he refocused his attention on the chapel. The move took all day, from sunup to sundown. And when the crew finally achieved its goal of relocating the chapel to its new foundation at the top of the rolling hill that overlooked the farmhouse and barns, everyone present felt like cheering. Once the chapel safely in place, Logan walked over to her father. The two men shook hands.

"That was an amazing thing to watch," Hank said to Logan. "I can't believe what you pulled off here, Logan. We couldn't have done this without you."

"It just took the right resources, sir," Logan said humbly.

"It was more than that," her father replied.

Her father admired Logan. He respected him. And it made her view Logan with a fresh perspective. She always dated tall. She was tall, her father was tall—everyone in her family was tall. So she gravitated toward tall men to date. She had always equated tall with masculinity and strength. But now, watching Logan with her father—even though he was shorter than Hank, he wasn't any less strong or masculine. Quite the opposite.

Her family had surrounded Logan like he was a rock star, thanking him and congratulating him. She hung back, feeling an unusual sense of shyness at the thought of coming face-to-face with him. And she knew that she hadn't felt this way for a man in a long, long time.

She had only felt this way one time before in her life, and that was when she first met Brice.

And then he was in front of her, looking directly into her eyes. He was dirty and hot and his shirt was soaked with perspiration. And it didn't bother her.

"What do you think?" he asked her. He seemed to want her approval.

The truth was that she was close to tears—happy tears. In a sense, Logan had rescued the chapel. Without planning and without thinking, Josephine hugged him. And then she kissed him on the cheek.

"Thank you." She let go of him.

He stood there, silently staring at her, as if he had forgotten what he wanted to say. Finally, he asked, "Do you want to get a closer look at her?"

"Yes."

The whole family walked over to the chapel with them, and Logan explained what the next steps would be to make sure the structure was sound. Logan estimated that they would be able to begin remodeling the chapel within the next couple of days, and the exterior of the chapel, at least, would be ready for Jordan and Ian's pre-wedding session with the photographer. Slowly, after the initial excitement dissipated and evening chores called, the crowd of people dwindled. Josephine lingered. She wanted more time with the chapel. And she wanted more time with Logan.

She found a spot of ground and sat down. While she watched the hired crew gather their tools and load them onto their trucks, she pulled blades of grass free from the earth around her. When she found two rather long pieces of grass, she wrapped them around her finger and then started to tie them into a knot. Her eyes followed Logan as he went about his business. And, she noticed, when he was working, the man was *all* business. Much like the day she first met him, when he threw the book at her and gave her three tickets. Maybe he wasn't ambitious in the same way she was, but he was a hard worker. That was undeniable.

The last of the workers piled into their trucks and left. Logan walked over to where she was sitting and offered her his hand.

"Were you waiting for me?"

She nodded, wiped off the dirt and grass from the seat of her jeans.

"Thank you. You're a sweetheart."

It was dusk now and the full moon was rising over the mountain range in the distance. They were standing together, alone on the hilltop next to the chapel. And that was when she had an impulse. Perhaps it had been there for a while. Perhaps it was something entirely new. But one minute she was standing next to Logan, and then next minute she was in his arms, kissing him.

Logan had been up late the night before and up early in the morning. He was hot and hungry, covered in dirt and mud. He was exhausted. But when Josephine started to kiss him, all of that was forgotten. Her lips were soft, her skin was soft, and she felt so good in his arms. Their first kiss, a kiss he had been worrying about, was gentle and tentative and more meaningful than he had imagined. He held her face in his hands and kissed her lips lightly; she rested her hands lightly on his chest.

When the kiss ended, neither of them spoke. Neither

of them moved. They stood facing each other, in the dusk, quiet with their own whirling, private thoughts.

She couldn't believe that she had done something so out of character as kissing Logan. But she had kissed him and she had liked it. It was exciting to kiss him. And it was exciting to have him kiss her back. His lips were strong, like the rest of him, but he was a surprisingly gentle kisser. And for the moment at least, she didn't regret stepping right over that friendship line. In fact, she was pretty certain that she intended to cross that line again.

Josephine heard the sound of the dinner bell and the silence between them, the spell, was broken.

"If we don't go down there, she'll just send up a posse to get us," she told him. "Are you hungry?"

"I'm pretty much always hungry."

As they started the trek down the hill together, Logan reached for her hand. His hand, so warm and strong and calloused, was starting to feel like a new normal. Holding Logan's hand was starting to feel like coming home.

"So...we're still on for tomorrow. Right? Snorkeling at Flathead Lake?"

"We're still on." Josephine didn't bother to hide her natural enthusiasm. She knew that she could be herself around Logan, without any pretense. "Actually, I can't wait."

Everyone in her family noticed that she was leaving for the day with Logan, but no one said a word against it. Perhaps they had all seen this coming, or perhaps they were just glad to see her with someone other than Brice. Either way, their quiet acceptance of the relationship, casual and fleeting as it would most likely be, was a relief. They took one of the ranch trucks and headed to the largest body of fresh water west of the Mississippi. Ever since Logan had seen a picture of Flathead Lake, which had gone viral, he had put it on his "must visit" list while he was in Montana.

They rolled the windows down, cranked up the tunes, and embarked on their first mini road trip together. The more she got to know Logan, the more relaxed she felt around him. He was a blast to be around. He wasn't uptight. He didn't have an agenda. He just wanted to have a good time and he wanted to get to know her better. To have a hot guy, one that her family approved of, no less, interested in her, was a boost to her wounded ego. That was the truth. Why shouldn't she have a romantic summer? Why shouldn't she act on the attraction that Logan felt for her and she felt for him? She was no longer attached. She was free to date. She was free to kiss. She was free to make love...

Her cell phone rang. She pulled it out of the front pocket of her shorts and looked at the screen. She stared at the name, unbelieving.

Brice.

Logan glanced over at her. "Everything okay?"

She pushed the decline button and slipped the phone back into her pocket.

"Yeah," she said. "Everything is just fine."

When they arrived at the park, Logan found a parking spot and jumped out of the truck. Whenever he was getting ready to do something out-of-doors, whether it was hiking or going into the cave or snorkeling, Logan would act as excited as a little kid. He was animated and pumped up and ready to take everything in.

"Man, look at this place! I love it!" Logan immediately walked over to the rocky edge of the massive lake and looked around. "I've got to come back here and scuba dive. Do you ever scuba dive?"

"Uh-uh. No." She shuddered at the thought. "I have a really bad fear of drowning. I like to be near my air source at all times, thank you kindly."

Logan laughed. "But you will snorkel."

"Snorkeling's doable. Yes."

They grabbed their gear and staked out a spot on the man-made beach. Even in the summer, the temperature of the water was only seventy degrees at the surface. They had brought wet suits so they could stay in the water for a longer period of time.

"I dare you to jump in." Josephine rubbed sunscreen on her face and neck.

"You're daring me?" Logan questioned her as if he had heard her wrong.

"That's right." She pulled her T-shirt over her head and exposed the top half of the Speedo she wore to swim laps. "I dare you."

Logan grinned at her, his eyes appreciative. "Child's play."

"We'll see," she egged him on.

Logan stripped off his top, and when he caught her openly staring at his beautifully developed torso, his smile widened.

"I like your tattoo," she said.

"I like you," he said easily. "Take off your shorts."

"Excuse me?"

"If I'm going in, so are you."

"So, wait a minute. Are you trying to dare me with my own dare?"

He nodded.

"Fine." Josephine took off her shorts, folded them neatly, and put them down on top of her folded T-shirt. "Montana woman." She pointed to herself and then pointed to him. "California boy. Who has the advantage?"

Logan looked down at her long, bare legs and his smile widened. She knew what he was thinking—he liked what he saw. "Well, I suppose we're about to figure that one out."

Without any warning, he scooped her up into his arms and carried her, legs flailing, mouth protesting, into the lake.

"Logan!" she commanded sternly. "Put me down!"

"In a minute." He kept on walking into the lake.

"*Not* in the water…on the *beach*!" she clarified her command.

"Sorry," he said easily. "No can do."

When he was waist-high in the water, Logan spun around and fell backward into the water, taking her with him. The minute they hit the water, he let her go. Her feet touched the lake bottom and she stood up. Being chest-deep in the frigid water felt like a thousand tiny needles were pricking her skin all over.

"Wooo!" Logan let out a loud whoop when he emerged from beneath the water and shook the water from his short black hair. "That's damn cold!"

"Ya think?" Josephine splashed water at him.

Logan only smiled in response, reached out and

pulled her toward him. Before she could think to stop him, he kissed her. Right there, in Flathead Lake, he kissed her. The moment his warm mouth touched hers, she forgot all about being cold, she forgot about the small audience on the beach, and enjoyed the taste of the fresh lake water on Logan's lips.

Chapter 12

The trip to Flathead Lake marked a shift in Josephine's relationship with Logan. They left that morning as friends with potential for more. They returned to the ranch as two people who were more than "just friends." She never returned Brice's call. His message was vague, but she had a feeling that the only reason he had bothered to call was because he saw the pictures on Jordan's Instagram. That kind of attention she didn't need from him.

"Good afternoon, Lieutenant Wolf," Josephine greeted Logan when he walked into the barn.

"Hey."

Josephine latched the latch to the stall door. "Have you seen the new baby?"

"Not yet."

Logan stopped beside her, slipped his arm around her waist, pulled her to his side, and kissed her on the lips.

"How are you?" he asked.

"Good. Things are on track. No major issues or meltdowns in the wedding situation room." She liked how he would just grab her and kiss her. He was an affectionate man, more affectionate than she was used to. "I was just coming up to see you."

"I was looking for you," he said. "Were you heading up to the chapel?"

"Yes. Were you looking for cheap labor?"

"I was just hoping you'd improve the scenery," he said.

Logan admired the new colt for a moment before he turned around and leaned back against the stall. Over the weeks, he had started to look less like a San Diego police officer and more like a Montana cowboy. His hair had grown longer and curled out beneath his standard-issue cowboy hat. He had traded shorts and hiking gear for jeans and cowboy boots. He always had a pair of gloves tucked into his back pocket; his naturally golden skin had turned a dark brown around his neck and his forearms.

The more time she spent with this man, the more handsome he became. There was a kindness in his brown eyes and sincerity in his smile. He was a go-with-the-flow kind of guy; it was refreshing. For now, for a summer fling, he was perfect for her. And when he kissed her, like she could tell that he was about to do now, her body felt pleasure all the way from her lips to the tips of her fingers. Since their trip to the lake, there had been a whole lot of kissing. It was that sweet, often excruciatingly slow, dance toward making love. Logan wasn't pushing her—if anything, she had been pushing him…a little bit further, a little bit further, every time they were able to steal away for a clandestine lovers' moment.

Logan was admiring her, as he always did, with his eyes. There was a small, intimate smile on his firm lips as he reached out to put his hands on either side of her slim hips. She took his hat off his head and put it onto hers.

"Can I have a minute of your time, cowboy?" she asked suggestively.

"You can have as many minutes as you want."

Josephine took his hand and led him over to a ladder that led up to the hayloft. She knew that he was staring at her derriere as she climbed up ahead of him. Enticing him, making him want her even more, was part of the plan. It was, she had recently discovered, part of the fun. She had been thinking about taking him up to the hayloft, something she had never done with a man, and today seemed like the perfect opportunity. They were the only ones in the barn—why not take advantage of the moment?

Logan knew what she wanted. He knew exactly what to do. When he joined her in the loft, he pulled a knife out of his front pocket, cut the twine off a fresh bale of green, sweet-smelling alfalfa hay, and spread the bale of hay over the old straw that was strewn across the wood floor of the loft.

Together, they lay down on top of the hay, facing each other. His eyes were smiling at her when he tucked a loose strand of hair behind her ear. He brushed his thumb over her lips, and then kissed her. Slow and gentle, that was how he always kissed her. She knew there was more behind those kisses, more to be discovered, but he held that part back. He was teasing her, in his way, building her anticipation, and driving her to come back to him for more. And it was working. She did want more. Her body wanted more.

Logan rolled her onto her back and then, for the first time, his body was on top of hers. His welcome weight pressed her down into the hay while his welcome lips left a trail of feathery kisses over her face and down her neck.

She couldn't help herself. She couldn't stop herself as she dug her fingertips into the muscles of his back, entwined her legs with his legs, and made a sound, a sound she had never made before. It was the sound of need. The sound of frustration. She knew her mind wasn't ready for them to make love, but her body was ready.

Logan lifted his head, put his hands on either side of her face, and dropped his hips down to hers so she could feel him. So she could feel the need she had created in him.

"Josephine…" The way he said her name, with so much reverence and care, let her know that she meant more to him than just a moment of a physical gratification.

Their eyes met and Logan shook his head as a private thought passed through his mind. "My God… Josephine…" He said gruffly. "Do you have any idea how beautiful you are to me?"

They kissed again, more deeply and longer than they had ever kissed before. She took his tongue into her mouth, just as she knew that she would soon take his body into hers. Logan broke the kiss, buried his face into her neck, and ground his hips into hers.

Josephine closed her eyes and enjoyed the feel of him. She loved the feel of his muscular arms and his muscular chest. From the very core of her body, a wonderful tingling spread. In her mind, she started to think—

Could I have an orgasm like this? Could I have an orgasm like this?

Usually, everything had to be *just right* for her to experience an orgasm. The lighting had to be right, the position had to be just right…

Yet there was a demanding ache between her thighs now, and she knew, unbelievably, that she was about to climax with Logan.

"Don't hold it back," he whispered in her ear.

She was too far gone in the moment to feel embarrassed that he *knew*. Logan's hands lifted her into his body and he took her higher and higher and higher until her head dropped back into the hay and she could sense an orgasmic moan rising from the back of her throat. She was so close…so close…

And then she heard her brother's voice.

Josephine's mouth clamped shut, her eyes popped open, and she stopped moving. She tightened her arms around Logan so he would stay still, too. They looked at each other, shocked that they were no longer the only ones in the barn. Once she knew that Logan was going to be quiet, she pushed on his shoulder to get him to move off her. Logan rolled carefully to the side. Josephine rolled onto her side and then got onto her hands and knees. She peeked through a gape in the floor and spotted her brother kissing London the intern.

Josephine scrunched up her face, sorry that she had witnessed a private moment between Tyler and London, while she lowered herself down onto her haunches. She shook her head at Logan and put her finger to her lips.

Logan, she noticed, looked like he needed to sneeze. He was pinching his nose in an attempt to stifle it. She shook her head at him again and mouthed the word "no." The last thing she wanted was for Tyler to catch her in the hayloft with Logan. She'd never live that one down with her brother.

While Logan made a valiant attempt to stifle his sneeze, she listened carefully for voices. Finally, she heard her brother say something to London, and she was glad that she couldn't make out the words. It was bad enough she had seen the kiss! From her vantage point in the loft, she saw Tyler leave. And then she heard the sound of the office door at the other end of the barn shut. London had gone into the office, which gave them a window of opportunity to make their escape.

Josephine grabbed the discarded hat and quickly stood up. "Time to get out of Dodge."

Right after Logan stood up, the sneeze he had been holding back came out.

"Bless you," she whispered.

"Thank you." He got the two words out and then sneezed again.

"Bless you," she repeated.

Once he started sneezing, he didn't stop. He sneezed again, and again, and then again. He sneezed so many times that she stopped saying "bless you," just so he wouldn't have to try to say "thank you."

She wanted to tell him to walk and sneeze at the same time so they could make a clean getaway, but she didn't have the heart to do it. His eyes were red and swollen and his nose was clogged. He looked miserable.

"I think…" he said between sneezes, "that I'm allergic to the hay."

She nodded. The romantic scene had taken a rather comical turn, and it hit them both at the same time. They started to laugh. And the more Logan sneezed, the more they laughed.

"Come on…" Josephine said to him. "Let's get you out of here."

Down the loft ladder, and out of the barn, they managed to leave undetected. Logan was still sneezing. He'd stop for a minute and it seemed like he was done, and then he'd sneeze again.

"Quit it." Logan ordered his sneezing to stop, but his body didn't listen. He kept right on sneezing for another couple of minutes.

"Holy mackerel," he said when the sneezing finally stopped. "I think next time we need to stay away from the hay."

"Agreed." She laughed.

Logan looked her over. "You have hay in your hair. And on your pretty little backside."

Josephine pulled her ponytail over her shoulder and picked the hay out of it. Then, she brushed off the seat of her jeans. She twirled around.

"Evidence gone?" she asked.

"You're good," he said. "How 'bout me?"

"I think we need to find you a Benadryl ASAP." She started to smile again.

He was smiling, too. He looked around to make certain that no one else would hear him. "I did enjoy the roll in the hay…"

His voice sounded different because his nose was completely clogged.

"Me, too," she agreed. "Until my brother interrupted us and all of the soft tissue in your noggin swelled."

"That wasn't sexy," he conceded with a self-effacing smile.

"Let's go ask Mom if she has an antihistamine, okay?"

Her mom did have the antihistamine. Josephine got the pills, poured a glass of water, and then handed them both to Logan.

"Thank you," he said after he took the pills and gulped down the water.

After she doctored him, Logan told her that he needed to go back to the chapel. Josephine wanted to stay behind and get some reading done, so she walked out to the front porch with him to say goodbye.

Logan paused on the top step. "Listen… I'm planning a trip up to the Continental Divide. I'm thinking that I'll be up there camping for about a week. If you think your mom and Jordan can spare you, I'd like you to come with me."

And there it was…the opportunity that they both knew they had been thinking about, the opportunity to be alone, the opportunity to make love.

Was she really ready for that? Were her mind and

heart healed enough to take that permanent step away from Brice and into Logan's arms?

"What do you think?" he asked.

"I think…" she said thoughtfully, "that if my mom and Jordan can spare me, I'm going with you up to the Continental Divide."

Later that day, after she had spent several hours reading, Josephine strolled up the hill to the chapel. Logan was on the roof of the chapel, stripped down to a ribbed, white tank undershirt, his tanned skin soaking in the late afternoon sun. He wasn't tall, which still bothered her, but what he lacked in height, he made up in pure strength. She had never seen such an incredibly built male physique up close. This was the kind of body that men had in the movies or magazines. They rarely existed in real life.

Logan spotted her coming up the hill. He waved and climbed off the roof.

"Hey…" He met her halfway. "I was hoping you'd come to check out the progress."

Josephine couldn't believe the change in the chapel. Logan had dedicated most of his free time to refurbishing the old family landmark. Yes, he had help from various hands on the ranch, and everyone in the family had pitched in, but Logan was the driving force behind the project. She didn't understand why he had put most of his vacation plans on hold to rehab the chapel, but she was grateful.

"It's incredible, Logan. Better than I ever imagined."

"I wanted to make sure that at least the outside is done by the wedding."

"Jordy was hoping that the inside would be done, too…"

"I know…but that's not going to happen. Honestly, I'm pretty surprised that we've almost got the outside squared away."

"What you've managed to do is a miracle. I never imagined—I don't know that any of us ever really imagined—that the chapel would get a new life. I think we had all kind of given up on it."

"No…" Logan's eyes were on the chapel. "You should never give up on something that you love."

He continued to look at the chapel, his eyes seeming to take inventory of all the details that still needed to be tackled. She looked at him. The profile of his face was strong and handsome, but there were deep lines around his eyes from smiling and squinting, and the nose had a bump on the bridge that made him look like a prize fighter who had taken one too many hits to the nose.

"How are you with a brush?" He turned toward her and caught her staring at him.

"Not bad," she said. "I can hold my own."

Logan handed her a brush and put her to work. He cranked up the CD player because he knew that she liked the Temptations. While he painted, he sang to her. Every once in a while, she joined in, singing with him—with Logan, she felt like singing again. And he encouraged it; he enjoyed the sound of her voice.

When the song "My Girl" began, Logan laid down his brush, took the brush from her hand, led her to a grassy spot nearby and took her into his arms. On the hilltop, with the chapel as their backdrop, he held her in his arms and sang to her.

She loved it. She did. But it also made her feel embarrassed and shy. He was so open about his feelings. He liked her, he wanted to sing to her, and so he did.

"What are you doing?" she asked, looking around for someone who might see them.

"Dancing with my girl…" He sang the words "my girl."

"I thought you couldn't dance…" Was she his girl? She wasn't sure about that.

"I can't," he admitted. "But I can sway back and forth like this. And I can dip you…" He surprised her by dipping her over his arm and then swinging her back up.

"Come on, Jo…" Logan said, still holding her in his arms. "It's okay to have a good time, you know. No one's going to see you. It's just you and me up here."

He was right. And so she danced with him. On the hill, in front of the chapel, with Logan singing the Temptations to her…she danced.

At the end of the song, Logan dipped her one last time and when he brought her up, he ended their dance with a quick kiss. Once the dance was done, they went back to their painting. Josephine still couldn't quite figure Logan out—and she told him as much.

"You were so…serious that first day that I met you."

"You mean the day that I pulled you over and wrote you several tickets?"

"And probably jacked up my insurance premium…" she added.

"I was on duty," he explained. "I have to be different when I'm in uniform."

"Do you want to climb up the ranks? Be a police chief?"

"Why do I sometimes feel like I'm on a job interview with you that's not going so well?" he asked. "To answer your question, I don't want to climb up the ranks. I'm happy with what I'm doing. And I want to retire when I'm young enough so I can do what I really love to do."

"Which is?"

"Working with kids...troubled youth. That's their label, but I know there's a lot more to them than that label."

"I think that's admirable."

"I got involved with the Big Brothers program a couple years after I joined the force."

"You're a Big Brother?"

"Yeah, I love it." Logan put his paintbrush down so he could pull his wallet out of his back pocket. He flipped the wallet open and showed her one of the pictures inside.

"Javier's school picture," he told her. "He's a big boy for eight, isn't he?"

She nodded, then pointed to another picture. "Who's that?"

"That's Mom."

"Red hair."

"Yeah. My dad, my biological dad—not my stepfather, whom I call 'Dad'—was a full-blooded Choctaw Indian. Got my coloring from him. Didn't get much else."

Josephine stared at Logan curiously. There was so much about this man that she didn't know, yet she had nearly lost control of her reason and made love to him in the barn loft earlier that day. If Tyler hadn't interrupted them, could she really say that she wouldn't have gone there with Logan?

No.

"You're a Big Brother, and you're fifty percent Native American. I didn't know any of that about you."

Logan read between the lines of her statement.

"And that bothers you…that you don't know everything about me."

It was a statement, not a question.

"Yes. I suppose it does. In a way, we've crossed a few boundaries lately."

Logan stopped painting and put down his brush. His arms were crossed in front of his body, which was a protective stance that she wasn't used to seeing from him.

"Let me ask you this…and you don't have to answer me. Just be honest with yourself about it. Did you really know everything there was to know about that guy Brice?"

Chapter 13

The morning that they were set to leave on their camping trip, Josephine headed to the barn to meet Logan. Jordan and her mom assured her that everything for the wedding was under control, so she decided to go on an adventure. When she arrived at the barn, she wasn't surprised that London already had two horses saddled for them and Easy Does It the mule was packed with supplies.

"Really?" Josephine asked when she saw her nemesis in mule form. "This was our best option?"

London patted the mule on the neck. "I had a talk with him and he assured me that he's up for the task."

Logan turned the corner carrying his rucksack. "Morning."

"We have to rethink this whole scenario," Josephine told him.

"What's the problem?" Logan packed his bag on the back of the mule.

Josephine pointed silently to Easy.

"She's holding a grudge against Easy," London, who was mucking out a nearby stall, said to him.

"Heck, yeah, I'm holding a grudge! He left me stranded...*twice*! I am not going all the way up to the divide only to have him take off with our coffee."

"Coffee?" Logan laughed. "Is that all you're worried about?"

"I have to have coffee first thing in the morning. It's non-negotiable."

"We need a strong, sure-footed pack mule and he's the best one we've got. We need him. Haven't you ever heard the phrase 'the third time's the charm'?"

In the end, Josephine conceded that they needed the mule for the trip, but she was holding Logan directly responsible for him. After they ran through their extensive checklist for the trip one last time, they set off on their journey. Logan had the trip planned out to the smallest detail. Planning for a camping trip to a high altitude location like the Continental Divide was something that Logan took very seriously. In this, he was not easygoing or go-with-the-flow. He knew it could be dangerous, so he tried to anticipate all of their needs. She had just basically needed to show up with her clothing and toiletries and get on her horse.

They stopped at the first camping sight, a spot on the ranch that her family had used over the years, in the early afternoon. Logan's plan called for them to take two slow travel days up to the peak, an overnight at the peak, and then two days for the return leg of the journey. She liked the slow pace that Logan had set for them. It forced her to relax and enjoy the moment. It forced her to get out of her own head, something that was very difficult for her to do.

"Do you know how to pitch a tent?" Logan asked her after he had unpacked the mule.

"Do I know how to pitch a tent? Does a duck like water?"

She had grown up on this land, surrounded by ranch hands, brothers, and a sister who was a tomboy. The only truly feminine influence on the ranch had been her cosmopolitan mother. She knew how to shoot a gun, fish, pitch a tent—she could even castrate a bull if she needed to get it done. It had been a long time since she had tapped into her inner woods-woman, but she was there.

Logan watched Josephine grab her tent and haul it over to a spot nearby. She had basically told him to mind his own business when he had offered to help her pitch her tent. When he had first met her, she was dressed like a fashionable, professional woman, with a designer dress and high heels. Now, she was in slim-fit jeans, boots, a button-up shirt with long sleeves rolled up to the elbow. Her long hair, hair that he loved to touch, was braided tightly into a thick braid down her back. Surprising to him, she now wore a large buck knife on her belt. He liked her in her business attire, but he really liked this side of her, too. He tried not to be too obvious about it, but it was hard for him not to stare at her long legs and shapely derriere in those jeans. He felt so attracted to this woman that it made him nervous. There had been no promises between them, no talk of continuing their relationship once they returned to California. Yet he had already, unintentionally, lost his heart to her. The question remained, was that a mistake?

Once she got started, her dormant camping skills came right up to the surface and she pitched her tent more quickly than Logan pitched his. She stood proudly next to her tent.

"Do you need some help over there?" she teased him.

"No, I got it," Logan said. "Thank you."

Josephine smiled at the rare display of Logan's fragile male ego. While he finished pitching his tent, Josephine went on the hunt for some kindling to start a fire. Logan was finished with his tent when she returned with a pile of dried sticks in her arms.

"Coffee?" she asked.

"Absolutely," Logan said. He had already started to assemble his fishing rod. They had agreed that they both preferred to eat freshly caught fish for dinner while they were on the trip.

"I'm going to head down to the stream. You good?"

"There'll be coffee when you get back. Catch something good. I'm starved."

When he returned to the campsite, he had caught something good.

"Look at the size of this guy!" Logan showed her his catch—a massive trout.

"I'd forgotten how big they could get up here," she said, impressed. "I hope you're hungry too, so this doesn't go to waste."

Without hesitation, she took the fish, put it on a makeshift cutting board and started to clean it. Logan, who usually dated women who liked the outdoors, had never been with a woman who would clean a fish just as soon as she would get a French gel manicure. It caught him off guard so much that he simply stood there and watched her.

Josephine used a sharp filleting knife to cut open the fish and in one easy, practiced motion, she gutted the fish. When she looked up from her task, bloody knife in one hand, fish head and spine in the other, Logan was staring at her with an odd expression on his face.

"Are you horrified?" she asked.

"No. Impressed."

"Oh…well, I know my way around a campsite."

"I'm picking that up," he said.

She put the head of the fish down and put the edible portion into a cast-iron skillet.

"Do you want to do the honors, or should I?" she asked.

He took the heavy skillet in one hand. "I'll cook it. You already did the dirty work."

That night, they sat by the fire, stuffed from the freshly caught and cooked fish dinner and several cups of strong, black campfire-brewed coffee. Perhaps it was the caffeine in the coffee, or perhaps it was the feeling of privacy and seclusion that being in the mountains created, but once Josephine started talking, she didn't stop. Not for a long time. She never used to talk very much with Brice. She had always thought that he was brilliant and what he had to say somehow mattered more than voicing her own thoughts. But with Logan—she liked to tell him what she was thinking. How she was feeling.

The moon overhead, nearly a full moon, was glowing large and bright in the expansive indigo sky. Josephine leaned her head back so she could stare up at that magical moon.

"I've always loved the moon," she told him. "My mom always stands under a full moon to get a moon kiss."

Logan liked to hear Josephine's thoughts. He liked to listen to the sound of her voice, to watch her facial expressions and the way her lips moved when she talked. No matter what time of day it was, he thought she was beautiful. To him, she was beauty personified. The firelight, and the light from the moon, only enhanced her natural beauty.

Silently, he stood up and extended his hand to her. She took it and he helped her stand up. Without pretense, he kissed her. He encircled her body with his arms, pulled her in, and gave her a sweet, gentle kiss. When he felt her arms tighten around his waist, when he felt her body sway into his, he deepened the kiss. His tongue danced with hers, one hand on her lower back, the other hand cradling her head.

Josephine loved Logan's kisses. She waited for them, looked forward to them. But even though he never hid his desire from her, he always held back. He had never tried to fondle her breasts or slip his hands between her thighs. There was a line he refused to cross. Even when she crossed that line, cupping the hard-on that was pressing against the material of his pants, he always kept his hands in "safe zones." His kisses, perhaps deliberately on his part, always left her wanting. Always left her needing more. Tonight was no exception.

Logan wasn't playing a game. He wanted her to come to him. He refused to push her into a sexual relationship with him. When it happened, it would be because *she* was ready. And it was not like she hadn't thought about it. She had. The idea of making love with Logan was very appealing. She knew the feel of his hard shaft through his clothes, but she had imagined what it would feel like, skin on skin, to hold him in her hands, to take him into her mouth—to have him inside of her body. She wanted that. And she had come close that day in the barn when she had almost let her libido take over. But perhaps that moment scared her, because they hadn't been that close since.

Just outside of her tent, Logan stopped to give her an enticing good-night kiss. Did she wish, in a way, that he would have at least *tried* to talk her into his sleeping bag? Yes. But that wasn't Logan's style. When it came to sex, she was the one who was in control. And even though it was an unspoken desire between them to make love on this trip, she still wasn't certain that she would.

"Good night, Jo." Logan's lips lingered on hers on last time, his fingertips touching her face.

"Good night." She unzipped the flap of her tent. "5:30?"

"5:30," he said. He waited for her to duck inside of her tent and zip it shut, and then she heard his tent flap zip shut.

Josephine climbed into her sleeping bag, but didn't fall asleep right away. She tossed and turned and kicked at her sleeping bag and pushed on her pillow. She couldn't get comfortable, but not because she was sleeping on the ground. She couldn't get comfortable because she was sexually frustrated and conflicted. She was having a silent debate, in her tent, in the dark.

Should she get up and go to Logan's tent? She knew he would unzip his sleeping bag and welcome her without question. And, after much debate, she actually kicked her legs out of her sleeping bag, unzipped her tent and took a step toward Logan's tent. But then she heard the soft sound of his deep breathing, signally that he was already asleep. Obviously, he wasn't as bothered by his frustration as she was, and that made her doubt getting out of her sleeping bag in the first place. Quietly, she turned around, went back to her tent and crawled back into her sleeping bag. It wasn't the right time; it wasn't the right night. Perhaps it never would be.

The next morning they broke camp early and headed to their second camp location farther up the mountain. They both liked to ride in silence, enjoying the sounds of nature surrounding them that could only truly be appreciated if talking was kept to a minimum. They stopped for lunch, and to water the horses and the mule, and then they were back on the trail. Very quickly, they established a system for their trip, one that worked for them both. As with the first day of the trip, they made camp in the late afternoon so they could prepare the campfire for dinner, make a fresh catch, and make the sure the horses and Easy Does It were well rested for the toughest part of the climb to the peak.

As with the night before, Logan caught the fish, she cleaned it, and he cooked it. They had piping hot coffee after dinner and toasted marshmallows, toasted on a stick Logan carved for her. It was, in her memory, one of the best nights she had ever had. There was an easiness to their relationship, with the way they moved around the camp, that made her feel like she was part of a couple that had been married for years. It was the kind of easiness she saw with her parents, as if they could read the other's thoughts and anticipate the needs of the other without words. How had she managed to achieve this with Logan, a virtual stranger, when she hadn't managed to achieve it with a man she had been with for over five years? If she had been able to carry out her plan to marry Brice, would she have *ever* achieved that with him? Why had she been so willing to settle for less than the relationship she had always wanted just because she had put so much time into the relationship and Brice fit the criteria she had created in her mind about what "husband material" should look like? It scared her, and shook her confidence, to think how close she had come to possibly making a major life mistake. She went to sleep that night, with the very real awareness that marrying Brice would have been exactly that—a major life mistake.

After they broke camp the morning they were going to make the trek up to the Continental Divide, Logan checked the girth on her saddle and lifted the stirrup length on both of her stirrups before he tended to his own horse. This morning, more so than any other morning, Logan was focused and had few words to say. She knew why—this leg of the journey could be treacherous. They had to be prepared. They had to respect the climb they were about to ask their horses to make. The ascent to the divide would take them up another eight thousand feet. The air was thinner, which would make it harder to breath, and the temperature would drop thirty degrees. Cell phone service for emergencies would be limited to none.

Josephine had a jacket and a long-sleeved thermal shirt rolled up behind her saddle. By noon, even with the sun heating up the day, she would need to start adding layers as they made the climb. She mounted her horse and waited for Logan to swing into his saddle. He was a skilled horseman, and she could appreciate how he handled his horse and sat the saddle. She had confidence in him and his ability to safely lead them up the steep incline to their next campsite.

"Are you ready?" Logan used the reins to turn his horse to the left so he could look at her.

"Ready."

She wasn't a nervous rider, but she had been raised to respect the steep, tricky footing of the trail as they climbed closer and closer to the peak of the divide. At the halfway point, they stopped to take a break from the saddle and used the water from their canteens to water the horses and the pack mule. She was relieved that Easy Does It had willingly carried their equipment up the mountain without any protest. She had to give the little mule credit—he was getting the job done and he was doing it well.

Josephine pulled on her thermal shirt and the jacket because the temperature had already dropped nearly twenty degrees, according to the thermometer she had hanging off her saddle. After she zipped her jacket, she yawned loudly. She wasn't tired, so the need to yawn was a direct result of the air being thinner. When she breathed in the cooler air, she started to cough.

"Are you okay?" Logan was also slipping on a jacket.

"It's the asthma. I have my inhaler."

"Best use it now," he said.

Josephine took a couple of quick puffs from her rescue inhaler and then they were back in the saddle. They both were anxious to get to the next campsite. Even though the scenery was majestic, from spotting wildlife along the way to the unusual foliage, they both respected the dangers of the journey. They climbed higher and higher, and it grew colder and colder, until they reached an altitude that was as high as the clouds.

She had last made this climb with her brother Daniel when she was in middle school, and she was relieved when they finally reached the peak of the mountain they were scaling and found flatter terrain. The air was very thin now, and it was very cold, and Josephine started to realize that the mild case of asthma she had developed in her early adult years was making it difficult to breathe now that they were at the peak.

"Do you think we're close?" she called to Logan, who was a little bit ahead of her.

Logan stopped his horse and Easy Does It, and waited for her to catch up with him.

"I think the spot I picked out is just up ahead. What's wrong?"

"It's a little tough for me…to breathe."

"Can you make it, or do you need a break?"

"I think I can make it. If it's just around the corner like you said." The idea of a break didn't appeal to her. She wanted to get to camp, get the fire going, and get some hot coffee into her body.

"It's close," he assured her. "What do you want to do?"

By her choice, they kept moving. And Logan had

been right—they were close. When they reached their destination, Logan grabbed a blanket from one of the saddlebags and wrapped it around her shoulders. He insisted that she sit down and conserve her breath while he made the fire. Once the fire was made, he settled her near it to keep her warm and put on the coffee. While she stayed warm by the fire, Logan quickly unloaded the horses and the mule and started the task of pitching the tents.

"We only need one," she told him. Her voice was weaker than normal, and he didn't hear her. She cleared her throat and said the words again, louder this time.

"Logan, we only need one tent tonight."

Logan straightened upright, her tent in his hands, and looked at her.

"Are you sure?"

She nodded her head in response.

Logan's eyes narrowed slightly as he contemplated her for a couple of seconds. Then he nodded one quick nod, put her tent down, and turned his attention to pitching his tent. *Their* tent. After he set up camp, he joined her near the fire. He poured them both a cup of hot coffee and joined her beneath the blanket. They sat together, quietly, at what seemed to be the top of the world.

"You can read about this. You can look at pictures." Logan looked off into the distance at the massive peaks that surrounded them for as far as the eye could see. "But actually being here…that's something else entirely."

Unexpectedly, without warning, tears began well up behind her eyes. Thoughts of her brother Daniel were so strong up here. Thoughts of the relationship—a friendship, really—that she had lost with Brice seemed more acute. Two men, two losses. She had no idea why it was hitting her so strongly right then, at that moment…but she was grateful that Logan was by her side and she was glad that he was so focused on the magnificent views that he hadn't noticed that she was fighting to hold back tears.

The weather, which had been in their favor for the first half of the trip, took a turn for the worse and forced them to go inside of the tent much earlier in the evening than they would have wanted. Logan had unzipped both of the sleeping bags completely and then laid them out like a makeshift mattress. They took off their jackets but left the rest of the clothing on. They lay down face-to-face and covered themselves with one of the sleeping bags and the blanket. Once they got situated, they looked at each other and started to laugh.

"It's damn cold up here." Logan reached out to pull her closer to him.

"The rain is making it colder…"

"How are you feeling? Better?"

Josephine nodded with a small smile. "I think I just needed a minute to adjust to the altitude."

"It's thin up here, that's for sure. It's tough for me, too."

"Logan?"

"Yes?"

"How do you feel about spooning?" she asked.

"Are you still cold?"

"Freezing."

"Then, come here, baby… I'll warm you up." He

scooted backward as far as he could so she could turn into his arms. He wrapped her up tightly in his warm arms and she immediately felt better.

"How's that?" he asked. "Better?"

She nodded again, but had another question. "Logan?"

"Yes, sweetheart?"

"Why haven't you tried to make love to me?"

Logan's body grew still; she could feel his strong heart beating against her back. "I was giving you space."

Josephine spun around again, snuggled into his body and hooked her calf around his lower legs.

She looked directly into his eyes and asked, "What if I don't want the space anymore, Logan? What then?"

Chapter 14

Her words were the green light Logan had been waiting for. He got rid of his clothes while she disrobed beside him. He was already aroused, and had been since they first lay down together. Now he just needed her body. But he knew that he wanted more than just her body—that was why he had waited for her. And the fact that there was a persistent voice in the back of his mind that was wondering if *she* wanted more from him than only a summer fling.

He rolled her gently onto her back and leaned on his arm to look down into her pretty, oval face. He didn't see doubt or hesitation in her light blue eyes—he saw desire. Pure desire, for him. He kept them both covered, he wanted to continue to keep her warm, but he needed to touch her. He had wanted to touch her for so long. He started at her lips, running his finger lightly over them, before he let his fingertips trail down the side of her face, to her soft neck, and down to her small, round breasts. He covered one breast with his hand, massaging it, teasing the hardened, sensitive nipple. Josephine closed her eyes, and Logan heard her sigh at the touch of his hand on her flesh. She was ready for the next step. She was ready for him.

Logan wanted to take his time exploring her body with his hands and she let him do it. Her skin was so silky and smooth, her legs and body so slim and finely muscled. He ran his hand along the side of her hip, down her leg, and then moved it back up. Without him having to say a word, Josephine opened her thighs, just a little, just enough, for him to slip his hand between them. She was wet, so wet, that he had to close his eyes, drop his head, and stop his own need to drive him to rush them to a quick release. He had waited too long for this to end quickly. He lowered himself down beside her, kissed the side of her neck, as he slowly slipped his fingers inside of her.

"Oh..." Josephine's head tilted back when he pushed his fingers deep inside of her. She reached down between them, encircled his thick shaft with her cool fingers.

He kept his fingers deep inside of her tight, wet center and worried her swollen clit with his thumb. She started to writhe against his hand, and bore down on his fingers, tighter and tighter, until she gasped loudly and her orgasm rained down on his fingers. His body wanted the same release he had just given her. But he made himself wait. There was only going to be one first time with his beloved Josephine and he had to make it count. He had to be the best she had ever had. He wanted her to believe, because it was true, that he was the best she ever *would* have.

Logan moved on top of her, but instead of entering her, as she might have anticipated, he moved downward, positioning his shoulders between her thighs with his hands beneath her tight rear end. Again, she didn't resist him. She welcomed him, relaxing her thighs and lifting her body upward to meet his mouth. Josephine dragged her fingers through his hair and it pleased him to hear how loudly she gasped when his tongue slipped inside of her. When he tasted the sweet aftermath of her orgasm, Logan growled low in his throat and lost himself in the feast. When Josephine's thighs tightened against his shoulders, her fingers pressed the back of his head into her core, and her fresh cries of release filled the small tent, Logan couldn't wait any longer. He quickly rolled on a condom and repositioned himself between her thighs.

Josephine looked up at him, a mixture of surprise and such uncertainty, that he almost stopped. But then she raised her hips upward, seeking, wanting, and that was the only encouragement he needed. With his hands positioned on either side of her shoulders, Logan locked his eyes with hers as he connected their bodies together.

Logan seated himself completely within her slick center. He closed his eyes so he could focus on the incredibly feeling of being joined with Josephine. She was a perfect fit for him. She was tight, and hot, but deep enough to take all of him inside of her. He pulled out of her slowly, torturing himself, then sank back into her again and again and again. Josephine's hands were on his chest, and the faster his rhythm became, the more she dug her fingernails into his skin. God help him, he felt her tighten around him and it drove him wild. His pace was frantic, crazy, driving into her harder and faster until she screamed his name. The sound of his name on her lips—that was the trigger that made him explode. One last hard thrust, he climaxed and, as if wrenched from his heart, he shouted her name.

"Josephine!"

After they made love, they had fallen asleep in each other's arms. It was cold inside of the tent, but beneath the sleeping bag and thick blanket, and with Logan's body generating heat, she awakened hot and sweaty. Still naked, Josephine carefully slipped out from underneath Logan's heavy arm and stood up. Bent over, she tiptoed in the dark, trying not to step on Logan's legs, and unzipped the tent flap. She stepped outside into the frigid air. Barefoot and without clothing, Josephine walked a few steps away from the tent. Tonight was the full moon. The ground felt hard and crunchy and stabbed at the tender skin of her feet, but it didn't stop her from walking toward the bright moon in front of her that seemed so close to the mountaintop that she could reach out and touch it with her hand. She found a soft, grassy spot. She stopped, lifted up her arms as if she were flying, and spun around in the moonlight.

Logan awakened and it registered, immediately, that Josephine was gone. He riffled in the dark until he found the lamp and switched it on. He yanked on his shirt, his pants, and stuffed his feet into his boots without socks. The tent was unzipped, and he noticed that her jeans were still folded neatly by the open flap. He stepped out of the tent; his breath curled out of his mouth like he had just exhaled smoke from a cigarette. He almost turned around to grab his coat from inside of the tent, but then he saw Josephine, naked, twirling in the moonlight, and he temporarily lost his ability to move. He could only watch, frozen in his spot, the woman he had fallen in love with. Her lithe, tall, athletic body, partially hidden in the mist, appeared gold from the reflection of the umber moon; her hair was long and loose, fanning out around her body. It was the most incredible thing he had ever seen. She was the most magnificent creature. For as long as he lived, he would never forget seeing Josephine Brand, dancing nude in the moonlight at the top of the world.

Josephine stopped twirling, appeared to be a little dizzy, and she laughed. The spell was broken. Logan grabbed the blanket out of the tent.

"What are you doing?" he asked her.

Josephine spun around, appeared to be surprised that she wasn't alone anymore. She didn't cover her nakedness, even though she was clearly shivering.

"I'm getting kissed by the moon."

Logan wrapped the blanket over her shoulders. "It's too cold out here for this, Jo. You're going to make yourself sick."

Josephine pulled the blanket tightly around her body. "I woke up so hot. I just wanted to cool off. We can go back now."

She was grateful to be back in his arms. At the time, she hadn't realized how cold her body had become. She hadn't felt it. All she had felt was joy. She felt happy and free and…beautiful. She had danced naked on the Continental Divide. It was a landmark moment. She was changed.

"Come here." Logan opened the sleeping bag for her to crawl inside. "Let me warm you up."

Josephine slipped into the sleeping bag and slipped into Logan's arms. They were facing each other; her breasts, small and pert, brushed against his defined pectoral muscles. She ran her hand over his arm feeling the muscles. She reached for his hand and threaded her fingers together with his. She was used to his hand now. It felt right to hold his hand now.

"My beautiful Josephine." He whispered in the dark. "You are more special than I ever hoped for…"

She pressed her lips to his. She untangled her fingers from his so she could touch his body. The tips of her fingers traced the ridges of his abdomen. Then, her hand moved to his groin. He wasn't aroused—not completely. She wrapped her fingers around his shaft.

"Your hands are freezing…" Logan said.

"Sorry about that." She laughed. "I need you to warm me up again."

"I can do this…" Logan kissed her before he grabbed another condom.

Josephine rolled onto her back and brought him with her. Logan slid inside of her, so slow, so deliberate. He kissed her slowly, sweetly, and he joined their bodies together.

"Josephine… I love you so much."

Those were the last words between them. Logan left

her body to guide her onto her stomach. He covered her body with his, one arm under her chest, hand over her breast, and entered her from behind.

"Ah…that feels so good, Logan. Please don't stop…"

Logan had no intention of stopping. He reached beneath her body and rubbed her swollen clit at the same time he loved her with his hard shaft. They rocked together and found a rhythm that felt like ecstasy to both of them.

"I feel you coming, Jo," Logan said in a strained voice. "Come for me…"

And when she did, when she began to shudder in his arms, he couldn't hold his orgasm a moment longer and they reached their climax together.

Breathing heavy from the effort, they collapsed into each other's arms and laughed. They both lay flat on their backs, hands intertwined, the cold air chilling their damp skin.

"I think this may be one of the best nights of my life," Josephine told him. Her feelings were still all over the map, so she couldn't say for sure that she loved him, but she knew that she loved *making love* with him.

Logan looked over at her; he could make out her profile in the dark. He remembered that he had told her that he loved her in the throes of making love. He had meant it, and he didn't want to think about the fact that she hadn't told him that she loved him too. He wanted to tell her that he was having the best time of his life with her, but he held back. Instead, he turned toward her, draped his arm over her stomach, and kissed her good-night. Right now he needed to sleep; the future would just have to take care of the rest.

* * *

Josephine wished that they could stay up on the divide for more than a day. The views were incredible and, at this altitude, she felt like she was closer to God. But her family knew their plan and they needed to pack up and start to head back down the mountain. Riding in the saddle, after a night of lovemaking, was difficult. Her body was tender and sore and it made sitting the saddle really uncomfortable. When they reached the first campsite on their return trip, she got out of the saddle as quick as she could. And she didn't even consider trying to make love with Logan that night. But by the time they reached the last campsite, her body had started to recover and all she could think about was making love. Once they returned to the ranch, they were going to be like bugs in a jar again; privacy and opportunity would be a problem.

They set up the camp and Josephine gathered up some toiletries so she could rinse off in the nearby stream.

"Coming?" she asked Logan.

"Yeah, I definitely need to rinse off."

"Why don't you grab the blanket…" Josephine asked with a mischievous smile, "…and a condom?"

On their trip together, Logan felt that Josephine had experienced her own sexual revolution. She was freer with her body, more assertive about letting him know when she wanted to make love again. And it seemed that the more frequently they made love, the more she wanted it, and even if he was tired, or not really in the mood, he never turned her down. He was going to take every opportunity to love Josephine. Whenever she wanted it, however she wanted it, he was going to be there for her.

Josephine stripped off her clothing, feeling more comfortable with her own body. Before this trip, before Logan, she would have never been naked outdoors. But she discovered that she liked it. It was exciting. Exhilarating.

Logan smiled at her. He loved that she had lost her self-consciousness and felt safe enough with him to stand before him completely exposed. When he took off his pants, Josephine looked down at his arousal with a pleased smile. Just looking at her for a few minutes and he wanted to be with her. No man had ever made her feel more desirable than Logan.

They both waded quickly into the stream. It was so cold that they washed as quickly as they could and then grabbed their towels and ran, laughing, back to the blanket.

"So cold!" Josephine shivered beneath her towel.

Logan dried off quickly, then lay down on the blanket and held out his arms to her. Josephine dropped her towel and unpinned her hair. She had never, in her life, considered making love outdoors, during the day, and she was about to do just that. With a lover's smile on her face, Josephine joined him on the blanket and took him into her mouth. When he was fully aroused, she pushed him back playfully and climbed on top of him. She rode him, rocking her hips back and forth, her long hair brushing his upper thighs.

He watched her pleasure herself with his body, mesmerized by her beauty. She opened her eyes, smiled at him, and then leaned forward so he could take her breast into his mouth. Perhaps it was because they were starting to know each other intimately—the way their bodies could work in unison—but this time was more intense. This time took her to a place that she didn't know existed.

"Oh," she moaned. "Oh, *Logan*…"

"I've got you, baby." He held her tight. "I've got you…"

She wanted him faster, she wanted him harder. She set the frantic pace until they were both panting and shaking and kissing each other breathless as they came together.

Josephine collapsed on top of him, laughing a joyful, tired laugh. Their bodies still connected, Logan rolled onto his side. He brushed her damp hair away from her face before he happily closed his eyes.

"Logan…" She felt so satisfied in his arms.

"Hmm?"

"I love you, too," she said tentatively at first, and then again with more conviction. "I do love you."

There was a strange feeling at the ranch when they arrived the next day. She was exhausted, but so happy and relaxed. She had laughed more with Logan, explored more, and loved more. The trip shifted her perspective. Everything looked just a little bit different. They took the horses and the mule to the barn to start to unload. At first, she didn't see London. After they had taken the tack off the horses and unpacked the mule, London appeared.

"How was your trip?" the intern asked.

"Amazing!" Josephine hung her bridle on the hook.

"You've got to go up there before you head back to the East Coast."

London gave her a placating half smile. It was then that Josephine noticed how swollen and red London's eyes were. She had been crying. Josephine's immediate gut response was that her brother was somehow involved. This was exactly why their father had a long-standing rule that no one on the ranch could get involved with the interns.

"Why don't you guys take off?" London said. "I'll take care of the rest of this stuff."

"Are you sure?" Josephine asked her.

London nodded and then turned her head away from them. Josephine sensed that London wanted to unpack for them so they would leave and she could be alone again.

"Are you coming up to the house?" Josephine asked Logan.

"I hadn't thought about it."

"At least say hi to Mom." She wasn't ready for their time together to be over.

They thanked London and then headed, hand-in-hand, up to the main house. Logan looked down at their linked hands.

"Are you okay with everyone seeing this?"

She was okay with it. Did she know where their relationship was heading? No. She didn't. But she did know that the friendship had turned into an attraction, and on this trip, had grown into love. She loved Logan—as a man, as a friend. And she was "okay" with everyone in her family knowing about it.

They were talking about the trip and laughing when they opened the front door and headed to the kitchen.

"Hey! Anybody home?"

They walked into the kitchen, still holding hands, but when Josephine saw that there was an uninvited guest sitting at the dining table, she stopped smiling and let go of Logan's hand.

"Hi, Josephine." Brice stood up and faced her.

She glanced at Logan quickly. His expression had turned stony as he checked out her ex.

"What are you doing here?" she asked.

"I came to be your date for the wedding." Brice took a tentative step toward her. "Can we go somewhere to talk?"

"You can use the study," her mother said.

Josephine stared at Brice unbelievingly. He shouldn't be in Montana. He shouldn't be in her family home. He had dumped her, left her dateless to her own twin's wedding. She should hate him for what he did to her. But she didn't. Seeing him now, she realized that she still cared for him. That hadn't been erased. They had been friends first.

She looked at Logan, trying to gauge his reaction.

He gave her a silent nod. She reached out, touched his arm to reassure him, before she addressed Brice.

"We can go to the study."

Brice wanted to hug her. He didn't, but she could see that he wanted to. There was sorrow in his eyes—and regret.

"Where are you going to be?" she asked Logan.

"The cabin. I'll come find you later," he promised.

Brice was in their space now, standing directly in

front of them. He was a head and shoulders taller than Logan, which registered in her head, right before she realized that she had been too stunned to introduce them.

"Brice…this is Logan Wolf. Logan… Brice Livingston."

They shook hands. Josephine crossed her arms tightly in front of her. She never imagined that these two men would ever meet.

After an incredible week together, their trip was ending with an awkward twist. Logan headed in one direction and she headed in the other, leading Brice to the study. She waited for Brice to walk through the door, and then she closed the door behind him.

"Welcome to wedding central." She stood by the closed door, arms crossed.

She watched Brice closely. He was such a handsome man—tall and sure of himself. He was the quintessential California man, with his stylish dusty-blond hair, strong profile, superwhite smile and blue-green eyes. Jordan always said he looked like a Ken doll. For the first time, she saw that maybe he did. Stiff and a bit plastic.

Brice turned to face her, hands in his pockets. "It feels strange to not hug you."

He was fishing for a hug, but she couldn't do it. She just couldn't do it.

"It's strange to see you with someone else," he said. "It's hard."

"I know." Her tone was caustic.

He took a step closer to her. "You look good. Happy."

"Brice…"

"Just hear me out...please... I need to apologize to you."

Josephine frowned, turned her head away, so he couldn't see the pain in her eyes, the tears that were starting to form. She had thought she was over Brice. She thought that she had put all of this pain behind her. And then he showed up, unannounced, with his perfect hair and his perfect clothes and his perfect apology.

"I made a huge mistake, Josie. I know I did. But do we have to throw away five years, Jo? *Five* years?"

A tear slipped down her cheek; Brice held out his handkerchief to her. She shook her head and wiped the tears off on her sleeve.

"Josie..." Brice tried to reach out for her, but she jerked her shoulder away from him.

"No! Shouldn't you be back in California with Caroline?" she asked bitterly.

Brice grimaced. "She's not the person I thought she was." He continued in a lowered voice, "She's not the woman you are, Josephine."

Josephine looked directly into his eyes. It was sincere. His apology was sincere.

He took a step closer to her. "I want us to start over."

"Brice... Logan and I have...been together." How easily those words came out of her mouth.

She saw the pain flash in his eyes. She had thought that causing him pain would make her feel better. It hadn't. Brice's eyes became hooded; his shoulders stiffened. "We both made mistakes..."

She pointed to her chest; she raised her voice to him, something out of character for her. "*I* didn't do this. *You* did this, Brice. This is all on you."

He held up his hands in surrender. "No, you're right. You're right. It was me. It was all me. But come on, Jo, I love you. We can start over...all you have to do is say yes."

Chapter 15

Logan didn't come to find her. Instead, she found him inside of the chapel, working. The wedding was only a couple of days away and he had said on their trip up to the divide that he was anxious to get it ready for Ian and Jordan.

"You said you were going to come and find me." She didn't want to engage in small talk with this man. After what they had shared on the mountain, it seemed like an insult to both of them.

Logan drilled a screw into one of the broken pews before he stood up and faced her. "I wanted to give you some space."

"You're really big on that, I know." Why was she taking this out on him?

Logan stared at her, and then with a small shake of his head, he knelt down again.

"Sorry…" Josephine sat down heavily in a nearby pew, leaned forward and rested her elbows on her legs. She felt weary and defeated. She had moved on during her trip with Logan, and then she came home, only to be slammed right back into her past with Brice.

"He wants to get back together."

Logan continued to work while they talked. "I know. A man doesn't come all this way without a motive in mind."

She looked down at her entwined fingers. He was right and they both knew it. But for once, she wished that Logan would get mad, ask questions, or demand answers. Why did he always have to be so calm and introspective?

"Brice is staying for the wedding."

When she told him that, she saw a small chink in his armor. His eyebrows drawn together, he stopped his work to look her way. "I'm surprised to hear that."

"I know… I know. So was I, frankly, especially with how my family has always felt about him. But he's an invited guest. Jordan never took him off the guest list—and he came all of this way. You've heard of Southern hospitality…we kind of have our own version of that in Montana." When he didn't respond, she added, "But he's not staying at the ranch, and he's not going as my date, Logan. I told him that we've been together…"

Logan's head dropped down and he breathed in deeply, like he was trying to gather his thoughts before he answered. His head still dropped, he said to her quietly, "I know you didn't invite him here, Josephine.

That's not what's bothering me." He stood up, drill still in his hand. "What's bothering me is that you didn't tell him to leave…"

Even though it felt like her private world was a mess, she didn't really have time to fix it, because life on the ranch had kicked into high gear. The list of last-minute preparations for the wedding had tripled, along with her mother's anxiety level. Everyone was busy, everyone was in a rush, and Josephine needed to put aside her problems in her relationship with Logan to focus exclusively on helping her sister prepare for one of the most important days of her life. Brice hadn't left Montana, which was a surprise to her. She hadn't promised him anything, she hadn't encouraged him to stay, but he was determined to attend the wedding anyway. The only positive she could find about him being nearby, contrite and willing to talk, was that she could ask him questions about what really happened between them. She could ask him questions about what had happened between him and the woman that was so appealing to him that he had thrown away their relationship and their future plans. But the answers he gave her always left her with a bigger question mark. He wanted her back, but she could never figure out exactly *why*.

"Oh, my goodness, Jordy… I've never seen you look more beautiful."

It was the morning of the wedding. The rehearsal dinner had gone off without a hitch, and now the day they had all been waiting for, the day that they had all been working toward, was here.

Jordan, who rarely cried, started to tear up when she

saw herself for the first time, fully dressed in her wedding ensemble.

"Wait, don't cry. You'll mess up your makeup!" Josephine rushed to grab a handkerchief out of her purse to hand to her sister. "Here, but blot, Jordan. Don't wipe, blot."

Jordan blew her nose into the handkerchief loudly completely bypassing the "blotting" instructions. Her sister looked at the handkerchief, saw the initials *BL* embroidered in fancy scroll on the corner.

"Ugh." Her twin wrinkled up her nose, balled up the handkerchief in her fist and then threw it in a small garbage can.

"Jordy…that wasn't mine!"

"Don't you *dare* fish that out of the trash, Jo. That's where it belongs," her sister said. "Why do you have it anyway?"

"I sneezed earlier, and he gave it to me. My gosh, Jordy, don't look so disappointed. I borrowed a handkerchief. I didn't have sex with him in one of the pews."

Jordan hugged her then. Tightly and for a long time. "I just want you to find what I have with Ian, Jo. You deserve that. I've never loved anyone like I love that man. I haven't had a moment of doubt about marrying him since the day he put this ring on my finger."

"I want that, too."

Still holding on to her arms, Jordan pulled back so she could look into her eyes. "I don't know if you could have that with Logan. I don't. But you're my sister and my loyalty is always going to be with you. But Logan's my friend, too, Jo, and Ian says he's really hurting over this whole Brice thing. Ian told me that, until you, Logan hasn't been serious about anyone since his divorce."

Logan had told her once before that he had been married, but she had never pried.

"Do you know anything about his ex?"

"Yeah…she was his childhood sweetheart. I think they were in a band together in high school or something like that."

Jordan adjusted her veil, which was her something borrowed. It was the veil that her mom had worn when she married their dad. "Is this right?"

Josephine helped her sister straighten the veil. She had known Logan was married before, but somehow it felt like she was hearing this information for the first time.

"Anyway…she did a real number on him, from what Ian tells me. She backed up a U-Haul while he was at work and cleaned out their apartment. She took everything. He got home and found her gone, along with everything they owned. Horrible, right?"

Josephine nodded. It was horrible.

Barbara Brand, followed by a posse of wedding planners, burst into the room and that stopped her from asking her sister another question about Logan's wife. Ex-wife.

"We're almost ready to start, my beauties!" Barbara's voice was higher and tenser than usual. "Hurry, hurry! You've got to get into place!"

"Is this straight?" Ian asked Logan to check his bow tie. The last time he'd had a tux on was the night he proposed to Jordan.

Ian stood still while Logan adjusted his tie. "Now it's straight."

Ian and Logan stood quietly together for a moment. There was a lot of commotion and voices on the other side of the door, but in their small room in the church, it was calm. Shadow, who was awaiting his next command, was sitting at attention by the door.

"Thank you for being my best man, Logan," Ian said to him.

"I felt really honored that I was the person you thought of when Dylan couldn't make it."

Ian gave a slight nod of his head. Then he said, in a lowered voice, "I'm sorry that Brice is here, Logan. If it had been up to me, he wouldn't have stepped inside the church today."

"It is what it is…" Logan tried to sound casual about it. But he hated the fact that Brice was at the wedding. He hated the strain Josephine's ex had already caused in his fragile relationship with the woman he loved.

A knock on the door stopped the conversation. They were ready for them to take their place in the church.

"You ready?" Logan asked his friend.

"I've been ready." Ian took hold of the handle on the special harness Shadow was wearing. "There're only two things I've ever been sure about in my life—being a photographer and marrying Jordan."

Logan and Ian took their place at the front of the church, and then waited for the rest of the wedding party to join them. Logan locked eyes with Brice, who was sitting next to Luke, Josephine's older brother, and his wife, Sophia, in the front pews reserved for the Brand family.

There was a challenge in Brice's look. Logan recognized it and knew that he hadn't abandoned the idea of reuniting with Josephine. The man was wealthy, privileged, entitled, and used to getting everything he wanted when he wanted it. He was definitely a problem.

The wedding procession started and Josephine, in a floor-length royal purple gown, started to walk slowly up the aisle toward them. He had never seen her look this lovely. She would, for the remainder of his life, be the most beautiful woman he had ever seen. Being separated from her like this since they returned from the divide felt like a third-degree burn all over his body that no one else could see. He was in pain, pure and simple, and he had sworn, after Alicia, that he was never going to put himself in a position to let it happen again. That pact he had made with himself was broken when he fell in love with Josephine Brand.

Josephine took her place at the front of the church. She hadn't been able to take her eyes off of Logan in his tuxedo. So strong and handsome—and this time, when she compared him to Brice, it was her ex who came up short. When the wedding march started, all of Josephine's attention was on her twin. Jordan, a statuesque and modern bride, stood next to their father. Hank looked more proud at that moment with her sister on his arm than she had ever seen him look before. As she walked down the aisle toward her waiting fiancé, her elegant twin sister seemed to be so much more mature since she met Ian Sterling. He was a good balance for her; he kept her grounded. Jordan had met her perfect match in Ian, and Josephine wondered, as the two of them began to exchange their vows, if she hadn't met her own perfect match in Logan. Now, when she looked at him, as he stood just behind Ian, all she could think about was how his lips felt on her skin, on her mouth, when he kissed her.

After the ceremony, a limousine took Ian and his new bride to the reception. A family friend, who owned a multimillion dollar spread just outside of Helena, had offered to hold the reception at his ranch house. This wasn't just any old ranch house; it was a Montana mansion in its own right. Tents had been erected outside and there was a large outdoor area, covered in twinkling lights and fragrant flowers, large enough for the band and for dancing. Tables were set up in the tent for dining and they all gathered there to eat before the dancing began. She was seated at a long table at the front of the tent that was reserved for the bride, groom, and wedding party. According to the seating arrangement, she was to sit next to Logan.

"Let me get that for you." Logan moved behind her and pulled out her chair for her.

"Thank you."

He took the seat next to her, and it occurred to her that this was the first time they were sitting down together since they returned from their camping trip. She couldn't stop looking at his hands—those hands had touched all of her body. Even though they hadn't made love since their return, she could still remember the feel of his lips on hers, and the weight of his body between her thighs, how amazing it felt to have his body completely fill hers.

"That's quite a dress." Logan's statement brought

her out of her own head and back into reality. That was more than he had said to her in several days.

She looked down at her gown. "I didn't want to get it. I thought it might come close to upstaging the bride, it's so beautiful. But Jordan insisted. She wanted me to look…beautiful."

"She succeeded."

"Thank you. You look handsome." She returned the compliment. "I've never seen you like this before."

"It's far and few between, trust me," he said. "I'm not normally a tuxedo kind of guy."

After the meal, and after the toasts, most of the guests moved out to the open dance floor where there was a free liquor bar and a live band. Logan had already left the table, so she headed outside. Brice followed her.

"As always, you look incredible tonight, Josie."

Josephine picked a spot away with an unimpeded view of the band. "Thank you.

Brice knew how to wear a tuxedo—that was his comfort zone, his realm of experience, and he presented a handsome, hard-to-resist exterior. But he was wearing the same tuxedo he was wearing in the picture when she first saw him with another woman. She couldn't bring herself to return his compliment.

"Did I ever tell you that I'm not really fond of the nickname Josie?" She looked up into his face, a face she had admired thousands of times before.

"What? No. You never have. Why would you let me call you by a nickname for all these years that you didn't like?"

"That…" Josephine responded, "…is a very good question."

Brice repositioned himself so he was in front of her, blocking the view of the band.

"Josephine, I came all this way to prove to you that I'm sincere. I made a mistake, and I want to make it up to you. I want to make things right between us. You're one of my best friends, Josie… Josephine… I don't want to lose that."

Logan returned from the men's room to discover that Josephine had left the table. When he didn't find her in the dining area, he looked for her outside. He spotted her, apparently in a deep conversation with Brice. Brice was standing very close to her with his head was bent down toward her. They weren't touching, but their natural comfort from years of being a couple showed. Logan almost turned and walked away. He almost did. But then it dawned on him. Perhaps Josephine had been waiting for him to fight for her. Perhaps Josephine needed him to show up, be present, and claim her for his own. He went to the stage and put in a request for a song. Then he walked directly across the dance floor to Josephine.

"Excuse me…" he interrupted. "I'd like to have this dance, Josephine."

Josephine glanced quickly between Brice and Logan, two men whom she loved, and two men who loved her. She was standing at an unspoken crossroad, and all three of them knew it.

"I'd like that. Thank you." Josephine didn't look at Brice when she took Logan's offered hand.

"We'll talk later," she told Brice.

Logan took her into his arms, and they began to sway together to Eric Clapton's "Wonderful Tonight."

"I love this song."

"I requested it for you," he told her.

Josephine smiled at him. With her heels on, she was a little bit taller than he was. She thought it would bother her, but it didn't. He was such a masculine gentleman that his lack of height seemed insignificant.

When Logan heard a certain part of the song, he pulled her closer to him so he could sing a line or two in her ear.

When he sang to her, all of the moments she had shared with him flashed through her mind. His voice, so rich and sexy, made her want to more than just dance with him. And she knew that he felt exactly the same way. Their bodies, whenever they were close, were a perfect fit.

Logan felt a tap on his shoulder.

"I'd like to cut in…" Brice had left the side of the dance floor and was standing directly next to them.

Logan slowed a bit, but didn't stop dancing, and he didn't let go of her. Her heart seized for a second, because there was something definitely brewing between these two alpha males.

"Not this time," Logan told him and then spun her away from Brice.

Brice turned red in the face and he grabbed Logan's arm. In an instant, Logan's officer training kicked in and the next thing she knew, Brice was taken down to the ground in his custom tuxedo.

Logan stepped back, prepared for a next attack. Brice was quickly on his feet; he'd boxed in college and she could see his stance. He was going to punch Logan.

"Brice! *Don't!* He's a cop!" she tried to warn her

ex. Assault on a law enforcement officer could derail Brice's career.

Brice ignored her warning, balled up his fist, and lunged at Logan. Logan ducked to the side, deflected the punch, grabbed Brice's wrist and twisted it around so his arm was behind his back and Logan had complete control of him. Logan took him down again, quickly lowered him to the ground, but this time, he wasn't gentle. He slammed Brice down, so he would *stay* down.

Instinctively, after years of being with Brice, she ran to his side and knelt down beside him to make sure he wasn't seriously hurt.

Logan stared at her with a look that could only be described as wounded and betrayed.

"Stay down," he told Brice, before he turned around and disappeared into the crowd that had gathered around them.

After she made sure Brice was okay, she searched for Logan, only to find out that he had decided to leave the reception early and return to the ranch. She wouldn't leave her twin's wedding reception to chase after him, but she did do the one thing that she should have done right from the start: she told Brice to leave.

The morning after the wedding, the ranch seemed so quiet compared to the pre-wedding chaos. Ian and Jordan had already taken off to start their honeymoon in the Caribbean island of Curaçao, where they had first fallen in love. And even her brother Luke and his wife, Sophia, had left for the airport because they both needed to get back to Boston for work and to take care of their three kids. Josephine had awakened with one thing on her mind: Logan. She skipped her usual stop, the kitchen, and headed straight to Tyler's cabin.

At the same time she was opening the front door, Tyler was coming out of his bedroom. They met in the kitchen and Tyler poured a cup of coffee for himself.

"He's up at the chapel," her brother said. "Coffee?"

"No, thanks." Josephine noticed several packed bags piled up just outside of the guest bedroom. She stared at them for several seconds, feeling sick to her stomach.

"Are those Logan's?"

Tyler nodded before he took a sip of his coffee.

Logan was leaving. She swallowed hard several times before she asked, "Did he say where he's going?"

"No. And I didn't think to ask," her brother said. "I take it you didn't know he was leaving."

Josephine shook her head. "I really screwed up with him, Tyler," she admitted.

"I doubt it's anything fatal. I think he's a really good guy. I'd go talk to him if I were you," her brother advised.

"Yeah…" She slid off the bench. "I guess I will."

Before she dealt with her own relationship issues, she knew she needed to talk to Tyler about his. "I've been so caught up with my own drama that I almost forgot to ask you…what exactly did you do to her?"

Tyler put his coffee cup down on the counter. "Who are you talking about?"

"London."

She saw it, the flash of pain on his face when she mentioned the intern's name. "She looked like she was crying the other day."

"She was?" Tyler seemed caught off-guard by her comment. "Did she tell you why?"

"No, but I do know you're involved with her, Tyler. Don't ask me how I know—I just do, okay? So what did you do?"

Tyler looked away from her, shook his head in thought, before he turned his face back toward her.

"She's pregnant."

"Oh…" Josephine stared at him, shocked. "Tyler, that's not good."

Tyler's face took on a stony appearance. "London would agree with you on that point."

"And you don't?" she asked him. Out of all of the siblings, Tyler had always been the slowest to want to grow up. He had always been serious about ranching, but he'd always sworn that he'd never settle down, get married, and have a family.

"No. Actually, I don't." Tyler dumped the rest of his coffee into the sink. "I'm in love with her, Jo. I want to marry her and raise our child here on the ranch. But until we've figured this out, I'd appreciate it if you'd keep this to yourself."

Josephine hugged her brother and promised to keep the secret.

"I'm having a hard enough time trying to fix my own life," she said. "Trust me, I don't think I'm in a good position to give relationship advice."

Chapter 16

Josephine rehearsed what she wanted to say to Logan on her way up the hill to the chapel. She knew that there were so many things that she needed to say...wanted to say...that they were all jumbled together. Even though her thoughts were jumbled, the main purpose of this encounter with Logan was perfectly clear: she owed him an apology. A big one.

Once she reached the chapel's door, she paused to collect her thoughts. Josephine put her hand on her churning stomach as she reached for the door handle. She felt nervous and upset mixed with a gnawing sense of foreboding. What if Logan didn't accept her apology? What then?

Josephine slowly pushed the heavy wooden door open. The inside of the chapel still needed a lot of TLC, but Logan and the rest of the crew had done a remarkable job getting the outside of the chapel picture-perfect for the wedding.

She closed the door quietly behind her and walked down the aisle. Logan, her Logan, was leaning against the podium, writing.

"Hi…" She stopped just on the other side of the podium.

"Hey," Logan said before he clenched the pencil between his teeth, grabbed a measuring tape, and walked to the other side of the chapel.

"I stopped by Tyler's. You're leaving."

Logan measured one of the thick stained-glass windows, before he returned to the podium to write down the window's dimensions into a notebook.

"That's right." Logan moved on to the next window and started to measure it.

Josephine crossed her arms defensively in front of her body. He couldn't…wouldn't…even look at her.

"Were you even planning on saying goodbye?" she asked caustically. "Or were you just going to up and leave?"

Logan let the measuring tape snap back into place. He turned around and met her eyes for the first time. "I wouldn't do that to you."

"No, I know." She contemplated the ground. "That's not your style."

This wasn't going at all like she had rehearsed. Instead of cleaning up the mess as she had intended, she was making it bigger.

"Could you just…stop…for a minute." Josephine put her hand on Logan's arm.

Logan looked at her hand on his arm. "I'm leaving today, Josephine. Let me finish what I started here."

"But that's what I'm trying to do…finish what we started."

With a frustrated sigh, Logan finally looked up at her.

"Look… I'm not up for any more drama, okay? I knew that you were fresh off a breakup, Jo. And I knew you needed more time, but I fell in love with you and I didn't want to wait. That was my mistake, not yours. I knew better. "

"I fell in love with you, too," Josephine told him quickly.

"Maybe you did. Maybe you didn't. Either way, I think we need to step back and give each other some space to think."

Josephine shook her head. "No. We don't need space. Quit giving me so much space! Why won't you fight for me?"

She saw a rare flash of anger in Logan's black, enigmatic eyes. She'd take the anger—it was better than the cold shoulder he'd been giving her ever since she had arrived.

"Fight for you?" he asked incredulously.

"Yes." She held his gaze. "If you want me, I'm right here. Fight for me."

Instead of talking, he acted. Logan grabbed her, pulled her into his arms, and kissed her hard on the mouth. When he kissed her this time, he was laying claim to her. His fingers, such strong, rough, calloused fingers, held her face while he deepened the kiss.

Logan broke the kiss, tilted his head back, and studied her through narrowed eyes.

"Where's the pretty boy?" he asked.

Josephine leaned into Logan's body, wanting more of his kisses. "I sent him packing…"

"About damn time," he said before he kissed her again.

Standing inside the rustic chapel, in the arms of the man she loved, Josephine truly knew, for the first time, exactly what she wanted.

"Logan?"

"Hmm?" Logan was nibbling on the side of her neck, breathing in the scent of her freshly washed skin.

"Will you marry me?"

The nibbling stopped. Logan leaned back, surprised, and stared at her.

"What did you just say?"

Josephine wiggled out of his arms. "You heard me. Will you?"

Logan rubbed his forehead and gave a little shake of his head.

"You're proposing to me?"

Her arms were crossed again. She gave a quick, silent nod.

"I'm not sure what I'm supposed to say here."

Her face felt hot—it had to be red and splotchy from the rush of embarrassment she was feeling.

"And now I feel really stupid…"

Josephine tried to escape, but Logan caught her hand and kept her from walking away from him.

"Wait a minute, you can't just spring a question like

that on me and then walk away. Jesus, Jo, you gotta give a guy a chance to process…"

"No. I waited for five years while Brice processed. I love you and I want to be your wife. What do you want?"

"I want to be your husband." Plain, simple, truthful.

"Then it's a yes," she said with a smile.

Logan kissed her in that slow, gentle way of his. "It's a yes. But… I get to propose."

"But I just proposed."

"Jo, we aren't going to get married until I propose. That's my deal." Logan grabbed the notebook off the podium and then he grabbed her hand. "I get to pick the time and the place for our official engagement."

"But we're engaged now, right? I asked and you answered."

Logan opened the door for her.

"You're a strong, determined woman, Jo…and I love that about you. But, sometimes, you're just going to have to let me be the man."

"Where do you think you left it?" Josephine asked her twin.

"I don't know. But we can't get in without that reservation card."

It was their birthday and Jordan, who wasn't into pampering, had, as a present to her, made them both reservations at a ritzy San Diego spa. But, when she met her sister in the lobby of their downtown penthouse, Jordan realized that she didn't have the reservation card in her wallet.

"Let's just go back up and look for it." Jordan waved at the lobby attendant and they got into the elevator to go forty-four floors back up to the penthouse.

"We're going to be late." Josephine followed her sister into the elevator.

"No, it's just right around the corner. We'll be fine."

Once inside the penthouse, they climbed up the stairs to the second story of the condo. Josephine was always struck by the views. The condo offered spectacular 180-degree views of the San Diego harbor.

"You check out on the balcony and I'll check my other purse," Jordan told her.

"Why would it be out on the balcony?"

"Oh, my *God*, Jo! You're so argumentative! I was out there yesterday and I think I may have left it on the table. Just *go*!"

Josephine opened the balcony door, and the first thing she saw was Logan Wolf standing by an enormous wrapped box, holding a sunflower. The balcony was covered with sunflowers. Everywhere she looked, she saw sunflowers.

"Happy birthday, Jo," Logan said.

Josephine took a step out onto the balcony, her eyes flitting from one huge sunflower arrangement to the next. "I thought you had to work…"

"I may have misled you a little there." Logan walked over to her, handed her the single sunflower, then he kissed her.

"All right, you two. Have a good time." Jordan appeared in the doorway.

"Where are you going?"

"Ian's flying me to New York for the weekend. The place is all yours." Jordan gave her sister a hug. "Happy birthday, Jo."

"Happy birthday, Jordy." She kissed her twin on the cheek. "You still owe me a spa day."

Jordan laughed, waved, and then shut the balcony door behind her. When they were alone, Jo pointed to the box.

"Is that for me?"

"I wrapped it myself."

Josephine laid the sunflower on the table and examined the box. "You're not an accomplished wrapper, are you?"

Logan laughed with good nature. "Just open the box."

Josephine pulled the giant white bow off the top of the box and stuck it on top of her head. She ripped the paper off the box and pried it open. Inside the giant box, was another, slightly smaller, wrapped box.

"Really?" she asked him. "That's how you're going to roll?"

Logan looked pleased with himself. "That's how I'm going to roll. Start unwrapping."

Box after wrapped box, Josephine ripped off the paper, only to discover a box within a box. Finally, she found what had to be the last box.

She raised her eyebrows playfully at Logan and shook the box. "This has to be the last one, right?"

"I don't know. Open it and see."

She quickly ripped the wrapping off the box and found a little black velvet jewelry box inside. She stared at the box for a second or two, her heart beating faster and faster with nervous anticipation of what might be inside of the box.

"Here, let me help you with that." Logan took it from her hands, took the jewelry box out, and put the empty one on the table.

Logan opened the box and showed her the contents.

She had expected to see a ring. Instead, she saw a folded piece of paper. Confused and curious, Josephine unfolded the piece of paper and realized that she was unfolding the form that San Diego police officers used to write tickets. In Logan's handwriting, in bold letters written across the ticket, there was a message for her: *Will you marry me?*

Logan bent down on one knee in front of her with a diamond ring in his hand. "Will you marry me, Jo?"

Josephine nodded her head quickly. "Of course I will."

Logan slipped the ring on her finger. It was a brilliant cut stone set in platinum. It wasn't a large stone, but it was nearly a hundred years old and in an antique setting. Just like Logan was the perfect man for her, the ring he had chosen was a perfect fit.

"I love you." Josephine hugged him tightly, kissed him sweetly. She had been waiting for this day for such a long time. "We're officially engaged!"

"I don't know how I got so lucky, but I'm glad that you do love me." He held her face in his hands and kissed her back. "I'm so glad that you do."

He had planned for them to stay in the condo guest room, but Josephine had insisted that they spend the night at his modest, sparsely furnished condo in Chula Vista.

Logan unlocked the front door, turned on the light switch at the door, and then let Josephine enter in front of him. He always felt a little embarrassed when Josephine came over. He knew she was used to much fancier digs, but this was the best he could do on his salary.

"We'll find a new place that works for both of us." Logan shut the door behind him. "I'm not expecting you to live in this dump once we're married."

"I don't think this is a dump." Josephine slipped off her strappy heels. "I like your place."

"Why?"

Josephine walked over to him, barefoot. She put her arms around her fiancé's waist. "Because it's yours... I love it here because I love you."

"It might not get much better than this on a cop's salary, Jo. Are you sure you can handle that?"

"Are you trying to back out of our engagement already?" she teased him.

He still had his hands in his pockets. His body posture was stiff and a little bit defensive. "I just want to make sure this is the life you really want."

"I want a life with you, whatever that brings. Okay?" Josephine grabbed his hand and led him to the small efficiency kitchen to find something in which to put her sunflower. "I'm going to be graduating soon, so don't forget, I'll have an income, too. Of course, I want to be a public defender and do a lot of pro bono work, so if you were thinking you were getting a high-priced attorney, you're barking up the wrong tree."

Josephine filled a large plastic cup full of water and stuck her sunflower in it.

Logan came up behind her, wrapped his arms around her waist, and kissed the back of her neck.

"Hmm…" She closed her eyes. "I've missed you."

At the end of summer, they had flown back to California together on Ian's private jet. Logan returned to San Diego and she went back to Berkeley to finish her degree. Their relationship had to be long-distance and sometimes they only saw each other a couple times a month. But they had spent hours getting to know each other by phone and Josephine believed that their forced distance had somehow made them stronger as a couple.

"I've missed you."

Josephine turned in his arms so she could kiss him on the mouth. She loved to kiss this man; she had to believe that she always would. There was something about the firmness of his lips; there was something about the natural scent of his skin and his taste that drove her senses crazy.

"Why don't we close the curtains?" she asked him.

Logan smiled at her with his eyes. He knew exactly what she wanted. She wanted to skip dinner and dessert and head straight to bed. They both closed the curtains to shut out the world temporarily. Josephine grabbed two glasses and a bottle of wine from the fridge before she headed to Logan's bedroom.

She pulled her short shift dress over her head and hung it up on one of the empty wire hangers in the closet. Next her bra and panties came off, her hair was let down, and the only thing she was wearing was her new engagement ring.

"You are too beautiful for words." Logan was watching her from the bedroom door.

"Don't you have too many clothes on?" she asked him, completely comfortable in her own skin before her future husband.

Logan undressed and tossed his clothing on the dresser. Then, he joined her, half-aroused, in his bed.

Josephine handed him a glass of wine and then held out her glass for a toast.

"Happy birthday, sweetheart," Logan said.

"Thank you. Logan, this is the best birthday I've ever had. I can't wait to be your wife."

They touched glasses and then Josephine took a sip of the red wine. She immediately made a disgusted face and looked at the wine in her glass.

"*Yuck!* What is this?" She put down her glass and grabbed the bottle.

"I don't know." Logan took another large sip of the wine. "It's not all that bad, is it?"

"No, don't drink that." Josephine took his glass out of his hand. "It's rancid."

"Hey, I wasn't done with that yet."

"Yes, you were," she told him. "Besides, you have some work to do, Lieutenant."

"Is that so?" Logan's eyes traveled from her eyes to her lips to her small, perky breasts. He reached out and encircled one nipple with his finger and he smiled, pleased, when it hardened and puckered beneath his light touch.

"Yes…" Josephine lay down beside him, offering herself to the man she loved. "That's so."

Logan skipped the foreplay and gave her exactly what she had been craving, a body-to-body connection. He slipped inside of her, filling her so completely. She liked it when Logan took control in the bedroom; she liked it when he manhandled her. Everything he did, everything he showed her, was pure pleasure.

Logan hooked his arm under her long leg and bent it toward her chest so he could go deeper within her. Josephine gasped, her head tossed back at the new sensation.

"Do you like that?" He was watching every expression that passed over her face.

"Yes…" she said urgently, not wanting him to stop what he was doing. "That…feels…so good…"

He loved her like that, stroking her, massaging her, filling her deeper and deeper, harder and harder, until he felt her grow completely still beneath him. He opened his eyes, and saw a look of unadulterated joy on her face.

Then she cried out and he felt a rush of wetness on his shaft. Wave after wave, her orgasm didn't stop. She was wild beneath him, drenching him with her love. Logan held her hands over her head and surged into her; the more she soaked him, the more excited he became.

"Josephine… Josephine… *Josephine…*"

She watched him, fascinated at the expression on his handsome face when he came. She arched her back and took him deeper inside of her. They were so close, so connected, that she felt his body pulse inside of her just before he cried out her name three times.

Logan collapsed on top of her and she hugged him

close to her. After a minute, he lifted his head and looked at her in amazement. They both laughed.

"What *was* that?" he asked her.

Satiated, Josephine laughed. "You hit my G-spot."

He looked at her in total amazement. That orgasm that they had experienced together, that they had created together, was beyond his experience.

He kissed her on the lips. "And here I always thought that was a mythical creature like a unicorn."

She laughed again. "Me, too!"

Logan rolled onto his side, still holding her hand, and lay flat on his back, one hand behind his head, on top of the sheets. Josephine scooted closer to him, pulled the sheet over her hips, and rested her head on his shoulder. She placed her hand, her left hand with a new engagement ring on her fourth finger, over his heart.

"It's still your birthday, Jo. What do you want to do? I'll take you anywhere you want to go."

Josephine flipped onto her stomach, rested her hand and chin on his chest so she could get a better look at his handsome face.

"I don't need to go anywhere. I'm exactly where I want to be. With you."

Logan's smile started in his dark, enigmatic eyes and then reached his beautifully shaped lips. He rolled her over onto her back so he could look down into wide blue eyes.

"Every day I love you more deeply than the day before, Josephine. I don't know how a guy like me managed to get a woman like you, but I'm the luckiest man I know."

Josephine put her hands on either side of his handsome face and smiled up at him. She knew now what true love felt like. She knew now what it was to feel layers upon layers of happiness and joy. When she had least expected it, when she hadn't even been looking, there he was, finally...her perfect match.

* * * * *

Mikey's fingers contracted. "Suppose I told you that the
hotel I own is actually a casino," he said slowly, "and it's
in Las Vegas?"

Bernie's eyes widened. "You own a casino in Las
Vegas?" she exclaimed. "Wow!"

He laughed, surprised at her easy acceptance. "I run it
legit, too," he added. "No fixes, no hidden switches, no
cheating. Drives the feds nuts, because they can't find
anything to pin on me there."

"The feds?" she asked.

He drew in a breath. "I told you, I'm a bad man." He
felt guilty about it, dirty. His fingers caressed hers as they

neared Graylings, the huge mansion where his cousin lived with the heir to the Grayling racehorse stables.

Her fingers curled trustingly around his. "And I told you that the past doesn't matter," she said stubbornly. Her heart was running wild. "Not at all. I don't care how bad you've been."

His own heart stopped and then ran away. His teeth clenched. "I don't even think you're real, Bernie," he whispered. "I think I dreamed you."

She flushed and smiled. "Thanks."

He glanced in the rearview mirror. "What I'd give for just five minutes alone with you right now," he said tautly. "Fat chance," he added as he noticed the sedan tailing casually behind them.

She felt all aglow inside. She wanted that, too. Maybe they could find a quiet place to be alone, even for just a few minutes. She wanted to kiss him until her mouth hurt.

Don't miss
Texas Proud *by Diana Palmer,*
available October 2020 wherever
Harlequin Special Edition books and ebooks are sold.

Harlequin.com

HSEEXP0920

SPECIAL EXCERPT FROM

LOVE INSPIRED
INSPIRATIONAL ROMANCE

An Amish man gets more than he bargained for when he moves next door to a large spirited family during the holiday season.

Read on for a sneak preview of
The Amish Christmas Secret
by Vannetta Chapman.

"Get back!"

Definitely a female voice, from the other side of the barn. He walked around the barn. If someone had asked him to guess what he might find there, he wouldn't in a hundred years have guessed correctly.

A young Amish woman—Plain dress, apron, *kapp*—was holding a feed bucket in one hand and a rake in the other, attempting to fend off a rooster. At the moment, the bird was trying to peck the woman's feet.

"What did you do to him?" Daniel asked.

Her eyes widened. The rooster made a swipe at her left foot. The woman once again thrust the feed bucket toward the rooster. "Don't just stand there. This beast won't let me pass."

Daniel knew better than to laugh. He'd been raised with four sisters and a strong-willed mother. So he snatched the rooster up from behind, pinning its wings down with his right arm.

"Where do you want him?"

"His name is Carl, and I want him in the oven if you must know the truth." She dropped the feed bucket and swiped at the golden-blond hair that was spilling out of her *kapp*. "Over there. In the pen."

Daniel dropped the rooster inside and turned to face the woman. She was probably five and a half feet tall, and looked to be around twenty years old. Blue eyes the color of forget-me-nots assessed him.

She was also beautiful in the way of Plain women, without adornment. The sight of her reminded him of yet another reason why he'd left Pennsylvania. Why couldn't his neighbors have been an old couple in their nineties?

"You must be the new neighbor. I'm Becca Schwartz—not Rebecca, just Becca, because my *mamm* decided to do things alphabetically. We thought you might introduce yourself, but I guess you've been busy. Mamm would want me to invite you to dinner, but I warn you, I have seven younger siblings, so it's usually a somewhat chaotic affair."

Becca not Rebecca stepped closer.

"Didn't catch your name."

"Daniel...Daniel Glick."

"We didn't even know the place had sold until last week. Most people are leery of farms where the fields are covered with rocks and the house is falling down. I see you haven't done anything to remedy either of those situations."

"I only moved in yesterday."

"Had time to get a horse, though. Get it from Old Tim?"

Before he could answer, a dinner bell rang. "Sounds like dinner's ready. Care to meet the folks?"

"Another time. I have some...um...unpacking to do."

Becca shrugged her shoulders. "Guess I'll be seeing you, then."

"Yeah, I guess."

He'd hoped for peace and solitude.

Instead, he had half a barn, a cantankerous rooster and a pretty neighbor who was a little nosy.

He'd come to Indiana to forget women and to lose himself in making something good from something that was broken.

He'd moved to Indiana because he wanted to be left alone.

Don't miss
The Amish Christmas Secret *by Vannetta Chapman,*
available October 2020 wherever
Love Inspired books and ebooks are sold.

LoveInspired.com